PENGUIN BOOKS

An Eligible Bachelor

Veronica Henry has written three previous novels, *Honeycote, Making Hay* and *Wild Oats*, all of which are published by Penguin. She lives in North Devon with her husband and three sons.

www.veronicahenry.co.uk

D0168170

An Eligible Bachelor

VERONICA HENRY

PENGUIN BOOKS

PENGUIN BOOKS

Published by the Penguin Group
Penguin Books Ltd, 80 Strand, London WC2R ORL, England
Penguin Group (USA) Inc., 375 Hudson Street, New York, New York 10014, USA
Penguin Group (Canada), 10 Alcorn Avenue, Toronto, Ontario, Canada M4V 3B2
(a division of Pearson Penguin Canada Inc.)
Penguin Ireland, 25 St Stephen's Green, Dublin 2, Ireland
(a division of Penguin Books Ltd)
Penguin Group (Australia), 250 Camberwell Road,
Camberwell, Victoria 3124, Australia (a division of Pearson Australia Group Pty Ltd)
Penguin Books India Pvt Ltd, 11 Community Centre,
Panchsheel Park, New Delhi – 110 017, India
Penguin Group (NZ), cnr Airborne and Rosedale Roads, Albany,
Auckland 1310, New Zealand (a division of Pearson New Zealand Ltd)
Penguin Books (South Africa) (Pty) Ltd, 24 Sturdee Avenue,
Rosebank, Johannesburg 2196, South Africa

Penguin Books Ltd, Registered Offices: 80 Strand, London WC2R ORL, England

www.penguin.com

First published 2005
1

Copyright © Veronica Henry, 2005
All rights reserved

The moral right of the author has been asserted

Set by Palimpsest Book Production Limited, Polmont, Stirlingshire
Printed in England by Clays Ltd, St Ives plc

I

Guy Portias knew the hangover from hell when he felt it.

He lay as still as he could and tried to rate it on a scale of one to ten.

As he couldn't even lift his head off the pillow it had to be at least an eight. The tight band around the back of his skull confirmed a port hangover, which was bad – that could possibly mean vomiting, followed by the shakes, depending on what he'd mixed it with. He tried to remember the night before. Hazy images came back to him, in no particular order.

He remembered the wrap party, to celebrate the end of filming at Eversleigh Manor.

He remembered suckling pig and syllabub and goblets of claret being raised in endless toasts in the huge marquee.

He remembered a mock sword fight on the lawn with the leading man. And being trounced – he wasn't to know that fencing was a prerequisite at drama school. Shit – he'd better make sure the swords had been put back safely in their place over the fireplace in the hall before his mother noticed they were missing.

He remembered Richenda, radiant in a white chiffon dress with a handkerchief hem, her glossy dark curls tumbling over her shoulders, looking as enchanting as some elfin . . .

Bride.

Why did that word strike a note of recognition? Why did he get a sense of discomfort and alarm? With a growing unease, he lifted his eyelids to see if he could gain a clue.

The first sign that things had got seriously out of control was the tapestry hangings round the bed. They could only mean one thing. He was in the master bedroom, in the master's bed – the bed that hadn't been slept in since his father had died in it four years ago. Guy groaned. That was sacrilege.

The second sign was the arm stretched across his chest. It was long and elegant, as slender and white as a swan's neck. His eye ran down its length to the wrist, on which was hung a pretty little diamond watch. Then he looked at the hand, his heart beating with trepidation. He had a shrewd suspicion of what he might see there, but was hoping against hope that it was the remnant of an alcohol-infused dream that was feeding his premonition.

But no. There it was, on the ring finger of her left hand. A whopping great ruby, as deep and dark a red as the port he'd been drinking, surrounded by a sprinkling of diamonds. His grandmother's engagement ring. The one that had, until last night, been incarcerated in the Portias safe awaiting a suitable recipient.

Beside him, Richenda stirred. Their eyes met. He knew without looking that his would be shot with tiny veins. Hers, by contrast, were clear: bright whites surrounding the mesmerizing green orbs that had been partially responsible for her meteoric rise to fame. Eyes you could drown in, agreed the press, rather unimaginatively. Eyes that could drive you mad and make you lose all reason, thought Guy. Eyes the colour of absinthe, that insidious liquor that had driven so many men to the brink of insanity. And like Toulouse, Vincent and Paul before him, he'd lost the fucking plot.

Her mouth curved into a smile. The full bottom lip and the pronounced bow above combined to give her a permanent moue that promised kisses of incredible softness; kisses that Guy knew kept their promise. But that wasn't the point. You didn't propose to a girl just because she kissed like an angel.

Richenda lifted her hand and ran her finger across his cheek.

'My nearly husband,' she murmured.

Guy gulped. Now was the moment he should retract his proposal. Put it down to a surfeit of Taylor's; explain that he was prone to acts of foolhardiness and impulsiveness when he overdid it. It was practically his party piece, proposing to girls when he was drunk. He never expected them to take him seriously. But Richenda obviously had.

He knew there would be a high price to pay if he backtracked. There wasn't a woman on the planet who would take kindly to a man reneging on his demands for her hand in marriage. It was, after all, the highest insult, the ultimate rejection. He imagined there would be hysterics, recriminations, tantrums, possible physical violence. But how long could that reasonably last? If she had any pride she'd take the first available train back to London. So he would have to tolerate two hours of torture at the most.

Compared to a possible lifetime.

He cleared his throat, then felt her hand with the incriminating heirloom slide up his thigh.

'I –' he started half-heartedly.

'Sssh,' she commanded softly, a mischievous twitch playing at the corners of that beautiful mouth. Then her head disappeared under the blankets and Guy felt his resolve slither away. He tried wildly to grasp at reason, but reason was telling him he'd have to be mad to reject her now. There wasn't a man in the country who wouldn't swap places with him. The most photographed lips in England were circling his cock. She'd been voted the country's sexiest woman by a leading lad mag, and that was without revealing any more than the most discreet peep of her décolletage. Only Guy knew the truth about her breasts, the perfect little handfuls like Marie Antoinette's 'coups de champagne'. She was the success story of the year. Darling of the small screen, the gossip columns and the paparazzi. It was rumoured that she'd just signed a seven-figure golden handcuff deal with ITV.

And that was the sticking point. Never mind the heavenly blow job. When you had a fifteenth-century manor house falling down around your ears, you didn't look a gift horse in the mouth.

Afterwards, Guy could never be sure quite why it was he hesitated. Was it because he was a coward, too afraid to face up to her bitter recriminations? Was it because he was mercenary, and saw in her newly acquired wealth the answer to all his problems? Or was it because he felt as if he was about to explode into a million exquisite particles of fairy dust?

As he let out a groan that was part despair, part ecstasy,

he knew he had lost his chance. He had to go along with it now. At least for the time being . . .

Strangely, once he'd reached his climax, his resolve stiffened again. Richenda protested as he slid out from between the blankets, but he patted her reassuringly.

'I'm going to bring you tea.'

He ran down the sweeping staircase to the hall, with its magnificent panelling and huge fireplace. He noted with relief that the swords were in their place. The production team had been told that when they left Eversleigh Manor, it should be as if they had never been there. Someone must have been sober enough last night to put them back. No one wanted to incur the wrath of his mother, the formidable Madeleine.

He slipped along the corridor past the dining room and through the swinging baize door into the warmth of the kitchen, where he filled the kettle and placed it on the Aga hotplate. All the time he was mentally assessing what damage limitation could be done without coming across as a total bastard.

He'd tell her he wasn't good enough for her. That he wasn't ready to settle down. That he was off on a mission to save a rainforest with Sting and that he might never come back – effectively widowing her before she was even married. She needed stability: a supportive husband who could stand proudly by her side at award ceremonies, who understood the pressures and the stresses and the strains of celebritydom. Not someone who hadn't watched television for five years, for God's sake!

He could hear the telephone ringing in the passage

outside. There was a little booth, with a shelf and an old-fashioned phone with a thick cord connecting it to the wall, and a proper ring that echoed through the corridors in the early morning quiet. He hurried to answer it.

'Eversleigh,' he announced.

'Morning.' A syrupy voice slid like molasses down the line. 'I wanted to be the first to congratulate you. Please tell me I am.'

Guy grasped the cord and wound it round his thumb.

'I'll tell you, if you tell me who you are,' he countered, oozing the equivalent amount of treacle. He was a great believer in treating like with like. There was no point in being defensive or aggressive or curt.

'Cindy Marks. The Bird Inside Your Telly.'

Oh God. Even Guy knew who she was, as her name had been bandied round the set with reverence by all and sundry. Television critic for the *Daily Post*, she could make or break a series by her recommendation, and had been the greatest champion of *Lady Jane Investigates*. Cindy had branded it 'the best reason to stay glued to your television since JR was shot. Correction, since JFK was shot.'

Guy smiled disarmingly, hoping that his charm would bounce back down the line.

'And why do I deserve your congratulations?'

Cindy responded with a throaty gurgle of delight.

'Your engagement, of course. I expect it's a bit early for a comment from the future Mrs Portias. I presume she's still ensconced in the old ancestral bedchamber. Just give her a big kiss from me, and tell her I expect an exclusive for Saturday's supplement. And I'm dying to check out the rock. She's a very lucky girly.'

The line went dead. Slightly nonplussed, Guy hung up, just as the front door bell jangled overhead. He opened the door to the most enormous bouquet of flowers he'd ever seen, a profusion of deep red roses and ivy intertwined with tiny twinkling fairy lights wrapped in gold organza.

The card read 'Congratulations on a fairy tale come true, from Cindy and everyone at the *Daily Post*.'

Who had blabbed?

Who indeed? There had been upwards of two hundred people at the party last night. He had been completely blotto. Discretion had been thrown to the wind. For all he knew he'd knelt down and asked Richenda for her hand in marriage in front of the entire cast, crew and associated hangers-on. It was hardly surprising if the press had got wind of it already.

Which meant that any hopes he had of damage limitation were well and truly scuppered.

Upstairs, Richenda was mentally redecorating the master bedroom. The tapestry hangings would have to go. Too heavy and ugly for words. She shook one experimentally and gave a tiny, ladylike sneeze as years of dust flew out. French grey silk, she decided. It was light, elegant and would hang beautifully.

She stretched herself luxuriously, and admired the glint of the ruby on her hand. She examined the ring more closely, unable to keep the smile off her face. Her engagement was the climax of what had undoubtedly been her *annus mirabilis*. It had started the previous September, when she had been cast as Lady Jane for ITV's glittering new series. This had been pitched to the Network Centre in six simple words: 'Miss Marple with her tits out.' The twin appeal of sex and nostalgia meant the series was immediately commissioned for thirteen episodes. The first episode had gone out before they'd even finished filming the series, and had been an instant hit, regularly pulling in more than fifteen million viewers – almost unheard of in this day and age. No sooner had the series wrapped than the cast and crew were pulled back to make a two-hour Christmas special. Filming had finished the day before. Richenda had known that time was running out; that she had to ensnare Guy while she still had a built-in excuse to be under his roof. And at the eleventh hour, he'd proposed!

She remembered the first time she had seen him, back in March. He was stripped to the waist, hacking at a sycamore which was overhanging the glass roof of the orangery, blocking out the light. She had held her breath as he dangled precariously from a rope and sliced seemingly recklessly through the offending branches with a chainsaw. She didn't think she'd ever seen such an overt display of masculinity: his apparent disregard for his own safety, his confidence as he slackened the hoist to lower himself down the tree. She'd presumed he was a gardener, or a tree surgeon.

Eventually, satisfied with his handiwork, he lowered himself to the ground and she was able to get a better look at him. His thick brown hair was tousled; his skin weatherbeaten. She watched as he lifted a bottle of mineral water to his lips and drank thirstily, then tipped the rest of the bottle over his head to cool down. Little rivulets ran over his torso, sliding over the corded knots of his muscles.

He looked up and their eyes met. Richenda blushed, realizing she was gawping at him. All she needed was a dirty old raincoat.

'Hot work?' she offered, her voice weak with embarrassment and longing.

'Yeah,' he nodded. 'Had to get rid of them, though. We're due some high winds next week – don't want them crashing through the roof.'

For a moment, Richenda was puzzled. She'd expected a country burr. His voice was slightly husky, the accent clipped, careless. And he had an air of confidence you didn't usually get with hired help.

He picked up a faded blue sweatshirt and wiped it over his chest to remove the residues of water and sweat. Then he shivered.

'Actually, it's chilly when you stop.' He tugged the sweatshirt on over his head. Richenda swallowed, thinking hard.

'Would you like a hot chocolate, to warm you up?' she offered. 'I was just about to get myself one.'

This was a monumental fib – she'd battled all week to resist the hot chocolate that the caterers were dishing up by the gallon. But she didn't want this vision to escape. She was intrigued.

Actors bored her rigid. They were self-obsessed, vain and insecure with only one subject of conversation – themselves. And even if they managed to achieve a perfect physique, they weren't real men. Richenda couldn't imagine any of the actors she was working with going anywhere near a chainsaw, let alone risking life and limb to climb a tree with it.

'I was about to go to the summer house and learn my lines for this afternoon.'

'Oh, right. So you're one of the actresses?' His eyes flickered over her with only a modicum of interest as he gathered up his paraphernalia.

Richenda was momentarily speechless. For the past three months she hadn't been able to walk out of the house without being recognized. She was practically a household name. The seminal photograph of her in nothing but a belted white trench coat, barefoot and sprawled on a tiger-skin rug, was hung in every garage and workshop in the country. Men drank out of mugs imprinted with her image; had her as their screensaver on their computers.

'Yes,' she replied faintly.

'Sorry, I should probably recognize you.' He gave her a fleetingly apologetic smile, accompanied by a cursory glance of appraisal. His eyes were navy blue, long-lashed, with deep lines that spoke of sunshine and laughter. 'I don't really watch the telly. Only the six o'clock news. Anyway, I've been out of the country.'

That would account for the tan, thought Richenda. He didn't look like the type to take advantage of a tanning cab.

'Really? Where?'

'Cuba. I've just spent six months there. Riding and diving. Before it gets totally ruined. Have you ever been?'

'No.'

'You should. Before it's too late.'

He was gathering up his things, ready to go. Richenda knew she had to pounce quickly. She held out her hand.

'I'm Richenda Fox.'

She tried to recollect the last time she'd actually had to tell someone her name. He took her hand in his – it was surprisingly warm and dry, not clammy as one might expect after all that exertion.

'Guy Portias.'

'Portias?' She couldn't keep the surprise out of her voice. 'As in . . . ?'

She waved an all-encompassing hand at the house and grounds.

'Yep. Couldn't ignore the irate telegrams from Mother any longer. I had to come home and do my duty. We're opening for business as soon as you lot have gone.'

'What sort of business?'

Guy made a face.

'Country house weekends. Aspirational bollocks for people with more money than sense.' For a moment his blue eyes looked bleak. 'You can't keep a place like this running without selling out.'

'It must be awful.'

'Yep. One up from prostitution, really.'

He replaced the safety guard carefully on the blade. When he looked up, his demeanour seemed more cheerful.

'So – where's this hot chocolate, then?'

That had been nearly six months ago. And of course, once Richenda had made up her mind that this was the man for her, there was little that Guy could do.

She slid out of bed and into the adjoining bathroom. There was just time to make herself look presentable before Guy came back with the tea. She spent two minutes with her whitening toothpaste, cleansed her face, applied a hint of mascara and lip gloss and ran some serum through her hair. Then she flipped out her contact lenses, studiously ignoring her reflection while she applied some drops. She could never bear to see those myopic, watery pale-blue eyes staring back at her. She stuck her lenses back in hastily and double-checked the results.

Perfect. She finished with a squirt of Bulgari to her cleavage then, satisfied that she had perfected that just-got-out-of-bed-but-utterly-irresistible look, slipped back between the sheets to wait for her fiancé.

The florist's van had woken Madeleine Portias. She peered out of the window of her flat in the coach house and saw it disappearing through the gates. The little green van with its distinctive logo, 'Twig', had been a familiar sight at Eversleigh Manor over the past few months. They'd done very well out of the recent filming, as they'd supplied all the floral arrangements for *Lady Jane Investigates* which, being a lavish period piece, had been many.

In fact, the whole community had done well. The inhabitants had moaned and groaned when the streets were blocked off for filming, but the truth is the local economy had boomed. Hotels, B&Bs, pubs and restaurants had enjoyed maximum bookings all year, whether through cast and crew or curious tourists. Now it was coming to an end, though Madeleine had been assured by the producer that *Lady Jane* was fairly certain to be recommissioned for another series.

When the location manager had come knocking at the

door eighteen months ago, Madeleine had been initially horrified at the suggestion that Eversleigh Manor be used for filming. Until the fee was mentioned, and it began to dawn on her that this would be the ideal way of financing her pet project.

After her husband's death four years before, it had soon become apparent to Madeleine that keeping Eversleigh Manor running just for herself was quite ridiculous. With Tony alive, there had been some point. But now her charming, absent-minded, genius of a husband had gone, the house felt as redundant and useless as she herself did. Its rooms echoed with emptiness. But Madeleine wasn't one to be defeated. She was determined to find some way to suppress the dreariness of grief. It was that or a bottle of paracetamol, and although sometimes she went to bed with a dread of waking up, she wasn't one for melo-dramatic gestures. She was a coper; a doer. She needed a challenge, a purpose, for herself and the house, some-thing that would bring them both back to life.

Friends urged her to do bed and breakfast. People would fall over themselves to stay the night in a manor, they insisted. But for Madeleine this didn't have quite enough glamour or cachet. It smacked of drudgery, watery poached eggs and bed-changing and having to be polite to people you couldn't stand the sight of. She had in mind something with more impact; something with a bit of style. After much deliberation, she hit on the idea of country house weekends. It was the perfect compro-mise, allowing her to live unhindered during the week and then pull out all the stops for forty-eight hours. Guests – a maximum of twelve – would arrive on the Friday night and enjoy a simple kitchen supper. The men would spend Saturday shooting, fishing or at the races. The ladies would spend the day shopping in Cheltenham or being pampered at a local day spa. Saturday evening would be a magnificent five-course dinner in the dining room, with fine wines and Havana cigars, and guests entering into the spirit of the occasion, with the men in black tie and the women in evening dresses. The very best of everything would be served, from Loch Fyne oysters to Prestat after-dinner chocolates. The shining mahogany table in the dining room would be laden with gleaming silver, glittering glass, the huge five-armed candelabra dripping beeswax, Waterford rosebowls stuffed with magnificent blooms, their scent mingling with the smoke from the fireplace. Then on Sunday, the guests would be gently nursed back to reality with a late breakfast, the newspapers, a roaring fire and the offer of a place in the family pew if any of them were in need of salvation before taking their departure.

Simple but opulent. Unashamed but tasteful luxury. Live like a lord for a weekend. A taste of the life that people craved, that they'd read about in Wodehouse and Mitford and seen in *Gosford Park*. It was an ideal fortieth birthday celebration, or anniversary, or an excuse for well-off thirty-something couples to escape their responsibilities for the weekend and totally indulge. Of course, it wouldn't come cheap, but Madeleine had a shrewd idea that she could get away with charging outrageous prices, as the sort of people she was likely to attract got a kick out of being thoroughly profligate. She knew it was new money she was going to be entertaining, and that more likely than not they wouldn't be sure which of the knives and forks they should be using, but she didn't mind exploiting the nouveaux riches, not at all. And if she could teach them something, so much the better.

So when the location manager sat down in the kitchen at Eversleigh and outlined exactly how much she stood to make, Madeleine grasped the opportunity with both hands. It was serendipitous. While *Lady Jane Investigates* was being filmed, the rest of the house could undergo a refurbishment financed by the hefty location fee. The film crew only wanted to utilize the exterior and the main reception rooms – the magnificent hall and stairs, the drawing room, the dining room and, for each episode's denouement, the library – and part of the deal was that they would decorate those to Madeleine's order, as well as leaving the curtains and furniture specially commissioned for the drama. The existing curtains were far too dull and faded and wouldn't show up well on television, so sumptuous, rich drapes were hung, and fat, velvet-covered sofas brought in. Meanwhile, six of the bedrooms upstairs were repainted – in some cases replastered – and thick, luxurious carpet was laid in a tawny, old gold the colour of a lion's mane. A joiner fitted wardrobes into awkward nooks and crannies along with discreet cabinets – televisions, DVDs and sound systems with hidden speakers were essential if she was going to get the price she was planning on charging.

Thank God Guy had come back in the middle of it. She loved her son dearly, but he exasperated her. He was always off on some madcap adventure, subsidizing his travels by writing articles for newspapers and magazines about his experiences, as bonkers and irresponsible as his father had once been. She'd finally mastered the computer in Tony's study, sending Guy subtle emails via his Hotmail account that hinted he was neglecting his filial duty; his two sisters had homes and families of their own to run, and couldn't really be expected to pitch in. He'd re-appeared eventually, deeply tanned and dishevelled, and together with Malachi, her gardener-cum-handyman, he'd been bringing the house and grounds up to scratch. It was incredible how quickly things deteriorated without a man about the place.

Madeleine drew on her dressing gown and went out into her little kitchen to make tea. When she'd first moved into the flat above the coach house, she'd thought she would hate it, and assumed she would move straight back into the main house as soon as the production team moved out. But now she'd decided she'd stay. The flat was warm and cosy and, above all, manageable, and she could keep an eye on proceedings while having her own space.

She realized she was feeling quite excited. Filming was finished; the production team were going to spend the next couple of days restoring order and then the Portias family would have Eversleigh to themselves. They then had a week to kick things into touch before the first of their weekends took place. Madeleine had scarcely needed to advertise. The success of *Lady Jane Investigates* had taken care of that – there had been no less than six articles in the weekend papers which meant they had a raft of book-ings already between now and next April, when the film crew was provisionally scheduled to film another series.

Madeleine was under no illusion that the next few months were going to be anything other than jolly hard work. But that had been the whole point of the project – to have something to throw herself into. Anyway, she wasn't afraid of getting her hands dirty. She did, however, need Guy's full attention. He'd been somewhat distracted lately by that girl. Madeleine thought Richenda was perfectly sweet, but was glad that after today they'd be seeing the back of her.

She poured herself a mug of strong tea and began to write a list.

A squeaking floorboard in the corridor outside alerted Richenda to Guy's return, and she snuggled back down under the covers, spreading her long, dark hair out on the pillow around her head and shutting her eyes.

He came in behind an enormous bouquet.

'Darling, you shouldn't have.'

'I didn't,' he replied. 'They're from Cindy Marks.'

Richenda sat up, batting her lashes in bewilderment as she read the tag.

'However did she find out?'

Guy sighed.

'I don't know,' he answered. 'I would have liked a couple of days to get used to the idea myself.'

Richenda buried her nose in the roses, hoping that the greenery would hide any hint of a blush on her cheeks. She might be an actress, but she wasn't all that used to deception. She'd already deleted any evidence of the call she'd made to Cindy at four o'clock that morning from the confines of the bathroom. Not that Guy had a suspicious nature, or would have a clue how to get into Call Register on her tiny Nokia – he was the only man she'd ever met who didn't know how to use a mobile phone – but it was better to cover your tracks when the stakes were this high.

She sighed.

'I suppose we'd better do a photocall. They won't leave us alone until we do.'

Guy was filled with panic.

'Not today. I'll need a shave. And a clean shirt. And . . .'

Richenda wound her arms around his neck.

'No, darling. Not today. Anyway, I want the world to see you as you really are. That's the whole point. That's why I love you. Because you don't pretend.'

'So what will the headline be? Beauty and the Beast?'

He scraped his stubble against her cleavage. She squealed with delight, then took his head between her hands, forcing him to look at her.

'Seriously. We need to do something official or there'll be photographers crawling all over the place.'

Guy's face clouded over.

'OK. But do me a favour. Can we wait until I talk to my mother? I don't want her finding out we're engaged when the hired help comes in brandishing the *News of the World*.'

'Not the *News of the World*,' corrected Richenda. 'The *Daily Post*. Cindy will have an exclusive.'

'Whatever,' said Guy, with a slightly sinking heart, and swearing inwardly that he would never touch Taylor's again.

2

Guy took his mother to the Honeycote Arms. The pub in Eversleigh was perfectly good for a quick pint, but the food was acknowledged as dreadful, serving either soggy baguettes or rock-hard scampi. The Honeycote Arms, by contrast, was an epicurean paradise, warm and welcoming, and Guy managed to secure a table in the bar by the fire that was well out of earshot of the other diners. He installed his mother in the more comfortable of the chairs, and went over to the bar.

While he waited to be served – the Honeycote Arms was always buzzing at lunchtime – he took a moment to ponder his predicament. Things had happened rather fast for Guy that day: in an ideal world after last night's party he wouldn't have been long out of bed, but waking up to find himself engaged had brought with it a sense of urgency that couldn't be ignored. Swept along by the momentum, this was the first moment he had had to draw breath and analyse his true feelings.

When he'd first met Richenda, he couldn't deny that he'd thought of her as a novelty, a delicious little pleasure to indulge in while he went about his daily tasks, a consolation prize for being dragged back to do his filial duty. They were, he considered, borderline obsessed with each other, but he had to admit the relationship was largely based on walks in the wood, fireside suppers in this very pub and rather a lot of furtive sex – they had to avoid the rest of the film crew and his mother, which of course made it all the more thrilling. Yet Guy had assumed that once filming had finished, Richenda would drift back to London, that their relationship would wither and die, like a holiday romance. Somewhere along the line, things had changed – to the point that she was about to become his wife!

It had certainly taken him by surprise, for he wasn't the type to be trapped into marriage. Indeed, he'd spent many years dodging commitment; had become rather expert at extricating himself from relationships as soon as they showed any sign of becoming serious. For Guy had a somewhat misguided conviction that women were buying into a package rather than him, that it was the lure of being the lady of the manor that made him attractive. It was why he spent so much time travelling. When you met a girl in the surf of Sri Lanka, or in a hot, sweaty club in Havana, they weren't aware that thousands of miles away sat a pile of Cotswold stone that made him the most eligible bachelor for miles around. But even then, he hadn't met the right girl for him, because at the end of the day he knew his future lay at Eversleigh. He couldn't escape that responsibility. And whoever he chose had to be able to deal with it in just the right way. Over the years, he could have had his pick of solid, sensible English girls who would have set to with gusto, chummed up the vicar and sat on committees and transplanted bulbs to their heart's content. But that wasn't really Guy's style. Whoever he finally married had to have a bit more about them.

And Richenda certainly had that. Her status was, in a twenty-first-century style, on a par with his. She was definitely no gold-digger. In fact, if anyone was going to be accused of gold-digging, it was probably him . . .

'Hello? Guy? Anyone in there?' His daydream was shattered by Barney, the landlord, grinning at him curiously.

'Sorry, mate. I was miles away.'

'What can I get you?'

Guy snapped out of his trance, ordering with alacrity, and ten minutes later he was digging into a slab of game terrine with pear chutney, while Madeleine picked at a plate of smoked duck breast. Madeleine scarcely ate. It wasn't that she didn't appreciate food. But she'd spent time in Paris before meeting Guy's father, and the city had had an influence upon her, which included an obsession with being painfully thin. On a more positive note, it had left her with a knack for choosing accessories — a knotted silk scarf, an artfully draped pashmina, suede loafers and always, always real jewellery — that stopped her from becoming the caricature of an English country woman, but also gave her an air of Parisian *froideur*.

Eventually she put her fork down and fixed him with a perspicacious glare.

'So,' she said. 'Lunch out. What's it all in aid of? I hope you're not planning to bugger off again?'

Guy took a slug of Honeycote Ale. It gave him both a hair of the dog and some Dutch courage before dropping his bombshell.

'I've asked Richenda to marry me.'

'I see.' She surveyed him frostily, her eyes as chill and

unforgiving as a winter's morning. 'This is all rather sudden, isn't it?'

Humour and cajoling, Guy knew, could restore her eyes to a softer blue. He smiled winningly.

'We've known each other nearly six months.'

Madeleine gave a disdainful sniff.

'Hardly under normal circumstances. It's not what you'd call a conventional courtship.'

'Well, no . . .'

'I mean, we've all been living in a fantasy world for the past few months. And I can see how easy it would be to imagine yourself in love . . .'

'Mother. Please. Give me some credit.'

'I'm just pointing out that when this circus has gone and you actually have to do some hard work, the reality might be different. For both of you.'

'We have taken that into consideration.' Guy lied glibly, infuriated with his mother for voicing fears he hadn't even voiced to himself yet.

She raised an elegant eyebrow.

'I know how impulsive you can be.'

'Impulsive, yes. But not stupid. I'm quite certain I'm doing the right thing.'

'How can you be so sure?'

Guy leaned forward, gesticulating with his knife.

'Because Richenda knows who she is. She's a person in her own right. She's confident, talented, successful. And I don't think she'll be intimidated by Eversleigh. Or swept away by it.' Guy chose his words carefully, knowing this was the only chance he had to convince his mother he was doing the right thing. 'I think we'll be an ideal partnership. We both have things in our lives that are incredibly important to us, that give us our identity. So we'll be able to support each other. But at the same time give each other enough space to be who we are . . .'

He cringed inwardly, knowing he was talking like some grim American chat-show host, but it seemed to do the trick. Madeleine sighed.

'Well, I suppose television stars are the new aristocracy,' she conceded, and lit a cigarette while he was still eating, another of her French affectations and one that Guy found deeply irritating. 'Does she realize what being mistress of Eversleigh entails? It's virtually a full-time job.'

Guy stabbed at an errant cornichon with his fork. 'Maybe you could talk her through it? You know what's involved far better than I do.'

'I'd be delighted. I think it's only fair to let her know what she's letting herself in for. And how irresponsible the Portias males can be.'

Guy smiled inwardly at this little dig, then realized that Madeleine was merely subtly shifting the balance of power by allying herself with Richenda. He put his fork down and pulled one of his mother's cigarettes out of the packet. He found he was suddenly nervous. He had won his mother over all too easily, for the time being at least. There were no more obstacles in the way, a prospect that was rather unnerving. He wondered whether he'd secretly wanted Madeleine to wade in and stop the proceedings, tell him she forbade it. But of course she wouldn't have. He was a grown man, after all, and she had absolutely no reason to object.

His mother's voice cut through his deliberation.

'I suppose you'll be wanting the master bedroom.'

Guy stubbed his cigarette out studiously. Anything rather than meet his mother's eye. He couldn't confess that he'd spent the night shagging the arse off Richenda in that very room.

'I suppose so.'

'I'll have it done out for you,' said Madeleine. 'I've been putting it off as it is. I couldn't bear the thought of it being used for paying guests.'

'Thank you,' said Guy faintly, not daring to ask if Richenda could choose the wallpaper.

'We'll have champagne in the small sitting room at six. It's just a pity your father's not here.'

Madeleine said it as if Tony was off on a fishing trip, not six foot under in the graveyard. Nevertheless, Guy managed a small smile at the thought of his father with Richenda. Tony would have had even less of a clue about what Richenda did than Guy, but he had appreciated a beautiful woman. It was amazing how sexually attractive the absent-minded professor act could be when executed correctly. His father had been utterly exasperating and totally charming. No regard for mealtimes or bedtimes, dress codes, deadlines; he had been a law unto himself. Guy suspected he'd never had to confront a bill or a bank statement in his life, let alone a leaky tap. Which was why Madeleine's life hadn't been any more difficult since his departure. Just empty.

'Then Richenda and I can have a little chat,' Madeleine carried on. 'I want her to be quite clear what she's letting herself in for.' She put her slender hand over Guy's in a rare moment of affection. 'I'm very pleased for you, darling. I hope you'll both be very happy.'

Guy's stomach gave a little flip. With his mother's seal of approval, he realized he was moving into the next phase of his life. Things couldn't stay the same, after all. He was thirty-five – he couldn't remain a bachelor much longer without attracting speculation. No, it was definitely time he settled down and faced up to his responsibilities. He told himself he was bound to feel nervous. He felt certain everyone had doubts. It was a lifetime commitment, after all – no one could ever be a hundred per cent sure they were doing the right thing.

'I'll go and pay.' He stood up and went over to the bar. While Barney totted up the bill, Guy wondered why his stomach was still churning. Had the terrine been too rich? Or was there a more sinister meaning? He leaned an elbow on the bar.

'Tell me,' he said to Barney. 'How did you feel when you proposed to Suzanna?'

Barney looked up, somewhat startled.

'What?'

'Were you shit scared?'

'Well, yeah. I suppose so. It's not every day you ask a girl to marry you. But I was excited too.' A smile spread over his face. 'Is there something you want to tell me?'

Guy scratched his head, grinning a bit bashfully.

'You'll read about it soon enough. In the papers.'

Barney gave him a playful punch on the arm.

'Congratulations, mate. And don't worry. You're bound to feel nervous.'

As Guy counted out the money for lunch, he tried to

feel reassured. But still he couldn't ignore the little nagging feeling of doubt. And he thought he knew what it was. He adored Richenda, that was certain. His heart leaped when she came into the room, or when he woke up next to her; he missed her dreadfully when she wasn't around. But he wasn't sure he knew her. She was mysterious, alluring, enigmatic – all things he found incredibly attractive and a turn-on, but he wasn't sure they were qualities you looked for in a wife. 'Wife' said to him comfort, cosiness, familiarity – knowing about each other's hopes, fears, bunions, childhood illnesses. When you looked at Barney and Suzanna, for example, you knew they knew each other inside out. But he hadn't a clue whether Richenda had had chicken pox, or whether she liked marzipan. Or even where she'd like to go on their honeymoon. It would be up to him to book it, but he wasn't sure of her ideal destination. Or even if she was afraid of flying . . .

As he drove his mother back through the lanes to Eversleigh, Guy told himself it was up to him to take their relationship on to the next level, to dig underneath the passion and the novelty for something more solid and sensible. He felt certain he would be reassured by what he found. And, he reminded himself, if it all went pearshaped he could always bail out. They were only engaged, after all, and engagements could be broken off. It wasn't as if they were getting married tomorrow.

While Madeleine and Guy went out for lunch, Richenda took the opportunity to wander round the house safe in the knowledge that she could explore for at least an hour before they got back. Not that she wanted to snoop, exactly. After all, she'd spent the best part of six months at Eversleigh. But it had been always teeming with cast and crew, lit by ferocious lights, crammed with cameras and cables and wires, its walls resounding with shouts and instructions. Panic and turmoil had reigned. Now a gracious calm had settled upon it, and apart from the few members of the production team who were restoring it to its former glory, and the men taking down the marquee, she had the place to herself. She wanted to revel in the wonder of its thick walls and take in the glorious fact that soon she would belong here. She would be Mrs Guy Portias, of Eversleigh Manor.

Loads of stars were buying up mansions in the Cotswolds. Elizabeth Hurley and Kate Winslet had already succumbed; even Kate Moss was rumoured to be looking for a place in the country. But there was a world of difference between buying a stately home and actually having the right to be there. The Portias family had inhabited Eversleigh Manor for five generations. Their coat of arms was set in stone over the front entrance.

There was no doubt that as houses went, Eversleigh was deliciously perfect, which was why it had made such an ideal location for *Lady Jane Investigates*. It was nestled smack bang in the middle of the village, next to the church, hidden by ancient trees and a crumbling, moss-covered stone wall. A pair of wrought-iron gates hung on two stout pillars, leading into a semicircular gravelled area in front of the porticoed entrance, though no one parked here – a drive led off round the side of the house to the garages and stable block. The house itself was symmetrical: each eave, each chimney pot, each mullion was perfectly reflected. The windows were leaded with squares rather than diamonds, which lent an air of elegance rather than chocolate-box tweeness. Everything was ancient and aged, smothered in moss and verdigris and lichen. The only hint of the twenty-first century was a small blue box tucked under one of the eaves that housed the necessary burglar alarm.

The huge oak front door led into a wood-panelled entrance hall that was large enough to hold a cocktail party, yet felt welcoming rather than cavernous. There was a stone fireplace big enough for a man to stand in, and a sweeping staircase that rose then split into two, leading back on itself to either side of the house. The flagstone floor was scattered with faded and worn Oriental rugs; a round mahogany table in the middle held a Chinese vase. There were three doors: one to the drawing room on the left, one to the dining room on the right and one to a corridor that ran the width of the back of the house leading to the library, the small sitting room and the kitchen.

Richenda wandered through each room in turn, reflecting with interest that the house was so gracious, so quietly authoritative, that there was no real need to decorate as such. Its features set the tone, so it was merely a question of choosing paints and fabrics that enhanced the atmosphere, rather than trying to impose one's own style. And Richenda couldn't deny that Madeleine had an excellent eye in what she had chosen.

The drawing room was painted soft ochre, with three large cream Knole sofas grouped around the fireplace. Conveniently placed occasional tables were home to pieces of silver and glass. Several landscapes adorned the walls. Richenda decided that this room, perfect though it was, was a little too formal for her liking. It was a room for polite conversation, not relaxing.

The dining room was more dramatic, its walls a peacock bluey-green of startling depth, set off by the golden Cotswold stone fireplace and mullioned windows. The curtains were a rusty red silk with a wide velvet self-stripe; a huge Persian rug under the table picked up the blues and the reds, while an enormous ormolu mirror over the fireplace reflected the entire room. The overall effect was dramatic, but not overpowering; a room that showed itself to best effect by candlelight.

Her favourite room of all was the small sitting room. Fifteen foot square and south-facing, with doors that opened out on to the garden, its walls were painted powder blue, and it contained two high-backed sofas smothered in cushions, a coffee table, a pretty little writing desk and a dainty piano. There was a bookcase crammed with paperbacks; everything you should ever read, from Daphne du Maurier to Wilbur Smith via George Orwell and Virginia Woolf. It was incredibly feminine; perfect for reading or writing letters, or kicking off your shoes and curling up with a magazine.

There were logs laid in the fire ready, and Richenda bent down to pick up a spill. It might only be early October, but there was a tiny chill in the air. Carefully, she lit the spill and thrust the flame into the centre of the kindling. She knew all about lighting fires. Once upon a time, it had been one of her many menial tasks. As the flames took hold, she smiled in satisfaction. The press might never know it, but her story was as close to Cinderella as it was possible to get.

Richenda's mother had had her as an act of rebellion. As the youngest daughter of elderly parents, living in a modest house on a quiet estate on the outskirts of Woking, Sally Collins had seen giving birth as a romantic gesture, a ticket out of her stifling existence, totally missing the point that a baby was a living, breathing ball and chain with twenty-four-hour needs. By the time that penny had dropped, the baby's father had done a bunk and the eighteen-year-old Sally was left stranded in a freezing caravan struggling on a mishmash of benefits. The bitter words of recrimination that she'd hurled at her bewildered parents, who would in fact have done anything to help her, precluded her from going back home. Besides, better a freezing caravan and the freedom to light up a joint if she fancied it than the claustrophobic, wallpapered walls of suburbia.

Sally looked like a Russian doll, with her sweet round face, her black eyes, pink cheeks and rosebud lips, her long hennaed hair parted in the middle. Sartorially she was hovering in limbo somewhere between a hippy and a punk: a lost soul when it came to style, in fringed skirts, fishnet tights and Doctor Martens, with tight crushed velvet tops and masses of silver jewellery – rings and bangles and earrings. But although she might look sweet and doll-like, she was actually selfish, lazy and not very bright, lurching from one disaster to the next, ill-equipped to think on her feet and always eager to take the easy way out, preferably at someone else's expense.

Living with her was an emotional rollercoaster. Sometimes she would hug her daughter fiercely, tell her it was just the two of them against the rest of the world, that she was all that mattered, and the little girl would go to sleep snuggled up against her mother's warmth. Until the next man came along. Then Sally would be besotted, and would make it clear that Richenda was no more than a nuisance. Richenda would stand her ground stoically, knowing from experience that Sally's relationships rarely lasted more than three months, and it soon would be the two of them again. But in the meantime she would be expelled from her mother's bed, left to shiver in some makeshift pile of blankets in the corner of whatever squat or bedsit or rented room her latest lover occupied.

Of course, in those days she wasn't known as Richenda. Sally had named her Rowan at birth, but by the time she was three she was cruelly known as Missy, short for Mistake, a tag that had been bestowed on her by one of Sally's many other mistakes, and it had stuck.

For ten long years the two of them struggled to survive. Occasionally, Sally would relent when things got really tough and would go back to her parents. Richenda loved these sojourns, for it meant proper food, a warm bed, regular bedtimes, the chance to watch telly. But it would only be a matter of days before a row broke out and Sally would have one of her tantrums, and their few belongings would be swept up into a holdall and off they would go again, to throw themselves on the mercy of one or other of Sally's friends. Richenda dreamed that her grandparents would one day have the strength to stand up to Sally and demand to keep her, but they never did. She would look back at them waving rather disconsolately and helplessly through the kitchen window, and as she grew older she came to despise them for their ineffectuality.

By the time Richenda was twelve, they were living in a damp flat in a house overlooking the railway line in North London. Sally supplemented her benefits by knitting jumpers that she sold at Camden Market – brightly coloured jumpers with cannabis leaves or Dennis the Menace or peace signs emblazoned on the front. She could knit without a pattern, weaving the colours in to create pictures with an expert eye, and the jumpers were very popular. It was Richenda's job to scour jumble sales and charity shops for old knitwear that could be unravelled and reused. She loved pulling the threads and watching the garments disappear before her very eyes, before winding the wool up carefully into neat balls which she stacked in colour-coordinated rows in orange boxes. One day Sally promised to knit her a jumper of her own, with the *Jungle Book* characters on it. Together they drew out a design, of Baloo with Mowgli, and Richenda watched in excitement as the figures emerged hanging from the needles. She couldn't wait for the day it was finished. Somehow this jumper represented the fact that their life was settling down, that Sally had got over her resentment of her daughter, that they were almost normal.

But before the jumper was finished, Sally met Mick . . .

Mick also had a stall at Camden Market, where he was selling bongs and pipes and all manner of smoking paraphernalia, and doing a roaring trade. The first day Sally met him she came home with a silly grin on her face. The second day she didn't come home until the next morning. Sally had repeatedly told Richenda she was old enough to stay in the flat on her own, and often left her alone in the evenings when she went to the pub, but all night was a different matter. Richenda had been worried sick, imagining that she had got drunk and fallen under a tube train. Sally had laughed, high on lack of sleep and too much sex and Mick's Lebanese red, and told her not to worry – they were moving to Mick's place. With a heavy heart, Richenda packed up her things, a strong sense of foreboding telling her that this move was not in her interests.

Mick's place was known as 'The Farm'. Not that anyone did anything remotely agricultural on it, unless you counted the spiky green leaves of the cannabis plants in the greenhouse. The farmhouse was built in unforgiving flint, and sat in an exposed position on the Berkshire Downs, ill-protected from the winter winds. It was a sort of idealistic post-punk commune full of middle-class twits in dreadlocks and combat trousers, trying to deny their origins and live their dream while picking up the dole, and in the meantime composing anarchic songs and trying to get gigs. The main room stank of cider, dope, garlic and stale sweat. Though Richenda could never understand why it smelled of sweat, for the house was freezing: there was a wood-burning stove that was constantly going out, as no one could be bothered to chop wood, and icy-cold flagstone floors and a howling gale that whipped through the windows. Now, more than anything, Richenda remembered the cold, and the unforgiving itchy lumps that came up on her fingers as a result.

The Farm also housed Mick's harem, a collection of

adoring females who came and went, ebbing and flowing in tune with some mysterious tide, bringing with them a stream of runny-nosed, unkempt offspring whom they proceeded to ignore as they sat round in stoned admiration, hanging off his every word. Richenda couldn't understand what they saw in him, with his matted dreadlocks and dozens of earrings in each ear. To her, his eyes were cold and dead. But he wove some sort of magic over these women, and her own mother was the latest to be under his spell. For two whole years Sally was queen bee, and shared his bed.

Richenda, being the oldest, was put in charge of the children. She wasn't sure how many of them were actually Mick's, but she found she quite liked looking after them. It gave her something to do. She commandeered the attic, a long, low room that ran the entire length of the house, and tried to turn it into a nursery for the children. None of them seemed to have any toys, so she went to the village jumble sale. There was a large box of toys left over at the end that nobody wanted. Richenda had looked round to make sure nobody was looking, then picked up the box and walked out. At least the kids had something to play with now.

She was surprised none of them were allowed to go to school, as that would have ensured they were out from under their mothers' feet five days a week, but the effort of getting them up and dressed, packing them a lunchbox, taking them to school and then picking them up was, apparently, too great. Much easier to leave them in Richenda's care.

She longed to go to school herself, but her mother had

told her she didn't need to go – she was being educated at home. Richenda realized the irony, that most kids would jump for joy at being let off, but she longed for a crisp navy uniform with a white blouse and tights and proper shoes. Not hand-me-down jumpers that had shrunk in the wash, and tie-dyed skirts and ugly old boots. Under this drab uniform no one seemed to notice that she was turning into a woman. She never had the fun of experimenting with clothes and make-up and hairdos, because there was little point.

When she was fourteen, she was given another duty: delivering parcels. Time and again, she'd clamber on to the bus in the village, change for Reading in the next village, then walk two or sometimes three miles to the address she'd been given – usually a seedy block of flats or a dilapidated terrace. The recipient would tell her to wait on the doorstep while they went to inspect the merchandise. Then she would make her return journey, often getting back in the dark, shivering with cold under her army surplus duffel coat. Looking back on it now it was obvious what was in the packages. She supposed she knew then, but it was easier to obey if she feigned ignorance to herself. What would have happened if she'd been caught?

As life is wont to do, one day it took a turn. Richenda had gone to the village post office to collect the family allowance – with seven children plus herself currently in the house it added up to a considerable amount, and there were plans for a party. For the grown-ups, of course. No plans for anything that might make the children's life any more comfortable, like proper new shoes or a radiator for the attic room. For a moment she wondered what would happen if she took the money and went into Reading, to blow it on bicycles and dolls and puzzles and a huge, enormous bag full of sweets. She didn't, of course. She didn't even dare buy a family-size bar of Dairy Milk to share out between them all. Mick would know exactly how much money she was supposed to bring back. For someone who declared himself anti-capitalist, he was very keen on money – as long as he didn't have to do anything for it.

On the noticeboard in the post office, there was an advert for auditions in the village hall, for a forthcoming production of *Oliver!* ALL WELCOME, it read. Richenda gazed at the poster for a full five minutes, turning the prospect over in her mind. The woman who ran the post office came up beside her.

'You should have a go,' she said. 'They're a good bunch. Not your usual am-dram types. It'll be a real laugh.'

'But I can't act. Or sing,' objected Richenda. 'At least, not properly.'

She could sing, she knew that. Sometimes, when Mick organized an impromptu jamming session, she'd join in. She'd received a couple of grudging compliments from the less self-obsessed inhabitants of The Farm. One had compared her to Stevie Nicks, which had earned her a scowl from her mother, who'd always harboured ambitions of stardom but couldn't sing a note.

'Nor can any of them,' said the postmistress cheerfully. 'You should give it a go. They'll make you very welcome. And if the worst comes to the worst, you can help paint the scenery. Whatever happens, you'll have fun.'

The postmistress watched Richenda go, hoping she'd follow her advice. The poor girl never seemed to have any fun. She was like a little Dickensian drudge, in her own way. She always looked pale and ill. It would do her good to get involved in something outside that dreadful commune she lived in.

For three days Richenda mulled over the prospect. The auditions were on a Saturday afternoon. Somehow, she managed to persuade one of the more sympathetic mothers at the commune to look after the kids, muttering that she had to go to the doctor. Then she screwed up her courage and began her journey to the village hall. The urge to run back home was overwhelming. But something inside told her it was time for her to take control of her life, grab this opportunity. Otherwise she would be facing a lifetime of drudgery at Mick and Sally's beck and call, a courier-cum-nursemaid.

To her surprise, she *was* made welcome. No one questioned her right to be there. When it was her turn to audition, the director made her feel relaxed, and thanked her warmly afterwards. His name was Neil Ormerod, and he was quite good-looking in a boyish way, in his collarless denim shirt and little round glasses, even though he was quite old; at least forty.

To her amazement, she got a part. She was the girl who sold strawberries in the market place, and she had a solo – 'Strawberries Ripe'. To add to her joy, she was to be Nancy's understudy. And Neil had hinted that she was good enough to have played Nancy. 'I can't give you that part, though,' he said regretfully, 'because you don't really have the experience and I'd be lynched. But stick with us and who knows what might happen next year? You've got a lot of promise.'

Richenda was beside herself with excitement. Each night, she managed to get the children in bed by half past six so she could slip across the fields to the village hall for rehearsals. It benefited her, as by getting a proper night's sleep they were better behaved the next day anyway. And even if she wasn't required at the rehearsal, she sat and absorbed every moment of what was going on; how Neil coaxed a better performance out of each member of cast.

One afternoon, Mick cornered her in the kitchen. She'd curled up to learn her lines as Nancy just in case. She thrust the script under a cushion as he came in.

'You seem very perky these days. You must be getting it from somewhere.'

'What?'

'Sex. A bit of cock. That's the only reason I know for a woman to be happy. Who's the lucky bloke?'

Richenda tilted her chin into the air indignantly.

'Don't be stupid. I'm only fourteen.'

Mick leered.

'If you're old enough to bleed, you're old enough to breed.'

Richenda recoiled in disgust. He tugged at her shirt.

'I bet you've got a nice little pair of titties under there.'

'Stop it!'

He wrenched the fabric and the buttons fell off, revealing her breasts. Mick guffawed in triumph.

'There you are. Told you. Beautiful.'

Richenda pulled the shirt back round her and went to

get off the chair and run away, but Mick grabbed her.

'Come on, sweetheart. Let me give you something to smile about. God knows I've been keeping your mother happy long enough . . .'

She was more surprised by her weakness than his strength. He was wiry, not particularly heavy, but she was still unable to push him away. Eventually, she submitted with a sigh.

'That's it. You've got to learn to relax a bit,' he said as he thrust away. After what seemed an eternity, he rolled off her. Richenda lay on the flagstones, staring mutely at the ceiling.

'Where do you fuck off to every night, anyway?' He looked at her with interest as he did up his flies.

'Nowhere . . .' Richenda replied dully. She couldn't think of a lie quickly enough. She sat up sharply as he pulled back the cushion on the chair to reveal her script. He studied it closely for a moment, frowning, then tossed it back on the chair and walked out.

He didn't mention the incident again, and neither did she, pushing it to the back of her mind. If it hadn't been for *Oliver!*, she thought she might have gone mad. While she was at the rehearsals, she could forget her miserable existence. She loved everything about the play, especially the camaraderie. Yes, there was competitiveness, but it was banter rather than bitchiness. There was no cynicism. Everyone was out to enjoy themselves. And she adored being on stage. Each rehearsal she gained in confidence; her voice grew stronger. One night she stood in for Nancy, who had a cold, and was praised warmly by Neil, told that she had real promise, real talent. And no one seemed to resent the fact that she had shone; they all told her she was brilliant. She felt filled with a warm glow that was pride and excitement – she'd found something she was good at and loved doing. She couldn't wait for the opening night. Each performer was given two free tickets to give to family or friends. She gave hers to the girl playing Betsy. No one at The Farm would want to come. They'd sneer and scoff. She didn't want them to come, anyway. This was her escape, her little world, and she didn't want it invaded.

The night of the dress rehearsal she came flying out on air and bumped smack bang into Mick.

'Thought you were up to something,' he taunted.

Richenda looked at her feet, her excitement withering away, knowing that somehow she was never going to end up back on the stage, that Mick would see to it that she wouldn't have her moment of glory.

Later that night she found herself being pulled out of bed by her mother, who'd turned into a screaming, hysterical banshee. She tugged at Richenda's hair, scratched her face.

'You fucking little slag!' she screeched. 'Mick told me you seduced him. Said you couldn't wait for his cock inside you!'

Richenda looked at Mick lounging in the doorway, surveying the scene with a mocking detachment. She was shocked by the brazenness of the lie, and was met with a cold, blank stare that told her he wasn't going to help her out of this situation. Her mother would never believe it if she told the truth, that he'd forced himself upon her.

Later, as she packed up her things, she found the *Jungle*

Book jumper, still hanging from its needles. It summed up her life so perfectly. Empty promises.

She ran. Across the fields and on to the main road. Her heart was beating so hard she thought it would burst. She pounded up the road through the village, past the post office where she'd seen the sign for the audition, past the pub and into the cul-de-sac of modern homes where she knew the director, Neil Ormerod, lived.

She ran over the crunchy gravel of the drive to his reassuringly sensible mock-Georgian house with lights that worked and curtains that closed and two neatly parked cars outside and a dog that did as it was told. She rang the bell. It had a merry, welcoming chime, and she felt heartened. He'd give her a bed for a couple of nights, she felt sure of it. He'd been so kind, encouraged her; he really seemed to care.

Ten minutes later, she was disillusioned.

'You can't stay here, love,' he said awkwardly, his eyes flicking behind him. Richenda wasn't to know that he had a history of affairs with his leading ladies that his wife didn't take kindly to; that she wouldn't look upon Richenda as a waif and stray but as a threat. Richenda didn't make a scene, just turned disconsolately to go.

'Wait!' he said and, thrusting his hand into his pocket, took out his wallet. He handed her two crumpled five-pound notes.

'I know it's not much . . .' he trailed off, feeling suddenly ashamed. 'If you get into real trouble, ring me at the office.' He fumbled in his wallet again and handed her a business card.

Richenda managed a grateful smile.

'Thank you.'

For the last time, she took the bus into Reading, where she changed and took a bus to Victoria.

It was surprising how easy she found life over the next couple of years, and how her existence had equipped her to think on her feet. She'd had the foresight to pinch the family allowance books before she left, which gave her a small lump sum to tide her over. The first thing she did was go into Top Shop and buy herself two new outfits and a pair of shoes, working on the basis that one had to spend money to make money. Then she booked herself an appointment at a smart hairdresser in Covent Garden – she went to the models' evening, so the price was minimal. By the end of the evening she had a head of shining hair and a job sweeping up and shampooing clients, cash paid and no questions asked. And a new name. When the boss had asked her name, she'd given the stage name she'd invented for herself in bed one night. From that day on, she was Richenda Fox.

By the end of the week she had feigned a terrible argument with her parents and moved into the flat of one of the stylists who needed help with the rent. She only had a sofa bed to sleep on, but it was better than moving from one late-night café to the next, snatching sleep on her folded arms until she was told to leave.

For the first time in her life she could relax. She was in control, and didn't have to live in fear of someone spoiling what she'd worked so hard to achieve. She loved working at the hairdresser's; the clients were glamorous and interesting and she picked up lots of tips on what to wear and how to look good. Soon she blossomed. She had a figure to die for, her hair was done for free and she spent carefully on bargains that she accessorized cleverly so she always looked bang up to date; a proper girl about town. Eventually, she was promoted to receptionist, which gave her a little more money. And to supplement her income, she did a stint as a tequila girl at a Mexican restaurant near Leicester Square, scarcely dressed but for a belt studded with shot glasses slung round her body, flogging slugs of eye-watering liquor to tourists who were already too far gone to know any better.

Two years later, she was offered her own room and bathroom in a wealthy client's house in Islington – not so very far away from where she and her mother had once lived – in return for help with the housework and children. It was a very carefree time: the family were noisy and loving, the children boisterous but affectionate, the parents overworked but very fair to her. And, to her surprise, they were interested in her as well. When they discovered that she had a burning desire to go to drama school that she feared would never be realized, they sent her off to evening classes to get some qualifications, pushed her to join the local drama group, took her out to the theatre, introduced her to friends of theirs who were involved in film and television. For the first time she saw that people didn't always have their own interests at heart. She stayed with them for four years. They were as close to a real family as she'd ever got. The day she left to join the Central School of Speech and Drama, she sobbed.

At drama school, she thrived. She emerged as one of the most promising students of her year, and straight away walked into a minor role as a nurse on a long-running hospital drama. She soon gained notoriety when a disc jockey on national radio began fantasizing about her on air during his afternoon show, stirring up a storm. Delighted by the publicity, the producers responded by giving her a storyline of her own. That Christmas she played Cinderella in a panto and legions of fans turned up. All the while she networked, smiled, gave polite interviews and waited for the plum role. Meanwhile, her character in the hospital drama embarked on a sizzling affair with a consultant and viewing figures rose.

The press called her the ice queen, but she didn't mind. Better to remain an enigma than embark on a string of failed showbiz relationships. Cleverly, she supported her leading man through his marriage break-up, using the old adage 'we're just good friends' to heighten media speculation. When he turned out to have been screwing another member of the cast, Richenda came out smelling of roses, and the press surmised that she might have been disappointed in love. She landed the role of Lady Jane not long afterwards.

She trod a fine line between maximizing her coverage, but not wanting anyone to dig too deep, to ferret about in her past for skeletons. She certainly didn't want Sally and Mick tumbling out of the woodwork. They would never watch TV or read the sort of magazines she appeared in. They lived in their own little self-indulgent bubble; a parallel universe that wasn't inhabited by TV stars. Anyway, she was certain they wouldn't recognize her.

For gone was the skin sallow from undernourishment

and fatigue. Now it was suffused with a glow that came from a healthy diet, several litres of water a day, daily exfoliation, moisturizing and regular skin peels. The long mousy hair with its frizzy cloud of split ends was a lustrous, gleaming chestnut brown. Her lips were plumped up with the minutest injection of collagen once every three months. And, courtesy of contact lenses, her once pale, insipid blue eyes were now a vivid green.

She'd invented an anodyne, uninteresting past for herself, a past that hopefully no journalist would want to go digging around in. And she'd neatly disposed of her fictional parents, by sending them off to Australia in pursuit of her fictional brother, where they were all living in the sun-drenched luxury of Adelaide, and where she joined them for family get-togethers from time to time.

Mousy little Rowan Collins had totally reinvented herself.

She was now the ravishing and successful Richenda Fox. And given her past, was it so surprising that she craved recognition, security and status? That the prospect of a mouth-watering manor house and a mouth-watering husband was so attractive to her, when she'd had anti-establishment claptrap rammed down her throat from an early age?

At the same time, she wanted to be sure that whoever she married wasn't after her for her fame and fortune. Guy certainly wasn't. He barely acknowledged the world she came from. He was in love with her for herself, not the face that graced magazine covers. He was confident enough in himself not to find her a threat, and he didn't want to ride on her coat-tails.

Richenda didn't think she'd ever been this happy. Which she found very hard to explain when Guy found her sitting in front of the fire, her arms hugging her knees, with tears streaming down her face.

Guy held Richenda tightly in his arms, any fears and doubts he had felt earlier evaporating. As he kissed away her tears, he realized she was as vulnerable as the next person, and he felt a surge of love. She might be a hugely successful actress, but in some ways that made her even more fragile.

'Sorry,' she gulped, her sobs finally abating. 'It's only because I'm happy.'

Guy stroked her hair. Women were weird sometimes.

'What happens when you're unhappy?' he joked.

Richenda smiled, brushing away the last teardrops. She didn't want to look red-eyed and piggy. She gave a delicate little sniff, then snuggled into Guy's chest.

'I've been thinking,' she said carefully. 'I think we should get married at Christmas.'

'What?' Alarmed, Guy looked at her closely to see if she was joking. It didn't seem as if she was.

'I've looked in my diary. Saturday the twenty-third. We can have the reception here, so we wouldn't have to worry about booking anywhere. And I'm sure the vicar will find us space.'

'But that's only two months away.'

'Which is why it's perfect. I've got two months off, virtually. All I've got to do is some voice-over work on *Lady Jane*, and all the promotional stuff. So I'll have masses of time to organize everything.' She didn't mention that the prospect of a Christmas wedding would add weight to her box-office appeal, that the magazines would all be falling over themselves to put her on the cover. 'And next year is a nightmare for me. The second series is due to start filming in April. And I've got to do a stint in the US promoting *Lady Jane* before that. And a guest appearance in my old hospital drama – a one-off special. I won't have time to breathe, let alone get married.'

Guy didn't answer, because he didn't know what to say. Richenda was pacing up and down the room, excited.

'It would be wonderful. A Christmas wedding! And personally, I don't want a huge affair. I've got no family here, after all. My parents would much prefer us to go out and visit them in Australia after the event, than for them to come over here.'

It came out so glibly. Richenda found that she almost believed in her fictional parents; she could almost imagine booking the tickets here and now.

'I've got hordes of cousins and aunts and Mother's got stacks of friends that will need inviting,' Guy warned gloomily.

'Well, that's OK. I've got the cast and crew of *Lady Jane*. I suppose they're my surrogate family.' Richenda rolled her eyes with a grin.

'So when you say small, you're talking about . . . ?'

'Two hundred? Ish? That's small these days.' Richenda was anxious to reassure Guy, who looked momentarily horrified. She wound her arms round his neck, smiling coquettishly.

'Please say yes,' she wheedled.

Guy had learned from his father that there was little

point in protesting when a woman had made her mind up about something.

'No problem,' he said amiably. 'Just tell me when and where and I'll tip up on the day.'

At six o'clock on the dot, Madeleine Portias glided into the small sitting room. She was wearing a dove-grey cashmere sweater, wide-legged tweed trousers and soft suede loafers. Three gold bangles on her left wrist emphasized her tiny bones. She looked the epitome of elegance.

Guy was hovering. Nervously, Richenda thought, which was interesting, because she'd never seen him nervous. She herself had dressed in a simple black wrap dress, her hair smoothed into a low chignon. She was wary of looking too showbiz. Someone had once mistaken her for Martine McCutcheon, and it had been an early warning for Richenda. Too much make-up and not enough clothing and she might one day be mistaken for a Slater sister if she wasn't careful.

Guy opened a bottle of champagne and Madeleine proposed a very gracious toast.

'I hope you'll be as happy together here as Tony and I were.'

The three of them exchanged kisses and hugs and smiles. A little awkwardly, because none of them could be quite sure what the others were thinking. Then Madeleine perched herself gracefully on one of the sofas, and indicated Richenda should sit opposite. Then she turned to Guy.

'Darling, please go and do something useful in the kitchen. There's a fish pie in the Aga. Why don't you make a salad to go with it? I want to talk to Richenda.'

The bracelets jangled as she shooed her son away. She turned to Richenda with a smile.

'Now, I need to talk to you about your wifely duties.'

Richenda looked at her aghast. Her future mother-in-law wasn't going to talk to her about sex, surely?

To her amazement, Madeleine broke into peals of delighted laughter.

'Heavens, don't look like that! I'm not talking about bed. I'm sure you've been road-tested already, knowing Guy.'

Richenda coloured furiously, not knowing where to look.

'I mean that as the lady of the house there are certain things expected of you. And I'm afraid that the responsibility will fall on you, once Guy takes over at the helm. I'll be here to guide you, of course. But you will be the one they all look to. And it can be quite a daunting task, I can tell you. Almost a full-time job in itself.'

She smiled brightly. Richenda looked at her warily, not sure what the message was.

'What sort of things?'

Madeleine opened a leather notebook, drawing a tiny pencil out from the spine.

'First and foremost is the village fête. We have it in the grounds here every July, and I'm afraid it's a political minefield. You have to be very diplomatic; make sure none of the committee members railroad you. Just be firm . . .'

Richenda nodded. She thought she could handle the village fête committee.

'The annual crisis is who to get to open it. It's usually

a toss-up between a celebrity gardener and a children's TV presenter. But obviously that won't be a problem any more. You can wield the scissors.'

Madeleine flashed her a quick smile before referring back to her list.

'Then the May Day bank holiday the gardens are traditionally open to the public. Via the National Gardens scheme. I'll introduce you to Malachi. He does all the planting here. He's a bit of a law unto himself. And he spends half of his time inside. Very light-fingered, I'm afraid. Not that he'd ever steal anything from us, so don't worry about that. The important thing is he's a genius in the garden. Though no doubt you'll have your own ideas.'

Richenda looked alarmed. She didn't have a clue about gardening; didn't know a dahlia from a dandelion.

'Then there's the Boxing Day meet.'

Richenda frowned.

'I don't know that I approve of hunting.'

'Doesn't matter whether you do or you don't. The hunt's met here on Boxing Day since 1611.' Madeleine had plucked this date out of nowhere, but she wasn't going to let the girl get any anti-hunting ideas. 'It's perfectly simple. I've done the same thing for years. *Vin chaud* and devils-on-horseback. And for the past three years I've used styrofoam cups. Get one of the kennel lads to go round with a black bin bag afterwards. Saves on the washing-up and no one cares, as long as they go off nicely anaesthetized.'

'Right,' said Richenda, who had absolutely no idea how to make *vin chaud* or devils-on-horseback, or even what they were. Though she would rather die than admit it.

'Then the school have a Teddy Bears' Picnic in about June; we usually do a summer concert in the grounds in August – a sort of bring your own picnic, Glyndebourne on a smaller scale sort of thing; then I do mulled wine and mince pies after the crib service on Christmas Eve . . .'

Richenda was looking utterly appalled.

'But I am going to be away a lot of the time. Filming.'

'You'll just have to work round it, I'm afraid. It is a big responsibility, you know, being a mistress of a house like this.' Madeleine softened momentarily. 'Don't worry – I won't throw you in at the deep end straight away. I'll be here to help, for the first year at any rate. Though I have to admit I'm rather looking forward to stepping back. I've been doing it for nearly forty years. It's definitely time for some fresh blood – I'm sure you'll have all sorts of wonderful new ideas.'

She closed her notebook with a satisfied snap and picked up her glass.

'Anyway, many, many congratulations. I'm utterly delighted. Here's to the two of you.'

'Thank you,' murmured Richenda, somewhat shell-shocked.

'Fish pie, anyone?' asked Guy hopefully from the doorway.

'Lovely,' said Madeleine.

'Did Richenda tell you that we've settled on a date?' asked Guy.

'No,' said Madeleine, looking from one to the other for enlightenment.

Richenda rose gracefully to her feet.

'December twenty-third,' she announced. 'After all, why wait? What would we be waiting for?'

And she swept out of the room with a brilliant smile, leaving Madeleine uncharacteristically speechless on the sofa.

3

The woman's breasts were spilling out over the top of her basque, her cherry-red nipples just visible. She was sporting a black G-string embroidered with rosebuds, and a matching suspender belt held up her fishnet stockings, revealing an expanse of smooth, creamy thigh.

Honor McLean picked up her icing nozzle and wrote 'Happy Birthday Nigel' carefully on the cake board underneath. The floozy cake was one of the most popular in her range: the freezer in her little outhouse was packed with sponge torsos awaiting decoration. They were fairly labour intensive – the criss-crossing on the fishnets took hours and a steady hand – but at sixty quid she didn't mind. She needed all the cash she could get these days. Who would have thought a decent pair of Startrites would eat up more than half of that? Six-year-old boys were seriously high maintenance: Honor couldn't remember the last time she'd spent that sort of money on herself. Not that she was going to start sawing away on a violin in self-pity. She'd learned to do without; weaned herself off the adrenalin rush that a new purchase used to bring. There was a time when she wouldn't have thought that was possible. Major expenditure had been part of her *raison d'être*. Two hundred quid on a jumper; double that on a suit – she'd never thought twice about passing the plastic.

Now she didn't even have a credit card. She didn't allow herself one as she knew how easy it was to slide it across the counter, ignoring the fact that fifty-six days later would come the day of reckoning. She only spent cash, because that way she kept an eye on how much was slipping through her fingers. Only the household bills and the council tax were paid by direct debit, because it was marginally cheaper. And when money was this tight, margins made all the difference.

She lifted the cake board carefully and placed it in a white cardboard box, closing the lid with a sigh. She could really do with putting her feet up in front of the telly tonight, but she had to go through Ted's spellings with him – he always had a test first thing Thursday morning – and make sure his PE kit was ready before forcing him into the bath. Then it was her favourite part of the day, when he snuggled up on her lap in his pyjamas and they read together – he would do one page, and she would do two, usually Dr Seuss or Roald Dahl. Once he was tucked up under his duvet, then she could flop down on the sofa and select her evening's viewing – a pointless ritual, because she would always fall asleep after two minutes.

Her days were long. Every morning she got up at six to put wood on the wood-burning stove so the house would be warm by the time Ted got up. Then she made her daily batch of three dozen scones: she supplied a local craft centre with freshly baked goods for the lunches and teas they served in their café. While the scones were in the oven she had a shower; she had it timed to perfection so that they were pale gold in the time it took her to wash her hair and rough dry it with a towel. Having extricated the scones, she made porridge or boiled eggs for breakfast, then she and Ted raced each other to get dressed. A ritual search for an essential item ranging from a Pokémon card to a plimsoll usually ensued, then Honor walked Ted down through the village to the school gates, where he joined the rest of his mates in the playground. Once she was back home, she embarked upon the rest of the day's orders, which the craft centre phoned through at about quarter past nine.

She often thought about going back to work properly, but she never wanted to have the dilemma of Ted being off ill. And she liked to pick him up at three fifteen. She didn't like the thought of him trooping into aftercare, even though many of his peer group did. And she'd want the holidays and half-terms off. Apart from teaching, which she was hardly qualified to do, there were few jobs that would allow that flexibility. So she muddled through with her scones and her birthday cakes, as well as dinner-party puddings for overworked hostesses who couldn't quite face the ignominy of serving up a Marks & Spencer cheesecake, but it was a lot of labour for the money – she seemed constantly to be covered in flour, hot from the oven. Or tearing round trying to deliver on time – once she'd dropped Ted at school she had a two-hour window to bake whatever else was needed and deliver it to the craft centre in time for lunch.

Today she'd done three quiches and two pissaladières and dropped them off at the craft centre, then rushed back to finish the birthday cake, which was going to be picked up later that afternoon by the wife of the unsuspecting Nigel. Taking off her apron and stuffing it into the washing machine, she looked at the clock. It was five to three – not long enough to do much about her appearance. She double-checked the calendar on the cork noticeboard to make sure there was nothing she'd forgotten. She was meticulous about writing things down because otherwise she'd never remember. Ted's social and sporting diary was hectic – certainly more than hers was. Beavers, swimming, football on a Saturday, parties most weekends, someone for tea at least once a week in order to help out some other working mother, and all of this underpinned by a complicated rota of lift-sharing. It was a social whirl, and Honor had to keep careful track of it all to make sure that she didn't forget to give another child a lift or take them home for tea. Once she'd forgotten to collect one of Ted's friends from a party, and she'd taken a long time to get over the trauma and the stigma.

Today, however, was clear of commitments. Honor breathed a sigh of relief, then looked along the squares of the calendar to the weekend ahead. In big red letters on Saturday was written CHARITY BALL. Her heart sank and rose simultaneously. She couldn't help feel excited by her first proper social engagement for nearly seven years. She'd been something of a recluse since she'd had Ted, and to be honest, once you got used to not going out, you didn't miss it. Which was why the prospect of the ball was so terrifying. Once, glittering social occasions had been the norm for her. The rails in her wardrobe had groaned with appropriate outfits. She had at one time suffered from ball fatigue, swearing that she couldn't face another evening of Buck's Fizz, chocolate roulade and insincere toastmasters raffling off trips to the local beauty salon. Those days, however, were long gone.

It was Henty Beresford who insisted she come and join their table. The moment Honor had met Henty at the school gates on Ted's first day at school the previous September, she'd known she was a kindred spirit. Henty was small and curvaceous and bubbly and spoke like someone out of a Famous Five adventure – 'golly' and 'crumbs' and 'crikey'. But her sweet nature was saved from sickliness by an acute observation and a wicked sense of humour. Ted and Henty's son Walter were as thick as thieves. They looked as if they'd stepped out of a cartoon strip: Walter with his white-blond pudding-bowl hair cut and wide blue eyes, and Ted with a thatch of red curls and freckles that looked as if they had been painted on.

Henty had been gently persuasive at first, then positively begged her.

'Please! I need someone to have a giggle with. Everyone takes these dos so seriously. And it's in a really good cause – the children's holiday farm. They give terminally ill kids and their families a chance for a break they'd never have otherwise.'

The emotional blackmail had clinched it, and Honor had given in, even though the fifty-quid ticket was more than she could really afford. Somehow Henty had sensed that, but she hadn't patronized Honor by offering to pay for her ticket. She'd ordered two cakes instead – one for her eldest daughter Thea's fourteenth birthday, in the shape of a sweetheart with 'Text Me' written in sugary pink, and one for her mother-in-law – which had covered the fifty pounds. Ted was to stay the night at the Beresfords', on a camp bed in Walter's room, and was unfeasibly excited. Honor hoped that the babysitter would cope, but – as Henty reassured her – they had mobiles and were only three miles away, and if anyone was going to cause trouble it was Thea.

Honor had contributed a prize to the auction as well – a bespoke cake done to the bidder's specification – because everyone who donated a prize had a free advert in the programme and as Henty pointed out it wasn't often that one had a roomful of potential customers.

'All these mothers buy their children's birthday cakes from Tesco, and wouldn't mind forking out a bit extra for something special.'

As she pulled on her duffel coat, Honor couldn't help feeling that the ball represented a turning point for her. With the cake business flourishing, her friendship with Henty, and Ted becoming more independent as each day passed, Honor found that after years of self-imposed isolation she was growing in confidence.

All she had to worry about now was what to wear . . .

As she approached the gates of St Joseph's, her heart sank. The only other mother waiting was Fleur Gibson, and she'd already seen her, so she couldn't turn round and go into the post office in order to avoid standing with her. Honor wasn't one to judge, but she'd taken an instant dislike to Fleur.

Fleur had opened a florist's in the nearby town of Eldenbury two years ago. After a slow start, Twig was now doing phenomenally, even though it was well known that it was Millie Cooper who had all the talent, a young girl she'd scooped up from the nearby college who was bursting with flair and imagination. Fleur just did all the deals, all the talking, while Millie sat in a freezing cold room at the back of the shop, hidden from view, creating wonderful bouquets and arrangements that ranged from the exotic to the fantastic. Honor imagined Fleur wafting about, poking the odd gerbera into place and taking all the credit, and couldn't help feeling it was unfair. But then Millie would never be able to afford to set up on her own. The overheads in Eldenbury were extortionate. She didn't have the contacts, the social connections. One day, Honor comforted herself, Millie would shoot to fame after being discovered on daytime television and would become the next Paula Pryke. Honor was a firm believer in fairy-tale endings.

She sidled up to the school gates, conscious that she looked less than glamorous in her duffel coat and wellies. Fleur was in faded jeans, a pristine white T-shirt with the Twig logo, and a cream mac, her razored bob perfectly in place and her matt lipstick freshly applied. She always managed to look crisp and chic, even though one would have thought the work of a florist was necessarily grubby.

Fleur gave Honor a tight smile, an insincere 'hi', and didn't even bestow an appraising glance on her outfit – Honor was clearly no competition. The mothers at St Joseph's were on the whole a sensible lot – jeans and muddy estates were pretty much the order of the day – but there was a small contingent who arrived in their convertibles fully made up and dressed to the nines. And Fleur liked to think of herself as leader of this pack, setting trends, dictating by example what should be worn, what car should be driven, what diet should be followed and what exercise regime adhered to. She repeatedly boasted that she was a size six, so tiny she had to shop in Gap Kids for her jeans. Not her tops, though, because on top she was a 36DD. She didn't mind telling anyone that she'd got her tits for her thirty-fifth birthday. Honor was desperate to ask her which birthday she'd had her nose for, because no one was born with a tiny little retroussé button that tilted up slightly at the end. But Fleur wasn't yet admitting to facial surgery.

Honor and Henty's friendship had been cemented by an intense hatred of Fleur.

'She shouldn't stand too close to fire,' murmured Henty, 'or she might melt.'

Honor and Fleur waited in awkward silence until a bigger crowd had accrued outside the gates and the atmosphere became more relaxed. It was only when Fleur was happy that she had a large and appreciative audience that she dropped her bombshell.

'Guess what? I delivered a bouquet up to the manor this morning. It seems congratulations are in order.'

Everyone looked at her, waiting for the revelation.

'Guy and Richenda.' Fleur held up her ring finger and rubbed it. 'Wedding bells . . .' she hinted, and waited for the reaction. There were gasps of amazement.

'Seriously?'

'Wow!'

'Oh my God!'

Honor frowned.

'Don't florists have a Hippocratic oath?'

Fleur looked at Honor blankly.

'What?'

'Shouldn't you keep your clients' details a secret? Like doctors? I mean, if people know you're going to blab, they're hardly going to order a bunch of flowers to send to a secret lover. Are they?'

There was a shocked silence. Fleur smiled frostily.

'I imagine, as the flowers were sent from the *Daily Post*, that it will be common knowledge soon enough. But thank you for your concern.'

She turned her back pointedly.

'Now. Only three days to go, girls. Have you all got your outfits?' This said with the smugness of one with a white silk Armani frock hanging in the wardrobe.

The crowd of mothers closed in around Fleur, managing to exclude both Honor and Henty from their circle. Somehow the word 'ball' turned the most sensible female into a gibbering wreck. Nearly everyone from St Joseph's was going. For the past few weeks, there'd been debates over the best crash diet as they all battled in vain to drop a dress size. The local gym saw its subscription rate flourish; the lanes were littered with joggers. The day spa at Barton Court was fully booked for inch-losing seaweed wraps and St Tropez tans.

Honor knew that she was, as usual, going to have to make do. She thought back with irony to all the dresses that used to hang in her wardrobe: some barely worn, one or two never worn, all carefully wrapped in dry-cleaning bags and hung in length order. She'd sold them all to a 'dress exchange' in Bath. It was scandalous really, what she had received in return – the full amount wouldn't have covered the price of one of the outfits. But to a jobless, homeless girl about to give birth, it was the deposit she needed to rent the tiny cottage she'd found in Eversleigh.

She looked down to see that Henty's little face was wrinkled in anxiety.

'I still haven't found a dress,' she confessed. 'Charles was supposed to take me to Liberty to choose something but he hasn't had time.'

Honor frowned. From what she knew of Charles, she was quite sure he had plenty of time. He just wasn't interested in his wife, which was verging on the criminal, as Henty was quite the squidgiest, funniest, most adorable little creature that walked the earth and Charles was a smug, self-satisfied pig. She didn't say that to Henty, though.

'Let's have a look through what you've got.'

'Nothing! Absolutely nothing!' squeaked Henty.

'You'd be amazed. You just need an objective eye and a bit of imagination.'

Henty didn't look convinced, but she needed no excuse for a bit of girly fun and the opportunity for someone to share a glass of white wine with. Ted and Walter were also delighted to have an impromptu play together, and piled into the back seat of Henty's Discovery. Honor leaped into the front, and Henty put on Thea's Pink CD. All the way back to the Beresfords' farm they sang 'Get This Party Started'.

There was one long plain black velvet dress in Henty's wardrobe that fitted.

'But it's so boring,' she wailed. 'I want to look sexy, not as if I've just buried my husband.'

Honor managed to stop herself from saying that really would be something to celebrate.

'Pass me the scissors,' she commanded, then proceeded to hack at the skirt until the hemline hung asymmetrically from mid thigh to ankle. Then she marched across the corridor to the bedroom that Thea and her younger sister, twelve-year-old Lily, shared. It was a treasure trove of pink girliness. The girls lay on their beds texting and glaring at Honor balefully as she rummaged around.

Eventually she pulled out a hot-pink feather boa from under Lily's bed.

'Hey!' chorused the girls in protest.

'Can you honestly, honestly tell me that you wear this?' demanded Honor, and neither of the girls had the nerve to say they did.

Quarter of an hour later, the boa was stitched round the hem.

'Are you sure I don't look like Lisa Riley?' asked Henty anxiously.

'You look gorgeous,' assured Honor. 'Go into Cheltenham tomorrow. Get yourself some killer strappy shoes and some long black evening gloves. And book yourself an up-do at the hairdresser's.'

Henty threw her arms round her.

'You're a life-saver,' she cried. 'We need a massive glass of wine. And why don't you stay for supper?'

When Charles walked in at seven o'clock, he found Henty, Honor, Thea and Lily practising dance moves in the kitchen, Ted and Walter taking the piss out of them behind their backs, and his oldest son Robin slugging the wine out of the second bottle that had been opened. And the potatoes stuck to the bottom of the saucepan.

'The potatoes are burnt,' he complained.

'Shut up, you old fart,' sang Henty, who was trying to do the splits but ended up falling in the dog's basket.

When Honor got home that evening, she put Ted to bed, keenly aware that they hadn't done his spellings but promising herself that they could squeeze it in if she got him up ten minutes earlier. Then she sat on her bed, immersed in the gloom that comes from having a drink too early in the evening and not carrying on. Which is always worse if you find yourself on your own.

'Be positive,' she told herself, and pulled back the chintzy curtain that hung in front of the rail she'd inexpertly put up in an alcove to house what remained of her clothes. Underneath were neatly stacked old shoeboxes that she'd covered in pretty wrapping paper, which held her accessories. Taking a deep breath, she started to rifle through.

Half an hour later, she appraised herself in the mirror and decided that, although she needed to double-check her appearance in the cold light of day and when she was sober, she hadn't done a bad job.

She'd unearthed a naughty black silk corset, tied with ribbons up the back, that she'd bought from an exquisite underwear shop in Paris at great expense. She'd kept it because she could hardly flog off her underwear, and of all the items in her wardrobe she loved this the most – the tiny, handsewn buttonholes, the discreet wiring and boning that gave her a minute waist and an impressive cleavage.

Round her waist she draped a black and white silk shawl. It had belonged to her grandmother, so once again she hadn't been able to part with it. She knotted it on one hip like a pareo, and the heavily tasselled silk hung beautifully. Then she slung on half a dozen pearl necklaces that she'd harboured from various charity shops: all different lengths and sizes. All she would have to buy was some cobwebby tights and false eyelashes. With some dramatic eye make-up and her short dark hair spiked, she'd look . . .

Well, different.

The one thing she wouldn't have to worry about was someone else turning up in the same outfit.

4

'Oh my God!' breathed Henty on Saturday night when Honor and Ted turned up. 'You look amazing! Like a punk princess.'

'You look beautiful too.' Honor gave her a hug.

Henty did indeed look stunning. The hairdresser had piled her dark curls on top of her head in an elegant up-do, and she'd added some of Thea's dangly earrings and some deep red lipstick.

Charles was draped languidly in a chair in the sitting room in his dinner shirt and braces, smoking a cigarette. He looked up as the girls trooped in.

'Wow,' he said. 'You look fantastic. You see,' he added to Henty, 'look what you can achieve when you make a bit of an effort. There's no reason to let yourself go.'

Honor saw Henty's little face cloud over at Charles's implied criticism. Why couldn't he just have told her she looked gorgeous and leave it at that?

She'd noticed that Charles always managed to burst Henty's bubble. She thought he was probably a bit of a bully. Henty had told her once that Charles wouldn't buy her a tumble-dryer because he liked his clothes line-dried. Honor had been horrified. With four children, two of them girls who changed their outfits at the blink of an eye, Henty did not need to be lugging baskets of washing outside only to have them rained on. But she didn't seem to be able to stand up to Charles.

He was shrugging on his dinner jacket now. Honor supposed he was good-looking in an oily sort of way, with his dark hair slicked back and his hooded hazel eyes. But didn't he know it. She'd put her life on him having wandering hand trouble.

'Who's going to drive?' asked Henty. 'We should have booked a taxi.'

'I'll drive,' said Charles magnanimously, wanting to look generous in front of Honor. He sometimes felt uncomfortable with the way she looked at him. Honor made him nervous, made him behave badly and say things he didn't mean because what he really wanted to do was flirt with her but he didn't quite dare. Henty had told him one night, rather aghast, that Honor had gone for nearly seven years without sex, and Charles had become rather obsessed with the information. Though he wasn't quite sure if he believed it. He suspected it was a myth Honor had built up around herself, to make sure other women weren't threatened by the fact that she was both single and incredibly attractive. He followed the girls out of the living room, running his eyes over the little buttons that ran down Honor's back, wondering how long they would take to undo.

In your dreams, mate, he thought wryly.

The ball was in an enormous marquee in the grounds of a nearby country hotel. The committee knew from experience that there was no point in knocking themselves out to decorate, as the guests were notoriously hardened drinkers and wouldn't notice their surroundings after about an hour. And the less that was spent on fripperies the more money would be raised for the hospice, which was, after all, the point. Half decent food, a decent band and plenty of booze was all that was needed to make the evening a success.

And tonight they had a bonus novelty which would make everyone feel they'd had their money's worth. Guy Portias had brought along Richenda Fox. Their engagement had been splashed all over the *Daily Post* that morning. The *Post* was one of those papers that no one admitted to reading but secretly did, full as it was of celebrity gossip and right-wing mantras. As long as you took their editorial with a pinch of salt it was a jolly good read.

Everyone had slavered over the pictures in the paper over their Saturday morning croissants. It was a typical *Hello!*-magazine style spread, with Richenda in sumptuous designer outfits posed in various different parts of Eversleigh Manor, while Guy hovered next to her in his jeans and a dark blue linen shirt, rumpled and bemused. Those who knew him well smiled inwardly, knowing he would have hated the attention. Guy was as popular locally as his father had been; both of them affable, charming, unaffected. Madeleine, of course, was a different story. She had an edge, though many of the wives locally protested that she had to stand her ground, as the Portias men were laws unto themselves. Utterly impossible in the nicest possible way.

Having had their fill of the tabloid gossip that morning and duly exchanged notes over the telephone, none of the guests at the ball were star-struck by Richenda's presence. They'd been used to having stars in their midst for the past six months with the film crew, after all, and anyway they were all far too well brought up to gawp. They all agreed, however, that the two of them made an absolutely stunning couple. Richenda was in a shimmering pale gold sheath; Guy looked as ever as if he had pulled on the first thing he could find when he got out of bed, in this case his dinner jacket. But they both looked incredibly happy, and couldn't keep their hands off each other.

Guy had indeed found the photoshoot a trial. He had resolutely refused to put on any of the clothes that had been brought along for him to wear.

'I'm not a bloody footballer,' he'd protested, chucking the cream satin shirt with the pointy cuffs back at the stylist, who'd winced.

'That's five hundred quid's worth of shirt!' she shot back, replacing it hastily on the hanger before it got creased.

'Says who?' said Guy amiably. 'Something's only worth what someone will pay for it and personally I wouldn't give you tuppence for it.'

In the end, Richenda had intervened, picking out the most understated shirt and agreeing he could wear his jeans.

'I'm not changing for every picture,' he warned. 'I never change! I wear the same clothes for weeks on end.'

'I had noticed,' said Richenda drily. 'And that's fine. You look gorgeous. Just smile.'

She kissed him on the nose as a hairdresser descended

once again to smooth down her already immaculate locks. Satisfied with her handiwork, the hairdresser turned to Guy, wielding her scissors.

'Could I just chip in to a few of your ends, give you a few layers, then put in some sculpting mousse?'

'Definitely not,' grinned Guy, running his hands through his curls. 'I've given it a good wash with some Vosene this morning.'

The hairdresser narrowed her eyes, not sure if she was being wound up.

'Leave him,' said Richenda, who was having eyelash extensions put on. 'I don't want him looking like David Dickinson. Anyway, the public might as well know the horrible truth.'

Guy had trailed round with long-suffering good humour, as the photographer ushered them excitedly from fireplace to sweeping staircase to gazebo.

'I've never sat in this bloody gazebo in my life,' he grumbled. 'It's a bloody charade.'

'I'm sorry, darling,' murmured his fiancée, 'but this is the price you have to pay for asking me to marry you.'

'He's got ten more minutes then I'm going for a pint,' said Guy, squinting into the glaring October sunshine.

Now, the two were enjoying their first outing as an officially engaged couple. The first hour had been taken up with congratulatory kisses and handshakes and back-slapping from people Guy had known all his life, and Richenda had been introduced to all of them. Now, however, everyone had forgotten the novelty and the two of them were regarded as just another pair of guests whose duty it was to have as good a time as possible. Dinner had been eaten, jackets were off and cigars were being lit, and the chairman of the committee was auctioning off the many items donated by local businesses in order to swell the money raised to renovate the kitchens at the hospice.

Guy had already unsuccessfully bid for a free pint every night for a year at any of the Honeycote Ales pubs. He'd drunk a bottle of Merlot and was itching to bid for something else. The mood amongst the bidders was of spirited competition, with everyone eager to outdo each other – not out of ostentation, but because the chairman was good at his job.

'The next lot,' announced the chairman, 'is a bespoke cake, decorated to your requirements. Donated by our very own domestic goddess, Honor McLean –'

At this point there was a resounding cheer from Honor's table and she had to stand up and take a bow.

'– who, I'm reliably informed, also does freezer fills – whatever they are, sounds rather uncomfortable – and dinner-party puddings. So, those of you who have an imminent celebration – birthday, anniversary, *wedding . . .*'

This last he said meaningfully, with an arch look over to Guy, and another resounding cheer went up. Guy grinned, and turned to Richenda.

'I'll have to bid for this now. We are going to need a wedding cake.'

Richenda opened her mouth to protest. She'd already decided on the cake she wanted, a towering concoction of white chocolate cherubs and rose leaves, hideously expensive but quite, quite stunning. But now was not the time to argue. Guy was obviously keen to bid for something. Hopefully he'd forget about it in the run-up. Or she could pretend she had forgotten. They'd be able to use the cake for something else – if he bid successfully.

Three minutes later, the cake was his.

'Three hundred and seventy quid!' he exclaimed. 'That'll be the most expensive wedding cake ever.'

Richenda didn't tell him that the one she had her eye on was over a thousand. The important thing was that the money had gone to a good cause. And she'd already decided that the most gracious thing to do would be to donate the cake to the hospice when they had the ceremonial opening of their refurbished kitchen. It would look lovely in the photos in the local paper.

The auction was soon over, and the chairman, smoke steaming from his calculator, announced delightedly that they had raised over fourteen thousand pounds and that the band was about to start. Chairs were pushed back and people hurled themselves on to the dance floor as the strains of 'Let Me Entertain You' urged them to their feet.

Guy walked past a table on his way to the bar and spotted the girl who had donated the cake he had bid for. She was sipping her wine, gazing at the dance floor – rather wistfully, he thought. She was a striking creature, with her short, dark hair and huge brown eyes. Elfin, he decided. Though tall for an elf. At least five eight. Fab legs. Coltish.

An elfin colt. Or a coltish elf.

Guy touched her on the arm. She looked up at him, startled out of her reverie.

'I bought your cake,' he said.

'Thank you.' She smiled, and her whole face lit up. 'You paid far more than it's worth. But I'm really pleased. I could never have afforded to make a donation like that otherwise.'

'We're going to have it as our wedding cake.'

'I'm very flattered,' said Honor. 'But if you change your mind I won't be in the least offended. I'm not professional. It's just a hobby, really. Pocket money.'

Pocket money was an equivocation. More than once the money from her cakes had meant the difference between beans on toast or a proper Sunday lunch.

'I'm delighted. I'll send Richenda to talk to you about it – she's in charge of all the wedding plans.'

Honor swallowed.

'Great. It would be . . . an honour.'

God – she'd start tugging her forelock or curtsying any moment. But there was something about Guy that made you feel deferential. An air of owning the place. He was very definitely in charge, but relaxed with it. Top of the pecking order but didn't put it about. Incredibly attractive. Honor realized that she was staring at him. And that he was staring back.

'Would you like to dance?' he asked suddenly.

Honor couldn't think of anything she'd like to do more. But at that moment she saw Richenda descending upon them.

'This is Honor, who's doing our wedding cake,' said Guy.

'Lovely,' said Richenda politely, looking straight through her, and guiding him away firmly by the elbow.

Honor was left feeling as if she was standing in her

underwear, which to all intents and purposes she was.

'Isn't he just totally edible?' breathed Henty in her ear.

'I think he's slightly spoken for,' said Honor ruefully, as Guy took Richenda in his arms on the dance floor.

'I don't know. There's plenty of time for it to go horribly wrong. Personally, I don't think she looks his type at all.' Henty analysed the happy couple critically. 'She's far too uptight.'

'Yeah, right,' said Honor. 'What would most men go for? A rich, famous and beautiful actress? Or a struggling single mother?'

'You're ten times prettier than her,' protested Henty. 'And he was dying to get his hands on you. You could see it a mile off.'

Honor just shrugged and smiled.

'Come on. Let's go and dance.'

Ten minutes later, Honor made her way back to their table in search of mineral water. It was boiling hot in the marquee – a relatively mild night combined with the heaters and vigorous activity on the dance floor had caused a mini greenhouse effect.

There was a particularly raucous table by the bar. Lots of extremely attractive blonde women in expensive black evening gowns, tanned and coolly confident. The men were equally complacent, their chairs pushed back, jackets off, bow ties undone. Honor's eyes flickered round the table. They weren't really her cup of tea – success stories who despite their charm she knew would have a ruthless streak – but they were interesting to look at. Honor loved people watching.

As she looked at the foot of the table, her heart skipped a beat. She had to blink twice to make sure, but yes – it was definitely him. He was leaning in to talk to one of the women, whose head was bent towards his. She was smiling in delight at what he was saying, and Honor could just imagine the innuendo, the flattery, the compliments, the suggestiveness that could relieve a woman of her knickers within minutes . . .

Johnny Flynn.

Johnny Flynn, with his thick, dark red hair that stuck up like a fox's brush no matter how hard he tried to stick it down, and his exquisite bone structure covered in perfect, porcelain skin.

Johnny Flynn, whose amber eyes burnt right through you, turning your defences to cinders and your resolutions to ashes.

Johnny Flynn, with his lilting Kerry brogue that had mockery and poetry in equal parts.

Like Cinderella, Honor turned to flee. She wasn't sure where she would go: she didn't have the number of a taxi on her. She could hijack a car but she was too drunk to drive. It was a three-mile walk to Fulford Farm, and she hadn't a coat. But she knew she had to get away as quickly as possible, before he saw her. The moment he clapped eyes on her, she knew she'd be lost. She was surprised she hadn't spotted him before. Or him her – her name had been read out by the auctioneer, she'd stood up to take a bow. Hadn't he seen her then? Though knowing Johnny, he was probably out the back groping someone else's wife during the auction.

She started to push her way back through the bodies

heaving on the dance floor. She felt a sweaty paw clutching at her arm.

'Come and dance,' commanded Charles, his hand like a vice on her upper arm.

Johnny was close. He only had to turn his head forty-five degrees to the left and she'd be spotted. She turned and practically threw herself into Charles's arms, to his surprise burying her head in his shoulder and pressing her body up against his.

She could feel Charles's hand in the small of her back, feel him slide his little finger just inside the shawl round her waist in a gesture that was so subtly intrusive she wanted to give him the slap he deserved. But she daren't move. Charles took her lack of resistance for compliance, enjoyment even, pressing his pelvis into hers. Oh God – what if Henty saw them and thought she was trying to get off with her husband? Honor peeped over Charles's shoulder; Johnny was looking away. If she made a run for it now –

'Excuse me – I need the loo.'

She pulled herself out of Charles's grasp before he could protest, and bolted through the back of the marquee.

She scampered up the steps to the loos. There were several mothers inside, indescribably pissed and dishevelled, swapping lipsticks and horror stories. Honor gave them a smile and rushed into the nearest available cubicle, where she put the lid down on the seat and collapsed into a heap with her head in her hands. Her head was spinning slightly, from unaccustomed alcohol and shock. Vivaldi's 'Spring' reverberated cheerily and inappropriately around the walls as she took stock of her situation.

Outside, the trickle of inane chatter disappeared out into the night air. She'd wait until someone else came to the loos, ask them to pass a message on to Henty telling her she didn't feel well and had gone home. Then she'd slip into the hotel and get the receptionist to call a taxi, praying that there would be one available. She could plead an emergency.

She slid back the bolt and stepped out of the cubicle. She ran some cold water to splash on to her face. She looked back at her reflection: pale, despite the alcohol.

As she put out her hand to grasp the rail and negotiate the steps in her unfamiliarly high heels, a soft voice greeted her.

'I thought it was you.'

Shit. Johnny was leaning against the rail at the bottom of the steps, rolling an unlit cigarette in his fingers.

'Don't you go running off now.'

'I've got a taxi waiting,' said Honor primly.

He grabbed her wrist.

'Fuck the taxi.' He pulled her towards him and raked his eyes up and down her. 'What the hell are you doing here?'

'I'm with friends . . .'

Johnny's eyes were burning a hole through her, so intense was his gaze.

'You're too thin.'

'There's no such thing.'

'You look like shite.'

'Thank you.'

'Jaysus, Honor – whoever he is, he's not making you happy.'

She couldn't answer. All she could muster was a bitter laugh at the irony.

'Are you married to one of these wankers? Show him to me.'

'He's not here.' She found her voice, pulled her hand out of his. 'And I've got to go.'

A figure approached, weaving slightly.

'Having trouble, Honor?'

Oh God. No. It was Charles.

'No.'

'Is this him?' asked Johnny.

'No . . .' said Honor desperately.

'I don't think we've met,' said Charles in a rather threatening tone, marking his territory.

'I was just asking Honor which was her husband,' replied Johnny.

Charles laughed smoothly.

'As far as I know she hasn't got one. Or so she'd have us believe.'

As the flame from Johnny's lighter lit up his features, Charles peered more closely at him.

'Bloody hell,' he declared.

'What?' asked Johnny, rather belligerently, as was his wont when drunk.

'You're the spit of Ted.'

'Who the fuck's Ted?' demanded Johnny.

There was a silence.

Johnny looked at Charles. Charles looked at Honor. Honor looked at the stars. For seven years, this was the moment she had been dreading.

'Ted is my son,' she said. '*My* son,' she repeated more defiantly, before turning on her heel and marching towards the marquee without a backward glance.

5

Honor whirled back through the marquee as if the hounds of hell were after her. The band were well into their stride, the dance floor was crammed and drunken guests dodged out of her path as she looked wildly round for Henty. She finally spotted her leaning up against one of the tent poles, slightly the worse for wear, her up-do now more of a down-do. Honor grabbed her arm urgently.

'Listen, I've got to go. Will Ted be all right with you tonight? I'll come and get him first thing . . .'

Henty struggled to focus on her friend.

'Of course. What on earth's the matter? You look as if you've seen a ghost.'

'A skeleton, more like,' said Honor grimly. 'I'll explain everything tomorrow. I've really got to go.'

She felt guilty, leaving Henty without an explanation. But there wasn't time. She had to make her escape. She hurried through the canvas tunnel that led from the marquee back to the hotel, and scurried through the corridors until she found her way to the reception desk.

'I need a taxi. As soon as possible. Please.'

She prayed that the receptionist was the cooperative type. The girl beamed at her.

'You're in luck. Someone booked a cab for midnight but decided they didn't want to leave. He should be waiting outside . . .'

Honor needed no second telling. She flashed a smile of thanks, pushed her way through the double doors and wrenched open the passenger door of the waiting mini-cab.

'Eversleigh, please. The high street. As quickly as you can.'

'Sure.' The driver started up the engine as she leaped in. 'What's the matter? Your house on fire or something?'

'Or something,' replied Honor, looking nervously over her shoulder. No one had followed her out. As the cab sped down the tree-lined drive that led to the hotel, Honor leaned back in her seat with a sigh of relief. With any luck, he wouldn't have a clue where to find her. Unlike Cinderella, she'd left no clues behind. She just prayed Charles would keep his trap shut. If he breathed a word, she'd kill him.

Inside the marquee, Henty was watching her husband on the dance floor again, this time clutching Fleur Gibson, his hands wandering freely over her bottom, which was like two hard-boiled quail's eggs wrapped in white satin. To her astonishment, Fleur didn't seem to mind. She was smiling up at him, tossing back her blonde bob, pressing her chest against his. Charles bent down to whisper something in Fleur's ear, and got a simpering giggle and a suggestive thrusting of the hips in return. Henty felt sick. How could her husband behave like that in public? He didn't even have the excuse of being drunk, because he was driving. And the thing that was most repellent was his choice of partner. She could have coped, could have excused, could even have laughed off this behaviour with most people. But for him to have chosen Fleur Gibson, so obviously the antithesis of Henty herself . . . a little golden sprite in contrast to a heffalump. They were both the same height, about five two, but Fleur must only weigh around seven stone, while Henty was ten and a half. Which was the equivalent of Walter. She was a whole six-year-old bigger than Fleur.

Miserable, she wished that Honor were still at the ball, because Honor could always be guaranteed to bring a smile to her face and restore her confidence. With one witty rejoinder she would dismiss Fleur, remove the threat, and Henty would feel reassured. She hated herself for needing constant bolstering, but over the years her self-esteem had slipped further and further until it was some-where down by her ankles. Her fat ankles.

Fleur's ankles were tiny. On one, just visible through the thigh-length split on her dress, she was sporting a chain with a diamond-encrusted padlock. Henty knew Honor would say ankle chains only meant one thing, and that it proved everything they'd ever suspected about Fleur, but Henty thought miserably that she would love to wear one, given half the chance. She picked up an unattended glass of wine from a nearby table. No one was keeping tabs on their drinks any more and Henty didn't care what she drank, as long as it obliterated her misery. As she swigged it back, one of the mums from school walked past her and gave her a smile of sympathy. She'd obviously seen what was going on. Henty felt her cheeks burning: she didn't want to be an object of pity. More to the point, she didn't want everyone saying 'Let's be honest, who would you choose?'

Bolstered by the half glass of wine she'd sunk, she marched up to Charles and tapped him on the shoulder.

'I'd like to go home, Charles.'

Charles's smile was rather fixed.

'Don't be silly, darling. We can't go yet.'

'I'm not feeling very well.'

'Go and sit down and have a glass of water.'

He hadn't even taken his arms from round Fleur's neck. Throughout the exchange, Fleur clung to his lapel, smiling patiently as she waited for his conversation with his wife to finish so they could resume where they had left off.

'I want to go,' repeated Henty patiently.

She saw Fleur and Charles roll their eyes at each other over her head. They obviously thought she was too pissed to notice. Charles fished about in his pocket and tossed her the keys.

'Go and wait in the car,' he said. 'I'll be out in a minute when I've said my goodbyes.'

Stuck your tongue down Fleur's throat, more like, thought Henty miserably as she picked her way across the field that was serving as a car park. She sat shivering in the Discovery for twenty minutes, until Charles finally emerged.

'Happy now?'

He slammed the door rather too hard and Henty winced.

'I can't help it if I feel ill,' she protested.

'You just can't bear anyone else enjoying themselves, can you?' he snarled, turning on the engine and spinning the wheels in the mud before roaring off.

This last remark was so patently unfair that it didn't

even merit an answer. Henty looked out of the window, chewing her finger, and wondered where on earth Honor had gone. Then a hideous thought occurred to her. Perhaps Charles had made a pass at her! They'd both been on the dance floor, then disappeared outside. Charles had reappeared just after Honor had made her hasty exit.

'Do you know what happened to Honor?' Henty blurted, rather belligerently for her.

'Ah. Honor.' Charles raised a quizzical eyebrow. 'The born-again virgin? She spotted a blast from the past. Couldn't get out of there quickly enough. She's a dark horse, if you ask me.'

He looked sideways at Henty, smirking, and for a moment the car drifted across the road.

'Charles!'

'Shit!' Hastily he corrected the steering, just in time to avoid a figure stepping out in front of them.

'Wanker!' he shouted.

'Charles, it's a policeman.'

Charles slammed on the brakes. There was a police car parked up in a gateway ahead.

'Fuck.'

'I thought you said you were all right to drive?'

'I am all right to drive. I'm just not all right to be breathalysed.'

'For God's sake . . .'

'Shut up. I'll deal with this.'

Charles wound down his window as the officer approached.

'Evening, officer.' He gave him his hundred-watt smile, the charm school special.

The officer nodded, and indicated his bow tie. 'I'd guess you're on the way back from the ball?'

'Yes. I drew the short straw tonight, I'm afraid. But you can still have fun without a drink. Oh yes.'

The officer nodded sagely in agreement.

'So you won't have had a drink, then?'

Charles faltered, not quite daring to lie.

'Ooh – just a glass of bubbly early on in the evening. To be sociable.'

'In that case, you won't mind blowing into this.'

Henty closed her eyes. That was all she bloody needed. Charles without a driving licence for the next twelve months. Where was she supposed to fit chauffeuring him around into her schedule?

The taxi drew up outside Honor's little house just after one o'clock. The village street was eerily dark, lit only by the occasional outside light from another house. Shivering, she dug inside her evening bag, praying that she had enough to pay him. The fare was thirteen pounds. She found a tenner and scraped up the rest of her change. There was just enough left over to give him a fifty-pence tip. She wasn't sure if that was insulting or not. In the old days she'd have given him a twenty and told him to keep the change.

'I'm sorry I haven't got any more,' she apologized. 'I didn't bring much money with me. I didn't think I was going to be taking a cab.'

'That's all right, love,' said the driver, who recognized that she was genuinely upset. 'I'll be getting a few more fares from the ball tonight – there'll be some of them who won't know what they're giving me, so I should make it up.'

He grinned at her as she shut the door and waved. As he drove away he wondered what had happened to make her so desperate to get away from the festivities.

Honor walked into the house. It was freezing: she had been expecting to stay over at the Beresfords with Ted, so she'd let the wood-burning stove go out. She was too tired to bother to light it again now, so she boiled a kettle quickly for a hot-water bottle and put a T-shirt on under her pyjamas. She climbed into bed and lay there shivering, chilled to the bone, scarcely able to believe that less than an hour ago she had come face to face with her nemesis.

The first time Honor saw Johnny Flynn she knew he was trouble. He was clinging on to the hotel reception desk, demanding a taxi, swaying from side to side as if on the deck of a ship in a force-nine gale. Kim, the panic-stricken receptionist, had summoned Honor, who was just about to slip off home. Weekends at the Jefferson were always hell, but things had usually calmed down by midnight. Not tonight.

'He's been with the racing lot,' Kim whispered. 'He wants a taxi back to Bath.'

'Tell her, will you, darling? She's saying it can't be done.' The brogue was unmistakable.

Oh God, thought Honor. Drunk and Irish. She surveyed her customer with a critical eye. A local trainer had been celebrating a win at the races in the restaurant. He'd spent a small fortune. It wasn't worth upsetting one of his party – Leslie Pinfield was a valuable customer, putting his entourage up at the Jefferson whenever they ran at Bath. A win meant copious bottles of champagne long into the night.

But there was no way she was going to let this specimen into a taxi. The firm the hotel used wouldn't appreciate someone tossing up in the back of one of their cabs. Honor didn't want to risk losing them; they were a valuable part of the service she provided, and reliable cab firms were hard to come by.

'I'm sorry, sir. We'll never be able to get you a taxi at this time of night. Perhaps we could get you a room instead?'

'Good idea, good idea,' proclaimed Johnny. 'I think I need to lie down.'

He tipped back his head and shut his eyes.

'Oh, Jaysus,' he groaned. 'Tell the bloody room to stop spinning, will you?'

Honor and the receptionist exchanged amused glances as Honor flicked quickly through the hotel register to find a vacant room, then slipped the key off the hook.

'Follow me.'

As he let go of the desk it was obvious he was unable to walk unaided. Honor grabbed an elbow, and found herself taking his full weight. Luckily, he wasn't a heavy man – about five foot eight, and slender. He slid an arm round her waist and dropped his head on her shoulder.

'Sure, you're an angel. How will I ever thank you?'

'By not getting into this state in my hotel again.'

'Your hotel, is it?'

'I'm the manager.'

'Oh.'

He craned his neck to peer at the badge on her breast pocket.

'Honor McLean. Manager,' he slurred. 'Well, in that case, Honor McLean, I have a complaint.'

'What?'

'Your bloody staff have been force-feeding me champagne. They've been pouring it down my neck, as if I was a fucking goose . . .' He stopped for a moment to regain his balance, as if the effort of walking and talking was too much. He gazed at Honor for a moment, and a smile spread across his face. 'I hate champagne.'

'Obviously,' said Honor drily. 'Come on. We're nearly there.'

'Nearly there!' Johnny sang, and made a supreme effort to put one foot in front of the other. Honor tried not to laugh. In spite of his appalling inebriation, there was something rather charming about him. With his Irish setter red hair sticking up and his boyish features, he looked like a squiffy teenager at his first sixth-form dance. Though on closer scrutiny Honor guessed he was in his late twenties at least. And what she had first mistaken for skinniness was wiriness; she could feel the hardness of his stomach muscles under his shirt. His arms were rock solid too. She wondered if he was a jockey – his build, the fact that he was Irish. But somehow she thought not. Although he could barely stand, see or talk, he still had an air of polish and sophistication that jockeys didn't generally have. His clothes and his shoes and his watch didn't say jockey either, though she couldn't come up with an alternative.

At long last, they reached the door of the room. Grateful that they hadn't passed any other guests en route, Honor managed to support him as she unlocked the door, then steered him gently inside and over to the bed. He sat down on it squarely, then fished around vainly for the packet of cigarettes in his shirt pocket.

'Don't even think about it,' said Honor firmly. 'This is a non-smoking bedroom.'

'Bollocks to that,' he said, and pulled them out of his pocket defiantly. Taking advantage of his slow reaction time, Honor snatched the cigarettes away from him, trying not to laugh at his indignant air as she put them into her own pocket.

'Hey!'

'I suggest you take your shoes off and get into bed. Sleep it off.'

Johnny needed no second telling and flopped back on to the bed, staring up at the ceiling.

'I think I'll have a full fry-up in the morning,' he declared. 'Will you bring it to me?'

Honor handed him the breakfast order.

'You'll have to tick off what you want and leave it on the door handle.'

She hid a smile as she pulled the door to. The last glimpse she had of him he was looking at the breakfast order, completely baffled. It was upside down.

'Who was he, anyway?' she asked Kim as she returned to the reception desk.

'Johnny Flynn,' Kim replied. 'Believe it or not, he's a vet. Specializing in horses. Leslie Pinfield thinks the world of him, apparently.'

Honor looked appalled.

'I wouldn't trust him with a guinea pig,' she said, 'let alone a bloody racehorse.'

But she couldn't help feeling rather intrigued, and wondered if he'd still be there by the time she came on duty the next morning.

Going into the hotel business hadn't been Honor's original career plan. She'd fallen into it rather by default. Her father had been an engineer in the oil industry, and as a result the family had led a rather luxurious ex-pat lifestyle, living in Dubai, Sri Lanka, Kuwait, Hong Kong – glamorous locations with a lifestyle to match. Nevertheless, every time they visited family in the UK, Honor had been left with the feeling that she was missing out on something. She would gladly have swapped the swimming pools and servants to live in the same place for more than two years running. She found the lifestyle superficial – which, of course, it was – and more than anything dreaded turning into her mother, queen of the ex-pat scene, living for nothing more than bridge and gin.

Honor was delighted when her parents had come home to England for a two-year stint while she was doing her A levels. Determined to put down some roots, she got herself a job as a chambermaid at a local hotel at weekends. She'd soon impressed them enough to fill in as receptionist during the holidays, and once she'd finished her exams was called in by the head of personnel, who persuaded her that she had just the right combination of patience, diplomacy, attention to detail and the ability to delegate for the hotel industry. She'd got a coveted place on their management course, and worked her way up, travelling the world that she already knew so well.

By twenty-five she was sick of the sunshine and beaches she'd already had her fill of. Once again she found herself longing for a place of her own in England, and a job she could get her teeth into, as well as the chance to exercise some creativity. She was tired of the hotel chain, tired of looking at the same décor whether she was in Thailand or Tahiti, although she was grateful for the training which had made her a desirable commodity. She scoured the trade journals, not interested in the salary so much as the challenge, and the ideal opportunity soon presented itself.

Maddox Jefferson was a Hollywood screenwriter and anglophile who wanted somewhere luxurious to stay when he visited the UK, and had hit upon the idea of opening his own hotel – partly as a tax write-off, partly because he wanted a change from the industry that had made him a millionaire several times over. He had fallen head-over-heels in love with Bath during research for one of his screenplays, and bought a crumbling Palladian mansion which he intended to convert into a luxury hideaway. He needed a crack team to help him do it, for what he knew about running hotels he could write on the back of a postage stamp. But he certainly knew what he expected from one.

As soon as he met Honor he wanted her on board. She knew what was important and what wasn't; the difference between flash and classy. He wanted understated style, and he could tell just by looking at her that she had a natural instinct for what was right and how to pull it together. Thus she was taken on as his right-hand girl, there as a sounding board and to mediate between the architects, designers and chefs, with a view to her managing the hotel when it was finished.

It was a thrilling few months for both of them – chaotic, nerve-racking, exhilarating and nail-biting – but finally the hotel was open. It was to be called the Jefferson – at Honor's suggestion, for Maddox's ego wasn't that big – as it sounded like somewhere you knew about, somewhere you had to be. It wasn't a large hotel, only twenty-four bedrooms, but the restaurant and bar were deliberately designed to attract non-residents. They also enabled Maddox to indulge two of his other great passions, art and wine: the rooms were hung with the hundreds and hundreds of paintings he had accrued, some great, some insignificant, and the cellars were spoken of in hallowed tones.

Once it was open, Honor ran the hotel like clockwork, and found she was never bored, because Maddox was constantly coming up with crazy and innovative ideas to attract new custom – screenwriting courses, jazz weekends, a 'Ladies Who Lunch' programme. With the money she'd saved by living in staff accommodation over the past five years, and Maddox's generous salary, she bought herself a garden flat in Bath. It was only tiny, because property prices in Bath were steep, but she was delighted at long last to have somewhere she could call her own home. And she soon had her own network of friends. She was thoroughly content. Over the next two years she had a series of semi-casual relationships and no lack of admirers, but she met no one she could imagine spending the rest of her life with. She enjoyed her own company too much; she liked to go home in the evening and eat exactly what she wanted without having to consult another person, watch what she wanted on television without a running commentary, go to bed at nine o'clock at night or two o'clock in the morning without considering someone else. It wasn't that she was selfish. She would happily sacrifice her independence if the right person came along. Only they hadn't yet . . .

The day after her skirmish with Johnny Flynn, she came in at nine to find he had already flown the coop.

'I got him a cab at about half six,' the receptionist told her. 'He looked pretty green.'

Honor felt a fleeting moment of regret. She'd been secretly looking forward to teasing him in the cold light of day, to see his reaction to her once the booze had worn off. Would he still be steeped in that warm Irish charm; suffused with irresistible affection and naughtiness? Or would he be cold, upright and sensible? Somehow, she thought not.

'Where was his taxi to?'

'Somewhere near Bradford-on-Avon, I think.'

Honor wondered if he lived there, or if he was staying with friends. Then she gave herself a shake. What was she thinking of, wasting time over a customer? She had work to do.

Two hours later, a magnificent bunch of yellow roses appeared in her office. Behind them a pale but ebullient Johnny, a rueful expression on his face.

'All I can remember from last night is you. I can't

remember what I said, but I hope it wasn't too filthy. It probably was, because even now I'm thinking what I might like to do to you. So I've come to pay for my room, and apologize, and say thank you. And ask you out for dinner.'

Honor was disarmed, charmed and intrigued. He took her bemused smile as an assent.

'Do you want small and intimate or loud and buzzy?' he asked.

'I've always wanted to go to the Hole in the Wall. But you'll never get a table.'

'I will.' Johnny looked into her eyes and smiled. 'I'm very good at getting what I want.'

It was such a cheesy line, Honor should have backed out of the date there and then. But somehow from him it didn't seem corny. Just horny. Those topaz eyes were burning right through her; she felt herself set alight inside, just as a magnifying glass sets light to a scrap of paper, suddenly and unexpectedly.

The table was duly booked for eight o'clock that evening. Honor, normally unexcitable, had tried on every single outfit in her wardrobe that afternoon, and finally fled into Bath at four o'clock to buy something new. She was usually confident in whatever she chose to wear, but nothing had seemed quite right. She wanted something soft, to detract from the hotel manager's image, but not too girly. Sexy, but not too obvious. Trendy, but not fashion-victimy. She whirled in and out of several shops before the manageress in her favourite boutique managed to calm her down and help her focus.

'I've never seen you like this before,' laughed Paula,

calmly working her way through the rails, pulling out Honor's size. 'Is it a special occasion?'

Honor looked sheepish. Normally she came in to the shop at the beginning of each season and coolly selected half a dozen outfits from the new collections to try on, from which she chose three to buy.

'It's just dinner,' she said lamely. 'But everything I've got seems too stuffy and grown-up. Or too casual.'

'In other words, you want to look like a fox. But not one that's touting for business.'

'Exactly!' Honor felt relieved that Paula understood. Which was why she always bought her clothes from her. It took Paula twenty minutes to kit her out, in a black pleated silk skirt splashed with red roses that came to just above the knee, and a short-sleeved black sweater.

'Wear your black knee-length boots – the ones you bought to go with the Jil Sanders suit,' she instructed. Paula was intimate with the contents of her best customers' wardrobes; they always went away happy if what they bought went with what they'd already got. It was one of the secrets of her success.

As Paula wrapped her purchases in monogrammed tissue paper it was heading for half past five. Honor realized she'd never have time to paint her nails, shave her legs *and* Immac her bikini line.

'Nails or bikini line?' she demanded.

Paula opened her eyes wide, and grinned mischievously.

'Well,' she said, 'I've never known a man take any notice of a decent manicure.'

By seven thirty, she was dressed in all her finery and pleased with the result. And before she left, she made sure her flat was immaculate. She'd changed her sheets earlier to her best set, put a jug of fresh tulips in the fireplace and replaced all the candles. As the taxi driver rang her bell to say he was waiting, she slipped a bottle of champagne in the fridge. Just in case. She was shocked by her own behaviour. She would never normally contemplate asking someone in after a first date, but there was something about Johnny that made her feel fluttery inside. She blatantly ignored the voice in her head warning her to be careful.

He was already at the restaurant when she arrived, in a stripy Paul Smith shirt, looking surprisingly fresh. But then he'd spent two hours in the gym, on the treadmill and in the sauna, sweating out the excesses of the night before, followed by a revitalizing aromatherapy massage. And now he was sipping gingerly at a glass of mineral water.

'I thought I'd better take it easy after last night,' he said sheepishly. 'I couldn't face champagne myself. But if you'd like a glass . . .'

Honor grinned.

'I would, actually,' she said. She definitely needed something to calm her nerves.

Over dinner, they talked nineteen to the dozen as they ate, the delicious food almost secondary as they shared their pasts between them. Johnny was indeed a vet, attached to an equine practice in Wiltshire, and had become the darling of the local horse set as he often seemed to work miracles. Healing hands, some said he had, but he pooh-poohed their theory.

'It's not magic. It's just a question of listening and looking. A lot of the time it's just common sense.' Like many people with a talent he made light of his gift, but it was obvious that he succeeded where others failed. Only the night before he'd been celebrating a win with a horse that had been on the brink of being destroyed.

'No one else had any faith in it. They were going to put the poor bugger down, get the insurance money. But I knew he could do it.'

By the time they'd finished sharing a pudding between them, Honor realized that she'd had the lion's share of the bottle of Sancerre they'd ordered – Johnny had only managed a glass. Yet the slight giddiness she felt, the thrumming of her heart and the pinkness on her cheeks weren't caused by the wine. As Johnny signed for the bill, a silence fell and they looked at each other, saying nothing but everything, as the waiter arrived at their table to tell them the taxi was there. Honor shivered as Johnny slipped her coat on, his fingers just lightly brushing her collarbone. They sat in the back of the taxi holding hands as the driver navigated the late-night traffic on the way to Honor's flat. Honor rested her head on Johnny's shoulder; he ran his thumb lightly over the back of her knuckles and she felt a delicious tingle run down her spine. When the journey came to an end, by tacit agreement Johnny got out too, paying the driver, and as Honor slid the key into the lock she was grateful for her earlier foresight.

In the hallway she turned to him, dropping her bag and letting her coat slide to the floor. He wrapped his arms around her and they kissed a kiss that she wanted to preserve for ever. It was so right, so full of promise:

it fizzed with anticipation, yet at the same time it cemented the feeling they obviously both shared, that they had each found something special.

And that first time Honor went to bed with him, she couldn't deny his touch was magical. She quivered at the mere brush of his fingertips as he ran his hands over her, knowing instinctively where to touch. For the first time in her life she lost control, begging him to stop yet pleading with him to carry on. Now she understood how ecstasy could be agony. He moved her to a higher plane. She'd always enjoyed sex, but this was something different. This was verging on the immoral. It turned her into an animal, driven by a new set of needs, with an insatiable appetite and constant craving for him. And he seemed just as hungry for her.

The first few weeks were perfect.

Out of bed, as well as in, they enjoyed each other's company. They had a hectic social life, combining her friends and his, and were out as often as they could be, bearing in mind they both worked sometimes unsociable hours. They ate out, drank out, danced, partied, entertained, went to the theatre and the races, and became must-have guests at most social events in Bath: charity dinners and balls, fashion shows and gala evenings, wine-tastings and concerts. Honor was getting by on an average of five hours sleep a night. She was as high as a kite on the thrill of it all, and it didn't detract from her work. If anything, it made her more focused and efficient – the Jefferson went from strength to strength, and Maddox was delighted. There was only one thing he had reservations about, and that was Johnny.

'Watch him,' he cautioned Honor strongly one day, and when she protested he said nothing.

After three months, Honor heard Maddox's words ringing in her ears. Johnny was becoming increasingly irresponsible and unreliable. He swore undying love then disappeared for days on end, not answering her calls. It drove her to despair and distraction. And he drank far, far, far too much. When she remonstrated, or voiced concern, he poured scorn on her, making her feel like a killjoy, a stick in the mud. His friends were on the whole like him – hard living, hard drinking – and Honor was never entirely comfortable in their company. They were wealthy, self-assured and rather ruthless. She found it disconcerting that Johnny fitted in with them so well. And gradually she noticed *her* friends drawing back – the supper invitations weren't quite so forthcoming. Was it because Johnny was a bit full-on, always having to be the centre of attention at the dinner table, coming on to all the women? On more than one occasion Honor had seen her female friends exchanging glances when Johnny had flirted with them. At first they had giggled and blushed under his innuendo; after a while they were just uncomfortable with it, presumably because Honor was their friend. Honor wondered what he got up to on the evenings out when she couldn't accompany him, when he hit on women who had no loyalty to her. It was obvious Johnny was a pathological flirt. The question was, how far did he take it when she wasn't there?

After six months, she realized she was thoroughly unhappy, as his cavalier attitude began to eat away at her. The more she complained, the worse he became, so she stopped complaining and became morose and miserable instead. When they were together she was twitchy and irritable; when they were apart she tortured herself, imagining him sliding those magic hands up another girl's leg. She knew he did it because she'd seen him, on numerous occasions, though when she remonstrated he just laughed. It meant nothing, he assured her. Then don't do it, she wanted to scream but didn't, knowing that to pull on the choke chain would make him strain further at the leash.

She began to wonder if she could live without him. No one had ever matched the thrill he could give her. Everyone else paled into insignificance. And he could still reduce her to putty. But was that thrill worth the accompanying agony? He was, she decided, like the most insidious class A drug, the one that gave you a high you couldn't live without, and a subsequent craving that superseded common sense. She had to make a decision. Were the few occasions that he made her feel a million dollars, brought her to the brink of mind-blowing, earth-shattering ecstasy, worth feeling miserable and worthless the rest of the time? After all, it wouldn't be long before her work started to suffer. She was keeping it together, but her increasing preoccupation and shattered nerves were going to take their toll eventually. She was jumpy and irritable, a constant knot of worry in her stomach. And she felt sick, couldn't eat. Maddox pulled her in and gave her a roasting.

'For God's sake, you look like a heroin addict. What are you playing at? Where's your self-respect? Dump him. This is not what it's all about.'

'You don't understand.'

'Yes, I do. He makes you scream when you come, right?'

Honor looked at Maddox in horror. He gave her a cynical grin.

'Honey, I wrote the movie. Ten times over, just changed the names. Trust me. The guy's a bum. He's never going to give you what you really want. And the sex thing?' He shrugged. 'If you want your pussy to rule your life, then carry on. But there's more to life than multiple orgasms.'

Honor managed a resigned smile.

'That's easy for you to say.'

'You just have to find something else to fill the hole. If you'll pardon the pun.' Maddox twinkled apologetically. 'It's like any addiction. You can recover.'

Honor found it chilling that Maddox had used the same metaphor she had. But it helped her realize she was addicted to Johnny, and he was doing her no good. As she drove back from the Jefferson that evening, she decided to take control. She'd talk to him that weekend, tell him she wanted a break. Then she'd be able to see if she could live without him.

Once she had made the decision, she felt happier. She fell asleep feeling calmer than she had done for weeks, and actually slept, instead of waking up and torturing herself about what Johnny was up to, how he would behave while they were out over the weekend, whether he would phone and cancel without telling her what he was doing instead: all the things that had reduced her to a nervous wreck over the past few weeks.

But the next morning she woke feeling sicker than ever. She drew on her dressing gown, stumbled to the bathroom and threw up. She finished retching and sat on the floor in front of the loo, pushing back her hair from her sweaty forehead with a trembling hand as a terrible thought occurred to her. She'd felt queasy for a few days. They had been out for a Chinese the previous Saturday and it hadn't agreed with her. But surely that still couldn't be making her feel ill?

There was another possibility.

Even sicker with dread, she pulled on a tracksuit and made her way down to the parade of shops at the end of the road, where there was a chemist. There was no point in speculating . . .

As soon as her suspicions had been confirmed, Honor phoned in sick, praying that Maddox wouldn't take it upon himself to call and interrogate her. When he had an idea he was like a dog with a bone, and she would have to be in a coma for him to leave her in peace. Thankfully, he was scheduled in for tennis, one of his other passions, and a lunch, so she should have the morning at least with no interruption.

She sat on the sofa cross-legged, clutching her tummy, while she decided what the hell to do, wishing for the first time in her life that her mother was in the country. Even though Rene wasn't the cuddly, comforting type, she was decisive and no-nonsense. She'd certainly have an opinion, and she wouldn't be shocked or judgemental.

At first, Honor couldn't believe that she'd made such a classic and clichéd mistake, when she was so organized and sensible. She never went overdrawn, was never late paying her credit card bill, double-checked her bank statements against her cheque book stub, had regular smear tests and dental appointments, serviced her car annually and kept it topped up with oil and water and checked her tyre pressure before a long journey. How could someone that efficient be caught out? But then her life recently, with its irregular hours, had played havoc with her body clock. The pill she was on required her to be meticulous. Somewhere along the line she had been too slapdash with her contraception. She was supposed to take her pill at the same time each day, but she remembered, with a twinge of regret, that twice she'd stayed over at Johnny's unexpectedly and had taken it eight hours late, reassuring herself that her body couldn't really know what the time was, and a third of a day couldn't really make that much difference. But obviously it could.

She'd taken a risk and she'd been caught out. And the consequences nearly took her breath away. She wondered just how many women had been in her situation, their lives turned upside down because of a split second, a fusing of two tiny cells. Millions, probably. Her only consolation was that many of them would have been in a far worse predicament than she was. Her eyes filled with tears as she conjured up images of terrified young girls subjected to hideous indignity with knitting needles and bottles of gin.

Without even thinking about it, she knew a termination was out of the question. Honor wasn't religious, but she was a very firm believer in what goes around comes around. She only ever did things that she was comfortable with. She knew absolutely that she wouldn't be able to live with having a baby aborted. That if she ever had trouble conceiving later, she would only have herself to blame. And if she ever had other children, she would never be able to sit down and tell them she had disposed of one of their siblings. She was twenty-nine. Hardly a gymslip mother. An abortion would just be for her convenience; the flushing away of a nuisance. That didn't sit well with Honor in the least. She believed in facing up to her mistakes.

Besides . . . a baby.

She might be shocked. She might have cursed herself for her carelessness. But, strangely, she wasn't frightened. She'd always wanted children one day: she wasn't one of those career girls who grimaced at the prospect of losing her freedom and her figure.

And obviously this baby was meant to be. After all, she could have gone on for years without making a conscious effort to procreate. There were hundreds of articles in the papers about desolate women who'd achieved huge success but failed to find their perfect partner and had therefore missed the baby boat. Honor couldn't think of anything sadder. What would be the point of her being the female equivalent of Rocco Forte, but without issue?

This baby wasn't a mistake. This baby was showing her the way forward. Otherwise, she might have been seeking the next step on the career ladder, spending another five years increasing her power and her salary – and for what? A few more designer suits in the wardrobe and the chance to boss a few more people around?

There was only one thing that made her falter, and that was what to do about Johnny. The night before, she'd gone to bed resolving to put their relationship on the back burner. But a baby turned all that upside down. A baby would mean some sort of commitment, perhaps moving in together, maybe even marriage.

It was this that made Honor uncertain. She tried to reassure herself. Perhaps it was what Johnny needed to calm him down. A sense of responsibility and duty might give him some focus; make him grow up. They could make it work. Their relationship wasn't all black: they'd had, still did have, some wonderful times. They could make each other laugh. She'd just have to find a way to deal with his dark side. Or maybe his dark side would dissipate.

She tried to think about it in practical terms. He had a good salary as a vet. She could take maternity leave. Between them they could afford a nanny when she went back to work. She could sell her flat – it would give them a good deposit on a house somewhere. Try as she might, Honor couldn't see a flaw in the plan. But then, she was a natural optimist.

To misquote Peter Pan, she thought to have a baby would be an awfully big adventure.

At five o'clock, Honor had a shower, got dressed and composed herself. She'd spent all afternoon mentally rehearsing her speech to Johnny. She would make it clear she wasn't putting any pressure on him. It was her deal; her mistake. But as she pulled on her coat and went out to her car, she felt excited. She had a vision in her head of a little stone cottage somewhere just outside Bath, with a cosy kitchen, babygros drying on the Aga, Johnny coming in from work and giving the baby its bath while she put the finishing touches to their supper . . .

She inched her way through the rush-hour traffic with everyone else trying to leave the city, and finally made it on to the road to Bradford-on-Avon. Johnny lived in a converted barn adjoining the farm of one of his wealthy clients, a barrister whose wife and daughters were horse mad. Johnny treated their horses in return for a nominal rent. The barn was thick with dog hair and mud, coffee cups and wine glasses, empty beer cans and take-away cartons. Honor had long given up trying to restore any order to the bachelor squalor. Her eyes flicked towards the digital clock on her dashboard. It was six thirty on a Thursday evening. He'd have finished his surgery by now; he'd be home having a shower or a power nap before going out. She turned into his drive, hoping against hope he would be there, suddenly needing his reassurance. He'd come through for her, she felt sure he would.

She breathed a sigh of relief as she drew up beside his filthy Audi estate. She jumped out of her car and ran to the back door. She could feel the tears welling up already; she knew she wasn't going to be able to break the news calmly and with dignity. She just wanted to feel his arms around her.

The news was on the telly; his jacket was on the breakfast bar, next to an open bottle of Becks. He must be in the bedroom getting changed.

'Johnny!' she called out, and pushed open the bedroom door.

Underneath his Homer Simpson duvet cover were two heads. Johnny and his client's leggy nineteen-year-old daughter Chloe. Chloe peered through the gloom.

'Oh fuck,' she said, then prodded the figure next to her. 'Johnny, it's the missus.'

Honor stood stock-still for a moment, surveying the scene with horror, and then turned and fled.

Later that evening Johnny had rung on the bell of her flat, wanting to explain.

'What, exactly?' she'd snarled at him over the intercom.

'It wasn't what it looked like,' he pleaded.

'Please,' said Honor wearily. 'Just leave me alone. I'm going away for a fortnight. I'm taking the leave that's owing to me. I'll talk to you when I get back and not before. OK?'

She hung up the phone. Thankfully, he seemed to get the message – she watched from the window as he drove away. Relieved that she'd bought herself some time by putting him off the scent, she sank down into the chair in her kitchen and put her head in her hands, wondering what on earth she was going to do.

She had to go away. She couldn't face seeing Johnny again. Not even for a moment. The nausea of pregnancy was nothing compared to the sickness she felt when she conjured up the image of him in bed with Chloe. She needed a clean break. She pulled a notebook and pen out of the kitchen drawer, and began to write lists. And, more importantly, do her sums. By ten o'clock that evening, she thought she had a plan. Utterly exhausted, she fell into bed, praying that she would sleep and wouldn't be tortured by images of her treacherous lover in bed with a nineteen-year-old nymphet.

The following morning she phoned the hotel to say she was going on sick leave immediately, and that she was handing in her notice. It was only half an hour before Maddox turned up. She let him in resignedly. She owed him at least part of an explanation.

'What's the little snake done?' he demanded. 'Dumped you? Cheated on you? Come on, Honor. I want to help.'

'Look, Maddox. It really doesn't matter what's happened, because you can't change it. But I've got to hand in my notice. I've got to move on.'

Maddox was beside himself. He threatened one minute to sue her, then the next tried to shower her with vast sums of money to lure her back.

'No one else understands how I want this place run,' he grumbled.

'I'm sorry.' Honor was trenchant. Then the colour drained from her face and she fled the room to be sick. When she came back, Maddox surveyed her beadily from behind his horn-rimmed glasses.

'You're pregnant,' he said accusingly. And when she didn't reply he knew he'd hit the nail on the head. 'No problem. I'll pay for a full-time nanny, and you can have a room at the hotel for the kid so you can see it whenever you want while you're working. And you only need to work part-time. Just to keep the place afloat. You're my right hand, Honor.'

But endless wheedling had no effect. Honor felt as if she was letting him down, this funny little East Coast American with his yellow jumpers and his crisp chinos and his hair parted on the side, who'd given her so many opportunities. But as much as Maddox was a mover and shaker, a man that made things happen, he couldn't turn the clock back for her.

'I've got to leave Bath, Maddox,' she said wearily.

'What's the bastard done to you?'

'Nothing. But if you tell him anything, or where I am, I'll burn your hotel to the ground,' she threatened.

Maddox knew when it was time to make a tactical withdrawal. Determined to win her over eventually, he gave her a hug and told her to call him any time of day or night for advice, counselling, 'or just confirmation that the guy is a grade A piece of shit'. Honor smiled. Maddox could always be relied upon to tell it like it was, though if he knew the real truth she shuddered to think what his reaction might be. Maddox was the kind of guy who had murky contacts. Not that he was tacky enough to rely on them except *in extremis*. But she could imagine Johnny being found face down in a slurry pit with cement in his wellies.

Over the next two days, she went through her flat like a dose of salts, despite the incredible tiredness that overwhelmed her and tried to lure her back under the duvet. She resolutely ignored what her body was telling her: time was not on her side, and she had to act fast before other forces intervened. She ruthlessly threw out anything she didn't want or need, called in a designer dress agency to dispose of her wardrobe, followed by a housing clearance company, until she had nothing left but two suitcases of clothing, a box of kitchen utensils, another box of personal effects and a portable CD player, all of which could be fitted into the boot of her car.

Then she put her flat on the market.

'I don't want a board up, or to have it advertised,' she instructed the agent. 'I want it sold discreetly.'

It wasn't a problem. They had five clients actively seeking a one-bedroom flat in the centre of Bath. Two of them came back within twenty-four hours and offered the asking price. One of them was in a position to proceed, so she accepted the offer. By the time she'd paid off her mortgage she would have seventy-five thousand pounds left in the bank. Not enough to buy somewhere else. But a reasonable buffer. And more than many single mothers.

At the end of the week, she was ready to leave. She called Maddox to say goodbye and he insisted on coming over. He handed her a brown padded envelope.

'It might come in useful. And please – if you ever need anything . . . I would do anything for you, you know that?'

Honor nodded, unable to speak because of the lump in her throat. For she was terrified, and it would be all too easy to throw herself on Maddox's mercy. But she knew she had to make a clean break. She threw her arms round his neck and kissed his cheek, not daring to look at the reproach in his eyes, then got in her car to leave Bath behind for the very last time.

She opened the envelope that evening. It contained three thousand pounds in pristine twenty-pound notes. Honor's instinct was to return it straight away, but she knew Maddox would refuse to take it back, and that it had been given with the best will in the world.

Besides, she was pretty sure she was going to need it.

She found the cottage advertised in *The Lady*. The owner was going abroad indefinitely – for at least five years, to work in the Middle East – and effectively wanted someone in the cottage to keep it lived in. Not only was the rent pleasingly low, but there was a substantial budget for running repairs and decoration. She only needed to ask and there would be more.

It was tiny – a little gingerbread house. Not unlike the little house she'd imagined for her and Johnny. It was in a remote Cotswold village, well off the beaten track, deep in the wilds of Gloucestershire. It had a porch with a stable door, leading into a living room with an inglenook fireplace, a small kitchen with a proper pantry off, and upstairs a bedroom and a boxroom and a bathroom. There was a little walled garden out the back, with a shed that had once been the outside loo. Sunny and south-facing. Safe and secure. The village, Eversleigh, had a post office, a pub, a school and a church. The village hall advertised yoga classes, mother and toddlers and Cubs and Brownies. Everything she was likely to need to keep body and soul together over the next few years.

And although her life had been turned upside down, she had been happy. Ted was the best thing that had ever happened to her, and to her surprise not once did she resent him, or blame him for curtailing her career, because to raise a child was the ultimate fulfilment. By making her life simple, she found she could manage financially. And the one thing she did have was time. Time to bake bread and cakes from scratch, grow things in the garden, teach Ted to read, make him home-made playdough, take him on long, splashy walks. The highlight of her week was when the mobile library came round. They would clamber on board, Ted would choose a new picture book, and she would fall with glee upon whatever new novel she had ordered. Even clothes didn't matter to her any more. Where once she'd been a label freak, now she wasn't ashamed to go to a jumble sale or a charity shop. Round here people often chucked out because it was last season or a mistake, and she wasn't proud. Once in the washing machine with a double dose of Lenor, and it was as good as new.

And now Ted was at school, she was really getting it together. As well as her work, she had a little bit of time for herself. Sometimes she would get back from dropping him at school and do her own home spa. Where once she would have wallowed in Clarins, now she used the supermarket's own body scrubs and face masks, and she had to admit that the overall effect was much the same. She'd cut her long hair off into a tousled crop which made her brown eyes look enormous and took two minutes to dry.

Her mother swooped in on a visit once a year or so, bringing overgenerous gifts that Honor didn't really need, like bottles of perfume and silk scarves, and took her out for expensive meals where Ted had to sit and behave. Honor would have preferred her to fill the freezer from the supermarket. But her mother only had one way of doing things and that was her way.

All in all, she'd muddled through quite nicely, learning a few hard lessons along the way, and not to take things for granted. But she'd also learned that people were kind. She felt safe in Eversleigh. She knew there were people looking out for her. Mr Potter three doors up came and trimmed her hedge because she couldn't reach. There was no shortage of volunteers who would sit with Ted if she needed to nip to the doctor or the dentist. And her friendship with Henty was wonderful. She sometimes felt guilty that she hadn't shared the truth about Ted with Henty, but she felt that if she didn't reveal her past, then it had never happened.

And now, she really couldn't believe it had caught up with her. Time and again she had told herself that the chances were remote. That although she hadn't exactly left the country, that in fact she only lived in the next county, the chances of Johnny falling upon her in a remote Cotswold village were slim. It wasn't impossible, of course. Honor had experienced enough coincidences in her life to know that the strangest things happened. But she had striven to keep herself to herself, had made a point of not mixing in circles that might seep into his social life, and had cut herself off from their old friends and acquaintances – about which she sometimes felt guilty, for she'd had some good friends, but it was a question of self-preservation. The only way she could survive was through total abstinence, like a recovering alcoholic.

Because Johnny was dangerously addictive. No matter how bad you knew he was for you, it was very hard to kick the habit. When you were in his thrall, you forgot all the bad bits. And like a drunk presented with a full bottle of whisky, Honor knew from just one look that evening that she wouldn't be able to resist him if she got too close.

Would he try to find her? Would he care enough to track her down? Honor suspected that his memory of her would have faded by now; he would have had dozens of girls since, all dazzling and successful. And anyway, if he'd really wanted to find her he would have done it years ago. It wasn't beyond him to have hired a private detective. They would have traced her easily through her national insurance. She hadn't gone to particularly elaborate lengths to cover her tracks. No, she was pretty sure he wouldn't be bothered. Mildly curious at best.

She realized that it was nearly dawn, and she was shivering with the cold. Eventually she relented and got up to light the stove. By half six a little warmth was seeping back into her bones. Usually on a Sunday Ted sneaked into bed with her at about this time and they would snuggle up together. She missed the warmth of his little body next to hers. She bunched up the duvet and hugged it to her for comfort. At long last she fell asleep, but it wasn't a peaceful sleep. Fears and worries danced in the corners of her mind, and all the while a menacing presence seemed to watch her from the corner of the room.

At half past eight there was a sharp rapping on the door. Honor started awake, immediately filled with panic. She knew there was only one person that could be. No one in Eversleigh ever came calling this early on a Sunday morning.

She pulled on a pair of jeans and looked in the mirror. Her eye make-up was smudged all round her eyes where she hadn't bothered to remove it the night before, and her skin was deathly pale. Good, she thought. The worse she looked, the better. Nevertheless, she rushed into the bathroom to brush her teeth. It was one thing looking rough, but there were limits to how unattractive you could voluntarily make yourself. As she brushed frantically the door knocker went again, louder and more insistent.

She opened the door without a greeting, her expression stony. On the doorstep stood Johnny, in jeans and a baggy Arran sweater. Without even breathing in she knew how he would smell: always of horses, because his car smelt of horses and he carried it with him wherever he went, and the oil of the waxed coat he wore when he was working, and underlying that a faint hint of the Kent cigarettes he smoked, mixed in with the scent of sandalwood from his aftershave.

'Where is he?'

'Who?'

'My son.'

'I don't know what you're talking about.'

'Come on, Honor. Your friend told me all about him.'

Bloody Charles, thought Honor venomously.

'Six years old? Skinny with red hair?' went on Johnny. 'I don't have to be a mathematician or a forensic scientist to work it out.'

'You're not the only redhead on the planet.'

'I'm the only redhead you were fucking seven years ago.'

'How can you be so sure?' demanded Honor. 'I wasn't the only person *you* were fucking, as you so eloquently put it. So what gives you the monopoly?'

'Because I know you, Honor.'

Honor folded her arms and leaned against the doorjamb.

'There's nobody here but me.'

'Don't you think we should talk?'

'I've got absolutely nothing to say to you.'

She glared at him, noticing how his jaw was clenched, the milky skin stretched over his cheekbones, the sprinkling of freckles standing out in stark relief. Seven years had awarded him a few more lines around his eyes, but he was still the picture of cherubic innocence, the spidery dark lashes fringing those hypnotic eyes. She'd always been in awe of his beauty, amazed that such feminine features could belong to someone so overtly male. For no one could ever be in any doubt about Johnny's sexuality. He only had to glance at a woman and she melted. Though she wasn't going to. Not this time. She was immune to his charms.

He was squaring up to her, thrusting his hands into the pockets of his jeans and throwing back his shoulders.

'I think you owe me some sort of explanation.'

'I don't owe you anything.'

'I'm not going until you do. I'll stand here all week if I have to.'

Mr Potter walked past on his way for the Sunday papers. He looked sideways at them curiously. Honor gave him a tight smile to assure him she was all right, aware that it was obvious from their body language that they were arguing. She hated the thought that she was rousing curiosity; couldn't bear to think that Mr Potter would go into the shop and start gossiping about her private life. She was going to have to let Johnny in if only to avoid further speculation.

She stepped aside with a sigh.

'You'd better come in.'

*

Johnny followed her wordlessly inside the cottage into the kitchen. She headed straight for the kettle. He took off his coat and sat down at the little breakfast bar, his eyes raking the room for further evidence of Ted. There was plenty enough. Paintings stuck to the wall – a robot made of pasta shapes sprayed silver, his name in Egyptian hieroglyphics. A selection of his shoes by the front door. His duffel coat on the newel post at the bottom of the stairs. On the breakfast bar was the see-through folder that contained his reading book and the spellings he had to learn for the week ahead. Honor cast a sidelong look at Johnny and saw him staring at the spellings intently. She could only imagine what he was thinking. That these simple four- and five-letter words – *shop, ship, shape, shine* – were being learned by the son he never knew he had. Honor chastised herself sharply for feeling a momentary pang of guilt. Johnny had given up all rights to Ted the moment he'd slid between the sheets with Chloe. She was going to stand her ground.

She made a pot of tea, darting round the kitchen in agitation, not wanting to stay still long enough for Johnny to scrutinize her and assess what damage the intervening years had done to her looks. Though why should she care what he thought of her, she thought savagely.

He was sitting on the stool Ted used for doing his homework, watching her quietly.

She plonked a cup of tea in front of him ungraciously. 'There's sugar in the tin.'

'Thank you.' He smiled at her. 'I don't suppose you've a spoon?'

She wrenched open a drawer and tossed a teaspoon at

117

him, then turned her back on him and picked up her own mug. Her hands were shaking slightly, but the warmth of the liquid reassured her. There was silence for a moment as he took the lid off the sugar tin and helped himself, then stirred vigorously. When he spoke, his voice was calm.

'So what have you told him? About his father? What am I? Dead? Some sort of legend you've created who died a heroic death?'

Honor opened her mouth to argue, but he cut in smoothly.

'Don't bother trying to deny he's mine. It'll be a waste of your time and mine. Let's cut to the chase, shall we?'

Honor put her cup down on the counter. She realized Johnny was right. There was no point in blustering; pretending Ted wasn't his. She'd been well and truly cornered. Now it was up to her to extricate herself from the situation as best she could.

'I told him that God decided to give me a little boy but forgot to give me a daddy to go with him.'

'That's sick!' Johnny looked genuinely appalled. 'He's going to work out that's total bollocks, as soon as he learns about the birds and the bees.'

'Then I'll explain a bit more about it. But not now. He's too little.'

'So what does he think he is? Some sort of immaculate conception?'

'He's six years old, Johnny. He's actually quite happy to accept that it's just him and me.'

'That's totally irresponsible. You've fobbed him off and it's only going to create problems when he wants to know the truth.'

'What should I have told him then? That his father was a feckless, no-good shagmeister?' Honor found herself spitting out the words that she'd been wanting to level at him for years. The bitterness hadn't faded. Now she had him in front of her, the anger was as strong as it had been the moment she had caught him in flagrante. 'How is the lovely Chloe?'

'Jaysus, Honor. I've no idea. She was a mistake –'

'No. *You* were a mistake.'

'We're not all paragons of virtue.'

'It's not that hard to remain faithful to someone you profess to love.'

'I admit I was a total arsehole, OK? But at least I would have had the guts to face what I'd done. Not run away.'

Honor drew in a sharp breath.

'You're not calling me a coward, surely?'

'You never gave me a chance to explain!'

'Johnny – no explanation in the world would have made any difference. You were in bed with a nineteen-year-old girl! How can you make that look anything other than despicable?'

'Do you really want to know?'

He looked at her defiantly. Despite herself, she was intrigued. What explanation would he come up with to absolve himself?

'You can say whatever you like. It won't make any difference.'

Johnny ran his hand through his hair, making it stick up endearingly. Harden your heart, thought Honor, here comes the whitewash.

'Chloe had me over a barrel, OK? I made the mistake

of sleeping with her when I first moved into the barn – way before I even met you. I had a house-warming party and she came along; everyone had too much to drink and it all got a bit out of hand. I made it clear the next day there was nothing between us, that it was just a fling, but she wouldn't get the message. She was obsessed with me. She'd come into the barn when I got home every evening. Twice I found her naked in my bed. I couldn't get it through to her that I wasn't interested. In the end she got heavy. She said if I didn't sleep with her she'd tell her father I'd raped her. He's a barrister, Honor. I wouldn't have had a hope . . .'

'Well, maybe you should have thought about that before you took advantage of her in the first place.'

'Advantage?' Johnny gave a yelp of indignation. 'Have you seen a nineteen-year-old girl with one thing on her mind? I didn't have a snowball's chance in hell!'

'There's only one little word you needed. But you've never been good with no, have you?'

'I was trying to protect myself, Honor. Sleeping with Chloe didn't mean anything.'

'So how long were you going to carry on?'

'That's the irony! I'd told her this was the last time. Because . . .' Johnny trailed off.

'Because what?'

'Because I was going to ask you to marry me.'

'Yeah, right.' Honor's tone was withering. 'I almost believed you up until then.'

'It's true!'

Johnny looked like an indignant little boy defending himself to the headmaster. Honor tried to hide a smile.

'What's so funny?' he demanded.

'It would be funny. If it wasn't so pathetic,' she said wearily. 'I'm not really interested in your elaborate explanations. After all, you've had long enough to think up a convincing lie –'

'You're so bloody sanctimonious, you know that?'

Honor looked taken aback. Johnny's voice was level, but she could see his fists were clenched.

'You can only think about yourself in any of this, can't you? Didn't I have a right to know you were carrying my child? A son who's been walking this earth for the past six years?'

'The second you jumped into bed with her, whether it was for the first or last time, you lost any *rights*.' She imbued the last word with heavy sarcasm.

'I want to see him.'

'Tough.'

'I've got legal rights. As his biological father.'

'Have you?' Honor raised an eyebrow.

'Of course I have.'

'I'm sure you haven't a clue whether you have or not. Because you've never given any sort of responsibility a moment's thought. There's only ever been one person in your life and that's Johnny Flynn –'

Honor realized she was shrieking like a banshee. Horrified by her lack of dignity, she stopped in mid flow, furious that Johnny had been able to reduce her to this in mere moments.

'You really don't think much of me at all, do you?' Johnny looked very pale, very serious, very young. Honor wondered how long he could realistically go on looking like a boy. Could you still be boyish at forty? Fifty? 'I'm going to do whatever it takes to see my son. Make up for what he's missed over the past six years.'

Honor tipped up her chin.

'He hasn't missed out on anything, I promise you that.'

'Only his father.' Johnny's voice was hard. 'Look, we can do this the easy way, Honor. Or the hard way. I can do the lawyer thing. Though I don't think that would be fair on Ted. Surely it would be best for him if we kept it civilized?'

'I don't know why you think you can just walk in here and start dictating terms.'

'Because despite what you think, you're the one in the wrong here. You've deprived me of my son, and my son of his right to have a father. And despite your low opinion of me, I would go to the ends of the earth to make him happy. And you, for that matter.'

'Really?'

'Jaysus, Honor, when you left . . . There's never been anyone to match you before or since. My only regret is that I didn't realize it at the time. I was a self-indulgent tosser who was finding it hard to break the habits of a lifetime. And I can assure you I've suffered for it since.'

Honor snatched their empty tea mugs off the breakfast bar and marched over to the sink. Her chin was wobbling uncontrollably. Shit – she was going to cry. She couldn't remember the last time she'd cried about anything. This was the worst thing she could do – show Johnny that he was getting to her. But her emotions betrayed her. Hot tears sprang from her eyes, and she could do nothing to stop them.

'Just fuck off and leave me alone,' she croaked. 'Leave us alone . . .'

As the tears started to course down her cheeks she turned the taps on full to drown out the noise. What the hell was she crying for? For a hundred reasons, but mostly because Johnny had stood in front of her and verbalized all the guilt and fear she had suppressed over the past years. Had she been wicked to deprive Ted of a father? Was she evil to lie to him about his paternity? And how long would she get away with fairy-tale explanations that defied all logic?

'Hey, hey . . .'

He was rubbing her back gently. There he was, with his bloody healing hands, turning her to putty. She could feel the warmth spreading through her bones. An alarm bell rang in her head as she turned off the tap.

'Get off.' She nudged him away with her elbow, wiping her runny nose with the back of her hand. Johnny smiled.

'That's not very attractive.' He fished in his pocket for a handkerchief and handed it to her. Reluctantly, she wiped her nose, sniffing inelegantly, realizing with fury that his close presence was making her feel quite peculiar. She should have felt revulsion, but it was far from it.

'What you need is some breakfast.' He gave her a final pat on the back and moved away. Immediately she craved his touch again. 'You've had a shock. And I don't suppose you slept last night because I certainly didn't.'

He went over to the fridge and opened it.

'What have you got?'

'Nothing. I was supposed to stay over at a friend's.'

'I'll go to the shop. We'll have eggy bread.' He grinned at her. 'You know that's the only thing I can cook better than you.'

It was true. Johnny had a way with eggy bread she'd never been able to master. The right amount of sogginess and crispiness. When she made it, it was always rubbery.

He picked up his coat.

'Go and have a nice hot bath. I'll be back in five minutes. Eggy bread, proper coffee and the Sunday papers.'

It sounded like bliss. She and Ted usually only had toast, because she took him swimming on a Sunday morning and if he ate too much it gave him cramp . . .

What was she thinking of? Johnny had only been here ten minutes and already she was capitulating. But he was being so lovely. *Don't be nice!* She wanted to scream. She could cope as long as he was the enemy. But she was tired and emotionally drained and frightened, which made her vulnerable. And it was too, too tempting to succumb to his charms.

6

Richenda woke at about nine on Sunday morning. Even though they hadn't got to bed until three, her body was still locked into the routine of waking early and going to have her hair and make-up done in the trailer while she learned her lines for the day. She lay still for a few minutes, listening to the sound of Guy's gentle breathing beside her, revelling in the knowledge that for the next few weeks it wouldn't matter what time she got up. She wasn't the type to lie in till lunchtime, but it was nice to know that if she wanted to she could.

She slid out from underneath the duvet and went to examine her reflection in the bathroom mirror. Not too bad, considering their late night. Her skin was gradually recovering from having heavy foundation slathered on it every day. She applied her cleansing grains with the special linen mitt, did her lymphatic drainage exercises with her fingertips, then dolloped on generous amounts of moisturizer.

Guy was still out for the count. She hovered over him, debating waking him with a kiss, but then she relented and decided to let him sleep. She'd make him a proper Sunday breakfast instead. She pulled on a pair of jeans and a sweater, tied her hair up in a ponytail, then crept along the corridor, down the sweeping stairs and along to the kitchen. By the stable door that led out into the rear courtyard were hung a selection of jackets. She shrugged on a Barbour, and wrinkled her nose. It was stiff and smelly. She considered going to the cupboard off the hallway where her ankle-length sheepskin was hung, but decided against it. She didn't want to thrust her glamour down the locals' throats: that was not the way to win their affection. She wanted them to realize that she was fresh, natural and down to earth; a country girl at heart.

Outside it was a glorious autumn day. The air smelt delicious; of sharp, fresh air, dead leaves that weren't quite rotted and the mingled woodsmoke from various chimneys. The glare from the sun made her squint and she wished she'd brought her sunglasses, then remembered she was trying to fit in. She wandered out of the gates and on to the high street. She hadn't taken much notice of Eversleigh while they were filming; it was hard to when the street was filled with film crew and cameras and trucks and lorries. Now the circus had departed, she could appreciate its charms.

She walked along the rank of oak trees that screened the manor, then past the squat, square Norman church whose stained-glass windows reflected the glory of Portias ancestors who'd given their lives in the First World War. On the opposite side of the street was a row of workers' cottages, some larger and grander houses, as well as a few modern additions which were fortunately in keeping. At the very end of the street was the Fleece, an ancient pub that was rumoured to be haunted, and opposite that the village shop. The road out of the village boasted several cul-de-sacs containing developments of executive homes that ranged from the modest to the elaborate but which shared over-inflated prices, courtesy of the sparkling Ofsted report enjoyed by the village school. People fell over themselves to send their children there, and the high property prices were more than made up for by what one saved in prep school fees, especially when there was more than one child to consider.

Richenda stepped into the village shop. It smelt of sugary sweets and the spilt box of washing powder that had been trodden into the black and white lino floor tiles. The shelves had a dearth of named brands, preferring the Happy Shopper label – you couldn't even get Heinz baked beans. Richenda wondered how on earth people put up with it. The shop down the road from her flat in Knightsbridge was like a mini Fortnum's. Rather reluctantly, she bought a packet of bacon and a packet of sausages, half a dozen eggs and a sliced white loaf. She decided against the mushrooms, which had almost shrivelled beyond recognition. There were piles of Sunday papers dumped on the floor by the counter. She thought about buying one, but then decided that she would only be tempted to scan the pages for gossip and speculation about her own engagement. She deserved a day off.

She joined the queue. In front of her was a man with rumpled dark red hair, stuffing his purchases into a too-thin carrier bag. Cheekily, he inspected her basket.

'Hangover fodder?' he grinned. He held up a carton of orange juice. 'Don't forget the OJ. It's vital to replenish your vitamin C.'

The Irish accent, the dissolute air and the dark rings under his extraordinary eyes – a clear golden brown, like

Jameson's whiskey – made a pretty devastating combination. He'd obviously spent the night up to no good at all, decided Richenda. She couldn't help but smile back.

Back in the kitchen, Richenda did battle with the uncooperative cellophane wrappers round the sausages and the bacon and spread her purchases out on the table. Then she turned to face the Aga. It sat there, smug and defiant, refusing to give any hint as to how she should proceed. There wasn't an explanatory knob in sight.

Sausages in a tray in one of the ovens, she decided. Then bacon and eggs in a frying pan on one of the hot plates. They terrified her – somehow she imagined the heavy lids crashing down on her hands, trapping them on the searing heat below, scarring her for life. Gingerly, she lifted one of them up by the handle. How did you control the heat, she wondered? She held her palm over the surface to gauge the temperature; it felt pretty warm. She decided to go for it.

By the time Madeleine came into the kitchen fifteen minutes later, the bacon was fried to a crisp, the eggs were hard as rubber, the sausages were still raw and Richenda was searching frantically for a toaster.

'This is what you need.' Madeleine produced something that looked like a medieval instrument of torture crossed with a fly swat. The bread was supposed to go between the two racks, and was then placed on a hotplate with the lid down. 'And you've put the sausages in the warming oven. Not the hot oven. They'll never cook in there.'

Swiftly, Madeleine rearranged everything. The bacon and eggs were binned.

'Never mind. I've got some more in my flat.'

Moments later she'd returned with a packet of organic bacon wrapped in greaseproof paper, a basket of free-range eggs and a paper bag full of field mushrooms the size of plates.

'We don't touch anything from the village shop,' she explained. 'Except in dire emergencies. Papers, milk and sugar are fine. Avoid anything else like the plague.'

Richenda nodded, hovering with the kettle. There didn't seem to be anywhere to put it. She'd have to wait until the toast was done before she made tea.

'An Aga is a whole new way of life,' explained Madeleine. 'Once you've got used to it, you'll wonder how you ever lived without it.'

No, I bloody won't, thought Richenda crossly, longing for her own kitchen, with its integral wok and a pizza stone. Not that she'd ever used either of them, but they were there if she wanted them.

Moments later she turned round to see black smoke billowing out. She threw up the lid to reveal two charred and blackened slices of bread.

'You do need to keep a close eye,' said Madeleine. 'You've got to catch it at just the right moment.'

Richenda bit her tongue and dropped the ruined toast into the bin on top of the bacon and eggs, deciding that the first thing she was going to put on her wedding list was a four-slice Dualit toaster.

Fifteen minutes later, when Guy came in stretching and yawning in his boxers, Madeleine served up a perfectly timed and perfectly cooked breakfast – sausages sizzling in their skin, crispy bacon and golden eggs that slid obligingly from the pan on to a plate that had been warmed in the very oven Richenda had been trying to cook the sausages in. Accompanied by a mound of buttery mushroom slices. Richenda was hot and flustered, and not a little crestfallen. This wasn't quite how she'd imagined it.

'Fantastic, Mum. You're a mind-reader.'

Guy tucked in appreciatively. Madeleine was having a poached egg on a piece of unbuttered toast. Richenda couldn't face any of it, but her fantasy had been to share Sunday breakfast with her husband-to-be, so she helped herself to some bacon and mushrooms.

'Right,' said Madeleine, leaving half her toast and the whites of her egg. 'We need to get cracking. I don't know if I need to remind you, but we've got eight guests arriving at four o'clock on Friday for the weekend of a lifetime. I've drawn up a list of what needs to be done and put the appropriate initials next to the task.'

She handed out three pieces of paper.

'Efficient as ever,' noted Guy, wiping his egg up with the last corner of toast and surveying his list with amusement.

'Question of having to be, after years of living with your father,' said Madeleine drily.

Richenda picked up the list and her heart sank.

'I've got to go to London tomorrow,' she said slowly. 'For some voice-over work. I'll do what I can, of course I will, but I won't be here for most of this week . . .'

'Oh,' said Madeleine, clearly put out. 'I thought you'd finished filming.'

'Filming,' said Richenda. 'But there's more to it than that.'

'Right,' said Madeleine. 'Then we're going to have to think again. There's absolutely no way you and I can do all this between us, Guy.'

Guy was looking at the list, frowning.

'Bloody hell – this is all a bit random, isn't it? Insurance, flowerbeds, wine cellar, transportation . . . music? What does that mean? I gave up the violin when I was nine.'

'I need a selection of CDs. For the dining room and the library. I haven't a clue what people want to listen to.'

'Norah Jones, Jamie Cullum, Dido and the Red Hot Chili Peppers,' said Guy decisively. 'That'll cover most people's tastes. Order it from Amazon. That's one job off the list.'

'I had you down for bedding, towels, napkins, books and magazines and bath things . . .' Madeleine pointed what Richenda felt was an accusing finger at her as she ran down the list, then gave a heavy sigh. 'I was supposed to be in charge of food – which, let's face it, is by far the biggest headache. But if you're not going to be available . . .'

'I'm sorry. I didn't realize you were going to be relying on me.' Richenda squirmed with discomfort.

'Come on, Mum. Richenda's got her own stuff to worry about. You can't expect her to make beds . . .'

'I wasn't expecting her to make beds,' replied Madeleine. 'Marilyn's in charge of housekeeping.'

'Marilyn's Malachi the gardener's girlfriend,' Guy explained to Richenda. 'They look after the house and grounds. They're a bit eccentric. Mad on the fifties. But they're not afraid of hard work.'

Richenda was about to protest that she wasn't either, when Madeleine cut in.

'There's nothing for it. I'll have to get someone in to help with the catering.' She picked up a pencil and began crossing things off on her list. 'I was going to give us the day off and start with a vengeance tomorrow, but it looks as if things have changed. Guy – I need you to bring up all the furniture we put in the cellar during filming, and all the spare glasses and crockery. While you're doing that, Richenda and I can whip down to Cribbs Causeway for the bedding and other linen. I'll have to ask Marilyn to come in and do more hours. It's going to be an added expense, of course . . .'

Madeleine managed not to shoot an accusing stare at Richenda, who felt racked with guilt nevertheless, and only just stopped herself offering to pay Marilyn's wages to make up for the fact that she wasn't going to be there.

Behind Madeleine, Guy mouthed 'sorry' at her with a grimace. Richenda gave a weak smile. She'd imagined a long bracing walk through the fields and woods, her fingers locked in Guy's, then lunch in a pub somewhere next to a roaring fire. Not a route march to John Lewis.

'So who are you going to get to do the grub?' asked Guy.

'Never mind about that. I've got an idea.'

Richenda started to gather up the breakfast plates.

'Where's the dishwasher?' she asked, and was rewarded with two blank stares.

'I suppose,' said Madeleine, 'that's something else we should look into. There's going to be an awful lot of washing up.'

Guy smirked.

'Something tells me Marilyn's going to be opening an offshore account before the year is out.'

Half an hour later, Richenda had changed into something suitable for her shopping trip with Madeleine while Guy put on yesterday's jeans. She swallowed as she looked over at him pulling a grey T-shirt on over his head, the fabric sliding over his muscles. For a moment she wished they were miles away in her apartment, feasting on out-of-season strawberries and warm brioches with apricot jam. They could have done something corny and touristy – an open-topped bus tour or the London Eye – before oysters and champagne at Bibendum, her favourite lunch spot. Somehow, the allure of Eversleigh Manor was already losing its lustrous appeal. Richenda couldn't see the point of being a slave to its walls. It was a bit like hiring a hat. She'd never seen the point of parading round in something that wasn't really yours. And she wasn't convinced that Guy was happy with the arrangements either. It was Madeleine who had hit upon the idea. She was the driving force; the one bossing everyone else around. Richenda suspected that Madeleine had been rather used to her husband and son doing what she wanted all of her life. Well, there was someone else in the frame now. And if it wasn't what Guy wanted . . .

'You know,' she said softly, sliding a finger between Guy's waistband and his brown skin, 'you don't have to do this if you don't want to.'

He started, whether from the cold of her fingers or her statement, she couldn't be sure.

'What?' he asked warily.

'All this . . . house party nonsense. It seems like an awful lot of hard work. And really, there's no need.'

His eyes narrowed.

'What do you mean, no need?'

She gave a little shrug, accompanied by a nervous laugh.

'If this is going to be our house . . . our marital home . . .'

'What?' His voice was stony.

'Well . . .'

'Go on. Say it.'

'I've got enough money . . .' Richenda faltered for a moment, then regained her courage. '*Lady Jane*'s about to transmit in the States. There's bound to be another series, and they're talking about a feature film. There's no need to put Eversleigh through this.'

Guy tugged a lambswool jumper off the back of a chair.

'Well, that's great. I'll go and tell Mum we needn't worry, shall I? That I'm marrying you for your money, and I'm going to be a kept man for the rest of my life. Perfect.'

He stalked out of the bedroom and the door slammed shut behind him. Richenda stared after him, appalled that her offer had been misinterpreted. It seemed perfectly simple to her. Why should they all be running round like headless chickens so half a dozen people could come and eat Beef Wellington and put their feet up on the furniture? All for a couple of thousand pounds. She could make that in five minutes doing a voice-over, for heaven's sake. Though something told her Guy wouldn't appreciate her telling him that.

Never mind, she thought with a sigh. She'd let them

go ahead with their plans. She was pretty sure they'd soon tire of people tramping through their family home, and one thing was for certain – Madeleine wouldn't take too kindly to being treated like the hired help. One click of the fingers from a jumped-up, Burberry-clad arriviste and it would all be over.

In the meantime, she'd keep quiet and play along with it. She'd go to bloody John Lewis with Madeleine and help her choose sheets. After all, while she was in there, she could pick up details of their wedding list service . . .

7

Sundays for Henty Beresford usually consisted of cooking a huge breakfast, washing up, ironing the uniforms,
cooking a huge lunch, washing up, trying to get all the
children to do their homework, doing the children's homework for them, cooking tea, bath-hairwash-nit-check-
fingernails-toenails and finally kitbags. Then, if she was
lucky, sandwiches and cake in front of the *Antiques
Roadshow*, which was spoilt for her by Charles trying to
outguess the prices and then arguing with the experts –
'Nonsense. You'd never get that. No one's touching
Meissen at the moment. Not unless it's mint.' 'He's trying
to pull a fast one. That's worth fifty grand of anyone's
money. Bet he'll try and make him a silly offer as soon
as the cameras stop whirring.'

Day of rest? Pah!

This Sunday, however, Henty was determined to make
a few changes. The night before had shown her just how
little respect her husband afforded her. And how little he
considered anyone other than himself. Why else had he
risked driving home like that? She wouldn't have dreamed
of going over the limit, because she knew how difficult
it would make life if she lost her licence. And that was
without going into the morality of drink-driving; it was,
after all, illegal for a good reason. Something that wouldn't
even occur to Charles.

Somehow, his being stopped by the police last night had given her the courage to stand up for herself. She felt she had the upper hand for once, the moral high ground, and she was determined to take advantage of it while she could.

Once breakfast was over, Henty sent the children off to clean out the rabbits. There was much moaning and groaning.

'Fine,' said Henty, determined not to let her children take advantage of her any longer either. 'I'll put an advert in the paper. Find some nice little children who want some pets. Free to a *good* home, I'll put.'

Startled by their mother's uncharacteristic steeliness, and recognizing that she meant business, the children scurried off to do her bidding. Or at least pretend to.

Charles was sitting at the kitchen table sipping coffee and leafing nonchalantly through the paper, as if he had not a care in the world.

'So,' said Henty. 'Last night. Where do we start?'

Charles looked at her, rather startled. This was a very assertive tone for Henty.

'Start?' he asked cautiously.

'You totally humiliated me, Charles.'

He frowned.

'When? How?'

'You and Fleur Gibson on the dance floor. Making it quite clear that if I hadn't been in the vicinity you'd have been at it like rabbits. I don't know where her husband was, but if you ask me you're lucky he didn't plant you one on the nose –'

'Hey, slow down a minute. Let's get this straight. I was

having a dance. That's what people do at *dances*.' Charles laid on the sarcasm with a trowel.

'You were groping her, Charles.'

'She was all over me. I was just being polite. She was plastered.'

'She wasn't the only one, was she?'

Strident and sarcastic digs weren't Henty's stock-in-trade, but for once she was determined to make her point. They hadn't got to bed until half past four. After his humiliation in the police station, Charles had got straight into bed, refusing to discuss what had happened.

Charles looked sideways at her, alarmed by the outburst.

'So,' said Henty. 'What are we going to do, now you've lost your licence? There is absolutely no way I'm going to be able to manage. It's not physically possible.'

She wasn't being difficult. It was true. Every morning, Charles dropped the girls at the bus stop that took them to their school in Cheltenham before he drove to the station, while Henty took the boys in the opposite direction to the school in Eversleigh. In the evenings and at weekends there was an elaborate rota involving both of them for swimming lessons, tae kwon do, ballet and Lily's flute, and that was before parties or other social events were taken into consideration.

But all that seemed to concern Charles was that he wouldn't be able to drive the horsebox.

'I'm completely buggered, aren't I? The hunting season's started and how the hell am I supposed to get me and the girls to the meet? It'll be OK if it's local – we can ride there at a push.' He looked at Henty, annoyed. 'I wish you'd learn to pull it.'

'Well, I can't and I won't.' Henty stood up and started banging plates on top of each other. 'And anyway, the hunt's the least of our problems. How am I supposed to pick Lily up from flute and Walter up from Beavers on a Thursday when they're fifteen miles apart?'

'Can't you do a lift share with the other mothers?'

'I already do!' Henty shrieked. 'For God's sake, Charles – you have no idea how complicated life is with four children. And you without a licence isn't making it any easier. Can't you take this seriously?'

Charles sighed. His head was pounding but he knew he wasn't going to get any sympathy for mentioning it. All he wanted was some bloody peace and quiet. Not his usually docile wife reminding him what a tit he'd been.

'OK. We'll get a nanny. Even better, a nanny-groom – one that can bloody well drive and pull a horsebox. She can take me to the station and pick me up every night. And help you out with the rest of it.'

Henty looked at him open-mouthed.

'What?'

'She can live in the stable flat. In fact, I don't know why we didn't think about it before.'

'Because we can't afford it?' ventured Henty, and was rewarded with a filthy glare.

'Actually, it'll be an economy. We'll save a fortune on babysitters. I think Mrs Potter's got a cheek charging us thirty quid for last night.'

'Charles – I had to give her extra because in case you didn't notice we didn't get home until four.'

'So how much will it cost?'

'I don't know. Three or four hundred quid a week?'

Charles winced.

'Well, make sure you get one that knows how to clean as well. This place is a pigsty.'

Henty fought down the urge to empty the teapot over his head. Charles was always infuriatingly arrogant and sexist when he was stressed. It was how she knew he was ashamed of his behaviour the night before. She decided to quit while she was ahead – she couldn't begin to count the amount of times she'd dropped hints about having some live-in help. It annoyed her that it was only visions of his hunting being curtailed that had made Charles capitulate, but she wasn't going to complain. It would be heaven to have an extra pair of hands . . .

'Where's the bloody review section?' Charles was rifling frantically through the paper.

'I think Thea took it to line the rabbits' cage,' replied Henty sweetly, and fled the room before she burst into giggles of triumph.

Charles couldn't quite bring himself to go and retrieve the review section. It was bound to have been weed on already. But he was annoyed, because he wanted to scrutinize the bestseller lists, analyse for the six millionth time what it was that the general public were buying to line their bookshelves, and see if he could get a glimmer of inspiration for the next big thing. The inspiration he had once had in spades.

Charles Beresford had always felt slightly second rate. He'd gone to a minor public school – not one grand enough to make him feel one of the elite, but one that made him feel like a bit of a knob. He wasn't smart, but he wasn't streetwise either. Pretty ill-equipped altogether. Then he'd failed to get into Oxford and had ended up going to Bristol, which had always piqued him, as at the time it was known as a dumping ground for Oxbridge rejects. And at Bristol, he didn't get into the posh halls of residence, but had ended up on the Downs with the hoi polloi. He was an also-ran, a wannabe. And rather than accepting his station in life, he always hung on the coat-tails of those he admired, and so had a constant reminder that he wasn't quite rich, glamorous or sophisticated enough to really belong.

When he left Bristol, he wanted to go into publishing, but singularly failed to get so much as an interview. So he took the back route, and went to work for a literary agent instead, hoping that the contacts he made there would open doors. Again, he failed to get into a top-rate agency, but ended up as assistant to the infamous Meredith Payne. She had once been a literary legend, champion of feisty, feminist writers, but at pushing sixty was becoming a little dotty, with her hennaed hair and mouth lined with plum lip-liner. Too many liquid lunches had puffed her up and she waddled rather than walked, her swollen feet stuffed into sandals, silver rings cutting into her fingers.

After just a few days it became clear to Charles that Meredith was losing the plot completely. He panicked, wondering if he should hand in his notice straight away, then realized that perhaps he could salvage something from the wreckage. For although she was no longer generating much business, she was good company and a fabulous source of gossip – what she didn't know, she made up, and it was really quite surprising she'd never been sued for libel. So she was often taken out for lunch, and she invariably took Charles with her, to relay the important things that had been said afterwards and to light her cigarettes. Thus he was given a personal introduction to some of the most important names and faces in the publishing industry. In the meantime, he sucked her dry for information; learned all her trade secrets – the ones she was more than happy to share with him after a good lunch – went through every single file, every single contract, read all the small print, clarified with her anything he didn't quite understand, until he was satisfied that he knew everything there was to know about being a literary agent. He made sure he was there to pick up after her, chasing up contracts and payments she had forgotten, reading and responding to manuscripts she had ignored, returning phone calls on her behalf, until the industry was quite clear that it was Charles holding things together. Gradually, clients, editors and publishers began to talk to him directly if they wanted anything done. Meanwhile, poor old Meredith tottered around oblivious in her own little world, slowly losing her grip on reality.

In the end, Charles reasoned that, as he was running the agency almost single-handedly, it was time to set up on his own. He was ready to jump ship. All he needed was a hot project . . .

One Friday evening, Charles was invited to dinner with his friend Dickon. They'd been at university together: Dickon had been part of the glamorous, moneyed crowd Charles had hovered on the edge of but never been quite comfortable with. Dickon had rather surprisingly kept in touch. He had an enormous mansion flat in South Kensington, was louche, immoral and bisexual with a penchant for matchmaking that was slightly out of character.

'Come and meet my new lodger,' Dickon commanded languidly. 'She's an utter sweetie. She keeps house beautifully, but she's wasted on me. I'm far too depraved for her. She'd be ideal for you, though.'

Charles was indeed immediately enchanted with Henty, who was like a Dresden shepherdess with dark curls, a creamy skin and a delightful naivety mixed with a sense of mischievous fun which proved a refreshing change from the rest of the world-weary thrillseekers at the table. By pudding, Dickon was reading from Henty's diary in a wicked imitation of her breathless, rather Sloaney tones. It had the entire table in stitches, as it depicted her madcap escapades around Kensington and Chelsea, trying to avoid the wandering hands of various baronets and viscounts and fighting off their advances.

'I'm the only virgin left in SW3,' she insisted.

Charles was transfixed, not only by Henty, but by the diary itself. It was startlingly well-written, in a style of its own. The descriptions of people and places were colourful, wickedly accurate and vivid; the antics were hilarious; the narrative thread was utterly compelling. And the world it depicted was glamorous, intriguing: a little slice of English life that fascinated people – minor aristocracy and wealthy layabouts behaving outrageously.

When the post-prandial white lines came out, Charles and Henty were the only ones who didn't indulge.

Charles went to help her with coffee in the kitchen.

'I made truffles,' she said, carefully laying them out on a plate, 'but I don't know why I bothered. Maybe I should have rolled them in coke instead of cocoa.'

She went to pick up the tray of coffee cups, but Charles put a hand out to stop her.

'Wait,' he said. 'I want to talk to you.'

She looked at him warily.

'It's OK. I'm not trying to get your knickers off. I want to talk to you about your diary.'

'God, it's so embarrassing. Bloody Dickon's always using me as his after-dinner entertainment.'

'So why do you keep a diary? Hardly anybody does these days.'

'I don't know. I always have. I find it sort of therapeutic. Besides, I've got the most dreadful memory and I can't remember a thing that's happened half the time and I think that's awfully sad, don't you?'

'The point,' said Charles, 'is that what you've written is brilliant. And I think it would make the most fantastic book.'

'What?'

'You should publish it.'

'Don't be silly. Who'd want to read it?'

'Lots of people.'

Henty looked at him doubtfully.

'Trust me. I'm a literary agent,' Charles equivocated smoothly. 'This is the best thing I've read for years. It's fresh, funny, different. Everyone's obsessed with Sloanes because of Princess Diana –'

'I'm not a Sloane!' protested Henty.

'Of course you are. You're posh and you hang out in Chelsea and you know people with titles. Don't knock it. This could be your meal ticket.' Charles paused for a moment. 'Surely you don't want to be hoovering Dickon's bedroom for the rest of your life?'

'Course not. I'm supposed to be going to Meribel next month. To be a chalet girl.'

'There you go. Classic Sloane behaviour,' Charles teased her gently.

By the end of the night, Charles had eight of the pink notebooks Henty used as her diary, filled with pages of her rounded handwriting littered with exclamation marks and smiley faces. Two days later, the manuscript was typed up. He knew he was on to a winner when the typist asked if there was going to be any more – she was desperate to know what happened next.

Then he sat down and composed a letter to an editor he'd been courting at one of the top publishing houses.

'I wanted you to be the first to look at this,' he wrote. 'It's called *The Diary of a Chelsea Virgin* . . .'

Diary of a Chelsea Virgin smashed into the bestseller charts a year later. Henty was fêted as a minor celebrity; there was a column for one of the society magazines and she did a what-to-wear-and-how-to-behave slot on breakfast telly when they did a round-up of the social season.

Charles launched his own agency off the back of it. Meredith was so gaga by then she barely noticed, and Charles was applauded for sticking by her for so long. Several of her clients wanted to jump ship with him, but he insisted that he couldn't do that to her – he wasn't that ruthless. He soon picked up new talent, Henty wrote a follow-up, and the two of them became an item. Charles just about managed not to capitalize on the fact that he'd deflowered the infamous Chelsea Virgin.

A year after that, they were married. And with her substantial royalty cheques, they bought a farmhouse in the Cotswolds.

'I want babies,' said Henty. 'Lots of them.'

Charles duly provided her with four.

Somehow, fifteen years later, life was not as perfect as it should be. After his meteoric rise and ten honeyed years of success, Charles was no longer the hot new kid on the block when it came to spotting talent. He hadn't moved with the times. He hadn't done a six-figure deal for three years. His client list was, frankly, rather embarrassing. When people asked at dinner parties who he looked after, they obviously expected a litany of chick-lit authoresses and Booker prize winners. Not that he wasn't making money. He had a client who wrote rather unsavoury sadistic thrillers that had a huge underground following and were lapped up by the Japanese in particular. Another specialized in lesbian porn – Charles was never quite sure if it was intended for women or men, but didn't enquire too closely, as they were exceptionally lucrative. He had plenty of projects that were ticking over, but what he didn't have was credibility. And Charles was very anxious about how he was perceived. It was why he'd taken up hunting; it was social death not to in Eversleigh, and he rather enjoyed shocking people with his exploits when he went out to lunch in London. He thought his approval of bloodsports gave him a certain cachet.

So lately he'd been rather tense. He was desperate for a project that would re-establish him and give him some respect. The hot new talent didn't even bother to send him their manuscripts any more, though he had plenty of crap from middle-aged women with empty-nest syndrome who thought they could write a bestseller. He just needed one hot project and he'd be back in the running.

In the meantime, he knew he was being beastly to Henty, but she always managed to make him feel such a heel precisely because she didn't nag and complain. He knew losing his licence like that was bloody catastrophic, but he couldn't bring himself to admit to being in the wrong. He just prayed that the nanny idea would be a success. Actually, how could it fail to be? A chauffeur on tap, hot and cold babysitting, someone to do all the mucking out that he had to nag Thea and Lily to do. Maybe he and Henty could have a life at long last. In fact, he didn't know why he hadn't thought of it sooner . . .

While Johnny went out to buy eggs and bread, Honor lay in the bath and came to terms with the fact that she was going to have to let him meet Ted. She simply didn't have any choice. She knew Johnny well enough to know that he wouldn't take no for an answer, and she wanted to avoid ugly scenes at all costs. To protect Ted, more than anything. In return for her compliance, she prayed that Johnny would accept that things had to go along at her pace. Surely he would respect that she would know what was best for their son? It was a delicate situation, after all.

She came down from her bath in fresh jeans and a

sweatshirt, her short hair still wet and slicked back. Johnny was flipping slices of eggy bread expertly; the breakfast bar was laid with two places, with glasses of orange juice and a pot of fresh coffee waiting. He'd certainly made himself at home already, she noted. He gave her a smile.

'Sit down. We're nearly ready.'

Honor perched on the other stool and watched him get out plates, then slide the golden triangles on to them.

'There you go.' He presented her breakfast with a flourish. She tucked in hungrily, eating it with her fingers as they always used to after a wild night out, dipping the corners into tomato sauce – he'd found that too. It was almost as if he was taking her on a journey back in time, reminding her of the good times they'd once had together. The infuriating thing was it was almost working. It was great to have breakfast cooked for you, great to have fresh coffee – Honor would normally never bother; the packet had sat in her cupboard for months – great to sit with someone who wasn't going to ask you how magnets worked, or what the gearstick on a car was for. Just for once, of course.

When she finished, she realized Johnny was staring at her.

'What?'

'You've got tomato sauce on your chin,' he grinned, and reached out a finger to wipe it off. She recoiled hastily, grabbing a nearby tea towel to wipe it off herself. She didn't want physical contact. She needed to keep a clear head.

'I haven't got leprosy, you know,' said Johnny reproachfully.

'I know,' said Honor. 'Listen,' she continued firmly, 'I've

decided you can meet Ted. But I don't want him to know who you are yet. I want to take this really slowly. I can't just spring it on him suddenly.'

'When?'

Honor knew she was going to have to stand her ground.

'Wednesday. After school. About . . . five o'clock. You can come for tea.'

Johnny frowned.

'Why not the weekend? It would give us more time.'

That was precisely what Honor didn't want. Plenty of time for Johnny to get comfy and get his feet under the table, and for her to be enjoying having him around, wanting him to stay longer. If it was a school night then she'd have to stick to their routine; she'd be able to kick Johnny out at half six saying it was bathtime.

'We're busy at the weekend,' she said firmly.

'Is there anything I can bring him? Does he collect anything? Lego or something? Do they still make Lego?'

'Don't bring him anything. You're just an old friend of mine, remember? He'll think it's a bit weird if you turn up laden with presents.'

'If he's a normal little boy he won't worry about it too much,' Johnny said. 'But if you insist.'

He took her chin in his hand and turned her to face him.

'You know what?'

'What?' said Honor, wary.

'I can't think of anyone I'd rather have as the mother of my child.'

'Thank you,' she said primly, because she couldn't think of anything else to say.

'I know you don't believe me, but there *hasn't* been anyone else since you, you know.' Johnny was gazing at her intently. 'I haven't been a monk, of course I haven't. But there hasn't been anyone who comes close to meaning what you did.'

He was staring at her, obviously expecting a reply, but she just smiled and shrugged rather helplessly.

'What about you?' he asked suddenly.

'What about me?'

'Has there been anyone else? Have you had . . . relationships? Have you got someone?'

Honor felt indignant. He was stepping over the line, poking his nose in where it didn't belong. She couldn't say yes, because that would be lying. And she certainly couldn't say no, because that would imply that she'd attached some great importance to her relationship with Johnny, that she'd been preserving herself in aspic ever since she'd left him. Which of course she hadn't.

'That is absolutely none of your business. Now if you don't mind I've got to go and pick Ted up, so I'd be grateful if you'd bugger off. And I don't want any funny stuff. I don't want you peering in the window to get a look at him or anything. You'll have to wait till Wednesday.'

'I'd forgotten just how tough you were,' mused Johnny. 'And how bossy.'

Honor picked up his coat and car keys and thrust them at him.

'Coat. Keys. Door.'

He backed out of the room reluctantly.

'Can I have your phone number? In case there's a problem?'

Exasperated, Honor picked up one of her business cards and shoved it in his top pocket. He rummaged in his coat and handed her one of his in return.

'My mobile number's on it,' he said softly. 'In case you want to talk. I'll be on the end of the phone any time of the day or night. I know you're pretending to be tough and in control, Honor. But there's a lot we've got to think about.'

'Johnny?' she smiled. 'Fuck off. I'll see you on Wednesday.'

Once she was quite sure Johnny had gone, Honor drove over to the Beresfords' to collect Ted. Against her better judgement, she allowed herself to be persuaded to stay for lunch by Henty.

'Please! Charles is in a bait – he got stopped last night for drunk-driving.'

'Oh no!'

'Yes. So he's not a happy bunny, even though he's pretending it wasn't his fault. Though how he works that one out I don't know. Anyway, if you're here for lunch he'll have to be nice. I've done an enormous leg of pork . . .'

Honor hesitated. She wasn't sure that she wanted to be a pawn in the Beresfords' marital battle, but Ted and Walter were having a fantastic time outside on the bikes and what was the point of dragging Ted away from a slap-up Sunday lunch when the fridge was empty at home?

Instead they had a hilarious time dissecting all the outfits from the night before. Honor noticed that Henty became very slitty-eyed when Fleur Gibson was mentioned, and Charles looked uncomfortable.

'She's a silly cow,' pronounced Honor.

'Tell Charles that,' slurred Henty, pouring herself another glass of wine.

'She's a silly, dangerous cow,' repeated Honor emphatically.

'I'm sure you're right,' drawled Charles, who knew when he was being got at. 'But she's got a fantastic arse.'

He sat back with a smirk to enjoy the look of outrage on Honor and Henty's faces.

'You should know,' said Henty. 'You had a good enough feel.'

Charles blinked slowly. Like a lizard, thought Honor.

'Perhaps it's small,' he said, 'because she doesn't sit around on it all day. Because she actually gets *up* off her arse and does something with her time.'

Henty gasped, as if he'd thrown a glass of ice-cold water over her. Honor narrowed her eyes and glared at him across the table.

'We could all open a shop,' she hissed, 'if we had rich husbands who put the money up.'

'Maybe.' Charles met her glare coolly. 'By the way, who was the Paddy last night?' He looked at her knowingly from under his heavy-lidded eyes, slipping the knife in when she least expected it.

'Just someone I used to know in Bath.' Annoyed with herself for not seeing it coming, Honor glossed over it as best she could. She'd thought for a moment the night before that Charles had suspected who Johnny was, but she'd hoped he'd been too drunk to actually put two and two together. Now she couldn't be sure.

'Someone you knew well?' Charles persisted.

'Just a friend.'

'Yeah? Well, he grilled me for a good five minutes. About what you were doing and where you lived.'

'I hope you didn't tell him anything!' said Henty.

'Of course not. I'm not going to give away Honor's secrets to a total stranger.'

Honor squirmed, not sure if Charles was toying with her, or if he was just being his usual smarmy self.

'You certainly didn't look too happy to see him. Had he got something on you?'

Honor shrugged.

'He's just not the sort of person I want to get mixed up with again. He's in with the hard-drinking, racing crowd. Too fast for me.'

'Ah, well, it's in the blood, isn't it? You can see that.'

Charles's final dig was so pointed that Honor stood up sharply to clear away, her cheeks flushing an angry red. She carried the vegetable dishes out to the kitchen. Henty followed her.

'I'm sorry about Charles. He's being completely obnoxious because he feels guilty about losing his licence.'

'What on earth are you going to do if he can't drive?'

'Every cloud's got a silver lining,' grinned Henty. 'He's said I can get a live-in nanny. I'm going to book it first thing in the morning before he changes his mind.'

'Good for you!' said Honor.

She stood by the kitchen window and took a gulp of fresh air. For a moment she wanted to confide in Henty. It was obvious Charles was suspicious and was going to spill the beans sooner or later. But she didn't feel ready to share her secret yet. Tempting though it was to throw herself on to Henty's comforting shoulder, she decided not to say anything. Henty had her hands full as it was. And she wanted to get things straight in her head before she shared the news with the rest of the world. She'd think about it tonight, when Ted had gone to bed.

But by the time she got home it was late and, exhausted from barely having any sleep the night before, she fell asleep watching *Heartbeat* on the portable telly in her bedroom with Ted curled up next to her and didn't wake up until eight the next morning.

8

It was a mad scramble to get Ted to school on Monday morning. Racing around trying to find either of them a pair of matching socks, Honor couldn't believe she had slept so soundly, given the traumatic events of the weekend. Eventually Ted was dropped off and she made it back to the solace of her little kitchen to drink a cup of calming camomile tea and take stock of the chaos that had become her life. She had the whole day to herself, as the craft centre didn't open for lunch on a Monday.

She was just about to sit down when there was a knock on the door. Hoping against hope that it wasn't more trouble, she answered it to find a slender, elegant woman standing on the doorstep. Honor recognized her at once – she'd seen her coming in and out of Eversleigh Manor on any number of occasions. But what on earth was Madeleine Portias doing knocking on her door?

'Honor McLean?'

Honor nodded and Madeleine held out her hand.

'Madeleine Portias. I hope you don't mind me not phoning first. I got your address from your advert in the ball programme.'

'Oh. Oh yes – wasn't it your son who bid for the cake? Did you want to order it now?'

'No, no. It said in your advert you do other catering.'

'Well, yes. Not on a grand scale, though.' Honor spoke

with a note of caution, wondering if Madeleine was about to ask her to do the wedding.

'I think you might be just the person I need to help me out of a tight spot.'

Intrigued, Honor stood to one side to usher Madeleine in.

'Come on in. I was just making camomile tea, if you'd like one.'

Honor led Madeleine through into the kitchen and pulled out a stool for her to sit on, then flicked the kettle back on. Meanwhile, Madeleine explained her predicament, outlining her plans for the country house weekends.

'I'm the last person to admit defeat, but I think I've overestimated my capabilities. I'd really like to try and delegate some of the catering. I can manage the main courses, because it's not as if I have to do something different every week. I can stick to what I know – pheasant, duck or venison. It's the other extras – the little things that are going to make a difference – that I worry I'm not going to have time for. And you'd be perfect.'

'So what exactly are you looking for?'

Madeleine extracted a list from her pocket and took a deep breath.

'Nibbles to go with drinks when they arrive. An easy pudding for Friday night. A home-made soup and home-made bread for Saturday lunch. Cakes and biscuits for Saturday tea. Starters and a fancy pudding for Saturday night. And petits fours. And often there will be a cake – people are going to be celebrating birthdays and anniversaries. And I could do with a hand in the kitchen on the

Saturday night – someone who knows what they're doing.'

Honor hesitated.

'It's an awful lot of work. I don't know if I'll be able to take it on, on top of everything else. And I've got a little boy . . .'

Madeleine leaned forward eagerly.

'You can do most of it in advance. You can use our kitchen for preparation and storage. Or you can do it at home and bring it in – whichever you prefer. You'd really only need to be there to help with the main course on the Saturday night – you'd be finished by eight thirty or nine. Your little chap can watch a video on the sofa . . .'

Honor took the list off Madeleine and tried to take it all in.

'I don't know. I wouldn't have a clue what to charge for a start . . .'

'I thought I'd pay you a flat weekly rate. Say . . . a hundred and twenty pounds? You can bill me for the ingredients separately. And you can work at your own pace.'

Honor turned the proposition over in her mind. The amount Madeleine was offering was generous and, even better, at least she would know exactly how much money she could rely on coming in each week. The craft centre was inconsistent: she hated the fact that some days she'd be thrown into a panic, while others, like today, she was left with nothing to do. Or worse, as sometimes happened, tied to the kitchen for a measly batch of shortbread or two quiches which weren't really worth the bother of getting her pots and pans dirty. With this proposition she would know well in advance how many she was catering for. She could plan what to do, make better use of her time. And she thought it might be quite good fun. She'd passed the manor house so many times and wondered what it was like inside. Of course, she'd be downstairs rather than upstairs. But what else did she do on a Saturday night? Bugger all. She might as well be earning money and Ted wouldn't mind watching a video.

'Why don't we give it a trial run? If it doesn't work out we can think again.'

'Can I have a think? And phone you this evening?'

'Better still, come and have a drink. I can show you the kitchen and so on. Say about six?'

'That sounds lovely.'

Madeleine left, leaving behind a faint trace of Cacherel. Honor sat down in disbelief. What a week this was turning out to be! She wasn't really sure what to make of Madeleine's offer, but she was grateful for one thing: at least it had stopped her thinking about Johnny.

Having said that, it was at times like this when the fact she was on her own was never more apparent. She always had to make the decisions, and there wasn't really anyone she could discuss things with – not things that really mattered. Her mother was always infuriatingly vague about anything important – Honor had known there was no point in even bringing up the MMR jab dilemma with her. So she was used to weighing pros and cons up in her own mind, and was quite prepared to take the consequences of her decisions.

But sometimes it was tiring. Sometimes, she just wanted someone whose opinion she respected to say 'Go for it!' Or 'Don't even think about it!'

Like this opportunity, for example. Once she'd written it all down on paper, worked out how many hours of her time she thought it might take up, it looked like a very attractive proposition. But there were downsides. What happened, for example, if there was a cancellation? Would she still get paid? And what if the whole venture was a failure, and she was laid off, having given up her arrangement with the craft centre? She'd just be left with the cakes, then, and although they were doing well they weren't a reliable source of income.

Honor sighed. Sometimes the incredible burden of her responsibility got to her. Not that she resented Ted for a millisecond. But occasionally she felt not exactly self-pity, but a bit wistful; a secret longing for a life where she could share things with someone. Not only the bad bits – she wasn't looking for someone to dump on – but the good bits too. Like when Ted had been Joseph in the nativity play, and when he'd got his hundred metres swimming badge –

She put her cup down with a bang, telling herself to pull herself together. She'd managed this long on her own, for heaven's sake. She'd better not go all wibbly-wobbly on Wednesday when Johnny came round, or he'd wheedle his way back into her life in seconds. She felt panicky about his visit whenever she thought about it, and she knew jolly well why.

Because she was looking forward to it.

And she didn't trust herself.

It was no good. She needed somebody to talk to. She'd give Henty a ring. The secret was going to be out before long, after all, and Henty would be mortified if she thought Honor hadn't confided in her. She picked up the phone and dialled, already feeling some relief that her burden was going to be shared. All she wanted was some objective guidance about the best way to tackle Johnny's reappearance in their life, bearing in mind that the only person that really mattered was Ted, who was not only an innocent bystander but the one who could be most affected in the long term.

Henty's phone rang and rang. Honor gave it twenty rings before she hung up. On reflection, maybe it was best to keep it all to herself. That was the only way she could be sure of controlling who found out the truth and when – not that she didn't trust Henty, but you just never knew. Some people found the responsibility of secrets just too great to bear. She might be tempted to tell Charles, and Honor certainly didn't trust him to keep his trap shut. Least said, soonest mended, she thought, and decided she would wait and see what Wednesday brought.

In the meantime, she prayed that Johnny had grown up enough not to play games . . .

Henty was in the flat over the stables. She'd rushed there as soon as the children had finally been got to school, to see if it was fit for human habitation. There was no point in organizing a nanny if they didn't have anywhere decent to put her, and the flat had been empty for years. In fact, it could hardly be called a flat at all – it was just a large room tucked into the eaves, with a shower and loo off. They'd converted it because Charles had thought at one point he might like to work from home, but had decided that it would be too complicated – the bit of paperwork you wanted would inevitably always be in the wrong place – so it had sat there empty. Now, looking at it, Henty decided it was quite comfortable. She'd turned on the heating and within half an hour it was as warm as toast. A good cleaning session, a lick of paint and a trip to Ikea, and it would be ideal.

It was going to be absolute bliss, thought Henty, to have someone around to help out. It would make all the difference to the children too. She often had to cart them all round in the car when she was picking up one of the others, and they always moaned and protested. But if the nanny was around, they could stay at home while she nipped out. And she and Charles could pop out for dinner whenever they felt like it. Or go to the cinema. She couldn't remember the last time they'd been to the movies, because it seemed a waste of a babysitter when things came out on video so quickly, but then she never managed to rent the films she wanted to watch. She was always outvoted.

Though all four children were at school, Fulford Farm was a high maintenance household. Not helped by the fact that Charles was very fussy and particular about how the house was kept. Because he had a dust allergy, the entire house had to be hoovered from top to bottom every day, and their bedsheets were changed twice a week. He changed every evening when he got home too, and those clothes always went straight into the dirty bin even though they'd only been worn a couple of hours. Then his shirts had to be ironed in a particular way. There was someone in the next village with an ironing service, and Henty had often longed to offload a mound of laundry, but Charles would be bound to notice, and quibble and complain. It was easier not to rock the boat.

He was fussy about what he ate as well. Meat had to be bought from the butcher's in Eldenbury; vegetables from the organic farm shop; cheese from the deli. And he had to have a proper meal every night. Thank God the children had decent school lunches and made do with sandwiches or spaghetti hoops on toast.

Added to all of this was the chore of looking after the horses. Five years ago, when Lily and Thea had started going to Pony Club, Charles had met some of the other parents and been talked into taking up hunting by the evangelical master of the local hunt, who happened to be a woman and far from unattractive. Within twelve months he'd learned to ride, bought himself a horse and the girls a brace of ponies, and joined the Eldenbury hunt. It was, Henty knew, one of his ambitions to become Joint Master, but he still had a long way to climb up the hierarchy. In the meantime, he and the girls hunted most Saturdays in winter, which strangely seemed to lead to an awful lot of work for Henty.

For Charles's allergy was peculiar, in that he seemed to be able to ride horses, but not muck them out or groom them. Which left Thea and Lily in charge, and it was always up to Henty to chivvy them along, to the extent that it was often easier to do it herself, even though she was terrified of horses. She didn't mind clearing out the stables once they'd been turned out – it was quite thera-peutic – but she couldn't stand handling the animals. It was the way they threw up their heads or kicked out their hind legs just when you least expected it. But if the nanny was going to help out there as well . . . A smile spread itself across Henty's face as she saw a new life opening out in front of her.

Maintaining the Beresford family had been a full-time job, and until now, Henty had never complained. Deep down she knew Charles was demanding and fussy and a bit of a tyrant, but she'd got used to his ways. As long as you went along with him and let him think he was in control, it was fine. His good points outweighed his bad – most of the time – and he couldn't help it if he was allergic to dust, and he did work hard. So the least she could do was provide support. Her role, after all, was wife and mother.

Now, however, with the prospect of some proper free time in front of her, Henty was determined to make some changes. She'd been stung yesterday by Charles's remark about Fleur. As Honor had pointed out, how hard could it be to open a florist's – especially when your husband had put up the money? But Charles was obviously impressed. Thus Henty was determined to prove that she was more than just a docile little housewife. She might not have a bum the size of a Cox's orange pippin, but hadn't she once been the toast of literary society?

Sometimes she found it hard to believe that really had been her. And other people found it even harder, when she revealed she'd had a six-week slot on TV-am giving advice on what to wear to Ascot and Henley. Over the years, Henty had convinced herself that *Chelsea Virgin* had been a fluke, that its success was one of those peculiarities of right time, right place. For after the second instalment of the book, when they'd moved to Fulford Farm on the proceeds and Henty had become pregnant with Thea, she'd tried to write a third. But away from the source of her inspiration, and bogged down with trying to renovate a farmhouse before the baby was born, Henty had struggled to string two words together. Charles had reassured her that everyone had writer's block, and the best thing to do was to put her typewriter away for a couple of months. That had been nearly fifteen years ago, and in the meantime her confidence had evaporated into thin air. Henty convinced herself her one-time success had been a marketing con engineered by Charles which had nothing whatsoever to do with any talent she might have . . .

A year or so ago, however, she'd listened to a programme on Radio Four about novel writing, and it had rekindled her ambition. A germ of an idea had planted itself in her brain, and on the advice of the programme she had rushed out to buy a notebook – pink, like the notebooks she had originally used for *Chelsea Virgin* – and started to jot down notes in the few quiet moments she had. Now the notebooks numbered three and were kept in the bottom of her tights drawer. Every time she thought about them she felt both fear and excitement, but she'd consistently had the excuse of lack of time to stop her doing anything concrete with them.

Now, however, it seemed she no longer had an excuse. And she was champing at the bit to get started. The time was right. She no longer felt fear, just the tingle of antici-pation, the itch to give some sort of shape to the ramblings she had begun.

Happy that she had somewhere to put her intended

addition to the family, she trotted back inside to the kitchen and found the Yellow Pages. There was an agency in Cheltenham that a lot of her friends used. She picked up the phone and dialled the number, idly doodling smiley faces over the pad she'd efficiently opened to make notes.

The girl at the agency was very apologetic.

'You've called at a very bad time. Everyone's been snapped up for the beginning of term.'

'Oh,' said Henty, deeply disappointed. 'But I'm desperate!'

'There is one possibility,' said the girl. 'But there is a slight snag that you might not be very happy about.'

'Try me,' said Henty.

Moments later, she put the phone down with a mischievous grin. Charles wouldn't like it, but sod Charles. After all, it was his fault in the first place.

The wind whistled up the platform at Eldenbury as Guy and Richenda stood waiting for the Paddington train. Richenda shivered, and snuggled down further into her sheepskin coat. Guy put an arm round her and hugged her to him.

'Chilly?'

'Freezing.'

She snuggled into him, grateful for his warmth. Thankfully, their little spat of the day before seemed to have been forgotten. By the time she and Madeleine had got back from John Lewis, Guy was resolutely cheerful. He'd restored all the furniture to its rightful place and put all the paintings back on the walls. The three of them had a roast chicken supper together in the kitchen, and the atmosphere had been far more relaxed than at breakfast. Richenda no longer felt as if Madeleine was trying to undermine her or score points – maybe they'd bonded somehow in the bedding department.

The train drew in and Richenda felt a pang. For two pins she wouldn't get on. She wanted to stay and muck in with everyone else; do her bit, prove that she didn't mind getting her hands dirty. But she was contractually obliged to turn up at the editing suite the next morning. She might like to think that her life was her own, but it wasn't. Far from it.

Guy opened the door into the first-class carriage. She picked up her holdall and climbed on board. Guy shut the door and they shared a long, lingering kiss through the window. The whistle blew and Richenda withdrew her head with a smile.

'Phone me when you get home,' instructed Guy, and she nodded, then made her way into the carriage to find a seat. Thankfully, she found an empty table. She didn't want to have to make polite conversation with anyone. Or worse, be recognized. She sank into the forward-facing seat gratefully, tucking her bag underneath her feet.

As the train drew out of the station, Richenda felt like crying. Hastily, she put on her dark glasses. What on earth was the matter with her? She should be walking on air. She was a star. She was engaged to the most gorgeous man on the planet.

The problem was simple: she didn't know who she was, or what role she was playing. Lady Jane? Richenda Fox? Nearly Mrs Guy Portias? For a moment she felt like mousy, plain nobody Rowan Collins again. Unsure, uncertain, unsettled . . .

Guy strode back through the station car park. He had that deflated feeling, an emptiness in the pit of his stomach that comes with a train-station farewell. And he felt angry with himself. The past couple of days had not gone as he'd planned. After the initial excitement of their engagement the week before, and then the official announcement in the papers over the weekend, the atmosphere between him and Richenda had become rather strained. Perhaps it wasn't surprising. There was bound to be a bit of an anticlimax after all the fuss and attention. But he felt annoyed with himself for letting it get to him.

He certainly hadn't meant to be so beastly to Richenda the day before by throwing her offer back in her face. It had been a sweet gesture, as she knew that deep down he hated having to exploit Eversleigh Manor's charms. But he'd had to come over all macho. He felt racked with guilt as he remembered her crestfallen face. Why had he humiliated her like that? He could at least have been gracious about it, thanked her but refused politely. More to the point, he could have accepted it. Guy had no doubt that she was making the sort of serious money needed to maintain a manor house like that. And if they were to be married . . .

But she had hit a raw nerve. Guy would have liked nothing better than to have the kind of money to keep Eversleigh going, to run it as it should be run. But he'd never settled down or stuck at anything, so now he was paying the price. He supposed he could have gone into the City, like a lot of his schoolmates, and made a killing – a killing that would amply underwrite the maintenance of a Cotswold manor house.

But then, he reasoned, he wouldn't be him. She'd told him time and again that it was his waywardness that she loved, his lack of convention, his scruffiness. The fact that he was his own master. So that wouldn't have been the solution. Guy told himself he should just be grateful that he and his mother had hit upon an alternative way of keeping their legacy going. And it wasn't such an awful fate – or at least, he hoped not. They'd know better after next weekend what they'd let themselves in for.

All he regretted now was that they hadn't had time to make up properly for their disagreement. Richenda had seemed a little subdued when he'd kissed her goodbye, and the last thing he wanted to do was hurt her. So he stopped off at the florist's in the high street and ordered some flowers to be sent to her flat; the assistant assured him they would be waiting for her when she arrived back.

As he drove back home, Guy realized it was the first time he'd ever sent anyone flowers, and he smiled to himself. This must be the real thing.

9

On Monday evening, Charles stepped off the train from
Paddington on to the platform at Eldenbury. As the rest
of the local commuters either trickled off to the car park
to collect the cars they'd left there that morning, or sauntered out to their waiting spouses, he stood by the ticket
office. He would either have to walk, telephone a taxi or
call Henty and be very, very apologetic and humble.

He knew she didn't deserve to be treated the way she
had. He'd walk up to the off-licence, buy a bottle of champagne. There were gallons of champagne at home, but
somehow walking in through the door with a chilled bottle
wrapped in tissue showed thought. And he'd get a big
bag of her favourite cashew nuts as a peace offering.

As he set off purposefully up the high street, he saw
with surprise that Twig was still open.

Two voices carried on a hot debate in his head.

Henty would much prefer flowers to champagne.

Not from Twig, she wouldn't.

*Take the label off. Tell her you got them from the florist's in
Charlotte Street and brought them back on the train.*

OK. But what if Fleur's in there?

What if she is? Anyway, she probably won't be.

*Of course she will! Anyway, you know that's why you're going
in. Because you want to see her. You're crazy, Charles. That way
madness lies . . .*

He pushed open the door, stepped over the threshold and into the hallowed atmosphere of Twig. The floor was limestone, the walls a very pale green, and along the back ran a dark wood counter topped with copper. In a huge semicircle in front of the counter were ranged zinc buckets stuffed with flowers whose names Charles couldn't even begin to guess. They ranged from the fragile to the exotic, from pale pink to raging red, flaming orange and deepest purple. The scent was overpowering. It made him feel quite peculiar. His pulse was racing nineteen to the dozen.

Fleur appeared, as if by magic, through a curtain of glass beads that tinkled back into place behind her.

Charles smiled awkwardly.

'Hi,' he offered. 'I've come to buy some flowers.'

Fleur brushed her hair back with one hand and surveyed him with amusement.

'Well, you've come to the right place, then.'

'What do you recommend?'

'Well,' she said, businesslike. 'That all depends. On who they're for. And why.'

She moved forward, and Charles resisted the instinct to step back.

'Um. My wife.' Flustered, he looked along the buckets and pointed to some fat, pale pink peonies. 'Those are nice.'

She nodded approvingly.

'They're sweet. They'd look lovely with some roses and some larkspur.'

'Perfect.'

Charles watched as she deftly assembled his chosen

blooms, snipping them to the required length and mixing them with a selection of frondy foliage until they were gathered into an artfully casual arrangement, as if they'd been plucked from the hedgerows by some willowy, Pre-Raphaelite maiden on a ramble. Charles frowned.

'She'll never be able to arrange them like that. They'll look a mess as soon as she gets them out.'

Fleur wound some hairy string around the stems.

'If she keeps the string tied, they'll stay like this. Just remember to keep topping them up with water.'

She pulled a length of dark green organza ribbon from a holder on the wall and wound it around the string, then tied it in a big, fat bow with a flourish, snipping the ends with her scissors so they formed an inverted v shape at each end.

Charles nearly fainted when she told him the price.

'They are out of season.'

'No – that's fine.' He handed over his credit card. While they waited for the machine to do its thing, he cleared his throat.

'You know, watching you . . . you make it look so easy. And it's got me thinking: there aren't any flower-arranging programmes on telly.'

Fleur raised an eyebrow.

'I can't imagine it would make gripping viewing.'

'I don't know – with the right person. Everyone's looking for the new big thing. Let's face it, cooking and houses have been done to death. Likewise gardens. And antiques. They're now reduced to making programmes about the best way to clean out your lavatory. I think it would be a winner. Everybody loves flowers and everybody thinks they can't do a thing with them. Give a woman a bunch of flowers and she panics.' Charles said it as if he thrust bouquets at Henty all the time. 'We should talk.'

Fleur looked at him, puzzled.

'I thought you just did books.'

'Well, primarily, but everything's very fluid these days. Books feed TV and vice versa. I've got contacts,' Charles assured her airily. 'And obviously we'd do a book to accompany the series.'

'There's masses of books on flower arranging.'

'I think there'd already been a few cookery books before Nigella came along. Hasn't affected her sales figures.'

'Nigella?' Fleur looked at him, amused. 'You're not comparing me to her, surely?'

'Same concept. Men want you, women want to be you.'

A less vain woman would have given Charles a slap at this point. But Fleur was rather warming to his idea.

'I was actually thinking about opening a flower-arranging school here. But a TV show would be much more exciting.'

'Let me draft a proposal for a format. Can you make a lunch in town to talk it over?'

Fleur thought about it.

'I could leave the shop with my assistant.'

'What about Thursday? I'll show you what I've come up with and you can add your ideas. Then we can think about a screen test. Get the whole package together.'

Fleur was looking a little shell-shocked, but Charles had gone into kick-ass mode. He could talk the talk when he wanted to; he made it hard to say no. Which she had no intention of doing.

'That sounds great,' she said, trying to keep the tremor of excitement out of her voice. The credit-card machine finally spewed out his receipt. Charles signed it with a flourish.

'See you Thursday. Oh — and best not to breathe a word to anybody. There's bound to be people still crawling round from *Lady Jane*. You don't want somebody else jumping on the bandwagon and getting in first with the idea.'

Fleur watched Charles go, feeling a little fizz in the pit of her stomach.

She was dangerously bored. She'd bagged her wealthy husband ten years ago, a dear little country solicitor with bright brown eyes and a gentle nature. She'd had her two children, one of each, immaculately turned out and well-behaved and now both at school. She'd started her own business to stop her going insane with boredom, and now it was turning out to be such a success with, it seemed, the minimum of input from her (for Fleur was nothing if not the mistress of delegation), she was ready for the next challenge.

Charles Beresford intrigued her. Half of her knew he was a bit of a knob, self-satisfied. But there was no doubt he was attractive, with those heavy-lidded eyes. And Robert, bless him, wasn't up to much in the bedroom stakes. If she put on underwear with strategic bits missing, he nearly had a heart attack. At thirty-six, Fleur knew she was at her sexual peak, and she wanted someone to peak with. Charles Beresford would definitely be up for it.

And if what he was saying about a TV programme was true, then so much the better. Fleur was shallow and, like most shallow people, craved fame. She'd been in agony throughout the filming of *Lady Jane*, wanting desperately to mix with the famous faces that passed through Eversleigh, but they'd looked straight through her when they passed her on the high street. She was a nobody, a Cotswold housewife with a flower shop. As the provider of flowers she'd hoped to be invited to the wrap party, but no invitation had materialized and it had stuck in her craw.

For a moment she indulged herself in a little fantasy. Her programme was a resounding success, propelling her, as Charles had hinted, to Nigella-like proportions (though not literally; Fleur would never allow herself to go an ounce over eight and a half stone). There would be a chain of Twigs across the country; perhaps even concessions in Sainsbury's or Tesco. No – Waitrose: that was the profile she was after. She would have as much influence on gerberas and lilies as Delia had once had on limes and cranberries. Buying flowers would become a weekly ritual for everyone. A necessary luxury. A luxurious necessity. You were judged no longer by what you wore or drove, but by what you had in your vase – as dictated by Fleur Gibson. Her book would be as de rigueur on the middle-class shelf as Jamie Oliver or the River Café.

She ran with the fantasy for a moment, imagining herself in a white, five-storey house in Notting Hill, with a driver who steered her from chat show to personal appearance to spa appointment. Robert would still be bobbing about in the background in a kindly way – she would never be so heartless as to get rid of him – but she would have her fair share of admirers who she would pick and choose for the occasional sinful fling . . .

Immersed in her dreams, Fleur happily counted the day's takings, tidied up the counter and switched off the lights, then mentally went through her wardrobe wondering what would be the best thing to wear for Thursday's lunch.

Bloody hell, thought Charles, as he sat in the back of the minicab he'd called from his mobile. That hadn't been his plan at all. He'd been so determined to wipe the slate clean and make it up to Henty. Now here he was with an arrangement to meet Fleur for lunch.

It was business, he told himself, looking down at the elaborate bouquet. He couldn't help it if inspiration had struck when it had. And it was an utterly brilliant idea. Of course, he wouldn't mention it to Henty, because she would be instantly suspicious. But he would keep his meetings with Fleur on a businesslike level. No funny stuff. If the idea came to nothing, then no harm would be done. And if it was a success, then he could think of some clever way of bringing it all out into the open that wouldn't rouse Henty's suspicions.

Henty thought the flowers were very nice, but wasn't quite as appreciative as Charles had hoped given the amount they'd cost. She plonked them in a vase and put them on the kitchen windowsill.

'Why don't you put them in the hall?' he asked.

'What's the point of that? I spend most of my time in the kitchen. I'll be able to appreciate them in here.'

He looked at her sharply, wondering just how pointed her remark was, but she was busy grating Parmesan.

'By the way,' she said. 'I managed to sort out someone to come and help us. It was only a stroke of luck. I just happened to phone at the right moment.'

'Experienced with horses?' Charles asked sharply.

'Very. Grown up with them. Plays polo back in South Africa.'

'Fantastic.' An image of a tanned, leggy blonde popped into Charles's head. 'Driver?'

'Yes. Obviously. That being the main criteria.' Henty's tone was sharp. Charles flinched. He hoped this newfound acidity was going to wear off soon. No doubt when the nanny arrived and smoothed things over . . .

'Great with kids, too. I'm sure you'll be relieved to hear.'

There it was again, that incipient sarcasm.

'Well, of course, that goes without saying, darling,' he replied soothingly. 'I know that's the first thing you'll have checked. When does she start?'

Henty stopped grating and looked up at him.

'She doesn't.'

'What do you mean, she doesn't?'

'*She* doesn't start. Because it's a he.' Henty flashed him a triumphant smile. 'Our new nanny-groom is called Travis, and he's arriving on Wednesday on the five-eighteen.'

At five to six that evening, having removed the traces of fish finger and baked beans from around Ted's mouth and forced him into a clean jumper, Honor led him down the road to Eversleigh Manor. It hadn't taken her long to decide to take Madeleine up on her offer. Never mind the economics, it was bound to be more interesting than catering for the coachloads of pensioners that pitched up at the craft centre. Honor had been itching for a challenge ever since Ted had started at school the previous September, but had been wary of taking on something with too much commitment. This was ideal; almost tailor-made. She'd popped in to see the manageress of the craft centre after lunch, and tentatively given her a week's notice – there had never been any formal arrangement between them, and she felt they often exploited her good nature, so she didn't feel too guilty. Then she'd spent the afternoon drawing up menu suggestions, until she had enough ideas for an entire year of house parties.

As they walked through the gates and crunched over the gravel, Ted looked up in awe at the sprawling manor. Uplighters in the flower beds illuminated the edifice; the golden stone was bathed in a soft glow. It looked warm and welcoming, and Honor felt reassured. She lifted Ted up so he could tug on the iron bell-pull, and they heard it ring deep inside the house.

Madeleine opened the door with a warm smile, and actually gave Honor a hug when she delivered her verdict.

'I can't tell you how delighted I am,' she gushed. 'Come on in. Come and see the kitchen. A lot of it's out of the ark, I'm afraid. But if there's anything you need, I'm sure the budget can run to it. I've spent a fortune already, so it won't make much difference.'

'Don't worry,' said Honor. 'I'm not really into modern technology.'

She realized minutes later that Madeleine hadn't been exaggerating. In relation to the grander reception rooms at the front of the house, the kitchen at Eversleigh was rather neglected. It was tucked away down a long corridor at the back of the house, and although it was cavernous – as big as the entire ground floor of Honor's little house – it hadn't undergone a revamp courtesy of the production company and was looking a little tired. The limed oak units screamed eighties, with their barley twist pilasters, leaded glass doors and integral spice racks, now with half the spice jars missing. The tiles were sprinkled with sheaves of corn and poppies; mug hooks and plate racks abounded behind decorative cornicing.

'It was the in thing at the time,' apologized Madeleine. 'But I haven't got thirty thousand to do it out again.'

'Don't apologize,' said Honor. 'It's a lovely room. It's bright and airy, and anyway, if you wait long enough all this will come back in again.'

In fact, the kitchen was so huge that you almost didn't notice the dated units and the rather dodgy cushioned flooring. The Aga was comfortingly enormous, and there was a long table in the middle covered in a Laura Ashley vinyl tablecloth, then two squashy old armchairs and a telly at the far end. And off the kitchen were various utility rooms and larders and cold stores, stuffed with all sorts of intriguing kitchen paraphernalia that had been part of the household for generations: jelly moulds and jam kettles and pie dishes; copper saucepans and mincers and mixing bowls large enough to bath a baby in. All of which Honor was itching to incorporate into her recipe ideas – it was like Mrs Beeton come to life.

Before long they had Honor's cuttings spread out on the kitchen table while Ted sat watching Cartoon Network.

'I've had to do the unthinkable and have satellite connected,' admitted Madeleine ruefully. 'It's what people expect these days. But I have to admit I've become rather addicted to the old reruns on UK Gold.'

'Ted would sit there till midnight, given half the chance,' admitted Honor. 'I keep thinking the poor child's deprived because he doesn't have Sky or a Playstation.'

'He has your attention, though,' said Madeleine. 'Which is more than most children get these days.'

'Maybe,' said Honor warily, who didn't like discussing her parenting skills, even when she was being complimented, and so changed the subject. 'What were you thinking of doing for the main meal on the Saturday? If we decide that then we can work backwards round it.'

'I was going to do fillet of local beef with wild mushrooms in a red wine sauce,' suggested Madeleine. 'I've done it a million times, but they aren't to know that. And at least I know it works. If we're going to have any teething problems, I don't want to be worrying about the food.'

'Quite,' said Honor. 'Let's keep it as simple as we can.

How about pan-fried scallops with crispy bacon to start? You can't really mess it up but it is absolutely delicious. And plum tart with home-made ice cream to finish. I can do little individual ones – they look gorgeous.'

'Perfect,' agreed Madeleine, who for the first time in her life felt excited about food. Not that she was going to be eating any of this, but she was delighted that the menu was falling into place and that Honor seemed as enthusiastic as she. How had she ever imagined she could cope with all this on her own?

'How about a glass of wine to toast our success?' she suggested, and Honor accepted eagerly. She'd thought at first that Madeleine was going to be a tricky customer – demanding and nitpicking – but she was pleasantly surprised.

They were just clinking glasses when Guy walked in.

'Ah,' he said. 'Perfect timing. Hello,' he said to Honor, frowning politely. He recognized but couldn't quite place her.

'You bid for my cake. On Saturday night.'

'Oh yes.' The smile of recognition lit up his whole face.

'Honor's going to help me out with the food,' said Madeleine. 'She's had some quite brilliant ideas.'

'Ah – so you were Mother's brainwave. Well, I hope you're going to take some of the pressure off. It's a bloody madhouse here.'

'I hope so,' said Honor. 'That's the idea, anyway.'

Guy poured himself a glass of wine.

'So you live in the village?' he asked. 'Sorry not to have a clue but I haven't been back home for long. I haven't caught up with who's who yet.'

'I live in one of the cottages at the other end of the high street. With Ted.' She nodded over to her son with a smile: he was totally absorbed in something lurid and fast moving, his hand dipping in and out of a bowl of crisps Madeleine had given him. Guy just nodded. He didn't raise an eyebrow or quiz her about her marital status.

'So when do you start?'

Honor looked to Madeleine.

'We hadn't got round to discussing it.'

Madeleine bit her lip anxiously.

'I was hoping you could start straight away,' she admitted.

'I'll have to give the craft centre a week's notice,' Honor replied cautiously, not giving away the fact that she'd already done it. She didn't want to look too keen. 'But I suppose I could manage both for a few days.'

'You're more than welcome to use the kitchen here. There's stacks of freezer space and masses of storage in the larder.'

'It would be easier than running up and down the road with batches of cheese straws,' agreed Honor. 'Have you got basic ingredients, or do I have to start from scratch?'

Guy and Madeleine looked at each other. Honor grinned.

'How about if I did a big supermarket shop for all the staples? Or better still, I've got a card for the cash and carry in Evesham.'

'Why don't you go with her?' Madeleine suggested to Guy. 'Then you can stock up on cleaning stuff and loo rolls. I've got Marilyn lined up to do a big clean from top to bottom on Thursday.'

'What about Wednesday morning?'

Honor mentally calculated that would give her the next day to bake whatever was needed for the craft centre for the rest of the week – she could bung most of it in the freezer. It was going to be hard work, but she could manage. She nodded her agreement.

'I'll come round to you as soon as I've dropped Ted at school.'

'No, I'll pick you up,' offered Guy. 'Say half nine?'

'There's so much to think about.' Madeleine sounded slightly panic-stricken, as she referred to her sheaf of lists. 'How many sorts of jam do you think we should serve at breakfast?'

'I think choice of jam's pretty low down on our list of priorities,' protested Guy.

'No, it's important. It's exactly the sort of thing that matters.'

'I quite agree. And the answer's three,' said Honor definitely. 'Marmalade, apricot and something fancy like loganberry. And a local honey.'

Guy gave a mock sigh of relief.

'Thank God – I can sleep at night now,' he said, then caught his mother's eye. 'Seriously, it's fantastic to have someone around who seems to know what they're doing,' he went on. 'Mother did rush into this somewhat.'

'I did not,' said Madeleine stoutly. 'I've got it all under control, in my own way.'

'There's no need to panic,' soothed Honor. 'It's only Monday. You've got four whole days before they arrive.'

'How can you be so calm?' asked Guy curiously.

'I used to run a hotel in Bath,' she admitted.

'I can feel a promotion coming on already,' said Guy. 'Forget being head of cheese straws. I think we should make you manageress.'

'You don't need a manageress. This place should run itself. All it's going to take is a lot of hard work.'

'Any time off for good behaviour?'

'We'll have to see,' said Honor, rather enjoying the banter, as Guy picked up the bottle of wine and filled up their glasses again.

'Why don't you stay for some supper?' said Madeleine. 'We can go through everything. I'm sure there's a hundred things I've forgotten. We can make a list –'

Guy smiled fondly.

'Mother's obsessed with lists. She even has a list of lists.'

'Lists are good,' said Honor. 'I couldn't live without them.'

'I've managed to limp through thirty-five years without ever making one.'

'That's because you're perfect, darling,' said Madeleine.

'No, no, no,' protested Guy. 'Not perfect. Perfect is boring.'

Honor surveyed the pair of them, amused. Actually, they were both pretty perfect: Madeleine with her cheekbones and her sleek bob, chic in a navy sweater and jeans, a classic silk scarf knotted round her neck; Guy, as dishevelled as his mother was pristine, but equally stunning. They both shared the same deep, periwinkle blue eyes. Honor had thought Madeleine's cold at first, but now she had relaxed they were softer. Guy's were filled with laughter – she wondered if he took anything seriously. He certainly didn't seem to.

She stood up reluctantly.

'I really should be getting home. Ted should have been in bed an hour ago.'

They tried to persuade her to stay, and Ted added his pleas, but she was resolute. A late night this early in the week wasn't a good idea, especially after such a hectic weekend, and supper would only mean more wine: she'd already drunk more in the past forty-eight hours than she usually did in a month. She needed her bed. She had a lot to think about.

'Guy will walk you back,' said Madeleine.

Honor protested that they would be fine, but Guy insisted. As they wandered back out of the drive, the autumn moon lit up the little high street. Ted held on to her hand, his steps dragging a little with tiredness.

'Thanks for coming to the rescue,' said Guy. 'She still misses my father dreadfully, and she's constantly looking for ways to fill the gap he's left. I think she's bitten off more than she can chew this time.'

'You'll be fine,' Honor reassured him. 'With a setting like Eversleigh, you can't go wrong.'

He saw her to the door with perfect chivalry, and they agreed he would pick her up at half nine the day after tomorrow.

'We've got an old pick-up that we use for carting logs and things around,' he said. 'We can shove everything in the back of that, if you can bear to be seen in it.'

'I'll wear my dark glasses and a baseball hat,' Honor promised solemnly.

Half an hour later, once she'd tucked Ted in, she snuggled up in her own bed with a pen and paper and started to draw up a shopping list, smiling to herself as she remembered Guy's disparaging remarks. She'd loved being in that huge kitchen, the banter between Madeleine and Guy. He obviously had a hugely irreverent affection for his mother, and it had made Madeleine seem less intimidating. Honor had been rather in awe of her at first, but it was dawning on her that the glacial elegance was just a facade. Though she wouldn't like to get on the wrong side of her – Madeleine was the type to know exactly what she wanted, and woe betide anyone who got in her way.

She'd also enjoyed having her opinion asked. Honor realized that she'd missed the power she'd once had, the adrenalin of decision-making, the buzz that came from a new project. It was going to be fun to be involved in Eversleigh, if only on the periphery. And from her point of view, there was no great risk attached to it.

She was halfway down the list when her eyelids became unbearably heavy. She put the papers on her bedside table and switched off the lamp, unfeasibly excited about her trip to the cash and carry. Oh dear, she thought, as she drifted into sleep, it really is about time I got myself a life.

At Eversleigh, Madeleine was washing up the supper things. Guy sat at the table, tipping back his chair and finishing off the last dregs of the second bottle of wine they'd opened.

'Well, I think Honor's arrival is timely. She's just what we need.'

'Yes,' said Madeleine. 'She seems very . . . real.'

'Real?' Guy looked puzzled. 'What's that supposed to mean? Real? Of course she's real.'

'You know what I mean,' answered his mother. 'She's got her feet on the ground.'

'Meaning?'

'I just think she's a nice girl, that's all.'

Somehow Guy got the feeling that Madeleine meant an awful lot more by her comments. He looked at his watch.

'I'd better give Richenda a call. She was having dinner with her producer this evening. She'll probably be back by now.'

He stood up and pushed his chair in, and went to give his mother a hug.

'Don't worry, Mum. This weekend's going to be brilliant.'

He kissed her on top of her head and sauntered off. She watched him go, her gloriously exasperating and loveable son. He was so like her beloved Tony, whom she'd spent years nurturing and cosseting. People laboured under the misapprehension that it was Madeleine who'd worn the trousers at Eversleigh Manor, but she had utterly adored her eccentric and amiable husband. His every wish had been her command, his every whim her pleasure. He had drifted through life answerable to nothing and nobody; she smoothed the path of his daily routine so he could wallow in his own genius. It was amazing, really, that he had been so charming; he could have been thoroughly spoilt and petulant. Even more lucky was that Guy had inherited his equable nature.

Madeleine felt a momentary fear curdle her stomach.

Tony had been allowed the luxury of being utterly delightful because she had made sure nothing had got in his way. Should she do the same for her son, or was that unhealthy? It was certainly unfashionable. But Guy was so carefree, so confident, she just hoped he knew what he was doing. If anybody hurt him, or worse still tried to change him, she'd rip them apart with her bare hands . . .

Richenda had just climbed into the bath when she heard the phone going. She sighed. About the only thing her apartment *didn't* have was a phone in the bathroom – she usually remembered to bring the handset in with her, but not this time. She clambered out again and pulled on her robe.

'Hello, gorgeous.'

It was Guy, and immediately she melted.

'I'm just about to get back into my bath,' she purred. 'I wish you were here with me.'

'Is there room for two?' he asked.

'At least.' She slid back into the rose-scented water. 'Fantastic flowers, by the way. Thank you.'

'They got there?'

'They arrived just as I did.'

'I'm glad you liked them.'

'They'll remind me of you all week.'

'Good. How was your dinner, by the way?'

'A tedious debrief with the director, and the producer droning on about plot ideas for the feature film. Not that I'm not interested, but I'm not an ideas person, so there's no point in asking me about it. I wanted to scream 'Just give me the script when it's done!' But I don't like being difficult.' She'd picked her way listlessly through char-grilled artichoke, then pumpkin gnocchi, wishing that she was having supper in the kitchen with Guy. 'How was your day?'

'Great. I spent the morning chopping logs with Malachi. Then Mother found this fantastic girl to help with the food. She used to run a hotel in Bath, so she knows what we should be doing.'

'Oh,' said Richenda, wondering when Guy said 'fantastic' just what he meant exactly.

'She's the girl who's going to do our wedding cake. Remember?'

'Oh yes. I wanted to talk to you about that.'

'Our wedding cake?'

'No. Just the wedding. We need to think about send-ing out invitations – or at least a "keep this date free" thingy.'

'Do we?'

'Well, yes – if it's so close to Christmas. It's already October and people start making plans so early, we don't want to find they're double-booked.'

'I suppose not.' Guy sounded wary.

'What's the matter? I thought we'd agreed . . . ?'

'Yes, I know. It's just . . . I'm so wound up with all this house party stuff, I can't take a wedding on board as well. Not just yet.'

'Why don't you leave it all to me?' said Richenda brightly. 'I'll organize everything, and you can just turn up on the day.'

Guy was silent for a moment. He knew he should be

taking an interest, but he didn't have the headspace. The last thing he wanted, though, was Richenda getting carried away – he had a sneaking suspicion that her idea of small, intimate and low-key might not be the same as his.

'Listen, why don't we talk about it at the weekend? You're coming down on Friday, aren't you? We should have got rid of the guests by midday on Sunday, so we'll have the rest of the day together. I promise to give you my undivided attention.'

'OK.' Richenda sounded mollified. 'By the way, I wondered if you could make it up here for dinner one night next week?'

'What for?'

'The *Daily Post* Entertainment Awards. I've been short-listed for Favourite Actress, remember?'

Guy had a dim recollection of Richenda and Cindy discussing something like that at the photoshoot.

'Oh yes,' he said enthusiastically.

'*Lady Jane*'s taking a table at the ceremony. The producer wants to know if you'll be able to join us.' She teased him gently. 'Tickets are like gold dust. If you don't want to come . . .'

'Is that one of those things where you have to look happy for the camera when you don't win? I don't know if I could do that. On your behalf, I mean.'

'Don't worry,' said Richenda. 'The *Daily Post* love me, especially now I've got a sexy, gorgeous fiancé. All they're interested in is photo opportunities and fodder for the paper. So I'm sure they'll fix it for me to win.'

'That's totally corrupt!'

Richenda laughed, a glorious, sexy gurgle. The one Lady

Jane used when she knew she'd got the villain stitched up like a kipper.

'That's showbiz.'

She sometimes forgot just how clueless Guy was about her industry. It delighted her. How refreshing it was to go out with someone who wouldn't know a Bafta if you hit them over the head with it, instead of some self-publicizing, scene-stealer with hollow aspirations and a determination to hang on to your coat-tails. A vision of his shocked expression came into her head and she felt a rush of fondness, together with a stab of longing for his taut body and his slightly roughened – but not too rough – hands on her breasts . . .

'Of course I'll come.' Guy's voice snapped her out of her fantasy. 'I'll be ready for a break by then. And it'll be good to spend some time together. I'm starting to forget what my own fiancée looks like.'

'Then let me remind you.'

Guy listened as Richenda painted a picture, with intimate and graphic detail, of just exactly what he was missing.

Clouds of sesame-scented steam billowed out of the kitchen of the Happy Wok in Reading. Outside in the waiting area, Sally Collins stared at an illuminated photograph of some jasmine blossom, her mouth watering. Mick had got some cash that afternoon and they were having a blow-out. She looked sideways at him. He was rolling a cigarette with his yellowed fingers. His dreadlocks, once a sign of youthful rebellion, now looked ridiculous on a man his age. The six o'clock shadow on his face was grizzled. There was no hope in his eyes any more. This wasn't a young man with fire and passion in his belly. This was a wasted no-hoper; a scrounger.

What did that make her? Sally sighed. She no longer had the bloom of youth to help her through life either. What would anyone want with her? The grey in her hair was more and more reluctant to take on the henna she applied, resulting in a matted, unattractive mane of brindled rust. Her skin was dull, lifeless and lined. Her eyes had lost any sparkle. Her legs were still thin, but despite the fact they rarely ate properly her middle had thickened and her breasts had sagged, giving her a top-heavy appearance.

She was sick of life. Why the hell had she stayed with Mick, with his schemes and dreams for fame and fortune that never bloody came to anything? A second-rate dope-dealing drop-out with nothing to offer her but his slightly rancid body. Even the farm had gone. They'd been evicted in the end; someone had found a loophole in the law and got them out, even though Mick had protested squatter's rights until the very moment their belongings had been hurled out of the door.

Now they had a grotty bedsit in Reading. They couldn't even cook, because the gas had been disconnected. Hence the need for a takeaway if they wanted something hot and proper. She was sick of Pot Noodles.

She reached out idly for the paper on the table. It was the supplement to Saturday's *Daily Post*. The day before yesterday's news – she couldn't imagine there'd be anything of interest in it. She never read the papers. Or watched telly. World War Three could have broken out and she wouldn't know about it. To be honest, she'd be hard pushed to name the American president.

But on the front cover was a face that seemed familiar. It was a mother's intuition that made her heart beat faster as she gazed at the girl, who glowed with happiness as she rested her head on the shoulder of what appeared to be her fiancé. You never really forgot the face of your own child – the set of the eyes, the shape of the nose, the curve of the lips, the features that were half your own. Not even if you were a bad mother who'd made terrible mistakes.

She prodded Mick urgently in the shoulder.

'That's Rowan. I'm sure of it.'

Mick peered closely at the photo. He was as blind as a bat these days, but there was no cash for an eye test. Let alone glasses.

'No. It says here she's called Richenda Fox.'

'Don't be stupid. That must be a stage name or whatever they call it. It's definitely Rowan.'

'Rubbish.'

'I think I know my own daughter when I see her.' Sally's voice rose in indignation that was bordering on hysteria.

Having made a closer inspection, Mick was inclined to agree with her.

'Do you know, I think you might be right. You know what this means, don't you? If it is her?'

'What?'

'Money.'

'Don't be stupid. She's not going to give us money.'

'*She's* not, no.' A sly smile slid across Mick's face,

showing several gaps where he'd lost teeth. 'But some-one would pay good dosh to know the truth.'

He pointed out a paragraph with a slightly shaking finger.

'Richenda had an uneventful childhood brought up in the Home Counties.' He gave an unattractive sound somewhere between a snort and a laugh. 'Her parents emigrated to Australia when she was seventeen, leaving her torn between a new life in Adelaide or drama school. Luckily for us, she chose the latter, and now she is the new darling of prime-time television, rumoured to have signed a golden handcuff deal worth . . . well, it would be vulgar to discuss money with Lady Jane. Not that money is likely to be a problem, as she has just announced her engagement to Mr Guy Portias, owner of the exquisite Eversleigh Manor where *Lady Jane Investigates* was shot . . .'

'Fucking hell,' said Sally.

Mick rolled up the supplement and stuck it in his pocket as the waiter appeared.

'Chicken chow mein beef in black bean sauce fried rice prawn cracker,' he recited as he dumped the already grease-stained bag down on the counter.

'Cheers, mate,' said Mick happily. Sally followed him out of the door in a daze, trying to take in what she'd just read and wondering just what it was Mick was up to.

On Wednesday morning, Honor woke with butterflies. She'd spent the whole of Tuesday doing batches of scones, quiches, carrot cakes and brownies in order to honour her commitment with the craft centre. She delivered half of them, then stored the rest in the freezer ready to be dropped over later in the week – she'd never resorted to freezing before, but she wanted her decks cleared before embarking upon her new role at Eversleigh. As she pulled on her jeans, she told herself that it was nerves about this new venture causing her stomach to flutter rather than the fact that Johnny was coming to tea that evening.

Several times since their agreement on Sunday, she had been tempted to call him and cancel. She had a good enough excuse, after all, starting a new job. But she knew that was only putting off the day of reckoning and prolonging the agony. Besides, she knew from experience that Johnny wasn't fobbed off easily. Now he knew of Ted's existence, wild horses wouldn't stop him from meeting his son. She was lucky Johnny had agreed to wait this long . . . All she could really be grateful for was that she had so much else to think about that she hadn't had time to dwell on the situation.

At half nine, Guy pulled up outside her house in a battered old red pick-up. She opened the door and he grinned at her doubtful expression.

'You've got to admit I do it in style.'

'I think it's cool,' she countered. 'Understated.'

'I had to fight Malachi for it. He's had to go off to the garden centre in his beloved Zodiac. He wasn't best pleased, I can tell you.'

Honor climbed into the front seat.

'Got your lists?' Guy teased.

Honor rummaged in her bag and held up a shorthand pad filled with scrawls, asterisks, arrows and exclamation marks. Guy smugly brandished a neatly typed sheet of A4, printed out by Madeleine.

'Mine's in alphabetical order.'

'Mine isn't in any order at all,' admitted Honor. 'I'm bound to forget something vital.'

'Well, you can send me out for anything you've forgotten. I've come to the conclusion that the best thing I can do in the run-up to this weekend is keep quiet and do as I'm told. Even Malachi's tense. He chewed me off a strip for being too ruthless with the hedge trimmers yesterday.' Guy looked aggrieved. 'I was only trying to help, but apparently I hacked off his peacocks' tails. How was I to know he was going in for topiary?'

Honor giggled.

'Too many chiefs and not enough Indians?'

Guy nodded.

'I hope you're not going to turn into a whip-wielding harridan?'

'I'll try not to.'

Honor gripped on to the edges of the seat as Guy took a bend. He seemed to drive down the middle of the country lanes oblivious to the fact that someone might be coming in the opposite direction. She was rather relieved when they finally pulled into the cash and carry.

'We might as well go our separate ways, and meet up at the till.'

Armed with their trolleys, the two of them set off with their respective lists. Honor had almost finished when she caught Guy shovelling bumper packs of peach-coloured loo roll on to his trolley.

'Stop!' said Honor, horrified.

'But it's on offer. And we need loads.'

'It's cheap and it's a hideous colour. You absolutely have to have white, and good quality. Not quilted, because that's naff. But soft.'

'Right. At least I know now.' Guy good-naturedly put the rolls back.

'Andrex or Kleenex,' called Honor over her shoulder as she headed for the refrigerated section.

'Harridan!' His riposte floated over the top of the shelves.

It was lunchtime by the time they got back to Eversleigh, and Madeleine rustled up tomato soup and toast. Afterwards Honor was given a guided tour of the four guest bedrooms. The overall feel was traditional English country house mixed with contemporary comfort; stylish, restrained, unfussy, luxurious. The walls and carpet throughout were a pale sand – neutral but warm – then each room was accented with a different colour scheme: russet, ochre, olive or aubergine were picked out in the chenille curtains and the upholstery on the chairs and cushions. The walnut sleigh beds were piled high with fat feather pillows and bolsters. Fitted cupboards and shelves hid away anything utilitarian or ugly, and were supplemented by dainty antiques: squashy button-back chairs, chaise longues, writing desks, dressing tables. Each room had a selection of botanical or architectural drawings hung in black and gold frames, and soft, flattering Venetian mirrors.

'They are absolutely gorgeous,' sighed Honor.

'Richenda was going to get all the little extras, but she's been doing voice-overs or something all this week.' Madeleine's tone was fairly disparaging.

'Why don't we go into Cheltenham tomorrow?' asked Honor. 'We can do candles, bath stuff, magazines . . .'

'And jelly beans,' said Guy.

'Jelly beans?' echoed Madeleine, mystified.

'Every good hotel should have an endless supply of jelly beans.'

'It's a gimmick, but it could work,' grinned Honor. 'We can get a load of jars with glass stoppers and fill them up – one on each bedside table.'

Madeleine wrinkled her nose.

'You don't think it's a bit tacky?'

'It's better than having a box of tissues by the bed,' countered Guy.

Madeleine sighed.

'Here's me killing myself to be tasteful and understated.'

'It's just a bit of fun,' Honor assured her. 'I think it shows you're not taking yourselves *too* seriously. It helps people relax. Some of your guests might be a bit intimidated by their surroundings, after all.'

Madeleine couldn't quite see why they would be, but it was obvious to Honor that anyone booking a country house weekend didn't have one themselves; that they were just buying into the fantasy for a couple of days.

More and more she was beginning to realize that the Portiases didn't have a clue what they were letting themselves in for. After years in the hotel industry she knew only too well how appalling people could be. Guy and Madeleine were obviously expecting their guests to behave as graciously as they themselves had been brought up to be. It was quite likely to be otherwise. Honor hoped she was wrong, then consoled herself that she would be there to pick up the pieces. It wasn't her place to be a harbinger of doom before the event. And maybe they'd be lucky – the prices they were charging should keep out the riff-raff. Though money and good manners did not necessarily go hand in hand these days . . .

All too soon it was three o'clock, and Honor realized that she could no longer take refuge in the preparations for the weekend. She had to confront the subject she had been displacing. Johnny was coming at five. Trying to suppress her panic as she walked down to the school to collect Ted, she concentrated on practicalities to avoid all the questions that were whirling round her head. What was she going to do for tea? She decided on macaroni cheese. It was substantial enough, Ted loved it and she could surreptitiously make it a little more exciting by putting some Gruyère on the top, snipping some Parma ham up into it, and mixing crème fraiche with the cheese sauce. And she had a bag of bitter leaves for the grown-ups to have on the side. For pudding they could have some of the extra chocolate brownies she'd made for the craft centre, with some vanilla ice cream . . . All of

a sudden she felt calmer. There was something thera-
peutic about planning meals.

Back at home, she changed Ted out of his uniform
into a pair of jumbo cords and a plaid shirt. He looked
adorable. She hugged him to her, feeling his warm little
body under the softness of the shirt. She couldn't help
being afraid, for him as much as for her. What did the
future hold for the pair of them, now Johnny was back
in her life? There were going to be some tricky questions
to answer, and some difficult decisions. The hardest of
which was going to be when to tell Ted Johnny was his
father. She prayed that Johnny would respect her wishes
and let her take things at her own pace. Though she
suspected that he didn't owe her that. Was it truly unfor-
givable, not to tell someone about their own offspring?

Or not to tell your offspring about their real
father . . . ?

'You know Mummy's got an old friend coming for tea?'

Ted nodded. 'Yep.'

'He's a vet.'

'Cool. Can he get me a guinea pig?'

Ted had pestered for a guinea pig for nearly a year now.
But Honor had resisted, because she knew they had a habit
of curling up and dying, and she couldn't bear the trauma.
Besides, they were singularly unattractive animals in her
view. Guilt, however, made her waver momentarily.

'You'll have to ask him.'

'You mean I can have one?'

'I didn't say that . . .'

'You said ask him. That means yes.'

'Does it?' Honor smiled.

'Yaaay!' Ted waved his arms in the air in triumph, victor of the long-running battle at last. Honor couldn't resist hugging him again. How simple life was at that age. She wished the prospect of a guinea pig could bring her such joy.

She looked at her watch. It was quarter past four. All day she'd told herself that she wouldn't bother changing, that Johnny could jolly well take her as she was. Suddenly, though, she panicked. She might not want to encourage him, but there was nothing worse than the look on someone's face when they thought you'd gone to seed. She hadn't looked her best on Sunday, but she'd had the excuse of a late night and being caught unawares. Maybe this evening she should make a bit more effort.

She bolted for the bathroom, leaped into the shower, smothered herself from head to toe in zingy shower gel, then towelled herself dry and rubbed cocoa butter all over her body. She grabbed a bottle of quick-dry nail polish and touched up her toes, which had chipped slightly since Saturday and looked rather slutty.

She stood in front of her wardrobe in her towel, dithering over what to wear and hating herself for worrying. In the end, she chose a pair of dusty grey velvet bootleg jeans and a long-sleeved T-shirt. She rough dried her hair with the dryer so it looked suitably dishevelled, then applied a small amount of smudgy green eyeliner and a hint of mascara.

She surveyed her reflection and added a belt with a big brass buckle. She looked a little bit rock chick on her day off, as if she wore this sort of thing all the time. She decided that going barefoot would look as if she hadn't bothered at all.

She heard the knock at the door.

'I'll get it,' shouted Ted.

'No!' Honor shouted back, and ran down the stairs. She wanted to be there when Johnny first clapped eyes on his son. She wanted to be in total control of the situation . . .

Johnny stood there, his keys in one hand. Honor was relieved to see that he hadn't come bearing an entire train set or a mountain bike. She wouldn't have put it past him to overrule her. He hadn't brought anything for her, either. No flowers, no bottle of wine. Good, she thought, because she wasn't going to be bribed.

He smiled, a tight nervous smile, his eyes darting over her shoulder.

'Hi.'

'Hi. Come on in.'

She stepped aside and he walked in past her. Ted was hanging on to the newel post at the bottom of the stairs, grinning with the self-conscious anticipation of a child awaiting a new guest. Honor went to put an arm around his shoulders and positioned him in front of Johnny, who'd stopped dead in the hallway.

'This is Ted.'

Honor couldn't describe the look on Johnny's face when he saw Ted. It was a mixture of wonder, terror and total adoration, while struggling not to express any emotion at all.

'Hey, Ted,' he said softly. 'How's it going?'

'We're having maccy cheese for tea,' Ted informed him

solemnly, 'but tell her now if you don't want bits in it, because she says we've got to have bits, and I hate bits.'

'Bits?'

'Ham and sweetcorn. Nothing weird,' protested Honor. 'I just like it plain.'

'Well, me too,' agreed Johnny. 'Whoever heard of macaroni cheese with bits in?'

Ted grinned in glee. Honor smiled, knowing when she was beaten.

'Come on in. Tea's nearly ready.'

Ted scampered ahead into the living room. Honor indicated that Johnny should go in ahead of her, but he stopped for a moment and looked at her.

'You look great. I like your hair short now I'm used to it. I wouldn't have thought it would suit you.'

Honor put a hand up to her hair and tugged at her fringe nervously. Even now she missed her glossy mane. Cutting it off had been symbolic of cutting off her former life.

'I don't have time to mess about with it long. It used to take me half an hour to blow-dry it.'

'I know. I remember.'

The corner of his mouth turned up in a wry grin. Honor's tummy did a somersault. That grin was so suggestive. It said there were a lot of other things he remembered as well. She swallowed hard, trying to remain calm, unflustered, thinking she should never have agreed to this meeting so soon. They should have sorted out the history between them before bringing Ted into the frame. Things were moving too fast. She was going to lose the upper hand. Why the hell hadn't she had the strength to withstand him? Cursing her weakness, she wondered if she should kick Johnny out now, tell him she wasn't ready.

But it was too late. He had already pushed open the door to the living room where Ted was showing off, diving over the back of the sofa and doing somersaults, waggling his legs in the air. Johnny picked him up by the ankles. Ted screamed with delight and fear, his shirt sliding up to reveal his skinny little body underneath. Johnny dipped him up and down.

'Let go! Let go!'

'OK. Whatever you say.'

Johnny obeyed, but carefully, so that Ted just plopped on to the sofa on his back and sprawled in a heap, giggling.

'Do it again.'

'I thought you didn't like it!'

'Agaaaain!'

Ted stuck his legs up in the air for Johnny to grab them. Honor watched from the kitchen doorway, her heart in her mouth. This was what Ted had missed – rough and tumble. She wasn't a cissy; she did as many things as she could with him. But she couldn't have picked him up by the legs like that, made him shriek with total abandonment. She wouldn't have had the nerve to drop him.

As she watched the pair of them, half of her wanted to tell Johnny to stop. It wasn't his place to rough-house with Ted like that, to step into the role so easily. For a moment, she felt overwhelmed with possessiveness. She wanted to snatch Ted out of Johnny's grasp. Tell him he could look, but he'd better not touch. She didn't, though. She went over to the stove and busied herself stirring the cheese sauce for the macaroni, dropping in handfuls of Gruyère and grating in some fresh nutmeg.

Ted was getting rough now, punching Johnny in the stomach over the back of the sofa.

'Doesn't hurt,' said Johnny. 'Harder.'

Ted obeyed, redoubling his efforts.

'Can't even feel it,' insisted Johnny, though Honor suspected that he was feeling pretty uncomfortable. Ted was getting overexcited, his face bright red with exertion over the freckles as he gave him a serious thumping. Honor managed to restrain herself from intruding. She didn't want to overrule their fun. Suddenly she felt like the outsider. Just as she was plucking up the courage to call a halt to the rumpus, Johnny beat her to it.

'Come on. That's enough now. Your mum's got the tea ready. Go and wash your hands.'

Ted slid off the sofa and trotted obediently upstairs to the bathroom. As soon as he'd gone, Johnny folded his hands over his stomach and bent double, groaning. Honor smiled, despite herself.

'I bet that hurt.'

'It certainly did. I couldn't tell him that, though.' He stood up, his expression more serious. 'He's fantastic, Honor. You've done a grand job.'

'I know. That he's fantastic, I mean,' she added hastily.

'It can't have been easy.'

'Not always, no. But it is now. I'm used to it.'

'I want to be part of his life. You know that.'

Honor stood stock-still in the middle of the kitchen, clutching the terracotta dish with her oven gloves. Ted bounded into the room.

'Mine's the red chair,' he warned, grabbing the back of the seat Johnny was hovering by.

'I'm so glad you told me,' said Johnny. 'I was about to sit there myself.'

The two of them sat down and looked at her expectantly. Honor swallowed. They were like two peas in a pod, with their freckles, their alabaster skin, their fringes that insisted on sticking up. She put the dish down on the table.

'I just need to wash my hands,' she said, and ran out of the room.

Upstairs, in the bathroom, she took several deep breaths. She wasn't at all sure how to handle the situation. They looked so bloody perfect together. She didn't have the right to deprive either of them of the other. But where did she stand in all of this? It was quite possible that she was destined to come out of it the most damaged.

For Johnny still had a magical power over her. She'd cared about what he thought of her hair, no matter how many times she told herself she didn't. She wanted his approval. And when he came near, he made her insides turn over. If he was to touch her, she'd jump out of her skin.

If only there was a pill she could have taken. An anti-Johnny tablet to make her immune, enable her to cope with his presence and deal with what was to come dispassionately.

'Pull yourself together,' she told her reflection sternly. 'He's a no-good, drunken, feckless bastard.'

And with that she marched back downstairs with her head held high.

*

Henty stood anxiously on the platform, all four children lined up behind her. Thea wanted to go to the station shop and buy one of her ghastly teenage magazines that gave advice to pubescent girls on how to give blow jobs, but Henty refused, and now she was sulking.

The train drew in. The heavy doors flew open and people started disembarking. Thea and Lily started guessing which one was Travis, giggling and pointing.

'That one!' shrieked Lily, pointing at a geeky-looking type with an anorak.

'God, no. Pleeease no!' Thea feigned praying, then wiped her brow theatrically as the geek walked straight past them. 'Phew.'

'Please, girls,' said Henty, anxiously scanning the platform. The guard blew his whistle, and started slamming shut the doors. Maybe he'd missed the train. That wasn't a very good sign. She needed someone reliable, not someone who couldn't turn up when they said they were going to.

Just as the train was about to depart, a door flew open and a tall, lanky figure hurled a rucksack on to the platform then leaped out after it. He scooped up the rucksack and looked around him. Shit, thought Henty. Talk about lock up your daughters. Tall and tanned, his dirty-blond hair curled down to the collar of his battered, dark brown leather jacket. An iPod stuck out of the top pocket; the earphones were slung round his neck. He sauntered up the platform towards them with an easy smile.

'Please let that be him. Please,' Lily intoned.

Henty stepped forward, hoping she looked business-like.

'Travis Cooper?'

'I nearly missed the station. I was fast asleep.' He grinned, showing perfect white teeth and took Henty's hand in both of his. 'Mrs Beresford, I presume?'

His accent was clipped, but somehow it didn't sound as harsh as she'd expected, perhaps because of the warmth of his smile.

'Yes,' she said. 'But call me Henty. This is Walter and this is Robin.'

'Hey, guys.' He ruffled Walter's hair and stuck his thumb up at Robin.

'And Thea and Lily,' Henty finished weakly. The two girls were gawping, for once at a loss for words. Travis ran an appraising eye over the pair of them, then shook them each firmly by the hand.

'How do you do?' he said with mock formality, and the two of them exchanged uncertain glances.

'Shall we go?'

'I'm not going to wash my hand for a week,' whispered Thea to Lily as they followed Travis's loping stride out of the station and into the car park.

By the time Honor came back down from the bathroom, Johnny had helped himself and Ted to macaroni. Ted was shovelling it up greedily with his spoon in his fist. Normally Honor would hear her mother's voice and tell him to stop eating like a navvy, but she let it go. She didn't want to come across like a nag. She sat down and helped herself, even though her appetite had mysteriously disappeared. Her stomach was too full of fluttering wings to allow room for food.

Ted put down his spoon and fixed Johnny with a look that said he meant business.

'Mum said you were going to get me a guinea pig.'

'I did not!' protested Honor. 'I said you could ask Johnny if he could get hold of one for you. There's a difference.'

'Funnily enough, I have a particularly fine specimen looking for a good home back at the surgery,' said Johnny. 'His name is Eejit.'

'Does he come complete with cage, feed bowl, water bottle, shavings and a supply of guinea pig food?' asked Honor sweetly.

'Well, of course,' said Johnny. 'Will I bring him over at the weekend?'

Honor shot him a warning glare, but it was too late.

'The weekend! The weekend!' sang Ted.

Honor wasn't going to allow herself to be out-manoeuvred that easily.

'Sorry. But I'm up to my eyes. I'm working at the manor.' Honor filled him in on her new venture. 'So Saturday's out of the question.'

'Not necessarily. How about I bring Eejit over and you can go up to the big house to work? Ted and I can stay here and I'll give him a lesson in how to look after guinea pigs.'

Honor sighed.

'Please, Mum,' said Ted.

'I'll think about it,' said Honor firmly.

'That means yes,' Ted informed Johnny.

'No, it doesn't.' Honor's tone was sharp. She was angry. She felt cornered, as if there was some conspiracy between the pair of them. Though she knew perfectly well it had been engineered by Johnny. She stood up sharply and started gathering up the plates. She wasn't going to let herself be manipulated. As she took the plates through to the sink in the kitchen, she heard the two of them start to play Paper, Stone and Scissors, thumping the table enthusiastically. They were as thick as thieves already, which was only going to make things more difficult.

Shit, she thought ruefully. She'd walked straight into Johnny's trap.

At Fulford Farm, Henty showed Travis to his room. She'd spent the day before trying to make it comfortable and appropriate for a bloke in his twenties. She'd bought chrome lampshades and a big stripy floor rug, a funky wall clock and a denim beanbag chair to match the denim duvet set. She'd moved the portable telly in out of the kitchen – at least that would wean her off Fern Britton and Phillip Schofield while she was doing the ironing. She'd listen to books on tape instead, from the library.

'Cool.' He looked round, nodding in approval, and Henty felt relieved.

'I'm not being funny,' she said nervously, 'but I'd rather you didn't allow Thea and Lily in here. I don't think it would be . . . appropriate.'

'I'm glad you said that,' said Travis. 'Teenage girls can be a nightmare.'

He chucked his rucksack down on the bed and shrugged off his jacket. Henty gulped at the sight of his broad shoulders underneath the faded grey sweatshirt.

'Supper will be at about eight,' she said faintly. 'Have a shower if you want. Or whatever.'

'I might go and look at the horses.' Travis peered out of the window into the stable yard below, showing a little hint of brown back above the waistband of his jeans. 'Then I'll come and give you a hand in the kitchen.'

'What?' Henty squeaked, surprised.

'That's what I'm here for, isn't it? To lighten your load?'

'Well, yes, I suppose so. I just thought you might be tired after your journey.'

'I've only come from Leamington Spa.' His green eyes were laughing. 'I'm not exactly jet-lagged.'

By half seven, Ted had got thoroughly overexcited and started trying to beat Johnny up again. Honor put her foot down and marched him upstairs to bed, despite voluble protests. While Ted was doing his teeth, she couldn't help interrogating him, despite herself.

'So what do you think of Johnny, then?' she asked casually.

'He's way cool!' said Ted enthusiastically. 'Is he going to be your boyfriend?'

'No!' said Honor, with a slightly hysterical laugh that she hoped indicated what a silly idea this was. She hustled Ted through into his bedroom, tucked him in under his duvet, then bent down and kissed him goodnight. He smiled and shut his eyes obediently, though she knew he always waited till she'd gone to slide his Gameboy out from under the pillow. She usually found him half an hour later, fast asleep with it still beeping in his hands.

She went down the stairs with trepidation. Her little

shield was in bed, the one thing that was allowing her to keep her distance. The kitchen was immaculate: the washing-up done and everything put away. Johnny was pulling the cork on a bottle of red wine.

'I found this in the wine rack,' he admitted. 'I think we probably need it.'

He poured it into two glasses and handed one to her. She took it warily as he raised his in a toast.

'To our absolutely gorgeous son,' he said. Then he drank deeply, and put his glass back down on the table. 'I've been knocked sideways, Honor. I didn't think I'd feel like this. I don't know how I thought I'd feel. But I didn't think I'd *love* him straight away.'

He looked into her eyes, his expression totally genuine. Which was unusual for Johnny – he usually had a hint of mockery or a glint of evasiveness when the conversation bordered on the serious. Johnny just didn't do mature, adult heart-to-heart debate. To him the answer always lay at the next party or at the bottom of the bottle. Life for him wasn't about making reasoned decisions.

'It's not just that I can see me in him. You'd have to be blind not to spot the similarity, with the ginger hair and the freckles and all,' he grinned ruefully. 'But I can see you in him as well. All the things I used to love about you. His warmth, his sense of fun, his ability to totally charm people . . .'

'Yeah, OK – enough of the flattery.' Honor cut him off with a wave of her hand. She was deliberately curt. She didn't want to be taken in by his hyperbole.

'I want to look after you both. What do you need? A bigger house? A bigger car? Is his school OK?'

Honor bristled.

'We're perfectly happy with things the way they are, thank you.'

'Come on, there must be things you need.'

'No,' Honor insisted. 'There's nothing we *need*. I've always made sure of that. Sure, there's things we don't have. Places we don't go to. But if there's one thing bringing up Ted has taught me, it's that you don't need half of the crap you're conned into thinking you can't live without. Ted has a better time when we go to Weston-super-Mare for the day than any of his friends do when they go to the bloody Caribbean.'

Johnny listened to her outburst with a half smile.

'Hey. There's no need to be defensive. I know you've given him the most wonderful life. That's why he's such a great kid. I bet you spend time with him for a start. I bet you spend hours building sandcastles with him.'

Honor didn't reply. Johnny was right: last time they went to the beach, she and Ted had made the most enormous and elaborate castle, studded with shells and peppered with little paper flags. Elsewhere on the beach she could see mothers stretched out on towels, immersed in lurid paperbacks, occasionally dishing out cartons of drinks or another dollop of suncream, but otherwise ignoring their children.

Johnny put both hands on her shoulders and made her look at him.

'I just meant . . . if there was something you wanted. Even if it's something silly. I'm not criticizing or even suggesting you haven't got everything you need. Because you're right: life's not all about what money can buy. But sometimes it's nice. Sometimes it's nice to say fuck it. I know you know that. Jaysus, I've been on enough shopping trips with you. *Fuck it, I can't decide which colour – I'll have both . . .*'

He did a wicked imitation of her in her former life. And she knew it was true. She'd always been profligate. She'd always had what she wanted: the best. And she couldn't deny that she didn't sometimes feel a pang for those things she couldn't afford. But getting them from Johnny was too high a price.

'Look, Johnny. This is all going too fast. Let's just stick with the guinea pig for the time being, OK? No great commitment. No sudden life changes. No promises we can't keep. Let's see how it goes.'

'Listen – there's no strings attached to my offer. I just want to help.' As Honor opened her mouth to protest, he put up his hand. 'And before you start, I'm not being patronizing. I'm a bachelor, and a well-paid one at that. My practice is doing incredibly well and I've got nothing else to spend my money on. Wouldn't you rather Ted had it than the bookie?'

'I suppose so . . .'

'Have a think about it. Let me know.' He paused. 'I can wait. I know it's going to take a long time to win you round.'

'What do you mean, win me round?'

Honor narrowed her eyes, wary. Johnny spoke softly: that was always a bad sign. It was when he was at his most persuasive. Usually prior to him being his most destructive. She tried to harden her heart to what he was saying.

'You know, Honor, you leaving like that was a serious wake-up call for me. It made me realize what a destructive bastard I was. Only it was too late. I'd done the damage. Lost the one person that really mattered to me . . .' He trailed off, looking sorry for himself. 'It's been a long six years. I've spent it searching for a replacement for you, but there wasn't anyone who came near. I was just coming to terms with the fact that there was nobody else out there for me. That I'd totally blown it and that I was going to face the rest of my life as a sad, lonely old git. And then . . . I look up and there you are.'

'I know. What is it they say? Small world?' Honor did her best to sound brisk and unsentimental.

'You don't think it means something? You don't think it means that we're meant to be together?'

'No. I don't want to burst your bubble, Johnny, but it was just a coincidence.' Honor was exasperated. Johnny was romanticizing, and no doubt hoping she'd get swept along. 'It's all very well trying to turn this into a fairy-tale ending. But don't try and tug on my heartstrings, because if anyone's had a tough time of it, it's me. Not that I'm looking for sympathy. It was my choice. I could have taken the easy way out after what you did. Most people would, finding out they were pregnant by a waster.'

She spat this out viciously, and was gratified to see Johnny look appalled by the implications of what she was saying. She carried on, finding that now she had started, she couldn't stop.

'But I chose to go it alone. And it's been tough, I can tell you. Carrying a child for nine months, not knowing if it's going to be all right. Giving birth on your own is no picnic either. And looking after a tiny baby is terrifying. I hardly slept at all for the first six months. Not because he didn't, but because I was so petrified he wouldn't wake.'

Honor found she was working herself up into a state, as the memory of all the years of worry and loneliness suddenly closed in on her. She was furious with herself. No doubt this was just what Johnny wanted – her breaking down, showing she was vulnerable. So that he could move in and comfort her.

But Johnny didn't. He just looked at her solemnly.

'I would have been there for you. For you both. If I'd been given the chance.'

They stared at each other, the atmosphere between them crackling with antagonism.

'You weren't fit to look after us.'

Johnny shrugged.

'Your verdict, Honor. Delivered without a judge or a jury, as far as I can see.'

'I didn't want to burden you with any more responsibility. You already had one child on your hands, after all.'

As soon as she delivered this final blow, an oblique reference to the girl he'd been in bed with, she realized she had gone too far, that her bitterness was unattractive, that she was losing face. Johnny gave a bleak smile.

'It was a meaningless fuck performed under duress, Honor. If you want to drag it up and throw it back in my face for the rest of my life, then fine, if it makes you feel better. I was hoping for a more positive outcome to all of this. Something that might be beneficial to Ted.'

Honor was silent, wary, her mind racing as she tried to work out how she could recover the ground she had lost. The bottom line was she couldn't change what had happened. Maybe Johnny was right. They had to make the best of it, for Ted's sake. But he had to understand how she felt. She couldn't just absolve him overnight. That seemed to be what he expected.

'You know what else?' said Johnny. 'I can't stand to see you so bitter. You shouldn't have to suffer because of my weakness. Give yourself a break – make the most of the fact that I'm back in your life.' He gave a cynical grin. 'Get the most out of me while you can – most women would.'

'I'm not –'

'Most women.' Johnny finished her protest for her. 'I know you're not. Which is why I'm here. Which is why I care so much. Which is why I came to find you both. Instead of doing a runner. Which would have been the easiest thing to do.'

Honor swallowed. Withstanding Johnny would add a huge pressure to her life. He wasn't easy to fight, she knew that. She couldn't cope with a battle of wills on top of her new job. And the luxury of having someone to share with – the luxury she had longed for so many times – was so tempting. And what did she have to gain by flagellating him, extricating some sort of eternal retribution for his errant ways?

She capitulated with a sigh.

'OK,' she said. 'You win.'

'No,' said Johnny. 'This isn't about me winning. Or you winning. This is about Ted. Hopefully, he'll be the winner.'

Honor nodded, hoping that she wasn't going to cry. She wasn't sure if it was the relief, or the suspicion that she had been somehow hoodwinked.

'You're right.' Her voice faltered a little. 'He is the only thing that matters in all of this.'

There was a small silence, while they both took in the fact that they had called a truce, neither of them quite sure what to do or say. Johnny cleared his throat awkwardly.

'So. Saturday's OK, then?'

'Saturday?'

'Can I look after Ted?'

Honor stared at Johnny in disbelief.

'You really don't know when to give up, do you?'

Johnny laughed.

'Never. I never give up. You know that.'

'I don't know . . .'

'For God's sake, Honor. What are you afraid of? That I'm going to kidnap him? Because I can assure you, I'm not. It wouldn't be too convenient, after all. I can't exactly bring a six-year-old boy into the surgery on Monday morning. And I won't try to brainwash him, either. I just want to get to know the guy, OK?'

Johnny ran his hand through his hair in exasperation. Honor bit her lip.

'You'll be two minutes up the road. And it'll be much better for you if you don't have him with you on the first night.'

He really did have a point there.

'OK.' She gave in with a sigh. 'Just promise me . . .'

'Promise you what?'

Honor didn't know. It was just a mother's reflex, to want reassurance. But she didn't want to come across as neurotic.

'Nothing. Come at four o'clock.'

Johnny put his glass down and scooped up his keys from the table top.

'Four o'clock it is.'

He moved towards her and instinctively she recoiled. He looked at her, hurt in his eyes.

'It's OK. I wasn't going to try anything on.'

His voice was brusque as he leaned forward and brushed his cheek against hers in a polite gesture of farewell, then turned for the door. She flushed with embarrassment.

'I'm sorry. I didn't mean –'

He put his hand up to say it didn't matter. Feeling thoroughly ashamed, she walked him to the door, and watched as he got into his car. She heard the engine start up and swallowed the urge to rush after him, tell him to stop and come back inside. She suddenly felt racked with guilt, and the need to explain. He'd behaved with such dignity this evening. Dignity and respect: he hadn't confronted her, or demanded an explanation, or condemned her. She was the one who had hurled accusations and harangued him, while he'd heaped praise upon her for how she had managed. Did that mean he was a better person than she'd ever given him credit for?

Could somebody really change that much?

She thought about how much *she* had changed in the intervening years. She'd gone from go-getting career-girl-about-town to unassuming single mother with no career to speak of. The high-maintenance, glamorous creature she had been had faded into the background; whereas once she had been groomed and coiffed, sleek and co-ordinated, now she was casual, with little make-up and comfy (though she hoped not frumpy) clothes. Jeans and hoodies and cardies and cargo pants in soft colours replaced designer dresses and trouser suits. And now her idea of a good Saturday night wasn't a fashionable water-ing hole or a dinner party attended by other success stories, but takeaway pizza and a video with Ted and a couple of his mates.

If she'd changed beyond recognition, then surely Johnny could have too?

When Charles came home at five to eight, Travis was, as promised, helping Henty in the kitchen with the supper. He stopped in the middle of chopping some garlic to shake Charles's hand, then carried on with his task. Henty smothered a smile as Charles looked a little nonplussed: Travis looked at home already, opening cupboards and drawers to find what he wanted. Henty decided there was nothing sexier than a bloke who was comfortable in the kitchen but didn't make a fuss about it. When Charles cooked, everyone had to know about it. He was constantly asking where things were, tutting if walnut oil or pine nuts weren't readily available, utilizing every utensil then expecting everyone else to clear up after him as if he'd done them all some huge favour. Travis just got on with it. Henty was doing steak, jacket spuds and salad for the grown-ups and the two girls – Robin and Walter had already had chicken nuggets and were fighting in the bath

– and he rustled up a salad dressing without any fuss. It was Henty's least favourite job. Charles hated ready-made, but she never got the balance right between oil and vinegar, no matter how many recipes she tried.

Travis got it just right.

'It's delicious,' exclaimed Henty when he asked her to taste it. 'The agency didn't tell me you were a demon cook.'

'I'm not really. But my mum trained us well,' he explained. 'I've got five brothers and sisters and she made sure we could all cook and wash and iron. Otherwise she says her life would have been hell.'

A bit like mine, thought Henty, deciding that she was going to start getting tough. Her husband and her kids were thoroughly spoilt. Whenever she asked them to do anything there was such a protest, it was painful. Take Thea and Lily. She'd asked them to lay the table earlier and they'd pleaded homework, but now they were sitting at the kitchen table drooling over Travis. They both had hideous shiny strawberry-scented lip gloss on and piles of eyeliner that made their eyes look tiny. Henty had been tempted to put on make-up too, but Charles would have spotted it imme-diately and passed some sort of sarcastic comment that would have made her squirm with embarrassment.

Lily insisted on putting Christina Aguilera on the CD player and turning it up, full volume. Charles turned it off and put on Dido.

'Yaaawn,' pronounced Thea, disgusted.

'Isn't there something we all like?' pleaded Henty.

'Which do you prefer, Travis?' asked Lily sweetly.

'We don't have music at the dinner table back home,' he said. 'We prefer to talk.'

What an angel, thought Henty, as he winked at her and the girls tossed their shiny hair in disgust.

Charles opened a bottle of wine.

'Not South African, I'm afraid,' he apologized. 'I'm a bit of an Old World traditionalist when it comes to wine.'

'Hey, I don't care where it comes from,' replied Travis, pointing to the little stubby Henty had given him earlier. 'I'll stick with the beer, if that's OK.'

'Sure,' said Charles, fetching him another out of the fridge.

'Can we have one?' chorused the girls.

'No,' chorused Henty and Charles.

'So what's brought you to England?' Charles swirled his wine round in the glass and sniffed appreciatively, whilst not taking his eyes off his new employee.

Travis leaned back against the work surface, one long leg crossed over the other, and took a swig from his beer.

'Mum's English, so I've got an English passport. I want to go to uni here, but I've got to save up some money first. I spent the summer exercising polo ponies for some family friends in Warwickshire, but the season's over now.'

'And what are you going to study?'

'Equine science.'

'That's what I want to do!' squeaked Thea.

'Since when?' said Charles, turning to her with a supercilious eyebrow. 'I thought you wanted to go to drama school.'

'No way. I never said that.'

'You did!' exclaimed Lily. 'You want to be an actress! You were hanging round Eversleigh Manor all summer hoping to be spotted.'

'I was not!'

'They've just finished filming a television series in the village,' Henty explained to Travis. 'It's been chaos. I don't know why, but the sight of a camera crew turns everyone into gibbering idiots.'

'Everyone wants their fifteen minutes of fame,' said Charles. Including Fleur Gibson, he thought, feeling a mild flutter of panic that the day he had been dreading and looking forward to in equal parts was so near.

Henty opened the oven door to get out the jacket potatoes.

'Golly, it's hot in here,' said Thea, and ostentatiously pulled off her top. Underneath she had on a tiny white singlet, and underneath that a bright pink bra. Charles nearly spat out his Shiraz. Since when had his fourteen-year-old daughter had a cleavage? Instinctively, his eyes turned to Travis. He was dicing peppers for the top of the salad, seemingly oblivious.

'Thea. Put your top back on. Now.' Charles muttered urgently under his breath, hoping his daughter would get the message and Travis wouldn't look up.

'Sorry, Daddy. Did you say something?'

Charles gestured wildly with his hands for her to cover herself up. She stared back at him in puzzlement. Travis caught sight of the exchange and picked up Thea's top from the back of her chair.

'I think your dad wants you decent at the dinner table. And when you've done that give your mum a hand with the plates.'

He turned away without giving Thea's chest so much as a second glance. Thea looked outraged and put her top back on without a word. Lily smirked. Henty concentrated hard on cutting crosses in the tops of the potatoes, once again trying not to smile. Life was definitely going to be interesting.

After supper, Charles and Travis shared a whisky at the kitchen table while Henty frogmarched the girls upstairs to bed.

'We might as well have this conversation now,' said Charles, rather pompously. 'Just so we start off on the right foot. But if you lay a finger on either of my daughters, you'll find one of your balls at Land's End and the other at John o'Groats. And just in case your geography's not up to much,' he added, 'they are a long way apart.'

Travis didn't look remotely offended.

'Hey, listen, you've got nothing to worry about,' he said. 'I'm not into teenage girls. I've always gone for the more mature woman.' He smiled at Charles. 'If you need to warn me off anybody, it's your wife.'

Charles laughed.

'Nothing to worry about, then,' he said. 'As long as we both know where we stand.'

He drained his glass, chuckling to himself at the thought of Travis giving Henty so much as a second glance.

Honor sat up late that evening finishing off the bottle of wine that Johnny had opened. Now she was alone, she could think clearly and weigh up exactly what had happened.

She began by reminding herself of all the reasons she'd wanted to keep him at arm's length. The times he'd stood her up. The times she'd watched him flirt with another woman across a room. The times he'd got disgustingly drunk with his mates watching rugby on a Saturday afternoon, and been incapable of attending whatever social occasion they had arranged for that evening. The time he'd forgotten her birthday. The times he'd borrowed money and not given it back. The times his credit card had bounced in a restaurant and she'd had to bail him out. The times she'd gone to his place for the evening and been disgusted by the state – the unmade bed with the sheets that hadn't been changed for weeks, the washing-up piled in the sink, the takeaway cartons in the living room. The times he'd lost money at the races and pretended he hadn't. The times he'd won money at the races and drunk the lot.

What on earth could a girl find attractive in that? Nothing, surely?

So why, then, had her heart skipped a beat when he leaned in towards her to say goodbye? Why had she been so disappointed when he merely touched his cheek to hers as one might a maiden aunt? Even though only moments before she had been flinging bitter accusations at him?

Because she knew the flip side of the coin. The Johnny that was passionate, loving, caring – the one that had been there this very evening. The one who used to look into her eyes with such fierce intensity when they made love, who'd reached right out and touched the soul she didn't really know she had. And once you'd had that passion, it was very hard to settle for anything less. Which was why Honor hadn't bothered looking. She'd rather be on her own than settle for the mundane and the ordinary.

Could she now go back? Could she steel herself for the chaos and the thrills, the constant turmoil offset by spine-tingling ecstasy? Would it be fair on Ted for her to be in a constant state of uncertainty, not sure whether she was going to spend the evening in disappointment, exasperation or exhausting, mind-blowing sex? Because that's the way it always was with Johnny. He was Mister Unpredictable. He might be putting on a good act for the time being, but his fickle, maverick nature ran deep.

Honor poured out the last trickle of wine, knowing that it was going to give her a thick head, but needing the security of being half pissed because that was so much better than facing cold reality. She could confront that in the morning. She sighed. If only she hadn't bumped into Johnny. *Stop it*, she chided herself. There was no point in saying if only. How far did you go back? If only she'd never gone to the ball? If only she'd never got pregnant? If only she'd never met Johnny in the first place . . . ? She leaned her head back on the sofa cushions. She just needed to be calm, cool and in control. Keep her distance. Businesslike, that was the key.

Honor gave a hollow laugh. Businesslike? Who was she trying to kid? How could she remain businesslike, when she knew all she really wanted was for Johnny to throw her on the floor, rip her clothes off and fuck what was left of her brains out? Bugger sex. She'd gone without it for nearly seven years, and now it was all she could think about.

12

Travis had been at Fulford Farm less than twenty-four hours before Henty decided that he had been sent from heaven. By seven thirty on Thursday morning, he'd fed the horses, let them into the top paddock, mucked them out, and had an in-depth conversation with Charles about their exercise regime whilst simultaneously making a huge saucepan of porridge for all the children. Which he then proceeded to make them eat, even Thea and Lily.

'All the top models eat porridge,' he'd assured them, and they'd scoffed a bowl each.

By eight o'clock he had taught Walter to tie his laces, a battle that Henty had lost on a daily basis and had given up all hope of ever winning, then left in the battered old Golf to drop Charles at the station and Thea and Lily at their pick-up point.

When Henty came back from dropping off Walter and Robin at half past nine, Travis was pulling on a pair of battered suede chaps over his Levis. Henty looked round the kitchen in disbelief. There wasn't a dirty plate or cup to be seen. Even the porridge pan had been scoured. Usually she spent at least half an hour clearing up after breakfast.

'I'm going to go and lick those horses into shape,' he explained, tightening up the buckles. 'Why don't you treat yourself to a day off?'

'A day off? But I don't work.'

'You're kidding, aren't you? That family of yours don't exactly do much to help. Go and have your hair done or something.'

Henty put her hands up instinctively to her nest of wild curls.

'I know it's awful.'

'That's not what I meant. You need pampering.' He grinned as he picked up his baseball cap and clamped it over his own curls. 'Isn't that why I'm here? So you can have a life?'

He sauntered out of the kitchen, whistling merrily, the soft, supple suede of his chaps moving with him, the faded blue denim of his jeans peeping out underneath. Henty smiled to herself. She bet it wouldn't be long before Charles rushed out to get himself a pair, but she doubted it would have the same effect. The leather would be stiff, giving him a stilted walk. And whilst Charles was trim, his legs weren't as long, his bum wasn't as . . .

Henty shook herself back into reality. What on earth was she doing, leering at Travis's bottom and taking the mickey out of her own husband for something he hadn't actually done yet? Instead, she stood still for a moment, and enjoyed the sensation of having nothing to do. The kitchen was immaculate; the beastly horses had been seen to. A gentle whirring from the utility room told her that a load of washing had already been put on.

She supposed there were things she could do. But nothing that wouldn't wait. Travis was right. She was going to put herself first for a change. She grabbed the phone to make herself an appointment at the hairdresser's in

Eldenbury. There was a choice of two – one rather old-fashioned establishment that was always full of old ladies having a shampoo and set, and a sleek, new salon, Gianni, that a lot of the mums at school raved about. Incredibly, she got an appointment straight away with Gianni himself, as there had been a cancellation.

Half an hour later she found herself sitting nervously in the chair as Gianni came up behind her. He was slight, in his late twenties, with a tight T-shirt tucked into designer jeans; good-looking in a stereotypically swarthy, Mediterranean way. From the moment he picked up her hair, she could tell he wasn't gay – his touch sent a tingle through her as he lifted the strands to see how they fell, pushed her parting from one side to the other, examined the ends, ruffled it up with his fingers to gauge its texture.

'It's beautiful hair,' he pronounced in an accent that still spoke of Sicilian lemon groves. 'But it's a mess. I need to take at least two inches off the bottom, and thin it right out.'

'I don't want thin hair!'

'It won't look thin – it will fall better. At the moment the weight is dragging it down. It's just doing nothing. If we slice into it, we give it body. Movement.'

'OK.' Henty was only half convinced.

'And we need to give it some colour. Some lowlights.' He pulled out a large folder. Inside were little swatches of hair in all the colours imaginable. 'You just want some subtle flashes – some nice autumn colours to make it rich.'

'And cover up the grey,' Henty laughed nervously.

For three-quarters of an hour she sat while a colourist

applied squares of tinfoil to her head, daubing on dubious-smelling gunk. Another half hour and Gianni inspected and seemed pleased with the results. He ushered her over to the sink.

His strong fingers were massaging her scalp and she closed her eyes, enjoying the luxury. To her amazement she was completely relaxed – a strange and not un-attractive man was touching her, and it felt natural. As she sat there she let her imagination wander – what might happen if there was no one else in the salon, if the lights were down low, the music soft . . .

'Hey – wake up. I'm finished.'

He was laughing down at her, and she opened her eyes in alarm. Something about the way he was looking at her told her he knew what she'd been fantasizing. Blushing furiously, she lifted her head obediently so he could tuck the towel round her neck, and as his fingers touched her skin again she jumped. She managed to compose herself as she walked back to the chair in front of the mirror and settled herself. What on earth had come over her? She never normally had erotic daytime fantasies about other men. Had the freedom gone to her head already?

Gianni was combing through her wet locks. She could see the colours, the copper and the bronze amongst her natural dark brown, and her heart beat in excitement. She felt already as if she was going to be a different person when she left.

Gianni picked up his scissors and began to snip with what Henty felt sure was gay abandon, but eventually she realized there was a rhythm in his work, that what he took off one side he went to take off the other, pulling out strands to make quite sure they were even. Then he swivelled her chair round so she was facing him. She gazed at his crotch, trying hard not to giggle, while he sliced into the hair at the front, giving her a soft, feathery fringe to frame her face. She panicked as she looked down at the floor and saw how much he had cut off.

'Don't worry,' he ordered, reading her mind and picking up his hairdryer.

Ten minutes later, she stared back at the mirror in disbelief. She looked ten years younger, but fifteen times more glamorous. The cut framed her face perfectly; her eyes peeped out from underneath the unfamiliar fringe, the ends fell to just above her shoulders, swinging jauntily as she moved.

'You look beautiful.' Gianni nodded in approval. 'When you came in, you looked like a middle-aged housewife.'

'Well, I suppose that's what I am.'

'No. You're very sexy.' There wasn't a trace of irony in his voice. He was totally matter of fact. He put both of his hands on her shoulders and she felt herself melt as he leaned forward. His warm lips brushed her ear. 'You need to go and have fun now with this hair.'

He gave her a wink – cheeky, not lascivious – and a moment later he was gone. Feeling like a million dollars, Henty floated over to the receptionist, and didn't blanch at the hefty bill – well over a hundred pounds. She'd have paid ten times that to feel like this. From behind his next client, Gianni smiled in approval. It was his job to make women feel like goddesses, to give them back their confidence. He loved that moment the best, standing behind them in the mirror as they surveyed their new appearance in wonderment.

Henty left the salon and stood on the pavement in a daze. From where she was standing, she could see her reflection in the shop window and she still found it hard to believe it was really her. With this haircut, she could be anything, do anything she wanted. It gave her the confidence to put her plan into action; the plan she had been nurturing for months without doing anything about it.

She went along to the cashpoint and punched in the number of her private little account, the one Charles didn't take any notice of. The one her royalties from *Chelsea Virgin* still went into, even though they were fewer and farther between nowadays. And the family allowance. It added up to a nice little nest egg. She smiled, satisfied. There should be enough in there for what she wanted.

When Henty had put her electronic Olivetti typewriter away in the cupboard all those years ago, it had been the machine of the moment. Now it was a museum piece. And she didn't have a clue how to use a computer. She knew there were some writers who still bashed away on an old-fashioned hunt and peck, but she secretly thought that was probably a bit of PR spin. If she wanted to be taken seriously, she'd have to get to grips with word-processing. And the Internet. At the moment, if Henty wanted to look something up she always got Thea or Robin to do it on the playroom computer.

There was a computer shop at the bottom end of the high street. She strode along the street purposefully, pushed open the door and marched in. There was a young lad in a white shirt and tie lolling against the counter, playing a lurid game. He stood to attention rather half-heartedly as she came in.

'I'd like to buy a laptop,' she announced. 'And I need someone to show me how to use it.'

'It's simple,' said the boy. 'You just turn it on and go.'

'But I'm a total idiot. I can type, but I don't know what a Window is. Or how to send an email.'

He grinned at her.

'I'll show you the basics. And we do telephone support if you get stuck.'

'Perfect. Right. What have you got?'

He took her over to a shelf of laptops, lids up, screens glowing. She pointed to the one on the end, sleek and silver, wafer thin.

'That's the most expensive,' the boy informed her solemnly.

'I'll have it,' said Henty.

'Don't you want to know what it does?'

'There's no point in telling me,' she said happily. 'I wouldn't have a clue what you were on about. But I like the colour.'

The boy nodded, a little warily, wondering if she'd indulged in a spot of lunchtime drinking, then reasoned that if she had he'd better take advantage of it while the going was good.

'What else do you need?'

'I don't know. You tell me.'

The boy didn't need any second telling. Mentally, he calculated his commission as he sold her a printer, a scanner, an ergonomic mouse, a mouse mat, some CDs, a CD case, a little vacuum cleaner for the keyboard, some anti-virus software – and a case to carry it all in.

'What are you going to be using it for?' he asked, as he booted up the software for her. 'Do you need spread-sheets? Graphics? Or what?'

'I'm going to write a book,' said Henty decisively. 'A big, fat, blockbusting, multimillion-pound bestseller.'

'Right,' he said, deciding that she was definitely pissed. 'What's your name?'

'Gary,' said Gary nervously.

'If you're very good, Gary,' she said, leaning in to him confidentially, 'and promise not to laugh every time I phone you for help, I'll put you in the acknowledgements.'

Ever since he'd made the lunch arrangement with Fleur on Monday, Charles had been battling with his conscience. Umpteen times he went to pick up the phone and cancel, but each time he told himself not to be silly, that this could be the one idea that turned his fortunes round. By the time Thursday arrived, any twinge of guilt had been thoroughly eradicated. It was a bona fide business lunch. He'd booked Chez Gerard in Charlotte Street. The food and the wine list were irreproachable, and the booths were nicely private. Perfect for discussing a programme proposal without fear of eavesdroppers.

At half twelve he descended the wooden stairs from his top-floor office in Brewer Street, and stopped in the cloakroom on the next floor that he shared with the rest of the occupants of the building. The mirror was speckled with age, but he was satisfied with his appearance. He had on a fine grey John Smedley jumper, a black jacket and jeans. He smoothed back his hair, touched each wrist with a droplet of Amateus and had a quick gargle with the mouthwash he kept for masking the scent of drink if he had an important afternoon meeting. Then he made his way out of the building and sauntered through Soho with a spring in his step.

He had two Kir Royales waiting at the table as Fleur walked in. She looked fantastic, in a beautifully cut cream trouser suit, enticingly low at the front. She slid on to the banquette opposite him and picked up her glass without question or protest. They chatted politely for five minutes, and ordered steak-frites and salad.

'Right,' said Charles. 'Let's get down to business.'

He unzipped his crocodile leather document wallet and slid the proposal across the table to her. He'd done a good job on it. He'd spent hours sourcing a stylish bouquet of flowers from the picture library up the road for the cover, which he'd then had laminated and spiral bound. But then Charles was very good at that – dressing things up to look like something when they weren't.

'*By Arrangement*?' she smiled. 'Great title.'

He shrugged modestly, then leaned forward, too impatient for her to read the document.

'Basically, the idea is you go into a celebrity home every week and do them an arrangement to suit some imminent social occasion. Or indeed several. Then deconstruct them for the viewers at home, making it look piss easy. So what we end up with is a bit of behind-the-scenes snooping – the *Hello!* magazine factor: check out the chintz – whilst giving the viewer the impression that they can recreate it for themselves at home.'

'Very clever.' Fleur nodded her approval as the food

arrived, together with a bottle of Charles's favourite Barolo. For the next half hour, they chatted round the idea whilst enjoying their steaks. Fleur refused dessert, as Charles guessed she might, but she enjoyed a glass of champagne while he finished off the last of the red with a plate of cheese.

'So . . .' Fleur picked up the proposal and put it in front of her, tapping the cover with, given her job, a surprisingly well-manicured finger. 'What's the next step?'

'We need to see how you look on camera. There's two options here. We go to a proper studio – fork out a good couple of grand for them to run us up a pilot we can show round. Or we do it ourselves.'

'Ourselves?'

'The home equipment you can get nowadays is as good as professional. I've got a digital video camera and an edit suite on my computer. And I've been around enough TV sets and studio sets in my time to know this sort of thing isn't rocket science. I reckon we could do a pretty good job.'

'We could do it at the shop. Or even better, in my conservatory at home.' She grinned. 'Like Delia.'

'If we do it, we can take our time; get it right without the meter ticking. The important thing is you are relaxed and confident. It's you we're trying to sell, after all.'

'I'll start getting ideas together,' said Fleur, thinking she'd get Millie on the case straight away. Something wild and autumnal; a dramatic centrepiece.

Charles looked at his watch and simultaneously gestured to the waiter for the bill.

'I'm so sorry – I'd better go. I'm expecting a call. One

of my clients is up to ghost an autobiography.' He named a famous racing driver, and Fleur raised her eyebrows, impressed. 'They said they'd let me know at three. Let's keep in touch, OK? I've got your mobile number. We'll speak.'

He put a hand on each shoulder and gave her a kiss on each cheek – a media kiss, a kiss that signified nothing. And as he strode back to his office, he felt filled with pride. Pride that he had exercised such self-control, and had managed to keep things formal. That must be a sign of real maturity, he decided. Two people who undoubtedly found each other attractive, being able to resist temptation and work together. He was a true professional.

On his way back into the office, he passed Gavin, the young producer from the production company on the floor below.

'Gav – I've got a seriously hot project for you.'

Gav sighed.

'If I had a penny for every time someone said that.'

'No, really. I'm going to let you have a show-reel and a proposal in the next couple of weeks.'

Gav nodded, stuck his thumb up and carried on down the stairs. He had fifteen proposals a day, all as crappy and ill-thought-out as the next. He wasn't going to hold his breath.

Rozzi Sharpe was exactly that – so sharp she'd cut herself one day.

She looked at the dishevelled man in front of her with distaste. It was amazing the maggots that came crawling out of the woodwork when there was a sniff of celebrity.

236

People quite happy to dish the dirt for a measly few hundred quid, about bedroom habits or childhood bullying. Slimy little Judases, the lot of them. It was strange, she thought. She might spend virtually all her waking hours digging for dirt on the rich and the famous, but she'd never dob anyone in it herself. She didn't mind exposing the people she wrote about: she owed them no loyalty. But it never failed to astonish her how happy people were to besmirch an otherwise unsullied reputation. No doubt jealousy was the prime motivation. Rozzi suspected that most people enjoyed the sweet taste of some warped revenge more than the tainted cash she gave them: the money her paper paid was handsome, but not life-changing.

Mind you, it might be in Mick Spencer's case. He was a particularly rancid specimen, but the story he had was good – if it was true. She had to stand it up, of course, but that was the same with any story: double-check the facts, make sure every accusation and insinuation was utterly watertight, get the legal boys to go through it all with a fine-tooth comb. Then you could make the splash.

'Got any photos? Pictures?' she asked him.

'Fraid not.' His lip curled unattractively. 'We weren't that sort of a family.'

'And you're still with her mother? Would you be able to get together for a photoshoot?'

'Well . . .' Mick hesitated.

'Is there a problem? There isn't much of a story without her participation. We need her side of it: the mother betrayed by her own daughter.'

'I'm sure I can talk her into it,' he smiled, showing

237

yellow teeth that wouldn't have looked out of place on a donkey. 'For the right price.'

Rozzi tried not to roll her eyes. Greedy fucker. She looked down at her notebook. She often smiled as she thought how much the pad would be worth in the wrong hands. That was why she'd devised her own version of shorthand, intelligible to no one but herself.

'OK. I'm going to get all this checked out. Then it's just a question of deciding the best time to spring the story – give it maximum impact. In the meantime, you keep schtum. Don't tell anyone what you've told me – or even that you've told me. Someone could easily run a spoiler if they got a hint, then we're all up shit creek. And you don't get paid.'

'I need a little bit of it upfront,' he whined.

Rozzi sighed and counted him out a hundred pounds cash. He looked at it in outrage.

'You could be lying to me,' she said. 'This could be the drug-induced ramblings of a psychotic maniac who's never gone anywhere near Richenda Fox.'

'But how do I know you'll pay me?'

'Ah, well –' she gave him a mocking glance from behind her heavy-rimmed glasses – 'there has to be an element of trust in all of this.'

Rozzi opened the window as soon as Mick had gone. The smell of sour sweat, old tobacco and patchouli oil had turned her stomach. She flipped back through her notes, underlining in red all the details she needed to check, then got out the file of press cuttings she already had and combed through them carefully, making more notes. If Richenda Fox had all these skeletons in her cupboard, then the chances were there were more to come. It wouldn't hurt to do a bit more sniffing around. Blowing apart fairy tales was what Rozzi was best at: once she got her pen out, there was no happy ever after.

When she got home from her spending spree, Henty decided that the boxroom where she did the ironing was perfect for her new project. After all, she thought wryly, no one else ever went in there, except in absolute *extremis* to search for an urgently needed item of clothing. It was only about eight-foot square, but there was a nice window that looked out on to the stable yard, and being next to the airing cupboard it was as warm as toast.

She spent half an hour mucking the room out. As well as an ironing room it had turned into a dumping ground for things that were no longer needed but hadn't quite made it to the dustbin. She ended up with three bin bags of clothes that no one wore any more, two old Hoovers, a cardboard box full of old Christmas decorations, an ancient high chair and three potties. She deposited them all in the utility room downstairs; Charles could take them to the tip at the weekend. Then she dragged the old table that had held her sewing machine underneath the window, and covered it with a length of chintzy fabric she'd once bought with the intention of making some curtains. She added a Lloyd Loom chair from the spare bedroom, a huge cork noticeboard that Robin never used and a soft rug from the landing to go under her feet. As a finishing touch, she lined up a dictionary, a thesaurus and her book of baby names on the windowsill. On the table, she laid a pad of A4 lined paper, a pile of index cards and a selection of coloured pens and highlighters.

She stood back and sighed with satisfaction. The room was light and airy – the perfect working environment. She didn't put up any pictures or photos, or add any ornaments. She wanted absolutely no distractions. The only thing that was likely to cause her attention to wander was the sight of Travis schooling Thea's pony: she could just see him in the top paddock, moving the mare from walk to trot to canter and back again with an imperceptible squeeze from his inner thighs . . . Henty gulped, then grinned. He wasn't a distraction, she corrected herself. He was a source of inspiration.

Then she got out her purchases. Her fingers were all thumbs as she wrestled with the leads and the cables, working out which plug went in which socket. But it was all quite logical in the end. With trepidation, she pressed the shiny silver button and waited.

Moments later the screen was up in front of her, with the daisy-strewn screensaver she'd chosen in the shop.

She telephoned Gary.

'Gary – it works!' she squealed excitedly.

'Of course it does, you pilchard,' he replied irreverently, and hung up.

With trembling fingers, she clicked on New Document. The blank screen came up in front of her. She smiled, bit her lip, and began to type the title: *The Diary of a Cotswold Housewife* . . .

13

Friday morning dawned with a crisp, autumnal perfection that made Madeleine smile with satisfaction as she drank her first cup of tea. Eversleigh Manor stood out in stark relief against the bright blue sky; it was cold enough to merit a roaring log fire in the entrance hall, but not unpleasantly chilly or damp. She felt calm. She and Marilyn had spent the previous day cleaning the house from top to bottom, and had made the beds up with beautifully crisp sheets spritzed with rosewater. Meanwhile, mouth-watering smells had wafted along the corridor from the kitchen, where Honor was baking like a demon. There was no doubt that the girl was a real find. She had brought a sense of calm to the proceedings with her quiet efficiency. The shelves in the larder were neatly stacked with Tupperware boxes and tins and plates full of the food they would need over the next few days, and she'd pinned lists of exactly what to do on the wall. She'd even drawn a picture of how to plate up the food, down to the very last sprig of flat-leaf parsley.

The sound of raised voices wafted up from the driveway outside. She looked out of the window to see Malachi remonstrating angrily with the milkman. Madeleine hurried outside to adjudicate.

'I've raked the leaves up three times this morning, and smoothed over the chippings.' Malachi was red-faced with indignation. 'Then he comes in and leaves his tyre tracks all over the drive. I've told him, tradesmen round the back from now on.'

The milkman looked in bewilderment at Madeleine for confirmation.

'I appreciate your high standards, Malachi, but we have got to live,' she chided gently. 'Of course Roger doesn't have to go round the back.'

Milkman mollified and Malachi muttering under his breath, Madeleine went to look for Guy. It was no good being complacent: there was still masses to be done, and she was going to have to deal with first-night nerves. In the kitchen she found Honor kneading the dough for bread rolls and Marilyn ironing a pile of starched white napkins, while Radio Two buzzed in the background. Madeleine felt a surge of warmth. It felt as if the house had come to life again, after being in limbo over the past four years. And even if taking in paying guests wasn't quite the same as having a proper family utilizing it as a home, she hoped that would be rectified one day soon.

Mick was lying stretched out on the hideous brown sofa that was one of the few items of furniture left in the bedsit – one of the few things they hadn't sold, because nobody in their right mind would have bought it, stained as it was with sweat and spillages. He was slurping from a can of Woodpecker cider, wiggling his toes with excitement. The nails were long and yellow, and he sported a toe ring, the skin underneath black with tarnish.

Sally paced up and down in front of the gas fire, desperate to know what was going on in his nasty little mind.

He'd been infuriatingly smug since they'd read that article in the paper. He'd disappeared off somewhere the day before and come back very full of himself. The only thing she could be sure of was that he would be the only one to benefit from his scurrilous plan. Whatever it was.

'What have you done, exactly? Blackmailed her or something?'

Mick gave an exaggerated sigh of satisfaction, and tucked his hands behind his head, smiling cheesily.

'I've sold my story. The truth behind the real Lady Jane.'

'You haven't!'

'Why not? The silly cow's been lying about her past. The public deserve to know the truth.'

'What did you tell them?'

His bloodshot eyes swivelled round to meet hers.

'I gave them lots of juicy details. About what a little prick-tease she was. About how she wouldn't take no for an answer. How could a red-blooded male resist, when she was flashing it in front of him twenty-four seven?'

Sally had heard the story so many times before. It was true, if someone repeated something often enough, you believed them. Especially if the other person wasn't around to defend themselves. But somehow, this time, his tone was so mocking, so sarcastic, so gleeful, that she knew it was a lie.

Suddenly, she found herself saying the words she'd never had the courage to say, all these years. Voicing the fear she had pushed to the back of her mind time and time again, because it was so much easier not to face the truth.

'She didn't come on to you, though, did she?'

'Huh?'

'Rowan. I bet she never even looked at you twice. You . . . forced yourself on her, didn't you?'

She couldn't bring herself to say the word 'rape'. It was too ugly. Mick just laughed.

'I gave her what she wanted. And she loved it, let me tell you.'

For a moment Sally was tempted to hit him, to pull back her arm and give him as hard a clout as she could manage. She resisted the temptation, though, because on the couple of other occasions she'd tried it, she'd come off far worse. Mick had no compunction about hitting a woman. Instead, she looked down at him in contempt, and he gazed up at her with his cold, dead eyes.

'You total fucking bastard,' she spat. 'To think I've wasted my whole life on you.'

'Yeah, well, the feeling's mutual.'

'I lost my daughter because of you.'

'Don't give me that. You never gave a toss about her in the first place.'

'How do you know? You've got no idea what I felt.'

Looking back, she'd suppressed any feelings she'd had after Rowan had left with as many drugs and as much drink as she could lay her hands on. She'd become a zombie; an emotion-free zone. Now, however, nearly ten years later, something clicked, and everything came flooding to the surface: rage, guilt, sorrow and loathing, both of herself and the monstrous man in front of her. And suddenly she felt strong enough to face the truth. The apparent success of Richenda Fox didn't absolve her from any guilt, but she felt empowered by the knowledge that her daughter had risen above what had happened and made something of herself. Sally knew she couldn't take the credit for any of that, but nevertheless she felt proud of her daughter. It gave her the courage to fight for once. She wasn't going to roll over and accept what Mick had done; let him perpetrate the myth he had created. It might be ten years too late, but she was going to atone for what had happened.

Mick had gone quiet. His head was drooping on to his chest; his roll-up had gone out in his fingers. Booze always made him conk out; he'd be snoring on the sofa for hours. She thought about setting fire to it while he was asleep. There was no doubt it would go up in seconds – if he wasn't burnt he'd soon choke to death on the fumes. And it would look like an accident; a careless cigarette. But she couldn't be bothered. If she killed him, there would be enquiries, questions, things to deal with – a funeral. She wasn't going to waste a second more of her time on him.

She went to his jacket and rifled through the pockets. There was a small wad of notes, courtesy no doubt of whichever rag he'd sold his lies to. She stood still for a moment, staring at the money, wondering how it had come to this: him betraying her, her stealing from him. They were scum, really. Could their life together ever have been different? Could one tiny little change in their fate have meant a fulfilling, loving relationship? She didn't think so. The truth was they were both losers. Wouldn't know an opportunity if it was presented to them gift-wrapped with a gold ribbon round it. She stuffed the notes quickly into her bag and left, closing the door quietly so he wouldn't wake up and follow her.

By two o'clock, Madeleine was starting to feel nervous. Guy had gone into Eldenbury with the final menus to see his friend Felix the wine merchant, to pick up the appropriate vintages for the guests to drink with their meal. Madeleine hoped he wouldn't spend too long sampling the wares. She needed Guy on his toes. He was, after all, front of house. He was going to do the meeting and greeting. Madeleine was old-fashioned and felt it was a job done so much better by a man – to be welcomed by one's host gave a sense of occasion.

To calm her nerves, she went into the drawing room to double-check it for the fiftieth time, and decided it had never looked so welcoming. The new upholstery had given it a long-needed lift. Marilyn had polished everything to within an inch of its life, and the scent of beeswax mingled with the magnificent flower arrangements that had been ordered from Twig – at huge expense, but there was no doubt that they looked the part. The effect was extravagant but relaxed: cream and orange lilies crammed into glass vases on the windowsills; a row of square pillar candles with a trio of wicks on the mantelpiece, each surrounded by a tangle of moss studded with coral-tinged roses.

For a moment Madeleine wondered wistfully what Tony would have made of the upheaval. He would have been slightly bemused but thoroughly enthusiastic and utterly unhelpful – not through want of trying, but because he would be incapable of keeping his mind on the task in hand, much to everyone's exasperation. Madeleine smiled fondly at his memory, then felt hateful tears brimming up. She blinked them back furiously. She didn't allow herself to cry any more. This was a new start, a new challenge, and she was throwing herself into it with all her heart and soul.

Someone pushed open the door and Madeleine hastily brushed away the remnants of her tears. It was Honor.

'I was going to do sandwiches for us all in the kitchen . . .' she said, and then peered at Madeleine, concerned. 'Are you OK?'

'Yes, yes, it's just . . .' Bugger. The tears were coming back uninvited. 'I was just thinking . . . my husband . . .'

Honor came straight over and enveloped Madeleine in a big hug.

'I know. It must be horrid. But I'm sure he'd be very proud of you. You've done a magnificent job, and it's going to be a huge success.'

Madeleine nodded, sniffing, and tried to smile.

'Sandwiches,' she said bravely. 'That sounds perfect. Let's all have a break and a glass of bubbly. I think we deserve a treat.'

It was a motley crew who gathered in the kitchen twenty minutes later. Malachi, his quiff wilting from the exertion of being a horticultural perfectionist, had stripped off to the waist and was flopped in a chair, displaying his magnificently tattooed torso. Marilyn was pink-faced from scrubbing, her peroxide hair wrapped up in a headscarf with a knot on top. Honor was covered in buckwheat flour from mixing up the batter for pre-dinner blinis. Guy had managed to extricate himself from Felix's clutches, and handed out champagne flutes to everyone. Madeleine composed herself, clearing her throat to gain the attention of the room.

'I want to thank each of you for putting your heart and soul into this venture,' she said. 'I couldn't have entertained it without your support. So this really is a toast from me to all of you.' She smiled. 'To my team.'

There was a collective clinking of glasses, and much hugging and kissing. Guy gave Honor a particularly grateful squeeze.

'You've done a fantastic job of keeping Mum's feet on the ground. Thank you.'

She smiled up at him.

'I've enjoyed every minute.'

Just as he bent his head to give her a kiss on the cheek, the door opened and Richenda stepped into the kitchen, immaculately groomed and fresh-faced. She smiled brightly round at them.

'I thought you'd all be busy, so I got a taxi from the station.' There was a rather awkward silence and Honor stepped away from Guy. 'How's it all going? Is there anything I can do to help?'

Everyone tried not to look pointedly at her white cashmere sweater and wide-legged wool trousers.

'I think everything's under control,' said Madeleine coolly. 'In fact, I think we'd be in trouble if it wasn't.' She looked at her watch. 'The guests are due to arrive in just over an hour.'

Everyone suddenly sprang into action.

'Will I light the fire in the drawing room, Mrs Portias?' asked Malachi.

'That would be lovely.'

Honor looked down at her grubby sweatshirt.

'I'm going to go home and make myself look more presentable. I'm filthy.'

'You don't need to be here if you don't want. It's tomorrow night I'll need you.' Madeleine rounded up the empty glasses.

'Don't be silly – I wouldn't miss it for the world. Ted's going to tea at Henty's, so you'll have an extra pair of hands. I'll see you later.'

Richenda stood awkwardly on the periphery as everyone melted away, thinking it would have been better if she hadn't come. She was quite obviously superfluous. Guy gave her a perfunctory kiss on the cheek then moved her gently out of the way.

'It's lovely to see you, darling. But I've got to dash. I need to go and make myself look like the gracious host.'

'Are you wearing a jacket and tie?' asked Madeleine, casually but hopefully.

'Bollocks to that,' said Guy. 'A clean shirt and cords is my final offer.'

Moments later the kitchen was empty. Richenda looked warily at the kettle. She wasn't going to risk making a fool of herself with the bloody Aga again. She picked up the bottle of champagne from the kitchen table. It was empty. Sadly, she put it back down again, feeling thoroughly crestfallen. She thought about going up to the bedroom to see Guy while he changed, but something about his half-hearted greeting stopped her. She didn't think she could bear it if he hustled her out of the way again.

She looked outside. It was going to be dark within the

hour. Too late to go for a bracing walk. She couldn't go and sit in the drawing room, or the small sitting room – they'd been put aside for the paying guests. She felt a burst of indignation. This was ridiculous. She shouldn't be made to feel like an intruder in what was virtually her own house. Once again she asked herself why Guy was putting himself through this. The two of them should be making preparations to have their own friends down for the weekend; their own bloody house party. She thought how wonderful it would be: choosing the food with him, laying the table and making it look pretty, deciding who was going to sleep where. They should be upstairs together now, sharing a bath before getting dressed, having a quick sneaky bonk so that their eyes would be sparkling when the doorbell rang –

Richenda strode out of the kitchen, along the corridor, through the hall and up the stairs to the master bedroom, where she threw open the door, about to confront Guy. But the room was empty. The jeans and sweater he had been wearing were on the floor in a crumpled heap. She walked over to the window and looked down.

He was outside already, smartly dressed as promised. Richenda thought how gorgeous he looked, master of his own home, opening the front gates with Malachi, the two of them laughing and joking. Feeling thoroughly deflated, she sat down on the bed. She'd lost her courage. She couldn't tackle him in front of the others. She didn't want to look shrewish. Maybe later, when they were in bed. She always managed to get Guy's full attention when they were between the sheets.

*

At half past four, a cream stretch limo with glittering fairy lights in the back window drew into the drive of Eversleigh Manor and pulled up in front of the house.

'Dear God,' said Madeleine faintly.

'I'll tell them we've double-booked,' said Guy.

'No!' said Honor. 'Get out there and charm the pants off them.'

'I don't think I can,' said Guy.

'Think of the money.' Honor put a hand in the small of his back and pushed him firmly out into the hallway. He gave a despairing look over his shoulder, stood at the front door, bracing himself, then pulled it open with a huge, welcoming smile as three forty-something bottle blondes fell out of the limo clutching monogrammed handbags. Madeleine looked on in horror as they tottered over the Cotswold chippings of the drive in their high heels. One was in three square inches of mock shredded Chanel tweed, another in a halterneck and jeans under an electric-blue bomber jacket, the third almost understated in a beige trouser suit – until she turned around to reveal a keyhole cut out of the back and naked flesh underneath. They were followed by three balding men in what seemed to be matching black polo necks and single-breasted leather jackets.

Guy stood at the top of the steps and gave an Oscar-winning smile.

'Guy Portias. Welcome to Eversleigh Manor.'

The host of the party stepped forward and gripped his hand firmly.

'Terry Spittle. We never knew Wolverhampton was so convenient for the Cotswolds. It took the limo driver less than an hour down the M5.'

'Good.'

'Just long enough to sink a few bottles of bubbly.'

That would explain the high spirits and the lack of balance, thought Guy. He suffered two more bone-crushing handshakes, then stepped aside as the women clacked past him into the hall. The ceilings rang with their high-pitched, sing-song accents.

'Wow – this is amayzing.'

'Look at the toiles, Ken. These are like the ones I wanted for our conservatory.'

'Mega stairs, look. You could do a real Scarlett O'Hara down those stairs.'

'How much does this place cost to heat?' the shortest of the men asked in awe.

'I've no idea,' said Guy, bewildered that anyone should think to ask.

'You want to get underfloor heating. It's much more cost-effective. That's what I've got in moy place.'

Guy nodded politely. Shredded Tweed clawed at his arm.

'You've got a really beautiful home,' she gushed. 'I don't know how you can bear to share it.'

Guy managed heroically to bite back a retort.

'I love that picture,' said Tasteless Trouser Suit. 'Where did you get it?'

'It's been in the family ever since I can remember.'

'It's not for sale, then?'

'Er – no.'

'Only sometimes when you go to these posh hotels everything's for sale.'

'Well, nothing's for sale here, I'm afraid,' said Guy firmly.

Trouser Suit's husband nudged him in the ribs.

'You'll have to watch Trudy. She's terrible when she sees something she wants. She'll have it in her handbag.'

The woman laughed at the look of horror on Guy's face.

'You're all right. I'm not a klepto.'

'More of a nympho.'

The entire group collapsed into giggles. Guy took a deep breath and picked up two suitcases from the bottom of the stairs.

'Shall I show you to your rooms?'

The three blondes surged forward eagerly and started up the stairs, twittering and giggling excitedly. A noxious cloud of their suffocating scents, all fighting for supremacy, engulfed Guy as he followed them. He showed them the three bedrooms, to exclamations of delight, and decided to let the six of them sort out who was sleeping where. As they were all virtually identical, he didn't suppose it mattered much, but they might have preferences.

'Right.' The man who was obviously the ringleader clapped his hands together decisively. 'I expect the girls would all like a bath before dinner.'

'Girls?' Guy looked round wildly. Had they brought their children? Then he realized that he was referring to the wives, who were protesting.

'We can't have baths. Not till tomorrow.'

'We all had a St Tropez before we got here.'

What was that? Guy wondered. A cocktail? Or rhyming slang for something obscene? He shuddered to think. He started backing obsequiously down the corridor.

'We'll be serving drinks in the small sitting room at half six.'

'Small sitting room? I wouldn't have thought a place like this had a small room.'

'It's a relative term,' said Guy kindly, and made his escape. Not before he was called back by the tallest and stockiest of the men, who looked uncomfortably like a retired boxer, with huge shoulders and a squashed nose. He put an avuncular arm around Guy's shoulder.

'Now listen. It's my Gaynor's fortieth birthday treat, this is. I want everything to go perfect for her. Whatever she asks for, just get it – all right? And add it to the bill.'

'Within reason,' said Guy.

'And by the way, she only drinks champagne. Krug. Is that a problem?'

Ten minutes later Guy was pacing up and down the kitchen with the telephone clamped to his ear.

'Felix – get up here now with a case of Krug. I've got some mad Brummies with a raging thirst on and they won't drink anything else. Cheers, mate. You are a life-saver. I owe you one.' He chucked the phone down on the kitchen table. 'It's a fucking travesty. I bet if I served them up bloody Asti Spumanti they wouldn't know the difference.'

Honor was putting the finishing touches to the blinis, which she'd topped with oak-smoked salmon, crème fraiche, finely-chopped egg and white onion, then arranged on a huge white plate.

'Look – it's money for doing nothing. Stick thirty quid on the price of each bottle they drink.'

'They won't pay that, surely?'

'They certainly will,' said Honor. 'Guy – those are the

customers you want. You keep them happy and they'll pay you. And they'll give you a whopping tip. Cash. So be nice.'

'I will be the personification of charm itself.'

Madeleine was looking shell-shocked. Honor grinned.

'Don't worry. They might be loud and brash, but they'll behave themselves. Only people who've been to public school know how to behave really badly.'

Richenda sat in her bedroom feeling sadly neglected. She wanted desperately to help, but it was obvious she wasn't needed. And she was absolutely starving, but she didn't dare go down to the kitchen and make herself some toast. Perhaps she should just slip out later and go down the road to the pub for something to eat? No one here would care. But then she realized her days of melting into the background were long gone. It would probably be plastered all over the papers the next day: Lady Jane on her own in the pub, nursing a glass of white wine and scampi in a basket. She was trapped.

She should have stayed in London. One of the other cast members was having a party that evening. It wasn't really her cup of tea, but at least she'd feel one of the gang, as if she belonged. Here she was neither one of the household nor a guest.

She got out her copy of *Wild Swans* and lay down on the bed to read. From down the corridor she heard a raucous cackle from one of the guests. She was glad someone was having fun.

*

Sally stood in the queue at the post office.

'I want a first-class stamp, please.' She shoved a fifty-pence piece under the window. 'Will it get there tomorrow?'

'Maybe. Maybe not.' The woman behind the counter shrugged as she poked a stamp and some change back towards Sally. 'Last post goes at half five.'

Sally licked the stamp and stuck it on as squarely as she could. Somehow it was important that her letter looked perfect; she'd printed the name and address out three times before being satisfied that it was neat enough. She stood for a moment in front of the red pillar box, her heart thumping, wondering if tomorrow her daughter would be holding this very envelope in her hands. And what would happen then. Briefly, feeling rather silly, she kissed it, then shoved it through the letterbox and walked away.

14

Honor treated herself to a luxurious lie-in on Saturday morning. She could hear the cartoons thudding up through the bedroom floor as she snuggled under the duvet, looking back over the week's tumultuous events and knowing this was going to be her only chance to recharge her batteries, both physical and emotional. She wanted more than anything to be strong for Johnny's arrival that afternoon. They might have signed a peace treaty, agreed to move on from the past, but she was still aware that Johnny was capable of railroading her, despite his reassurances. She was sure he was genuine when he said that Ted came first, but he wouldn't put himself far behind.

She'd gone to collect Ted from Henty's the night before, but there hadn't been a quiet moment to ask her advice, or seek her reassurance. It wasn't a scenario you could blurt out in ten seconds flat, and there was too much going on at Fulford Farm for a heart-to-heart. Henty had looked amazing, for a start. She'd had her hair done, and it made her look totally different. There was a definite gleam in her eye that hadn't been there before.

'Wow,' said Honor.

'Travis made me,' explained Henty.

'Travis?'

Henty beckoned to her with a mysterious grin, opened

257

the door to the playroom and pointed to Travis, who was supervising an elaborate Meccano construction with Ted and Walter.

'My new nanny.'

'You're kidding.' Honor couldn't fail to be impressed. She did a mock swoon. 'He's divine.'

'He's Mary Poppins on testosterone. He's totally changed my life.'

'What are you going to do with yourself?'

'Oh, I don't know,' said Henty, half wanting to spill the beans about her new project, but knowing that Charles was likely to be earwigging. 'Some of the house could do with redecorating for a start.'

'That's deeply dull,' protested Honor. 'You should do something for yourself.'

'Something will come to me,' Henty assured her. 'If not I can always just sit and look at Travis.'

Honor smiled at the memory of her friend's transformation, and snuggled deeper down into the blankets. Just as she'd managed to doze off again, the phone rang.

'Sorry,' said Guy. 'Complete emergency. It's Gaynor's fortieth. We need a cake. Tell me to fuck off and go to Marks and Spencer if you like, but I thought I'd try you first.'

'It's OK,' Honor sighed, pulling on her dressing gown. 'I've got just the thing in the freezer.'

The cake took her the rest of the morning to decorate. By the time she and Ted had cleared up and had some lunch, the doorbell rang. Honor opened the door to find Johnny proudly bearing a state of the art Perspex guinea pig run that was going to take up the entire living-room floor. And a cardboard box stuffed with hay.

'Eejit!' shouted Ted. 'Eejit's arrived!'

'Have some respect,' joked Johnny as he carried in the guinea pig palace.

'It must have cost a fortune!' Honor exclaimed, as Johnny carefully slotted the myriad pieces of see-through tubing together, Ted hopping up and down with excitement beside him.

'Nah. One of my clients was getting rid of it. One of the perks of being a vet.'

Finally the palace was assembled and Eejit was ceremoniously removed from his cardboard box.

'There, now hold him gently but firmly, under his tummy.'

Honor felt a lump in her throat as she watched Johnny show Ted how to handle the little bundle of fur. The look of pure delight on Ted's face as he watched Eejit scurry through his new home matched the look of delight on Johnny's as he surveyed his son. Her heart contracted slightly with guilt – she'd deprived the two of them of this joy for the past six years. How selfish did that make her?

'I've got to go,' said Honor hastily, before she lost it.

'No problem,' said Johnny. 'We'll be all right, won't we, big guy? Did you get the beers in?'

Ted looked slightly baffled.

'Mum said we could have Coke.' He went over to the fridge and pulled it open, lugging out a big bottle of Pepsi.

'Not too much,' warned Honor. 'Or he gets hyper.'

'On Pepsi?'

'You've obviously never seen a roomful of kids with a sugar rush.'

Johnny grimaced.

'Jaysus,' he remarked. 'I've got a lot to learn.'

'I've left chicken drumsticks and jacket potatoes in the oven. Will you be able to manage?'

'Oh ye of little faith. I'll have you know I can now cook a mean Thai chicken curry.'

'By piercing the film lid three times and putting it in the microwave?' Honor couldn't resist teasing him.

'From scratch. With fresh coriander on top. I'll prove it to you. I'll cook for you one night.'

'I shall look forward to it,' said Honor drily.

It would be highly entertaining to watch Johnny in the kitchen. Apart from his superiority on the eggy-bread front, he was a culinary klutz. He used to survive on take-aways and cheesy Wotsit sandwiches, until Honor came along and urged him to up his fruit and vegetable intake. The prospect of becoming a fat bastard convinced him, for if Johnny was anything it was vain – when Honor wanted to really wind him up she used to pinch his waist and tell him he was putting on weight.

She picked up the cake box on the breakfast bar. Curious, Johnny peered inside, then recoiled in horror at the man's torso clad in leopardskin underpants.

'What the hell is that?'

'Don't ask,' said Honor. 'I know it's hideous. But these cakes are de rigueur when you hit your fortieth.'

She put the lid firmly back on the box, and took forty candles and a packet of sparklers out of the drawer where she stored them.

'Be good,' she said to Ted, and gave him a kiss on the nose. 'And you,' she said to Johnny. 'You've got my mobile number if there's a problem.'

'There won't be,' Johnny assured her. 'We're going to be fine.'

As Honor walked up the road to Eversleigh Manor, she suppressed the urge to run back and peep in through the window. It was obvious that Johnny had no real experience with children, but as he was little more than a child himself in hundreds of ways, she thought they would probably get on. And Ted was no trouble. A lot of the kids that came back to play were absolute horrors -- unable to take no for an answer, with appalling manners and a tendency to tantrums if they didn't get their own way. Ted was polite, easygoing, happy to share: she knew that because she'd been told so by other parents, who marvelled at her doing such a good job when she was bringing him up on her own. But then she had time to spend on him. She wasn't a mad career woman who had to overcompensate by showering him with toys and treats, like many of the other mums in the area. So she was quite happy that Johnny's few hours of childminding wouldn't be too traumatic for him.

What was making her really anxious, though, was what was going to happen if they *did* get on? Where on earth did she go from here?

She didn't have very long to dwell on the matter. As soon as she arrived at Eversleigh, it was quite clear that somebody needed to take control. Madeleine might seem redoubtable, but she had moments when her judgement and her nerve failed her. Honor suspected Guy didn't *quite* care enough about what he was doing – he had a tendency to sneak off for a fag at a critical moment. And there was nothing Honor liked better than choreographing the behind-the-scenes chaos necessary for people to really enjoy themselves. So by six o'clock she had nominated herself in charge, and delegated appropriately.

By seven o'clock the Portiases and Marilyn, who'd been drafted in to wash up, realized they were in the hands of a ruthless taskmaster whose attention to detail was second to none. But they had to admit she had a flair for the job, an unerring instinct for the momentum needed.

'It's all about timing. The anticipation is as important as the reality,' she explained. 'Drinks should last long enough for everyone to become relaxed, but not totally sloshed. There should be enough canapés to take the edge off their appetite, but not fill them up. So when they go into dinner they are convivial and hungry.'

'Convivial and hungry,' repeated Guy obediently, as if it was a mantra. 'Then what?'

'Not too long a wait once the starters are cleared. Then everyone should get their main course at roughly the same time,' Honor continued. 'As they're all having the same this should be easy, but I suggest we serve up in here and each take in two plates, so everything stays hot.'

'OK.'

'Then we have a good ten or fifteen minutes before pudding, so everyone can have a fag and a wee.'

'Charming.'

'Seriously – everyone will be dying for one or the other by then. Followed by cheese. And tonight, with coffee –

the pièce de résistance. Gavin the Groin. At this point you can also try and ply them with more champagne, though it might be worth assessing how far gone they are, and whether you want to add a carpet cleaner to your overheads.'

Mick sat in the lounge bar of his local. It was dingy, run-down and unwelcoming, so it suited him down to the ground. He was grinding his teeth with rage. Rozzi Sharpe had phoned him earlier, putting the pressure on. Jesus, didn't she think he'd have been in touch by now if he'd sorted it? Women had no bloody patience. They wanted everything done yesterday. He'd placated her in the end, telling her Sally had gone to stay with a friend for the weekend but she'd be back Monday, and they'd come in then.

'She can't wait to set the record straight,' he assured her. 'Tell the world what a fraud her daughter is. This is the chance she's been waiting for. Her chance to get her own back.'

If he could only find Sally, he could talk her round, he knew he could. He'd always been able to control her. And once she realized how much was in it for them, she'd soon comply. But he had to find her first.

He couldn't believe she'd gone. She wasn't answering her phone either. He shouldn't have had a skinful the day before, but he hadn't been able to resist celebrating. He'd woken up on the sofa at three o'clock in the morning with a stiff neck and a blank memory. He couldn't remember for the life of him what he'd told her or what had happened. Had they had a row? They must have done, else why would she have disappeared like that? Along with the money out of his jacket. That had gone too. He'd had to scrat around in the pocket of his dirty jeans to get enough for a pint this evening. What was she thinking of, leaving him with nothing?

Bitch. She was an evil bitch, just like her daughter.

At Fulford Farm, the atmosphere was surprisingly genial for a Saturday. Usually there was squabbling (Lily and Robin), sulking (Charles and Thea) and tears (Henty and Walter), as everyone tried to negotiate what they were doing for the evening. But with the arrival of Travis, calm seemed somehow to have descended. He and Charles had spent the afternoon schooling Charles's horse, with Thea and Lily happily looking on. Charles was feeling so affable as a result that he offered to take Henty out for supper. Thea, who would usually be desperate to go to some hideous teenage gathering in a highly inconvenient location, was for once happy to stay in, so Henty was spared the trauma of the teenage hysterics which she always found utterly exhausting. By the time she'd finished remonstrating with her daughter she'd usually lost any desire to go out and socialize herself, but tonight she'd actually been able to have a long, luxurious bath without any interruptions.

As she put her make-up on, she decided that this week had been a real turning point in her life. Any doubts she'd had about Travis's suitability had evaporated: although he was utterly drop-dead gorgeous, he had an underlying steeliness and self-control that convinced her he was no threat to her daughters. He took absolutely no crap from either of them. Henty wasn't sure how he did it. Whenever she tried firm and no-nonsense with Thea and Lily, they wiped the floor with her. But Travis had them jumping to attention. They didn't even attempt to answer him back. It was quite extraordinary. Like now, for instance – he'd actually got them cleaning their tack. In the kitchen, admittedly, which was always a mess – there were reins and stirrup leathers strewn everywhere, sweaty girths draped over the backs of the chairs and horrible grass-encrusted bits in the sink – but Henty didn't care because she was going out and Pizza Pete had already been contacted and was delivering in an hour.

Even more gratifying, she'd already typed nearly three thousand words of her new opus the day before. She'd been thoroughly excited by the word count facility on her laptop. At first she'd clicked on it after virtually every paragraph, but now she'd restricted herself to every half an hour. Three thousand words in just one day! If she carried on at that rate, she should have a sizeable chunk done before long. The words just seemed to be spilling out of her, just as they had when she'd written *Chelsea Virgin*. The bare bones were there already, in the note-books she'd extricated from her tights drawer, but Henty had been pleasantly surprised how lucidly it all came together. It was as if there was a voice in her head dictating to her, and all she had to do was type it in. It was the most glorious feeling. She'd sneaked back into her little room this afternoon, just for an hour, and reread what she had already written, terrified that it would be the most utter rubbish. But it wasn't. It was funny. Sexy. Slightly outrageous. Naughty but nice. She couldn't wait for

Monday, for an empty house, when she could sit back down at the keyboard and have another bash.

It was incredible how the hideous events of last Saturday, when Charles had made such a fool of her and then lost his licence, had turned out to have a silver lining. And the nicest surprise of all was that when she dried her hair it actually looked almost as good as when Gianni had done it. As she surveyed the final results in the mirror, Henty felt on top of the world, the happiest she'd felt for a long time.

Her euphoria was short-lived. She spotted Fleur's sleek navy-blue Mercedes convertible as they drove into the car park of the Honeycote Arms, and her heart sank. Henty prayed Charles wouldn't notice her – that the Gibsons would already be seated in some dark little corner. Luck, however, was not on her side. As soon as they walked in, Charles's eyes lit up.

'Look who it isn't!' he exclaimed, and bounded straight over to the bar, where Fleur was perched on a stool swinging her legs carelessly as her husband ordered their drinks. She slid off her stool as soon as she spotted Charles and snaked a sinuous arm round his neck.

'Charles – darling. What a surprise. I didn't know you ate here.'

'Who doesn't?'

'I know. Isn't it fab? We come here every Saturday if we're not going somewhere else. Robert, look – it's Charles and Henty.'

She managed to make 'Henty' sound like 'fat lump'. Robert, standing patiently at the bar with a twenty-pound note folded between his first two fingers, greeted them genially.

'Hello, you two. What'll you have to drink?'

'Hadn't we better go through?' asked Henty anxiously. 'Our table was booked for eight, and it's already quarter past.'

'I know! Let's see if they'll push our tables together,' Fleur was trilling excitedly. No! Henty wanted to scream. I don't want to sit here while my husband gawps at your unfeasibly large and suspiciously upright breasts.

But it was too late. An amenable waiter was nodding as Fleur outlined their desire. Moments later two tables were conjoined and the Gibsons and the Beresfords were ushered into the dining room. Trailing miserably behind, Henty surveyed Fleur's champagne suede mini and high-heeled boots with the diamanté studs, and immediately felt enormous and a total frump. She didn't suppose she could get Fleur's minuscule skirt over one of her thighs. Her combat trousers and the silky knit sweater that had made her feel svelte and a little bit trendy now made her feel stumpy and middle-aged and as if she was trying a bit too hard. Deep down she knew that Fleur looked as if she was touting for business, but superficially she desperately wanted to wear an outrageously short skirt and silly boots. Fleur's legs were bare, and even though it was October they were toned, silky-smooth and tanned. Henty knew hers were flabby, dimpled, blotchy, hairy and white. She shuddered with revulsion at the thought of them being exposed.

Henty sighed as she sat down and took her menu from the waiter. She was going to feel utterly inhibited now. If she ordered anything more substantial than a rocket and red onion salad for starters, she knew Fleur would look at her pityingly as if to say it was no wonder she was the size she was. And Henty desperately wanted the wild mushroom tortellini. And bugger – here came the waiter with a basket of warm home-made breads and a big pool of green olive oil to dunk it all in. The men helped themselves eagerly.

'Don't you want bread, Henty?' asked Charles.

'No – I'll never be able to manage my main course otherwise. The portions are huge here.'

'I don't know how you can resist,' said Fleur. 'This bread is totally scrumptious.'

She ripped off a hunk of tomato focaccia and dipped it in the oil, then ate hungrily. Henty was sure she was taunting her. She bent her head and studied the menu, wishing she was at home with Travis and the kids, with pizza and Ben and Jerry's.

At half nine, Richenda couldn't ignore her hunger any longer.

She'd stayed out of the way during the day. It seemed the most tactful thing to do, so she'd taken a cab into Cheltenham and consoled herself by buying some extremely expensive nightwear. Guy wouldn't be up *all* night seeing to his guests' needs – at least she hoped not – so when he came off duty she could see to his. But in the meantime, the party still seemed to be in full swing. The last time she had peered down the stairs over the banisters she'd seen Guy racing through the hall bearing a perfectly hideous cake on a silver tray.

If they'd reached the cake stage, she thought things might have calmed down in the kitchen by now, and there might be something left over that she could have. She was slipping down the stairs, hoping not to be noticed, when a vision in coral-pink stretchy lace and four-inch perspex sandals, en route to the loo, caught sight of her.

'Oh my God!' she shrieked, clasping her hands to her chest. 'It's Lady Jane!'

Richenda smiled as graciously as she could. There was no point in denying it.

'Oh please. Will you come and say happy birthday to Gaynor? It'll make her day, it really will.'

Richenda hesitated, not really wanting to be drawn into a public appearance situation – she hadn't put any make-up on. But what was the alternative? Being in the way in the kitchen, or going back to the bedroom on her own? She smiled.

'Of course I will.'

Her reception in the dining room was very gratifying. They all made a fuss of her, but in such a warm and welcoming way that she couldn't begrudge them her presence. Terry pulled her up a chair and gave her a glass of champagne, and Gaynor insisted on cutting her a piece of cake.

'Though I bet you never eat cake. Look at you.'

Richenda was actually starving, so she ended up eating two pieces and nibbling at the remnants of the cheese-board. In the meantime, the three women regaled her with the intimate details of their sex lives, bank accounts and cosmetic surgery, much to their husbands' excruciating embarrassment. They were an absolute scream.

'After three kids I had no pelvic floor left,' Gaynor was saying. 'But then I discovered these little weights. They're fantastic, honestly. I've got a grip like a vice now. Haven't I, Terry?'

Terry was mortified, not knowing where to look. The women collapsed with laughter, and Richenda with them.

'He can pretend not to know what I'm talking about,' screeched Gaynor, 'but he calls me the Gin Trap.'

'That's because of your drinking habits,' quipped Terry drily. 'Nothing to do with your performance in the bedroom.'

Richenda wiped her eyes. She hadn't laughed so much for years. Or enjoyed herself so much. On the surface, she wouldn't have thought these people were her type at all, but they were warm, funny, raucous and obviously had a deep sense of loyalty to each other. Their marriages, she guessed, were as strong as a rock, even though she'd heard some of the most outrageous sexual anecdotes. She wished she could take a leaf out of their book, relax and let herself go a bit. But then all her grown life she'd been putting on a performance, both on and off camera. Or had she – was this the real her? She supposed that by now it was. She'd created who she was: the image of perfection who could do no wrong. She had absolutely everything that the public craved for themselves: beauty, celebrity, talent, true love . . . everything the media told them repeatedly was important and was to be striven for. But was it enough?

Or perhaps it was too much? Perhaps she'd be better off with only one of those things, like these people. They obviously had a bit of money and they had love . . . but not a modicum of talent or fame. Or beauty. Yet they were clearly happy.

It was at this point that it struck Richenda that she wasn't. Not really. There was something deep inside her that felt unsettled. Whenever she thought of the future – even though on paper it held so much promise – she had a strong sense of foreboding.

'Are you all right, bab?' Gaynor was looking at her anxiously.

'I'm fine. Sorry – I just drifted off for a second.'

'Give her some more champagne, Terry.'

Terry jumped and did her bidding, topping up her glass with a flourish in a camp imitation of the most obsequious maître d'. Out of the corner of her eye, Richenda saw Guy enter the room with a tray of liqueurs. He did a double take when he saw her.

'We found her in the hall,' said Gaynor. 'She was bored, poor kid. You shouldn't keep her locked away like that.'

Guy wasn't at all sure what to say.

'I know,' said Trudy. 'Let's have a toast to their engagement. We saw those fantastic photos in the *Daily Post* last Saturday. You looked beautiful.'

Richenda smiled her thanks as the six of them raised their glasses.

'To Guy and Richenda,' proposed Terry. 'May you be as happy together as we all are.'

Henty was really struggling to enjoy herself. The bitter irony about your spouse losing their licence was that they proceeded to be chauffeured around for the next twelve months getting as pissed as they liked. Where was the justice in that? It was no punishment at all.

This, however, was hell. Sipping Malvern Water and watching Fleur and Charles get more and more drunk and more and more outrageous. Robert was sweet, but dangerously dull. Frankly, she didn't know how he put up with Fleur's blatant flirtation. Or would he remonstrate with her later in the privacy of their bedroom? Would he put her over his knee, pull up that ridiculous little skirt and give her a good spanking with the back of her hairbrush? One that she would no doubt enjoy –

'Henty? Are you with us?'

The rest of the table was looking at her. Henty realized that she'd drifted off into a rather warped little fantasy, and blushed furiously. What on earth was happening to her? This was becoming a bit of a habit.

'Do you want pudding?'

'Yes,' she said stoutly. If she couldn't drink, then she certainly wasn't going to deprive herself of the house speciality. 'I'll have the chocolate trio.'

Fleur took in a sharp breath through her teeth.

'Calorie city.'

'So?' said Henty. '*I'm* not drinking.'

She looked pointedly at the two empty wine bottles upturned in the ice bucket next to their table. Charles frowned.

'There's no need to be rude.'

'I'm not being rude,' said Henty. 'I'm just pointing out that a bottle of Chablis is easily worth a dollop of chocolate mousse.'

She wasn't going to pull her punches any more. She hadn't missed Fleur's patronizing little smirks throughout the meal; or the conspiratorial smiles she'd flashed at Charles when she thought no one was looking. The more Henty thought about it, the more convinced she was that this evening had been a set-up. That Charles and Fleur had cooked it up between them. Henty and Robert were just pawns in their sordid little game. Well, she'd play along for the time being and act dumb. Fleur obviously thought she didn't have a clue, by the way she was behaving.

By ten o'clock, her instructions obeyed to the last letter, Honor's duties were over. Madeleine urged her to go home, but there was a little bit of her that felt rather deflated. Instinct told her to see the evening through – at the hotel she wouldn't have been happy until the last of the guests was safely tucked up – but that wasn't what she was being paid for at Eversleigh. Reluctantly she left them all to it, missing the kitchen camaraderie that came after service, the wind-down, the debrief, the banter.

On the way back home, she became filled with a sudden panic. She'd meant to phone halfway through the evening and make sure everything was all right, but there hadn't been a moment. All sorts of hideous eventualities involving spontaneous combustion and anaphylactic shock flashed through her mind as she raced up the road and burst in through the front door, breathless and panting, wild-eyed with alarm. Johnny was stretched out on the sofa, hands behind his head. He jumped up immediately.

'What's the matter?'

'Is everything OK?'

'What?'

'Is Ted all right?'

'Of course he is. He went to bed at half eight, as good as gold. I haven't heard a squeak out of him since.'

'But you've checked him?'

'Of course. He's fine.'

'Thank God!'

'What the hell did you think was going to happen?'

'I don't know.' Honor collapsed on the sofa. 'I just panicked, that's all.'

'Well, don't. Sit down there and I'll get you a drink.'

'Thank you. Sorry.' Honor wriggled out of her coat and flopped back with a sigh.

'How did it go?'

'Fantastic. As far as I know. They're all still hard at it.'

'Good.' Johnny nodded his approval. 'Tea or coffee?'

Honor looked at him askance.

'I'd quite like a glass of wine, actually. I think there's some left in the fridge.'

She shut her eyes for a moment, trying to regain her composure, while Johnny went into the kitchen and emerged with a glass of white wine.

'There you go.'

Honor accepted it gratefully.

'Aren't you going to have one with me?'

Johnny looked at his watch.

'Actually, I better go. I've got rugby first thing in the morning.'

'Oh.'

'Anyway, you must be exhausted.'

'Not really. I think I'm overwound.'

'Why don't you take yourself upstairs and have a nice, warm bath? You'll fall asleep before you know it.'

To Honor's chagrin, Johnny started picking up his keys and his mobile. She really felt like sharing the rest of the bottle of wine, chatting over the evening's events. But no – he was standing in front of her, putting on his coat. He really was going.

He bent down and gave her a kiss on the cheek.

'Don't worry about seeing me out. How about I see you Wednesday?'

'Wednesday?'

'Thai chicken curry, remember?'

'Um . . . I'm not sure.'

Wednesday seemed too soon, somehow. She longed for the chance to take stock, maybe talk to someone, get an objective opinion on her situation. She could never think straight when Johnny was around.

'Come on,' he cajoled. 'It'll do you good to have someone cook for you. You spend your whole life cooking for other people after all.'

'OK,' she agreed reluctantly.

'I'll see you then.'

And a moment later he was gone.

As soon as she heard the front door click shut, Honor felt desolate. She looked at the clock. It was only just past ten, for heaven's sake. When had Johnny ever left anywhere at ten because he had to be up the next morning? He had ridiculous stamina. He could go to work on two hours' sleep.

Then the penny dropped. He had somewhere else to go to. Of course. If he put his foot down – which he would – he'd be back in Bath within an hour. Just in time to slip into the pub before closing time and get the low-down on where the party was happening. There'd be a pretty girl who would have spent the evening looking at her watch, wondering if he'd keep his promise, whose face would light up as he walked in through the door . . .

She sat on the floor of the living room with her arms round her knees, sipping the rest of her wine even though she didn't really want it, but hoping it would make her sleep.

She was at his mercy. She was trying to call the shots, set the pace, but every time Johnny took the upper hand. She didn't want him to come on Wednesday. It felt suspiciously as if he was trying to set a routine – subtly insinuating himself into her life with a rhythm she would come to find comforting until she couldn't do without him.

And as much as she didn't want him to come on Wednesday, she hadn't wanted him to go tonight. Honor felt infuriated with herself. How could she expect to call the shots when she wasn't consistent? She shivered. The woodburner had gone out. She was usually in bed by now. Reluctantly, she double-locked the front door, switched off the lights and made her way up the stairs, somewhat dreading her empty bed.

All the time she'd lived here on her own with Ted, she'd never felt lonely. But tonight she did.

During pudding, Charles felt someone drop something discreetly in his lap underneath the tablecloth. He waited for a suitable moment to discern what it was.

He looked at the scrap of fabric in his hand. It was a

tiny little triangle of black lace held together with silk ribbons that had been untied.

Jesus, he thought. He'd got Fleur's knickers in his lap. What the hell was he supposed to do with them? If he dropped them on the floor, someone might see. He looked over at her with a question in his eyes, but she just gazed innocently back at him. He stuffed them hastily in his pocket, feeling a slight sense of rising panic. He thought he was losing control of the situation. He was, both literally and metaphorically, no longer in the driving seat.

'I'm so sorry,' said Guy later, when he'd managed to extricate Richenda from the dining room. They were sitting in the kitchen finishing the remains of a bottle of Krug that had been left after pre-dinner drinks. 'I won't let anything like that happen again. You're not supposed to be on public display. This is your home. I would have thought they'd have respected that.'

'It's fine. It's not a problem,' said Richenda, biting back the urge to retort that it was actually the most attention she'd had all weekend. And at least they'd bloody fed her. She was trying very hard not to behave like a spoilt princess. Guy had, after all, been working his socks off.

'Show me what you bought this afternoon.' Guy, who sensed a certain frostiness in the air, knew that most women were mollified if you showed an interest in their retail activities.

Richenda held out her hand.

'Come upstairs.'

Guy followed her out into the hallway, where they were

greeted by the sight of Gaynor sliding naked down the banisters wearing nothing but a diamanté G-string and her high heels.

'Sorry,' she giggled. 'We're playing Truth Dare Kiss or Promise.'

She looked at them, eyelashes batting furiously.

'I don't suppose you want to come and play?' she asked, then collapsed in a drunken heap at their feet.

15

At midday on Sunday, the limo arrived to take the some-what subdued house guests home again. They said their farewells, with many pleas to come and stay both in the Black Country and their timeshare in Majorca.

'I became almost fond of them, in a funny way,' said Guy, as the tail lights disappeared through the gates.

'I think we can certainly call the weekend a success,' countered Madeleine, who didn't quite feel the same, but was willing to concede that they had shown their own brand of courtesy.

They walked back into the hall and shut the door. Madeleine pulled open a drawer in the table that held the post.

'By the way, I forgot. This arrived for Richenda yester-day – a bit of fan mail, I think.'

Guy took it absently. He was going to have to make it up to Richenda now. The poor thing had looked so forlorn all weekend, and then last night's fiasco had only added insult to injury – he shuddered as he remembered having to give Gaynor a fireman's lift back to bed. Now hopefully they had the whole day together. They'd go for lunch at the Honeycote Arms. They needed a bit of time on their own. Quickly he phoned Barney and booked a secluded table, then ran up the stairs to the bedroom.

Richenda was drying her hair. He plonked the letter on the dressing table in front of her.

'Lunch at the Honeycote Arms at one. That arrived for you yesterday – Mum forgot to give it to you in all the uproar.' He planted a big kiss on her cheek. 'You get ready. I'm just going to go and add up what we've made over the weekend.'

He rubbed his hands together in mock glee, and Richenda giggled.

'You old Scrooge,' she teased.

'Don't knock it. Lunch is on me.'

The next moment he'd gone. Richenda smoothed some serum on to her hair, absently picking up the envelope. Her heart skipped a beat as she read the name on it. *Richenda Fox.* Then, in brackets next to it, *Rowan.*

She slid her finger under the flap, her hands shaking slightly, and drew out a piece of blue notepaper. Both sides were covered in the awkward scrawl of one who rarely put pen to paper but was trying to be neat. And without looking at a signature, she knew who it was from.

Dear Rowan

I saw your picture in the Daily Post last week. I can't describe my feelings. Relief, mostly, that you were all right. And guilt – again. There hasn't been a day when I haven't wondered where you are and what you are doing. Now I know you are a star! Of all the things I imagined might have happened to you, this was beyond my wildest dreams.

I know you probably don't want to hear from me, or care how I feel but I need to warn you – Mick's sold his story to the papers. I don't know what he's told them, exactly, but if I

know him it's not going to be nice. And that's the last thing I
want. I don't have a clue how these things work, but I want to
make it right for you. And if that means telling my side of the
story then I will. I'm ashamed of what happened, more than
you can ever know, but I'm not afraid to admit it. So I want to
do whatever I can to help.

I've wanted to say I'm sorry for years. But I never knew
where to find you. If nothing else comes of this at least I know
now that you are all right. More than all right! Not that I
deserve peace of mind.

I've put my mobile number at the top of this letter. Ring me.
I want to help. Though I understand if you want nothing to do
with me.

Sally (Mum)

It was the word 'Mum' in brackets that creased her.

She'd denied herself the memories for so long. Even
though Sally had been dreadful at times, she was still her
mother. All her young life, her mother had veered between
aggression and affection, sometimes smothering her and
sometimes seeming to fight her off. But they had had
moments of incredible closeness – usually when there
wasn't a man in her life – when they'd snuggled up in
bed together, Sally hugging her from behind, scooping
her up in her arms, and they'd sleep in a lovely warm ball.
Then she'd felt cosy and cared for and warm and safe.
She used to wake first in the morning and watch her
mother sleeping, praying that they could stay like this for
ever. There was no other feeling like it in the world, and
Richenda had long come to terms with knowing she
would never feel it again.

Looking back on it, she realized she'd blocked out all the good memories of Sally in order to cope. She'd erased any trace of a mother's love, the delicious warmth that came from being nurtured and cared for, until she was entirely self-sufficient; an emotional island.

Not that she was incapable of loving. The feeling she had for Guy, and the love she got from him, was different. Their relationship was a partnership, a balancing act, fuelled by the sweet, all-invasive power of sex. It bore no resemblance to the unconditional love she'd shared with her mother until things had got totally out of hand. When she was small, she'd forgiven her cruelty and unkindness, the little acts of spite and thoughtlessness. But that final betrayal had been the last straw. She'd lost the power to forgive; the scales had fallen away from her eyes and she'd seen her mother for what she really was.

Reading the letter now, she wondered if perhaps she'd been too harsh. Her mother was fallible, human, she made mistakes. As a little girl, she wouldn't have had the wisdom to realize it, but now Richenda was older she saw how difficult it must have been for the easily-led and insecure Sally, who'd been a mere eighteen when she'd had her baby. Maybe it wasn't surprising that the pressure became unbearable and she took it out on the person closest to her. That was human nature.

Instinctively, Richenda knew that somehow this letter held the key to her disquiet. That all the time she had been lying, both to the public and to herself. And that really all she wanted was to be small again, to have Sally's arms around her, feel the total reassurance that only a mother can give. But surely the chance for that was long gone? She was nearly twenty-five; Sally must be forty-three. Too much time had passed for them to resurrect that relationship.

But perhaps the time had come to forgive . . .

She was hastily flinging the few things she'd brought down for the weekend back into her bag as Guy came into the room.

'The good news is I can afford to buy you roast beef *and* Yorkshire pudding.'

'I've got to go.'

'What?'

'I've . . . got to go and do a press conference thingy. They just texted me. I can't get out of it. It's for the American launch – some big magazine . . .'

She was improvising wildly and improbably, but Guy didn't seem to notice. He just looked thoroughly crestfallen.

'Well – shall I drive you to the station? Better still, why don't I drive you up to town? You can do your thing and I can take you out to dinner afterwards.'

'No – it's going to drag on. I've no idea what time we'll finish. Just take me to the station.' Richenda looked at her watch. 'If we hurry I can get the one-eighteen.'

'Well, I'll buy you a KitKat for the journey. And I'll see you Wednesday. We'll do something special then.'

'Wednesday?'

'The award ceremony? You do still want me to come, don't you?'

Richenda smiled weakly.

'Sorry. I'd forgotten. Yes, of course I want you to come.'

She couldn't bear to think about that at the moment.

God knows what sort of shit would have hit the fan by the time Wednesday came around.

As they drove to the station, Guy realized that Richenda was very quiet. She seemed preoccupied with something. Or perhaps she was sulking? He thought he'd already apologized for neglecting her somewhat over the weekend, but maybe that wasn't enough. He knew there were girls who made you suffer indefinitely if something displeased them. His younger sister had been a sulker, capable of the silent treatment for days on end if things didn't go her way. But he didn't think Richenda was that type.

Anxious to mollify her, he squeezed her leg affectionately.

'Listen, it's not always going to be like this. The first weekend was bound to be chaos. We'll settle into a routine soon, and I'll be able to delegate a bit more.'

She hardly seemed to be listening.

'What?'

'This weekend. I'm really sorry it was so boring for you.'

'It was fine. Don't worry.'

She looked out of the window and chewed the side of her finger. Guy frowned while he decided on a different tack, then gave up. He couldn't think of one. He'd find a way of making it up to her. Wednesday night, the award ceremony, was going to be her night – he'd make sure she felt like a total princess. She'd have his full undivided attention.

He pulled up by the ticket office.

'You go and get a ticket. I'll find a parking space.'

'Don't bother. You don't need to wait. The train will be here any second.'

Richenda jumped out of the car and went to slam the door.

'Hey! Don't I get a kiss?'

She tapped her head in mock forgetfulness, then leaned in through the door. Their cheeks just managed to touch over the gearstick.

'I've got to rush.' She put her hand over his in a momentary gesture of affection, and Guy saw the ruby ring glint in the autumn sunshine. 'I'm really sorry. Bloody career women.'

Her rueful smile as she shut the door and waved made him realize that she hadn't been sulking at all. She was probably just stressed about work; psyching herself up for her press conference. It must be hell, being on public display, he mused. Watching your every move, thinking about your appearance, your behaviour, hoping you weren't ever misconstrued or taken out of context. Richenda always seemed so calm, it was easy to forget she must be under constant pressure. Her world was so alien to him, and it occurred to Guy that it was going to take him a bit of time to get used to being part of it. When they were together, having fun, making love, it was as if she was a normal person, not a superstar. But that stardom wasn't going to vanish. It was part of the package. Just as Eversleigh was part of his package, he supposed. They were going to have to work hard to incorporate their respective responsibilities into their relationship.

He drove back home, wondering what on earth to do with the rest of the afternoon. He ought to be knackered, after all the running around, but he felt full of energy. Restless. There wasn't really any clearing up to do. Malachi and Marilyn had arrived at eleven and done a sterling job. The beds were all stripped, the rooms vacuumed, the glasses and crockery were gleaming and in their proper place.

It was his mother who finally came up with a suggestion.

'Why don't you take some of these flowers up to Honor? There's too many here for just us to enjoy, and they're still perfect. She might as well get some pleasure out of them. They won't last till next weekend – I'll have to get more.'

'Good idea.' Guy didn't suppose Honor had fresh flowers very often – not ones as elaborate as these at any rate. And she wasn't the type to be offended by hand-me-downs; this past week had shown him she was a practical and down-to-earth girl. He had to admit to a sneaking admiration for the way she managed her life. She didn't seem phased by anything. Yet somehow she managed to evade being Girl Guidy or prefecty. She still retained a slight air of mystery; as if you were only getting part of the story. Guy was intrigued. Taking the flowers up to her would give him a chance to peep behind the scenes. Not that he wanted to snoop, but there was nothing else to do and it would fill the afternoon.

Guy felt a bit of a plonker walking down the high street with an enormous vase of lilies, but it was worth it for the look on Honor's face when she opened the door.

'Oh my God. They're completely divine. Are you sure I can have them? Come in! It's chaos, I'm afraid. Ted and I are doing fairy cakes for tea and he's absolutely insisted on black icing. Don't worry – we won't be offended if you don't eat one.'

Guy came into the warm fug of her kitchen to find a dozen fairy cakes cooling on a rack and Ted stirring a bowl full of something suspiciously grey and unappetizing.

'Don't you ever stop? I'd have thought you'd have your feet up, exhausted, after the past couple of days.'

'You can't, with children. Don't you know that?' She grinned at him impishly. 'I can collapse tomorrow, when he's at school.'

'No, you can't. Mum's asked you up for lunch. Though you don't have to come, of course. I expect you're sick of the sight of us.'

'No. It would be fun to have a post-mortem.' A thought occurred to her. 'Isn't Richenda still here?'

'She had to go back to London. Press conference or something.'

'Oh. Poor thing. I suppose she's always at their beck and call.' Honor plonked a yellow liquorice allsort in the middle of a fairy cake. 'Can I tempt you?'

Guy took one politely and bit in.

'Delicious.'

Manfully, Guy managed to swallow the whole of the fairy cake. Ted solemnly offered him another one.

Honor giggled.

'I'll make you a cup of tea to take the taste away.'

Guy leaned back in the kitchen chair and surveyed his surroundings as subtly as he could, looking for clues to

Honor and what made her tick. She had a rapier-sharp brain and huge amounts of talent which she'd obviously sacrificed for Ted's benefit, and he admired her for that. It was probably far harder than succumbing to a demanding career and depending on others for childcare. Yet it was obvious that the child benefited from his mother being around: Guy didn't have much contact with kids, but Ted was utterly charming without being precocious.

Presumably the biggest downside of not working was financial. Yet Honor's surroundings had more flair and imagination than most of the grand houses Guy had been inside over the years. The kitchen was a necessary mix of Ikea and junk shop: brightly coloured mismatched crockery, mugs and glasses, shelves she had painted herself in a rainbow of colours using sample pots, a long Shaker peg rail along one wall where everyday items from brollies to shoe-bags were hung. There was an aura of organized chaos – Guy felt sure Honor could put her hand on whatever was next needed amidst the muddle and spontaneity.

He watched as she piled the mixing bowl and the baking tins into the sink. She must be worn out, he thought, but she still looked fresh-faced, with a sparkle in her eye. And that was without a scrap of make-up on. There was no doubt about it, she was quite beautiful, with those large, dark eyes and that enviable bone structure. He wondered if she ever went out on dates. He didn't remember seeing her with anyone particular at the ball.

His question was answered a little while later, when Honor was pouring tea into two spotted mugs. Ted came running into the room with an olive-green ribbed scarf, clearly alarmed.

'Mum – Johnny left this! It was under the cushion on the sofa.'

Honor took it from him absently and hung it on one of the pegs.

'Never mind. We can give it back to him on Wednesday.'

That answered that, thought Guy. Whoever Johnny was, he had good taste in accessories and his feet under the table. He told himself he was pleased. Honor deserved the love of a decent man. He just hoped this Johnny knew how lucky he was – Honor was definitely a very special person.

When Guy got back to Eversleigh later, Madeleine was jubilant.

'The Spittles have just phoned. They had such a fantastic time they want to know if we can do New Year's Eve for them. They want to bring some friends – ten altogether.' Madeleine raised her eyebrows and shrugged her shoulders tentatively. 'What do you think? It could be lucrative. They seem to expect to be charged double.'

'Why not?' replied Guy cheerfully. 'I know we said we wouldn't do Christmas, but I loathe New Year's Eve. Might as well make some money out of it.'

'I'll phone them back and say yes, then. If you're sure we can manage.'

'Yes. We'll be old hands by then.'

It was only later, as he drifted off to sleep, that he realized if things went according to plan, on New Year's Eve he should still be on his honeymoon. How on earth could he have forgotten that?

16

In the living area of her luxury Knightsbridge apartment, Richenda paced up and down on the maple floors until she couldn't stand the sound of her heels on the wood any longer. Why the hell hadn't she insisted on carpet? The brochure had boasted of the ultimate in urban relaxation, but she didn't think she'd relaxed for as much as a moment in this room. She flopped back on to the white leather 'seating module', wincing at the cold, and thought longingly for a moment of the cushion-strewn sofas in Eversleigh and the roaring log fire. She could turn up the flames in her fire if she wanted, but as usual she couldn't find the remote.

For the hundredth time that afternoon, she smoothed out the letter from Sally and read it again, wondering if perhaps it was a trap; if some clever journalist somewhere was trying to smoke her out. It was inevitable that she'd be found out sooner or later. Someone only needed to start rummaging about for facts prior to drama school to find out that the glib back story she had invented for herself had no founding; that it was a thinly-veiled smokescreen with no substance. It was obvious that her marriage to Guy was going to create huge media interest, and there would be some sleazy reporter out there who had her in their sights.

Yes, she decided. It was definitely best to come clean

now, before the stakes got too high. Assuming this letter was from Sally – and she thought it was genuine; the writing was faintly familiar – then they could work something out together.

She looked at the number on the top of the letter, wondering what Sally was doing, where she was. Was she sitting somewhere now, waiting for the phone to ring, anxious, excited? Was she filled with trepidation, expectation, hopeful of a long-awaited reunion with her glamorous daughter? For a moment Richenda hesitated. Wasn't this classic – people coming out of the woodwork at the first hint of success? Would her mother be so keen to get in touch if she was an assistant in Top Shop?

She couldn't think like that. Paranoia drove you mad in the end. And either way, she had to address the issue. The problem wasn't going to go away. Mick had set the pace by going to the press already. The bomb was ticking. Only by contacting her mother did she have the chance to defuse it – or at least control when it went off and how much damage it did.

She took a deep breath, picked up the handset and dialled, withholding her number just in case.

It was answered on the second ring.

'Hello?'

She would have recognized her voice anywhere. The Home Counties drop-out accent; the wariness.

'It's –'

Who was it? Rowan? Richenda? What should she say?

'It's me,' she said simply.

There was a pause, then a sigh.

'Rowan . . .'

'Yes. I got your letter.' She laughed nervously. 'Obviously.'

'Oh God.' Sally sounded totally overwhelmed. 'I've been waiting for this for so long, and now I don't know what to say.'

'Nor do I.'

'It's just so weird . . .'

There was silence for a moment as both of them floundered for what to say next.

'I . . . think we should meet.' Richenda decided she had to be businesslike. She didn't want to descend into an emotional free-for-all. And the situation was so sensitive; it needed to be dealt with face to face, not over the phone. Besides, now she'd heard Sally's voice, she wanted to see her.

'Sure. OK. Where? Whereabouts are you?'

'I'm in Knightsbridge.' Richenda realized how snotty she sounded. She hadn't meant to. But what else could she say? Just off the Cromwell Road?

'Right. Well, I'm in Uxbridge. Staying at a mate's. So I'm not that far.' There was a note of amusement in Sally's voice. 'Shall we meet somewhere in the middle?'

Geographically or socially? Richenda wondered.

'Why don't you come to me? I'll make us something to eat.'

'OK.' Sally sounded slightly unsure. 'When?'

Richenda thought for a moment. Time wasn't really on her side.

'As soon as you can, I suppose.'

'I reckon it'll take me about an hour.'

'OK . . .'

She gave Sally instructions on how to get to her apartment, then put the phone down.

This was totally surreal. In less than an hour's time she was going to come face to face with her mother again. She wondered if she'd done the right thing, having the reunion in her apartment, but she preferred to stay on home territory. She had security here – no one else could get in. And she knew there were no hidden cameras or microphones. Yet again she chastised herself for being overcautious, but then she could only trust herself to act in her own best interests.

She rushed to examine her appearance. She didn't want to look too intimidating. She wasn't going to play the big star. She changed out of her wool trousers and into a pair of jeans, adding a red polo-neck sweater, then tied her hair back in a low ponytail. She didn't have time to rush out and buy food, so she inspected the contents of her freezer. There was a packet of tortellini and a tub of arrabiata sauce. And some mango sorbet. That would do as a makeshift supper for the two of them. Sally had never been big on food, as far as Richenda could remember. And they could always order a takeaway. She took a bottle of wine out of the wine rack and stuck it in the fridge, wondering if she should have a glass before Sally arrived – she was amazed at how nervous she felt.

She tried to analyse her feelings. What was she hoping for? A happy reunion with total forgiveness on both sides? All these years later the pain of her mother's treatment of her had finally abated – when she thought about it now, it was like watching the re-run of a film in her head: a hideous incident that had happened to someone else. Did she have the strength to confront everything she had so successfully buried? They would have to talk about it; they couldn't pretend nothing had happened. Could they? Of course not, Richenda told herself. Besides, she wanted the chance to set the record straight, and convince Sally that she had never seduced Mick. Although somehow she thought her mother had known it all along. In which case she had to face the ugly truth – that Sally had chosen Mick over her own daughter. For a moment her stomach filled with the red-hot bile she had felt in those first few days after running away: a gnawing pain that seemed to eat away at her insides, fuelled by insecurity, panic, fear and the knowledge that she was very much alone . . . The pain had gone, eventually, once she had found a job, a purpose, an identity. But feeling it now, Richenda was reminded of the hell she had gone through. She told herself she was only human; coming face to face with her mother was bound to churn up bitterness and resent-ment. Did she have the strength to deal with it graciously, and remain in control of her emotions?

The buzzer went, and for a moment Richenda wished that she hadn't been so hasty, that she had slept on the contents of Sally's letter. She'd invited her into her home, back into her life, without really considering the possible consequences. It was too late now. Sally was standing on the steps downstairs, no doubt looking at the buzzer with the number five next to the bell. No name. When you were a TV star, you didn't advertise your whereabouts.

Steeling herself, she lifted the entryphone.

'Come on up,' she said, and pressed the button that released the lock.

It took thirty seconds for Sally to come up the stairs, and they felt like the longest of Richenda's life. Slowly she opened her front door, and the two of them looked into each other's eyes for the first time in ten years, mother and daughter.

Superficially, Sally hadn't changed at all. She had the same hair – long, shaggy and hennaed; the same clothes – leather jacket, short skirt, biker boots; the same make-up – black kohl, pale foundation, plum lipstick. She even smelt the same, of some earthy, exotic essential oil that came out of a tiny blue phial. But Richenda was shocked at how unkind the intervening years had been to her. Her mum had always been glamorous in a punky, rebellious way; her clothes slightly outrageous. Now she just looked horribly dated, as if she'd been stuck in a time warp. And faded. Her make-up made her look older: the foundation highlighted the wrinkles, the dark lipstick bled into the lines around her mouth.

For what seemed an eternity they surveyed each other warily. Then Richenda managed a smile.

'Hello, Mum.'

Sally blinked, looking slightly shocked, as if this was the last thing she'd expected. Then her whole expression crumpled, and she put her hands up to her face.

'Oh God,' she choked. 'I'm sorry. I'm so sorry.'

Instinctively, Richenda put an arm round her and drew her inside, shutting the door on the outside world. Sally collapsed against her, and Richenda held her, uttering soothing noises, feeling her mother's fragile frame shaking with sobs. After a few moments Sally pulled away, half laughing with embarrassment through her tears, wiping her face with the back of her hand.

'I was going to be so cool,' she laughed shakily. 'Look at you,' she went on in wonderment. 'You're so beautiful. Oh God, I'm going to cry again . . .'

'It's OK,' Richenda assured her. 'It's allowed.'

'You're not,' said Sally.

'I know,' said Richenda. 'But I might any moment.'

It was true: she did have an enormous lump in her throat. But Richenda was used to staying cool. Her acting training had enabled her to mask her feelings as well as put them on. There wasn't a person in the world who could tell what she was thinking or feeling. She was serene, implacable. A blank canvas.

Masterfully, she swallowed the lump and cleared her throat so her voice would be steady.

'Come on in. Come and sit down.'

Sally followed her out of the entrance hall and into the open-plan living area. Her eyes widened at the sight. It was pretty impressive: a huge, open space, with gleaming wooden floors, white walls, recessed lighting, a sleek, state of the art kitchen and a few carefully chosen pieces of Italian furniture. It was truly fit for a star.

'Wow. Is this all yours?'

'Yes. I hate it, really, but I needed a London base. So this is ideal. As well as being an investment.'

'Shit. It's amazing.' Sally ran her hand along the back of the white leather sofa. 'Convenient for Harrods,' she added drily.

'I never go there,' grinned Richenda. 'Do you want a cup of tea or something?'

'Actually, I could do with a drink,' admitted Sally. 'Have you got any in, or shall I nip to the offie?'

'I've got wine. But it's probably not cold enough yet.'

'I don't care.'

'I'll stick a couple of ice cubes in it.' Richenda walked over to the kitchen area, pulled the bottle out of the fridge and plucked two glasses off a shelf, then filled them with ice from the dispenser on the front of her fridge-freezer. Sally hovered awkwardly, looking round the kitchen in awe, stroking the black marble work surfaces.

'I've left him, you know,' she announced defiantly. 'It took me ten bloody years, but I finally did it.'

Richenda pulled the cork and poured the wine.

'Good.'

'I just wish I'd had the nerve to do it ten years ago. But I was scared. When you're mad about someone, you can put up with a lot.'

'I'm sure you can.' Richenda passed her mother a glass. Sally took it and gulped gratefully. Richenda saw her hands were shaking. She wondered if it was just nerves, or if her mother had a drink problem. Sally saw her looking and smiled.

'It's all right. It's not DTs. I'm just a bit of a nervous wreck. I didn't know what to expect. I thought you might have a go at me. And I wouldn't blame you if you had.'

Richenda shrugged.

'What would be the point? It was ten years ago. I've moved on.'

'Yes,' said Sally. 'You really have. I wish I could say the same.'

Her face was bleak; her voice bereft of hope. Richenda panicked; she wasn't quite ready for soul-baring. She decided to move on to a safer subject.

'So where are you living?'

'I slept on my friend's floor last night, but I can't really go back. They haven't got room for me. And I haven't got any of my stuff. I'm not bloody going back for it either. I don't want to see that bastard again.' She smiled grimly to emphasize her point. 'So I suppose I'm officially homeless.'

'Oh.' Richenda was shocked that Sally was so matter of fact. She'd forgotten all about her mother's world, how she'd always lived on the edge, with no security, and how it never seemed to phase her. Even now. She opened her mouth to say that she could stay with her, then stopped herself. She needed to be cautious. They'd got a lot to talk over, and she didn't want Sally getting too comfortable until she was certain of her motives. Her mother was quite capable of using her, she was sure. The people she mixed with had always thought the world owed them a living; they were takers, not givers, and their attitude was bound to have rubbed off.

'So,' she said briskly. 'Tell me about Mick. Who's he sold his story to?'

Sally looked stricken.

'I don't know. He wouldn't tell me. But he reckoned he was going to make a few quid out of it. He wanted me to tell my side of the story – how I was betrayed by my own daughter.'

Sally looked down at the floor, unable to meet Richenda's gaze, ashamed of the memory. Then she looked up.

'I'm ready to tell them the truth,' she announced. 'That it was me who betrayed you. That I was stupid and gullible and selfish. That I sacrificed my own daughter for a total . . .' She groped around for a suitable word. 'I don't even know what to call him. Scumbag. Arsehole.'

'Let's not even think about him,' suggested Richenda. 'Let's see how we can turn this round. The one thing we don't want to do is give him an opportunity to capitalize on the situation. If we move quickly, we can come out of this smelling of roses.'

She was surprised at her own efficiency, how she was able to take control so swiftly. But time was of the essence: although she'd had the press on her side up until now, she knew how quickly they could turn the tables if there was a juicy bit of scandal in the offing. No one was safe if there was an opportunity to boost the circulation figures.

'I think what we need to do is come clean,' she said quietly. 'If we go to the press with our story first, then whatever Mick's got up his sleeve won't have the impact.'

'How do we do that?'

'I've got someone I can call straight away. We can have a meeting first thing tomorrow. Which gives us this evening to work out exactly what we want to say. We've got to make our story watertight; make sure Mick can't get his twopence worth in.'

She looked at her mother. Sally looked bewildered, as if things were moving too fast for her. Which they probably were. Richenda decided it was best if she was out of earshot while she dealt with things.

'You look shattered. Why don't you go and have a nice hot bath while I call my contact? I can lend you some clothes. Then we can have supper; talk everything over.'

Sally's voice was shaky.

'I don't know if I deserve this . . .'

Richenda stood up.

'Let me make it quite clear. I'm doing this to save my career. Not out of loyalty to you.'

Sally winced. Richenda regretted the harshness of her words, but she was only going to get through this by keeping Sally at arm's length. Once it was all over, then she could afford to let her guard down.

'Come on,' she said briskly. 'I'll show you the bathroom.'

Ten minutes later, Sally wallowed in the water that came up to her chin, looking round in awe at the marble bathroom with its two inset sinks, the enormous shower-head the size of a car wheel. This was like some peculiar dream – and God knows she'd had a few of those in her time, courtesy of the mind-altering substances she'd shoved in her system.

She'd often had nightmares, too – dreams about babies being ripped from her arms, little girls crying for help, screaming for their mummy. She would wake up drenched in sweat, shivering with fear, guilt souring her stomach. Then she'd look at Mick sleeping beside her and try to convince herself her daughter deserved everything she got: what sort of a child seduced her own mother's lover?

Now she'd faced the truth, she wondered if it was too late to salvage anything of their relationship. The beautiful creature who had answered the door to her bore no resemblance to the mousy little girl she remembered. They had nothing in common; their worlds couldn't be farther apart. Sally had no hope of entering Richenda's territory, and Richenda wouldn't want to go back to the world she had done so well to escape. Was a mere umbilical cord strong enough to reunite them, bind them together and allow them to rebuild the love they had lost? Or had so much time passed that the cord had withered and shrivelled to nothing, become meaningless? She hoped not. She'd longed to fill the empty space she'd carried inside her for so long. At one point she'd thought about another baby, but she'd been too afraid that it might look up at her with reproachful eyes; that rather than filling the void it would be a constant reminder of the daughter she'd rejected. Where had she gone wrong, she wondered? Why had her life been so filled with regret and mistakes and disappointment and guilt? And so lacking in hope? She wasn't wicked. Just weak.

This was her one chance, decided Sally. This was an opportunity to atone, and to start again. She didn't have Mick filling her head with cynical nonsense, exerting undue influence over her. Now she was free of him, it occurred to her that was what he'd done for years: controlled her every move, her every thought. But now she was in charge of her own destiny. She could do what the hell she liked. Sally felt flooded with excitement as she looked to the future.

There was a big fluffy towelling robe on the back of

the door. Sally stepped out of the bath on to the mat, and slipped it on, then wrapped her wet hair in a towel. She looked in the mirror: a weary, malnourished, haunted face looked back at her. She was going to look dreadful in the photographs next to her radiant daughter. The optimism of a moment ago suddenly drained away. Who was she trying to kid? Richenda wasn't going to be interested in rekindling their relationship. She'd salvage what she could from the story to save her career, then send her packing. Which, after all, was no more than she deserved . . .

Richenda's head was spinning. Wearily, she wondered if she should capitulate and call in a publicist, someone who could engineer this unfortunate turn of events to her best advantage and cash in on it at the same time. But she decided not to: she really didn't want to make more of this than was necessary. A heart-warming tale of a mother and daughter's reunion and a few pictures, that was all they needed. If you got greedy and made a big deal, it encouraged the press to dig deeper for dirt. This was about damage limitation. She realized she needed a plan of action before Sally came out of the bathroom. She had to be in control. She fished about in her bag for a notebook and pen, and made a list of people to call.

Cindy Marks. There was a pleasing symmetry to her giving Cindy the story, when it had been the spread in last Saturday's *Post* that had essentially reunited her with her mother. And she thought she could trust Cindy, as much as you could trust any journalist. Plus they could tie it in with the *Post* awards this Wednesday, if they got their act together. If she got her mother together, more like. She had to do something drastic about Sally's appearance. She looked dreadful: twenty years out of date yet at the same time in clothes that were far too young for her, as if she was clinging on to some vestige of lost youth. Richenda didn't want to be cruel, but being photographed next to that wasn't going to do her image any good. She added the names of her hairdresser and her make-up artist to the list, and the owner of the little boutique where she bought a lot of her clothes. Then she flipped through the address book on her phone until she got to Cindy's mobile number.

'Cindy Marks.'

'Cindy? It's Richenda.'

'Richenda! I hope you've got a serious dress for Wednesday. Not that I'm giving anything away, of course.'

Richenda's heart began to beat faster. The stakes were creeping higher. If Cindy was hinting that she might have won an award, the spotlight really was going to be on her.

'Listen, I've got a story for you. I want you to promise me if I give it to you, you'll handle it sensitively. And I want copy approval.'

'Darling, you haven't broken up with that gorgeous man. Not already?'

Shit, thought Richenda. She hadn't even begun to decide how to break the news to Guy. Where was she going to fit that into the scheme of things? Later. First things first. She laughed smoothly.

'Of course not. We're still going strong. I'll still be wearing my ring in the photos.'

'Thank goodness for that. I'm relying on your wedding

pictures for a Christmas special. So what's the story?'

'It's about my mother.'

'She's in Australia, isn't she?'

'Um – no. She's here, in my apartment. And she's never been to Australia. I haven't seen her for nearly ten years.'

'Ah,' said Cindy. 'Have you been telling me porkies?'

'I think they call it lying by omission,' admitted Richenda. 'Give or take the odd white lie. But I'm ready to set the record straight.'

'Bloody hell,' laughed Cindy. 'Call me naive, but I genuinely thought you had no skeletons in the cupboard. And me a muckraking journalist.'

'That just goes to show you what a good actress I am,' said Richenda lightly. 'Come to my apartment at nine tomorrow. I'll give you all the gory details.'

She hung up, feeling rather drained. She'd committed herself now. There was no way out; if she reneged on the deal, she risked losing Cindy's loyalty, which at the moment was the most valuable commodity she had.

Behind her, Sally appeared in the doorway, dwarfed in a huge white robe. Richenda was surprised. With her hair wet, face devoid of make-up, she didn't look old, but incredibly young, her eyes wide with awe and uncertainty.

'You said you might have some clothes . . .' Sally looked awkward and embarrassed, and Richenda suddenly realized how uncomfortable she must feel. And how brave she must have been to come here.

She got up off the sofa.

'Of course. Jeans and a sweater OK?'

Sally nodded hesitantly. 'Um – I didn't bring anything with me at all. I came out in such a rush . . .'

She couldn't quite bring herself to ask for underwear. Luckily Richenda took the hint.

'That's OK. I've got stacks of everything.'

As she rummaged through her wardrobe, she thought how weird this was. Here she was lending clothes to the mother she hadn't seen for ten years, whose parting words had been a spiteful tirade of abuse. She pulled open the door of the walk-in wardrobe that was custom-fitted with shelves, shoe racks, rails and drawers, where everything was neatly hung or stacked the moment it came back from the laundry service. She took a white T-shirt off one pile, a pair of Earl jeans off another, and slid a black velour hoodie off a hanger. She stood for a moment with the clothes in her arms, steeling herself. They had a long evening ahead of them, and a lot of painful ground to cover. Was she ready for it? She'd imagined this eventuality so many times, usually in the early hours of the morning when she woke and couldn't sleep, yet was too tired to stop the unwelcome images creeping into her mind. She might have walked out on her mother, cut herself off from her past, totally reinvented herself and become, to all intents and purposes, an entirely new person. But the bond was still there. Even now, despite everything, she yearned for Sally's reassurance, to be told that she was loved, unconditionally and for ever. Would that happen?

Again, Richenda felt the hot lump rise in her throat. She smoothed her hand over her throat to swallow it down. Cool. Calm. Serene. She repeated the words to herself over and over until she felt composed, fixed her brightest smile on to her face and went out to her waiting mother.

*

An hour later, they sat one either side of the marble-topped breakfast bar, each with a steaming bowl of tortellini and a glass full to the brim with white wine. For the first few minutes, as they ate their meal, they kept the conversation light and trivial, skirting round the deeper issues that would inevitably be touched upon. But for the moment they needed to eat.

'So what have you been doing?'

'Working in a pub,' admitted Sally. 'Just behind the bar. But it's all right.' She made a face. 'I've screwed that up, though. I should be there now. But I can't go back, because I don't want Mick to find me . . .'

'What's he been doing?'

'Still dealing. Smalltime. Not that I see much of that – he drinks most of it.' She took a swig of wine. 'Not that it matters now. With any luck I won't see him ever again.'

Richenda picked up her glass and took a sip to give her courage.

'You know I didn't . . .' she faltered. 'I didn't . . .'

She couldn't bring herself to say it. Vocalizing what had happened would make it real. Even now she could feel his heaving, sweaty body on her, smell his sour odour, taste his rank breath. She'd never spoken of it to another human being, because that way she could pretend it had never happened. But didn't that mean Mick had won? By burying the memory, she had allowed him to get away with it. She had to speak the truth.

She looked Sally in the eye.

'Mick raped me,' she said, unable to believe, now she had made the decision, how easy those three little words were to say. Three little words that would hopefully change her life.

Sally put her fork down. She looked at her half-eaten tortellini as two big fat tears rolled down her cheeks.

'I know,' she said. 'I think I always knew. I just never wanted to admit it. It was too horrible to believe. It was much easier to tell myself it was you . . .'

Richenda slid off her stool and ran round to Sally's side. She put her arms round her neck.

'It's OK,' she said. 'It wasn't our fault. It was Mick's. He had total control over us both. But it's OK. We're going to show the bastard . . .'

17

On Monday morning, Henty had to force herself to address her household chores before disappearing into her boxroom. Travis had seen to the breakfast things and was going to drive into Eldenbury to the feed merchant's to get some supplements for the horses that he thought would enhance their performance. He was also going to call in at the supermarket to pick up a few things, like coffee, milk and jam. He was a godsend, thought Henty. If it wasn't for him she'd be tied up with household dross all morning, quite unable to hit the keyboard. Looking forward to the prospect of unleashing the torrent of words that was waiting to escape via her fingers, she hurried through the few things she had left to do. It was incredible, she thought, how much better she felt now she had a purpose.

It was only when she went downstairs with the laundry basket that it all went wrong. She was doing a jeans wash, and going through everyone's pockets, which she now did religiously, having laundered several irreplaceable and apparently vitally important bits of paper over the years – though to her mind it was other people's responsibility to check their own pockets before they put their clothes in the dirty-washing basket. She was rummaging through Charles's Levis when her hand came across something soft, bunched up in his left-hand pocket. Expecting a handkerchief, she drew out a little scrap of black ribboned silk. She held it aloft, frowning. It took her some moments to realize that what she was holding was a pair of knickers, and immediately she dropped them on to the floor with a little squeal of revulsion.

There was only one person these could belong to. Only one person who would sport such a minimal, impractical and screamingly expensive item on her nether regions. How the hell had they found their way into Charles's pocket? Panic made her phone the only person who would provide the cool, calm voice of reason that she needed.

'Honor!' she gasped. 'I need you to tell me I'm not going mad.'

'What's the matter?'

'Come for coffee and I'll show you,' said Henty dramatically.

Honor needed no second telling. Five minutes later she was pulling up to the front of Fulford Farm, to be greeted by a wild-eyed Henty, who dragged her into the scullery to inspect the evidence still lying in a scrumpled heap in the middle of the flagstone floor.

'Are you sure they're knickers?' queried Honor, not convinced.

'Yes!' said Henty. 'You tie the ribbony bits up at the side.' She pointed distastefully at the tiny triangle in the centre. 'I presume that's the gusset.'

'And they were in Charles's pocket?'

Henty burst into tears.

'They're bloody Fleur's, I know they are,' she wailed. 'We went out for supper on Saturday and the Gibsons were there. I'm sure Charles and Fleur set it up. It wasn't just a coincidence. And you should have seen them slavering over each other all evening. Honestly, it was disgusting. She practically ate him alive!'

She knew she was exaggerating, and overreacting, but she had to get how she felt off her chest.

'Calm down,' said Honor. 'It doesn't necessarily mean anything.'

'What – the fact he's got her pants in his pocket?'

'Why don't you ask him what he was doing with them?'

'I don't think I want to know the answer.' Henty was gloomy. 'Anyway, he'll only deny it.'

'How can he?'

'You know Charles. He can talk his way out of anything. He'll just say he hasn't a clue how they got there. And then I'll end up looking stupid. Suspicious and parochial.'

The two of them stared down at the incriminating garment.

'I've got an idea,' grinned Honor.

Ten minutes later, mollified by the wicked simplicity of Honor's plan, Henty made a big pot of coffee and got out a packet of chocolate digestives.

'I suppose it's his mid-life crisis thing,' she announced, dunking her biscuit in her coffee just long enough for it to become slightly soggy. 'I know he's panicking because his hair's starting to recede and he's put on a bit of weight. And he'd deny it till he's blue in the face, but I know he feels a prat about losing his licence. So I suppose having Fleur thrusting her tits in his face makes him feel better about himself. It's a bit of an ego boost.'

'I'm quite sure if she did anything about it he'd run a mile,' Honor reassured her.

'I know, but it's still humiliating, watching him drool over her.' Henty wasn't entirely convinced. 'How would he like it if I came on to Travis over the breakfast table?'

'It's no wonder Charles is behaving badly. He's obviously threatened.'

'He's got no need to worry. I wouldn't humiliate myself by throwing myself at Travis. He'd run a mile.'

'He might not, you know.' Honor hated the way Henty always put herself down. She obviously had no idea how attractive she was; she exuded warmth, voluptuousness and mischief, a pretty irresistible combination where most men were concerned. Far more attractive, in fact, than Fleur's rather contrived and clichéd attributes. But it would take more time than Honor had got to convince Henty of that.

'Anyway, enough about me. I've hardly seen you at all since you started at the big house,' Henty complained. 'How's it going?'

'It's been fantastic. The first weekend was a huge success,' said Honor. 'At least I think so. I'm due for lunch with Madeleine for a debrief.'

'Madeleine, is it?' said Henty, impressed. 'And what's Guy like? From all accounts he's an absolute dreamboat.'

'Very charming,' agreed Honor. 'And,' she added as Henty's eyes lit up, 'very devoted to his fiancée.'

'Bugger,' said Henty. 'I could see you ensconced in the big house, popping out heirs and running the village fête.'

'I'm afraid the position's already been filled,' said Honor with a grin, pulling another chocolate digestive out of the packet. It was half an hour until she had to go to the manor. Just long enough to explain to Henty the re-appearance of Johnny in her life. She was, after all, Honor's best friend, and if she was prepared to air her own dirty linen – quite literally – it was the least Honor could do to reciprocate. And she was so unsure about what path to take. She knew Henty would be sympathetic and she longed for some guidance, or at the very least some reassurance.

Honor knew the day was drawing nearer when she would have to make a decision about when to tell Ted the truth. It wasn't fair on him or Johnny to allow them to build up a relationship based on a false premise. But once Ted knew, it meant the presence of Johnny in her life was cemented, and she wasn't sure how she felt about that. She needed to establish some ground rules, a clear framework within which to operate. But until she could be sure of her feelings, that was impossible.

Sometimes she felt a surge of affection for Johnny, beguiled by his charms, and then she would remind herself that that was his speciality, casting a spell that made you blind to his faults. That was when she tried to step back and be objective, counting his many failings, chief of which was his conviction that the world revolved about him. And Honor knew that attitude did not make for good parenting. She didn't care if he let her down, messed her about, but it could be only a matter of time before he did it to Ted. And that was when the trouble would start . . .

In the meantime, it would be nice to have someone else's opinion. She opened her mouth to spill the beans when Henty leaned across the table, eyes shining.

'Can I let you into a secret?'

'Of course.'

'I can't keep it to myself any longer, but you must promise not to tell anyone. Especially Charles.'

'I won't breathe a word.'

Henty took a deep breath.

'I'm writing another book.'

'Good for you.'

'It's fallen into place all of a sudden. I've had the idea for ages but I haven't done anything about it. But now I'm ready. I want to prove that I'm not just a wishy-washy overweight housewife –'

'Nobody thinks that of you!' protested Honor.

'Want to bet? That's exactly what Fleur thinks.'

'Well, don't do it for her benefit.'

'I'm not. I'm doing it for me.'

'So what's it about?' Honor was genuinely curious. She'd read and loved *Chelsea Virgin*.

'It's sort of semi-autobiography mixed with fantasy.'

'Whose?'

Honor grinned.

'That would be telling. But I'm having quite good fun with the research.'

Richenda had never believed in miracles until today. But the transformation that had taken place in front of her very eyes was almost on a par with turning water into wine.

Cindy Marks had arrived promptly at nine o'clock, whereupon Richenda had swiftly and efficiently given her the version of events that she wished her viewing public to read. It wasn't far from the truth – there was little point in lying. But to give it a satisfying twist they focused on Richenda and Sally at long last being able to rekindle their relationship, having been kept apart by a controlling monster all of these years. A monster who had rebuffed their individual attempts to make contact with each other (this was exaggerated, but impossible for Mick to deny); a monster who had at long last been put to rest. That way any attempt at a backlash from Mick would just look like the spiteful revenge of a man whose wicked plan had been foiled.

By eleven o'clock they had concocted a masterpiece between them: a thoroughly heart-warming fable of reconciliation. Richenda was at pains to ensure that Sally was happy with the content, because the last thing she wanted was for her mother to start retracting statements and making denials. After all, it wasn't impossible that Mick might get her back into his clutches. Unlikely, but not impossible.

Cindy, meanwhile, was ecstatic. She arranged a photo-shoot for five o'clock that afternoon, and gave Richenda a substantial budget for a total make-over. By midday, a rather dazed Sally was in the chair at Richenda's favourite hairdresser in Beauchamp Place, who had strict instructions to take off at least six inches and as many years. The hairdresser put a rich chocolate brown vegetable dye over the hennaed grey, then, despite Sally's alarmed squeaks of protest, lopped off half her straggly mop. The end result was a glossy, layered shoulder-length bob with a long, sexy fringe falling over one eye.

'Steady on,' murmured Richenda *sotto voce* as she paid the hefty bill. 'I don't want her looking too good.'

They galloped up the road to the boutique where she bought her more casual clothes. The rails were stuffed with beaded cardigans, customized jeans, silk tops, luxurious sweaters and the most mouth-watering array of accessories from earrings like crystal chandeliers to dainty pearl bracelets: a veritable dressing-up box for grown-ups. Sally's eyes widened when she looked at the price tags, wondering if perhaps the nought was in the wrong place. She picked up a mohair sweater, fine as a cobweb. It was four hundred pounds.

'Jesus. I could knit that in half a day,' she whispered, scandalized.

'Ssh – don't worry about it. The *Post* are paying,' chided Richenda. 'Right – let's decide what look we want to go for. I'm thinking rock chic, rather than rock chick. I know Lulu can carry it off, but you don't want to look like Chrissie Hynde on a bad day.'

She knew she was being blunt, but the pictures were going to be vital. And the look that Sally favoured was rather harsh – black leather was unforgiving. The idea was to retain her image – Richenda didn't want to turn her mother into something she wasn't; that would be humiliating – but soften the look up to make it more flattering. And Sally seemed excited by the idea, exclaiming with delight over the clothes, eager to try on whatever Richenda suggested. In the end, they chose a dark-red silk chiffon top with wide sleeves that looked perfect over a white T-shirt and jeans, teamed with a pair of high, pointed suede boots, some strands of amber beads and an armful of bracelets.

Sally stood slightly self-consciously in the middle of

the boutique for everyone's approval. It was incredible to think that this was the same woman who had appeared on Richenda's doorstep the day before. That Sally had been faded, drawn, dated, a ghostly apparition of times past. Now she looked bohemian but glamorous. And the thing that did most to enhance her appearance was her smile; all day long she beamed with happiness and excitement.

'Right,' said Richenda, looking at her watch. 'We've got just over an hour before we need to get to Kensington. Nail bar, then make-up. Hold on to your hat!'

Outside St Joseph's, the crowd of mothers was gradually expanding as half past three came closer. Henty stood on the periphery, unnaturally quiet, trying to suppress the bubble of mischief inside her. Every time she thought about what she was going to do, she wanted to laugh. But she needed a deadpan expression if she was going to pull it off. Not that it was really that funny, when you thought about it. Charles's behaviour was disgraceful, but he was a weak, vain and silly middle-aged man insecure about being the wrong side of forty. Fleur, meanwhile, was a traitor to the female of the species. They both needed teaching a lesson, before things got out of hand. Henty could just about handle the situation as it stood at the moment, but she knew if it got any more serious she'd be devastated. Which was why Honor's idea was so perfect – it would bring them to their senses, and make them realize how ridiculous their behaviour was.

Honor was by the gate. Henty didn't dare catch her eye

or she knew she would collapse, so she stuffed her hands deep into her Barbour pockets and kept her head down. Out of the corner of her eye, she saw Fleur arrive at the gate, her hair immaculate, her expression supercilious. She gave her a smile, and strolled over to her.

'Hi. Great evening on Saturday. I really enjoyed it.'

'Yes. Me too.' Fleur was cautious, aware that people were listening, curious as to what they might have been up to. 'I love the Honeycote Arms.'

'By the way, I think you might have dropped these while you were there.'

Henty held the knickers aloft by one of the ribbons. A dozen pairs of eyes widened as they realized what they were.

'They certainly aren't mine. They wouldn't fit me,' continued Henty sweetly.

Fleur turned white, and then bright red.

'I don't know what you mean. They're not mine either.'

'Well, they must be Charles's then. I found them in his pocket. I never knew he was into women's underwear.'

The pants dangled in mid air between the two women. Eventually Henty tossed them into the wastepaper bin outside the school gates that usually held drinks cartons and sweet wrappers.

'Pity. They must have cost a fortune.'

The rest of the mothers turned away, smiling and exchanging scandalized glances. Fleur turned on her heel, her jaw set, her lips tight, clearly furious but unable to admit it.

Honor sidled up to Henty.

'If that doesn't warn her off, nothing will,' she

murmured. 'There's nothing like a bit of public humiliation to put the likes of Fleur in her place.'

The reunion photoshoot took place in a smart little townhouse hotel in Kensington – neutral territory where everyone could relax. They ordered proper tea, with tiny triangle sandwiches filled with cucumber and egg, and scones, and cakes oozing cream, all served on delicate bone china. Cindy ordered champagne as well, to give it a sense of occasion.

Richenda and Sally sank back into the comfort of the hotel's sofa, smiling and laughing for the cameras. And it wasn't put on – they each felt a genuine sense of elation at being together, combined with a sense of glee that they had triumphed over Mick. Cindy was quite delighted. It was so refreshing to do a positive story once in a while. She did occasionally weary of muckraking, but as a tabloid journalist it went with the territory. There was just one more question she had to ask. She came and sat on the arm of the sofa, then leaned down and picked a tiny chocolate éclair off the cake stand.

'By the way,' she said casually. 'How does Guy feel about all of this?'

There was a pause. Richenda smiled.

'He's absolutely delighted, of course. We've arranged a reunion for the weekend. In the country. He wanted us to have a few days alone together to get to know each other again.'

It was almost like reciting a script; as if she'd been up all night rehearsing her lines. Cindy would have no idea that she hadn't mentioned a thing about her mother's reappearance to Guy. Not that she was hiding it from him, exactly, but the time had to be right. After all, she'd been lying to him as well as the rest of the nation.

Unfortunately, Honor and Henty had severely misjudged their opponent. By showing Fleur up in front of the other mothers, Henty had merely thrown down the gauntlet. Fleur was determined that this was now war. She'd prove to that frumpy little dollop who had the upper hand. She arrived back home, put out milk and biscuits for her two children, then draped herself over the sofa in the living room while she made a phone call, admiring her reflection in the glass of the enormous plasma-screen television, stroking her flat stomach and running her hand over the generous curves of her breasts.

'Charles . . .' she purred. 'It was gorgeous to see you at the weekend. We need to meet.'

'Of course.' Charles sounded a tiny bit nervous. After Fleur's performance on Saturday, he felt uncertain about what he'd begun. Not that he wasn't incredibly flattered, but she was a bit scary.

'What about this pilot?' she continued smoothly. 'I was thinking Wednesday. It's a quiet day for me at the shop. I can leave my assistant in charge. If you came here then we could get the cameras rolling.'

Charles hesitated. A week ago he would have agreed with alacrity, but he was getting cold feet. While he still thought the pilot was a great idea, he was a little wary of Fleur's motives. There was something slightly unhinged about her, something –

'You're not getting cold feet, are you?' she enquired.

'I'm sure I could take the idea to someone else.'

Charles opened his mouth to protest that it wasn't her idea to take elsewhere, but knew that if she did there was bugger all he could do about it. Terrified that she might, and that he would miss out, he hastily reassured her.

'No, no. I'm just checking my diary. Seeing if I can rejig.'

Charles flipped through his diary. He had one appointment on Wednesday morning – a fresh-faced graduate who was convinced she was the next big thing, who'd described her work as magical reality meets chick-lit. Charles knew she was unlikely to have any talent whatsoever, but there were worse ways of spending time than imparting your wisdom to suggestible young girls hungry for fame. However, Fleur was a better prospect, so he put a line through the appointment and declared himself free.

'I'll email you a rough script,' he said crisply, trying to sound businesslike. 'You don't need to follow it to the letter, but it'll give you something to bounce off.'

Fleur smiled to herself. If she had her way, they'd be bouncing off the walls, the ceilings, the floor . . .

'Fantastic. What do you think I should wear?'

'Um . . .' Charles swallowed hard as a number of possibilities ran through his mind, none of them suitable. 'Something practical but pretty?'

Fleur snorted in disdain.

'How deeply dull. I was thinking thoroughly impractical but sexy.'

There was a teasing note in her voice. Charles laughed lightly, realizing he sounded as if he was taking the whole thing too seriously.

'Maybe you're right. I'll leave it up to you. We can always

have a costume change if it doesn't look right on camera.'

'And you'll bring all your equipment?'

Again her voice was syrupy with suggestion. Charles tried to inject a little of it into his response, hoping he didn't sound too like Leslie Phillips.

'Oh yes. Don't worry about any of that. All you need is your secateurs.'

'Perfect. Shall we say ten o'clock?'

'Ten it is.'

Charles put the phone down with a shaking hand. The innuendo had oozed back and forth down the line between them – he felt the blood pounding in his head, his veins tingling. He picked up the phone again to rearrange his appointment for Wednesday, wondering if he was completely and utterly insane. There was no doubt that Fleur was a bit of a loose cannon. She had to be, to drop her knickers in his lap like that on Saturday –

Shit! Her knickers! What had he done with Fleur's knickers? He'd been pretty drunk by the time he got back on Saturday – he'd meant to secrete them somewhere safe. But had he? He couldn't remember now. They must still be in his jeans. Over the back of the chair in the bedroom. He hoped against hope that Henty hadn't washed them. He was always having a go at her about remembering to check his pockets. How ironic it would be if this was the one time she did remember . . .

He couldn't phone her and tell her not to touch his trousers. That would be asking for trouble. He'd just have to pray that they hadn't made their way into the laundry basket.

*

Sally really couldn't believe what was happening. Mick was going to go ballistic when he saw this in the paper. Totally ballistic. And serve him right. She helped herself to another glass of champagne. She shouldn't drink too much, because she didn't want to make a fool of herself. She didn't want to let Richenda down. Besides, her head was already starting to throb from the unaccustomed bubbles. And the stress – believe it or not, it was very stressful being made up, pampered and photographed. She wouldn't want to do this every day.

Sally leaned back on the sofa and shut her eyes. She was trying to drown out the persistent question that kept popping into her head: what the hell was going to happen to her when all this was over? She might have been fêted and fussed over today, but Richenda wasn't going to want her hanging around. She had nothing to offer, after all. What use was a raddled, addled, out-of-work barmaid to an international superstar?

When Charles got back home, Henty was in the kitchen, straddling a chair, while Travis manhandled her from behind.

'You've got to relax here,' he was saying, motioning down her spine with his tanned and capable hands. 'And you don't want any tension here.' He grasped her hips firmly, then smiled as he saw Charles come into the room. 'Hi. I'm just convincing your wife she should learn how to ride.'

'Oh.'

Charles noticed Travis wasn't in any hurry to take his hands off Henty's ample curves. And that Henty seemed quite happy.

'I've told him I'm terrified of horses,' she declared, her eyes wide.

'You just need a good teacher.'

Travis finally released his grip, and Henty clambered off her imaginary steed.

'You'd need to sedate me, I'm afraid.'

'You don't know what you're missing.'

'I'll just have to imagine it then, won't I? I've got a very good imagination.'

She walked over to Charles and gave him a kiss on the cheek.

'Hello, darling. Good day?'

'So so.'

Charles kissed her back warily. He couldn't tell from her reaction whether he had any reason to panic. She wasn't behaving like a woman who'd found another woman's pants in her husband's pocket – but then presumably she wouldn't give anything away in front of Travis.

'I think I'll just go and change.'

'OK. Supper's ready in ten minutes.'

'Lovely.'

He escaped from the room, ran up the stairs, threw open the bedroom door and looked at the chair where he usually slung his clothes.

No matter which way he looked at it, it was empty.

18

Fleur's knickers hung suspended in the air between Henty and Charles for the next couple of days. Neither of them mentioned a thing. Henty because she was quite happy that she had marked her territory, and besides, she had other, more important business utilizing her brain power. If she behaved a little distantly, it wasn't because she was worried about the predatory Mrs Gibson. On the contrary, the incident had spurred her on. The moment the house was empty she hit the keyboard, metaphors and similes flying from her fingers.

Charles, meanwhile, mithered himself almost stupid all of Monday night and most of Tuesday wondering where on earth the offending garment could have got to. In the end he decided that they had come apart from his jeans in the wash, and that Henty had assumed they belonged to either Thea or Lily and put them in the appropriate drawer. If she didn't actually recognize them it was nothing unusual: their friends were always leaving half their stuff behind when they stayed the night, and the girls were constantly borrowing clothes – their wardrobes were thirty per cent other people's. He didn't quite have the nerve to go rifling through their drawers to put his mind at rest, but by Wednesday morning he had decided that if there was going to be a scene, it would have happened by now. Thus he was able to set off for Fleur's house with impunity. He let Travis drop him at the station as usual, then called a taxi to take him to the Gibsons' house, set in a little hamlet down a leafy lane between Eldenbury and Eversleigh.

He sighed with envy as the house came into view. It was chocolate-box Cotswolds and absolutely pristine – there wasn't a hedge or a leaf or a chipping out of place. They must have legions of underlings keeping on top of it, thought Charles, alighting from his cab. He admired the immaculately creosoted gates as they swung open, the shining wrought-iron letter box, the crunch of the thick gravel as he strode up to the front door. The first thing he would do when he pulled off his next big deal, he decided, would be to get a landscape gardener in for Fulford Farm, which was shambolic in comparison to this. They had a chap to help with the lawns and hedges, but apart from that, it rather ran to seed.

Charles lugged his recording equipment up to the front door and rang the bell.

Fleur answered the door wearing an off-the-shoulder dress with gathered sleeves and ruffles galore, splashed with brightly coloured flowers. She was obviously going for the peasant look, decided Charles, though it had undoubtedly cost more than any peasant earned in a year, and the strappy pink sandals that went with it would have been useless for toiling in the fields.

'Charles.' She gave him a hundred-watt smile, showing perfect white teeth, and ushered him inside. 'Come through into the conservatory – I've set everything up in there. You can tell me what you think.'

She whisked him through the hallway, and Charles

followed at a gentle trot to keep up as she disappeared down a long passage, rather alarmed at the brisk pace she set.

She threw open a pair of double doors.

'Here we are.'

The word conservatory didn't quite do the room justice. Charles recognized the handiwork of a well-known local architect in the spectacular floor-to-ceiling glass room she led him into. It was simply, almost sparsely furnished in cream and gold, giving it a washed-out, dream-like effect, with pale flagstones, wicker chairs covered in bleached linen cushions, muslin drapes tied up in thick knots and an impressively large Moroccan-style chandelier. The only real colour was provided by huge distressed terracotta pots stuffed with lush, exotic greenery. In the centre was an antique butcher's block, the wood scrubbed and gleaming, on which Fleur had laid out the tools of her trade – buckets and vases and scissors and oasis, as well as several bunches of flowers and assorted greenery.

'I thought we could shoot it here, with the garden as a backdrop. What do you think?'

'Perfect,' agreed Charles. 'I just need to check the light and so on.'

He started taking the camcorder out of its case. He found himself fumbling. Somehow Fleur being so crisp and businesslike, with no hint of flirtation, was making him even more nervous. He told himself to pull himself together.

'Right,' he announced briskly. 'I'm going to need power.'

Fleur pointed at the floor, where the sockets were covered up with neat little brass covers.

'Perfect. Now if you want to get behind your work-station . . .'

Fleur slid a dark-green florist's apron over her head, tied it round her waist and took up her position with a rather unnatural, fixed smile that made Charles's heart sink. This was going to be a total waste of time. An utter fiasco. What on earth had made him think she might have even a modicum of talent? Sighing inwardly, he realized he'd have been better off lunching his ingénue writer, who would no doubt have hung off his every word and been thoroughly grateful for his time.

Henty leaned back in her Lloyd Loom chair and stretched luxuriously, then circled her head to release the tension in her neck. She'd been typing solidly since Charles and Travis had left for the station that morning, and only the rumbling of her stomach had roused her from the dream-world she was creating. She looked at her watch and was amazed to see it was midday – not quite lunchtime, but she hadn't even stopped for elevenses. She decided to break for a pot of coffee and a sandwich, then press on until it was time to pick up the children. Conscientiously she clicked on the 'save' icon. She still didn't entirely trust her new silver machine not to swallow up everything she'd done and refuse to relinquish it. It always amazed her to find her work still there, exactly as she'd written it, every time she turned it on.

In the kitchen she found Travis sawing inexpertly at a bloomer on the kitchen table with decidedly unclean hands.

'Are you making enough mess?' she teased.

'Where I come from the bread comes in slices,' he complained, handing her the knife. 'You do it.'

Henty carved off several neat doorsteps and spread them with butter.

'What do you want on it?'

'Peanut butter?'

Henty wrinkled her nose in distaste and found peanut butter for him and lavender honey for her. The two of them sat at the table, munching contentedly. Travis looked at her curiously.

'What are you doing locked away up there in that room, anyway?'

'Writing a book.'

'You should have regular breaks, you know,' he chided. 'You'll get repetitive strain injury.'

'Will I?'

'My mum did. She types up stuff for the professors at the uni in Cape Town. She was in agony.'

'I don't think I've been at it long enough to get RSI. I only started it last week. When you arrived.'

'Well, you should make sure you keep altering the height of your chair. And get outside for some fresh air every couple of hours.'

Henty gave him a mock salute of obedience.

'OK, sir.'

Secretly, she felt rather pleased that someone was actually bothered about her wellbeing. She spent so much time fussing and clucking over everyone else, it was strange to be on the receiving end. But not unpleasant.

'So what's it about, this book? Can I read it?' Travis was asking.

'It wouldn't be your sort of thing. It's a novel for middle-aged housewives like me.'

'Am I in it?'

He gave her a cheeky grin. Henty tutted.

'No,' she lied.

'Well, I should be.' He slathered another piece of bread with a thick layer of peanut butter. 'I know exactly what middle-aged housewives like.'

Henty choked on a stray crumb.

'Do you?'

'Oh, yes. Back home was crawling with yummy mummies. My mates and I had to beat them off with a stick.'

Henty looked at him, slightly appalled but curious.

'That's awful.'

'Nah – it's just the way it was. They were bored and rich, looking for their next thrill.' His eyes were twinkling with mischief. 'We quite liked it too.'

Henty was scandalized.

'That's totally immoral.'

'Don't worry – we were all over the age of consent. And it was a fantastic education. That's the great thing about mature women. They show you exactly what they want.'

Henty's eyebrows nearly shot through the roof.

'I'm not sure that this conversation is appropriate,' she said, hating herself for sounding so prim.

Travis looked anxious that she was getting the wrong end of the stick.

'Hey, listen, don't worry – I'd never make a pass at you or anything.'

Henty couldn't help feeling a tiny bit piqued at his

matter-of-fact tone, as if it was an utterly ridiculous eventuality.

'Good.'

'Don't get me wrong. It's not because I don't fancy you. But because I like you too much. And I like it here. And I'm always falling in love – if I fell in love with you, it would be a disaster.'

'Well, it's not going to happen, so we don't need to worry, do we?' Henty stood up briskly.

'No – but if you want any gory details, I've got a pretty good idea what your age group likes . . .'

Henty stared at him, tipping back in his chair, chomping on his bread. He was still skinny with youth; everything he ate was instantly burned up, but his shoulders, his biceps and his thighs were bulking out from the physical work he undertook every day. For a moment her mind wandered, imagining his hard, boyish limbs entwined with softer, more yielding curves, and she felt a twitch of excitement.

'For example?' she ventured, unable to contain her curiosity any longer.

Charles's suspicion that the morning's work would be something of a travesty was not unfounded. Fleur was wooden and forced, and she couldn't talk and arrange flowers at the same time. She kept dropping her secateurs and fluffing her lines. And when she wasn't fluffing, she was hamming it up with exaggerated facial expressions and innuendo. He wasn't even going to look at what they'd recorded, let alone try and edit it. It was totally cringeworthy. By two o'clock he was squirming inwardly with embarrassment and panic. How the hell had he got into this situation, and how was he going to get out of it? He'd promised her fame and fortune – or at least that's what she seemed to understand. And he'd totally compromised himself by coming here furtively. Why hadn't he been open and honest with Henty: told her up front that he was shooting a pilot with Fleur?

Because she'd suspect that he was trying to get something else out of it, that's why. And he had to admit that he had enjoyed the game so far, playing the Svengali, lapping up Fleur's attention, telling himself he could have her if he wanted her . . .

And now here he was, with Fleur convinced she was hovering on the brink of stardom. How was he going to persuade her otherwise? People like Fleur didn't take kindly to rejection or criticism.

'So,' she said as he put away his camcorder. 'What do you think?'

Charles took a deep breath. He might as well get it out of the way now. Nip it in the bud.

'I'll have to have a proper look when I get back,' he said carefully. 'But I think . . .'

The look on her face was so full of expectation. He swallowed. Be cruel to be kind, he thought. There's no point in stringing her along. It's not fair.

'I think there's a lot of promise,' he finished lamely. *For God's sake, man. Put the knife in. You're not supposed to be giving her hope.* 'But if I do a good editing job, and we get some decent music and graphics . . .'

Fleur flushed with delight.

'You really think we're in with a chance?'

'Um –' Had he actually said that?

'I thought you were going to say it was awful! I thought I was really wooden . . . I certainly felt it. But didn't it come across?'

Charles's mouth hung open for a moment. She'd given him an open invitation to say what he really thought.

'Well, obviously it's your first go, so there's room for polish . . .'

'But you think it was OK?'

'Well, obviously, it's not down to what I think.'

'No. But you think it was good enough to put forward?'

'Yes, yes. Absolutely. No question.'

You fucking twat, thought Charles desperately, as a beaming Fleur pulled another bucket from under the table. It was filled with ice, and on it was perched a bottle of champagne.

'Well, I think this calls for a celebration, don't you?'

Charles nodded. He wasn't sure about a celebration, but he could certainly do with a drink.

Guy had forgotten how completely frustrating London was when you were in a hurry. He usually wasn't – he only came up to town when he wanted a new suit, or to have lunch with a friend or see an exhibition, so time was generally on his side and he could enjoy the metropolis, feel charged by the energy that buzzed through the streets and fantasize for a moment about city living. He'd flirted with the idea once or twice – there were people who'd wanted him to go in with them on business ideas, and he'd nearly convinced himself that London was for him.

But today, when he was late, he thanked God he hadn't

succumbed. He'd queued for fifteen minutes for a cab at Paddington, and now it was crawling through the traffic – every time the driver dived down a side street to take a short cut he came across a delivery lorry blocking the route, or roadworks. Several times Guy was tempted to jump out of the taxi and walk, but then they would be on the move again. It was no good for his heart, he decided, as he watched the long hand speed round his Tag.

It was lucky he'd made the train at all. It was only this morning that it occurred to him to check out his dinner jacket, which he found hastily flung on to a hanger in his wardrobe where he'd stuffed it unceremoniously after the charity ball the other week. His mother had been horrified by its crumpled appearance.

'You can't be seen in public like that. I'll take it to my cleaners – they do an emergency service.'

His dress shirt was unlaundered too, but the saintly Marilyn put it on a quick wash, tumble-dried it and ironed it beautifully in just over an hour. He managed to polish his shoes himself, and hunt down his bow tie, which was under the bed.

'Honestly, Guy,' tutted Madeleine. 'You're worse than your father.'

'I can't think of anything more boring than being the sort of man who sends his suit straight to the dry-cleaners the morning after a ball. Where's the adrenalin rush in that?' Guy retorted, scooping up a pair of wafer-thin gold cufflinks from his dressing table and shoving them in his pocket. 'Anyway, isn't that what a wife is for? I'll have one of those soon.'

He accompanied his deliberately sexist comment with a cheeky grin. Madeleine raised an eyebrow.

'I hardly think Richenda's going to have time to tend to your laundry, what with shooting schedules and award ceremonies,' she remarked.

Guy didn't reply. He wasn't going to give his mother the benefit of seeing her slurs sting. Madeleine did, after all, belong to another age, when women didn't really have careers and put their husbands and children first. Guy knew better than to expect that in the twenty-first century. Theirs would be the most modern of marriages, not least because her earning power would dwarf his. But that didn't mean they couldn't find a way of being happy.

He was looking forward to talking all this through with Richenda. He realized that tonight was the first time they would be together away from Eversleigh; the first time he had been to her flat. They could spend the next twenty-four hours pleasing themselves – Guy had wangled himself the day off, confident that his mother and Honor could hold the fort, and he was determined to spoil Richenda. He'd spoken to her a couple of times on the phone since she'd flown the coop on Sunday, and she'd seemed extraordinarily distracted. He wanted to reassure her that everything was going to be all right.

At last he could see Harrods up ahead of him. Richenda's apartment was only round the corner. He debated jumping out and buying her some flowers, but decided against it. Besides, if she won an award tonight she would be inundated with blooms far more elaborate than anything he could afford.

She came to the door in a silk dressing gown, a towelling

turban round her wet hair, ready for the attentions of her minions. Guy noticed she looked rather pale and subdued as he gave her a kiss.

'Darling – there's no need to be nervous. If you don't win, you don't win.'

'It's not that.' Richenda drew him inside and looked at him with large, troubled eyes. 'I've got something to tell you.'

It was amazing, thought Charles, just how quickly two people could demolish a bottle of champagne and find themselves halfway through a second. By which time it was far too late to put a sensible head on. He'd protested mildly at half three when Fleur had produced another bottle, wondering if she had to go and collect the children. But they were, apparently, going to friends for tea.

'Don't worry, I've blocked off the whole day. They won't be back till seven – Robert's picking them up on his way home. So we've got hours yet.'

A little voice told Charles that he should call a cab now. But he'd just slid into that delicious state that only champagne can bring, the bubble-fuelled sense of total relaxation combined with the hint of sexual promise. Now she'd taken off her apron, Fleur's breasts were spilling precariously over the tightly ruched neckline of her peasant dress.

As she leaned over and topped up his glass, she smiled at him provocatively.

'After all, we've worked hard all day. I think we deserve a little reward, don't you?'

*

Initially, Guy made light of Richenda's revelation. She'd looked so full of dread when she answered the door that he thought her news was going to be of some life-threatening illness or financial ruin. So hearing that the mother he'd thought was in Australia was actually up the road in the Capital Hotel was something of a relief. But as further details came out, his face darkened.

'What I really don't understand is why you didn't tell me any of this before?'

She was nervous. He could see that by the way she was rolling the silk sash of her dressing gown between her fingers.

'There . . . never seemed to be a right time. Things have happened so fast between us. You . . . swept me away. I didn't have time to stop and think.'

'We've been engaged for over a fortnight.' Guy's voice was icy. 'Presumably you were going to mention it before the actual wedding?'

'Yes . . .' Her reply was a little too slow to be convincing.

'Or were you going to wait till we were on our way to Heathrow? For our trip to Australia? To see your imaginary family?' His tone dripped bitterness and sarcasm.

'Stop it! Of course I was going to tell you.'

'When?'

'I don't know. To be honest, I didn't think it was that important.'

'Important? Of course your past's important. And don't tell me you never had an opportunity to set the record straight. Am I that unapproachable? Don't you trust me?'

'You don't understand, do you?'

'Frankly, no.'

Richenda jumped off the arm of the sofa where she had been perched.

'It's all right for you, brought up in the manor house. With your gracious mother, and your father everyone thought the world of –'

'Hang on a moment. Dad wasn't perfect. And I'm sure my mother's not either. Nobody is. And some of my ancestors behaved like absolute fiends.'

'It's not quite the same, is it? It's not seedy and squalid. You weren't brought up by a load of drunken drop-outs in a disgusting squat. If I didn't tell you about them, it's because I wanted to put it all behind me. Do you begrudge me that? Or do you want me to be reminded of just how awful it all was? All I wanted to do was forget!'

Her voice trailed off in a desolate wail. Guy looked thoughtful.

'Well, maybe that's what we should do. Forget the whole thing.'

'What?' Richenda looked dumbfounded. This wasn't the reaction she was expecting.

'Why not? You obviously can't think much of me. Marriage is about trust and respect and having a bloody sense of honour. I wouldn't have thought any less of you because of your upbringing. I'm not that judgemental.' He paced up and down the apartment, furious, while Richenda looked on helplessly. 'And now I don't know what to think. I mean, what else haven't you told me about? My imagination's doing overtime here –'

'Stop it! I'm still the same person. Nothing's changed

except . . . a load of stuff that happened years ago that wasn't my fault. And that I wanted to forget. Is there anything wrong with that?'

'Yes. I don't appreciate being lied to.'

Guy knew he was being harsh, but Richenda had to understand how strongly he felt. If she couldn't understand that, then there was no hope for the two of them. He looked at her. She was standing with her fingers pressed to her temples, as if she was trying to clear her head of all the accusations that had been flung at her. Finally she looked up, white with distress.

'I'm sorry,' she whispered. 'I can't say any more than that. I'm really sorry. But if you must know, I was ashamed. And I thought once you knew the truth, you might break off the engagement. That I wouldn't be good enough for you.'

Guy looked at her in astonishment.

'What on earth was there to be ashamed of? You can't help your background any more than I can help mine. It's an accident of birth. And I don't take kindly to being thought of as that shallow.'

'Please don't shout.'

He hadn't actually realized he was, but Richenda was shrinking back from him almost in fear. Appalled by the anger the incident had provoked in him, he took a deep breath and gathered himself together.

'Look, you've got a big night ahead of you. I don't want to spoil it. We can talk about it later.'

'I don't want you to come to the ceremony if you're still angry. I couldn't bear it.'

There were tears shimmering on the end of her lashes.

Shit, thought Guy. He didn't want to be responsible for her turning up all red-eyed and blotchy.

'I'm not angry, OK? I'm just a bit . . . shocked. I haven't had time to take it in. I'll be fine.' He managed a glimmer of a reassuring smile that he didn't mean. 'Can I use the shower?'

She nodded, her bottom lip trembling, then bursting into tears she threw her arms round his neck.

'I love you so much. I'm sorry . . .'

He patted her awkwardly on the back as she sobbed against his chest.

'OK. It's OK. You're forgiven, all right? Now dry your tears – you don't want to look all piggy for the cameras.'

She gave a shaky little laugh as he pulled a handkerchief from his pocket and began to wipe her eyes, just as the buzzer went. Richenda slid away from him.

'That'll be my hairdresser.'

Guy watched in amazement as she swiftly composed herself, injecting a smile into her voice as she answered the entryphone.

'Hello, Michelle. Come on up.'

Pretty rapid recovery, he thought wryly to himself as he made his way into the bathroom.

'I can't do this,' Charles was protesting weakly. 'I've never cheated on Henty.'

Fleur had kissed him. Just to say thank you, she'd said, and it would have been churlish to refuse. Not to mention impossible. It had been quite a delicious experience. Kissing was so intimate, so tantalizing – one could inject so much passion and promise into a kiss without actually

339

incriminating oneself. It was a pastiche of the love act itself – possibly even more enjoyable. Sex could, after all, be something of a disappointment by the time your mind and body had worked themselves up into a frenzy of anticipation. With a mere kiss, you could always imagine that it would have been perfect.

But Fleur didn't seem inclined to stop there. One minute they were snogging on the sofa, the next she'd managed to wriggle herself out of her dress – she seemed to specialize in clothes that were easy to get out of. She stood in front of him in a strapless bra and another scrap of lace masquerading as knickers.

'Seriously,' said Charles, a wobble in his voice. 'I think we should leave it at that.'

Fleur ignored him and unfastened her bra, revealing the breasts he'd been slavering over since the day he'd met her. They were incredible, even more magnificent than he'd imagined: perfectly round, plump but firm, with dainty coral-tipped nipples placed exactly in the centre, they seemed to defy gravity. They truly were a master-piece. Charles wasn't naive enough to believe they were real, but who cared? Real meant floppy, saggy, wrinkled. These were like ripening peaches ready to be plucked from the tree: sweet, delicious, soft-skinned, irresistible.

She knelt in front of him and unzipped his trousers, then carefully extricated his penis over the waistband of his Hom briefs. The delicate touch of her fingers caused it to swell in front of their eyes, unfurling itself slowly and deliberately until it stood upright in all its magnifi-cence. Looking down in awe, Charles felt relief and a hint of pride, then watched in amazement, hardly daring to breathe, as Fleur wrapped each breast either side of his cock until it was nestling in the deliciously warm, soft cradle of her cleavage.

'It's OK,' she whispered. 'This doesn't count. Officially you haven't been unfaithful.'

Charles wasn't entirely convinced. Wanking yourself off between a woman's tits was about as intimate as it got. Suddenly he imagined Henty's dear, sweet, shocked expression: what if she could see him now?

'I can't do this!' he insisted, pulling away.

'Oops!' said Fleur. 'Too late . . .'

In a steaming hot shower, Guy had a chance to wash off the grime from his journey and go over what had happened. He thought he had every right to be angry. Bloody furious, in fact.

The whole thing unsettled him. Not so much her murky past – he'd said himself she couldn't help that – but her lies. And the fact she'd obviously only come clean to him because she'd been found out. And he hadn't liked the way she'd dealt with it subsequently; her behaviour had turned his stomach slightly. He wondered about the tears. Were they real, or just for effect? In fact, he felt wary about her whole performance. She'd made him feel unreasonable, almost a monster, then wheedled forgiveness, albeit reluctant, out of him. Was this going to be a pattern in their marriage? Her using subtle emotional blackmail on him to get what she wanted, with her wily, actressy ways?

Pumping a generous handful of her shampoo into his hand, Guy scolded himself for being too hard. It was

pretty normal female behaviour, he supposed, to manipulate men. They started young by working on their daddies:
he remembered seeing his own sisters at work on his
father, and being amazed at what they could con out of
him – and even more amazed that he didn't see through
them. Now he realized that of course he *had* seen through
them – it was just so much easier to give in. Guy had
capitulated as his father had before him. He hadn't had
the strength or the energy to withstand Richenda, and
she had won.

In the past, he'd never gone for the manipulative type.
His preference was for straightforward girls with a bit of
spirit. No nonsense. Richenda had been something of a
departure in that she was an unknown entity, but he had
been entranced. Bewitched and intrigued. Besotted, even.
He'd fallen for her head over heels, but perhaps he'd been
mistaken to let things move along so quickly.

All in all, he felt rather foolish, especially when he
considered all his resolutions on the journey up – his
determination to make up for his neglect over the past
few days, even though that had been out of his control.
And she had repaid his goodwill by betraying him. Not
that he thought she'd deliberately set out to con him. But
he did feel aggrieved that she obviously didn't feel she
could trust him. And he still had a sneaking suspicion
that if she could have kept her secret for a little longer,
if not for ever, then she would have. That really wasn't
great grounds for a marriage.

Sighing, Guy picked up a bar of soap. Maybe he
shouldn't judge her too harshly. He'd known all along that
they needed to get to know each other better. He had to

give her the benefit of the doubt. And he certainly wasn't going to spoil her evening. He was too much of a gentleman to do that.

Charles sat bolt upright in the back of the taxi feeling thoroughly sick. He wasn't sure whether it was the surfeit of champagne, the smell of Fleur's scent that his own skin seemed to have absorbed as if by osmosis, or the thought of what he had allowed her to do to him and what that meant. Shit! He had been so perfectly in control of their relationship. He had only meant it as a minor diversion – a little flirtation to boost his ego.

He'd been feeling rather depressed lately, as if he'd reached a point in his life where that was it – no more excitement, no more achievements. The heady rushes that went with love and success belonged to the next generation; it was his turn to bow out gracefully. Charles certainly hadn't felt ready for slippers and gardening and Radio Four. He was only forty-one. Fleur had made him feel young and attractive and successful again. Giving her the prospect of fame had turned him on, even though he knew it had been a long shot. But he'd decided to play on it in the meantime: it gave him the chance for a few clandestine encounters that had given him the frisson he yearned for, even though he'd had no intention of letting it go anywhere.

Now it had gone way too far and he was panicking. He must have been mad! He didn't trust Fleur one little bit. She was, he knew instinctively, the type to cause trouble if she felt like it. And what made him feel even sicker was the fact that she had known exactly what she was doing all along. He'd played right into her hands. Or rather, her breasts. Basically, he'd jeopardized his marriage for thirty seconds of semi-pornographic self-gratification, and now he was panicking.

The incident only served to remind him just how much he loved Henty. Of course he did. It was just that the magic had gone out of their marriage. The spontaneity. The romance. Which wasn't surprising with four demanding children. He remembered why he had fallen in love with her in the first place. Her guilelessness, her naivety, her humour, her gung-ho attitude to life. Of course four children and nearly fifteen years hadn't been kind to her, but Henty wasn't the type to freak over it. Not for her the facial peels and brow-smoothing injections that Fleur obviously relied upon. But so what if she looked a little plump, a little worn round the edges; if her sloppy sweatshirts and down-at-heel loafers weren't cutting edge? Henty, his lovable squidgy Henty, was real. And he'd neglected her, kicked her to one side. He was a vain, self-centred monster. What right did he have to think the world owed him an endless injection of self-indulgence and thrills? Which, if this afternoon's encounter was anything to go by, made you feel hollow and empty.

For a moment, he compared the two women.

Fleur: artificial, grasping, manipulative . . . that just about summed her up.

Henty: loving, giving, patient, kind, tolerant, happy-go-lucky, undemanding . . . the list went ever on.

As the taxi slewed heavily round a corner, Charles groaned. It was all very well him realizing he should appreciate what he'd got. It might just be too late.

344

The driver was looking at him in alarm.

'You're not going to chuck, are you, mate? Only, if you are, you can get out here.'

Guy sat on the sofa dressed and ready, sipping from a bottle of St Miguel he'd taken out of the fridge, wondering what on earth all those people were doing. He estimated that it had taken him approximately fifteen minutes to get ready. Richenda had been ensconced in her room for over an hour and a half with no less than three minions.

Finally she emerged. And he had to admit that now he could see what had taken the time. She looked absolutely breathtaking. Her dress was very simple, cut on the bias in pale grey-green silk chiffon shot through with silver, so that it shimmered like a moonbeam. Her skin reflected the milky glow of the three-strand pearl choker round her throat; her hair was smoothed back into a knot tied loosely at the nape of her neck, with just a couple of strands falling free. She looked like an ethereal apparition that had sprung from some legend – a mermaid princess.

'You look beautiful,' said Guy, and he meant it.

Her responding smile lit up her features, doing more for her than any make-up artist. She took his arm in hers, and he breathed in the scent of ripe figs. He had, for the time being, forgiven her.

'Let's go,' she said. 'The limo's waiting.'

Charles stumbled up the drive to Fulford Farm filled with resolve. He was going to take the day off tomorrow. He'd take Henty shopping, treat her to whatever she wanted, then they'd go somewhere for lunch. Stratford. He thought Stratford would be nice. They could even try and get tickets for a matinee at the RSC. They hadn't done that for years.

Delighted with his plan, too drunk to realize that it was the plan of a guilty man and that Henty might think it was strange, he slipped in through the front door, deposited his camcorder in the study so as not to arouse suspicion, then made his way to the kitchen.

The atmosphere hit him at once. Sultry Latin jazz was oozing out of the sound system. Henty was sitting on one of the kitchen units with a glass of white wine in one hand, swinging her legs. Her eyes were sparkling, her cheeks slightly flushed, and she was giggling at something Travis was saying. He was sprawled carelessly in a chair, nursing a bottle of beer and looking very much at home.

'Hi, Charles,' Henty said, matter-of-factly, no hint of warmth in her voice. 'We started without you, I'm afraid.'

Charles swayed slightly, blinking, trying to assess the situation.

'Looks like he's started already,' drawled Travis, and the two of them burst into laughter. It rang mockingly in his ears, and he started to protest, but his words came out slurred. He must be drunker than he thought – he had a dim memory of Fleur topping his glass up more often than her own.

'Another one of your boozy media lunches?' asked Henty lightly, and the words sliced through him like a knife. It was true – he often came home half cut from schmoozing. But there was no need for her to be so disparaging. It was part of the job. Ninety per cent of deals were done over a restaurant table.

It was just a pity *he* hadn't managed to pull one off lately.

Fear turned the champagne in his system to acid, burning through the walls of his stomach and seeping into his bowels. He couldn't bring himself to burst in through the bubble Henty and Travis had drawn around themselves. They'd been having fun before he arrived, he told himself. Now they looked wary, unsure how to accommodate the intruder.

'I'm going to bed,' he managed to mumble, turned on his heel and shut the door.

19

Just as Honor had known he would, Johnny forgot the ingredients for the Thai chicken curry that evening.

Or didn't forget, exactly. He'd been held up tending to a horse with a tendon injury. He could have stopped off at the supermarket for all the stuff, but then he would have been late. Or even later than he already was.

'I'm sorry,' he said. 'I'll run into Eldenbury for a take-away.'

'Don't worry,' said Honor, resigned. 'I've got plenty of stuff in the fridge.'

How had she known that the promised meal wouldn't materialize? Because she knew Johnny only too well. This was familiar territory. Promises, promises. Followed by excuses. The eternal let-down. It was almost as if, once he'd made a vow, he had to break it. Oh well, she told herself. If you didn't expect anything from Johnny, then you weren't disappointed.

He had, however, brought a DVD player together with a load of pirated movies he'd got from one of his clients.

'Isn't that illegal?' Honor asked.

'Yes,' said Johnny, but before she could protest Ted had spied a copy of the latest Disney movie and she'd had to give in. They were sprawled on the sofa together now, laughing uproariously at the animated antics. Their mirth was infectious: Honor found herself smiling as she whisked up the batter for toad-in-the-hole and poured it carefully over the sizzling sausages in the baking dish, taking care not to let the hot fat sputter up on her skin. She slid the dish back into the oven, then selected two round onions from the string hanging off one of the butcher's hooks in the ceiling and sliced them thinly for the onion gravy.

Minutes later the onions were browning nicely, well on their way to becoming caramelized, and Honor leaned back on the kitchen cabinets to draw breath for a moment. She picked up the glass of wine Johnny had poured her and sipped it contemplatively, looking at Ted. He was sitting with his legs crossed, his head on Johnny's shoulder, trying to fight off the fact that he was tired, for he knew the minute he showed signs of fatigue he'd be packed off to bed. Her heart constricted inside her. Ted was so like Johnny. Surely he looked at him and saw himself? How much longer could she keep up this pretence?

She saw the little boy's lashes finally give in and fall on to his cheeks. It always amazed her how he could be laughing one minute and fast asleep the next. Honor went to scoop him up and carry him up the stairs, but Johnny nudged her gently out of the way.

'I'll take him.'

He lifted him up effortlessly – Honor had to admit that it was becoming more and more difficult for her to lift him – and in his sleep Ted put his arms round his father's neck and his head flopped on to his shoulders. Her heart was in her mouth as Johnny reached the door.

'Johnny –' she began.

He turned.

'He . . . hasn't brushed his teeth,' she finished lamely.

Johnny grinned.

'I'm sure it won't hurt just this once. He can do them twice in the morning.'

He disappeared through the door, her one-time lover, carrying their son. She took another big slurp of wine, hoping to dispel the questions and doubts that were whirling round in her mind.

I'm not a celebrity, get me out of here.

Guy was hating every minute of the evening but trying desperately not to show it. From the moment their limo had arrived at the hotel and they'd walked in through the entrance, past the roped-off area that held back the straggle of paparazzi, he'd been squirming in discomfort. It was all so fake; a tawdry attempt by the newspaper to emulate the glitter of the more prestigious award ceremonies in order to boost its circulation. And the tragic thing was that the actors and actresses and presenters that it was purporting to celebrate went along with it happily despite the fact that it was a total set-up and the winners were bound to be rigged. The lure of column inches, it seemed, was a strong one. They were more important than talent in this day and age. Celebrity and notoriety could fast forward a career; no one with any ambition turned down the opportunity to be in the public eye. So the place was packed out with wannabes, has-beens and the faces of the moment, all of whom had spent at least the last week planning what to wear and being groomed for the occasion.

Inside, the hotel's ballroom was crammed with hundreds of tables barely twelve inches apart. The place mats were miniature versions of the *Daily Post*, printed with copies of their most famous headlines over the past ten years. At each place was a shiny bag stuffed with goodies. Guy was astonished to find a silk tie, a badger shaving brush and a leather-bound notebook in his, as well as a selection of luxury male-grooming products. This was obviously big business; the suppliers were banking on celebrity endorsements. Either that or they were getting rid of old stock . . .

Comely waitresses were circling the room with trays full of some filthy, lurid cocktail. Guy took one sip and gagged. Sickly, oversweet and artificial. Nobody else seemed bothered, presumably because the cocktails were free. If you wanted something else, you had to pay for it. He found another waitress and sidled up to her with a winning smile and a twenty-pound note.

'Do you think you could possibly get me a bottle of beer?' he asked politely. 'I'm seriously allergic to whatever's in that.'

The waitress nodded eagerly, obviously mistaking him for some big-time, small-screen star, and rushed off to do his bidding. Happy that he would at least have something decent to drink, Guy looked around him. Through the crowds, he could see Richenda talking to the executive producer of the company who made *Lady Jane*. The simplicity of her outfit and her natural make-up were, he realized now, an act of considerable cunning, for next to her every other woman in the room looked overdressed and obvious. Fake tans, false hair and elaborate scaffolding abounded. There were unnecessary acres of exposed flesh – some firm, some flabby. In this day of stylists and personal shoppers, there really was no excuse for fashion blunders. But in the battle for attention, most actresses made the mistake of revealing as much as they could to ensure they were the focus of every camera. Richenda had done quite the opposite, and as a result all eyes were upon her. Of course, you had to be stunning to pull that trick off in the first place, but she had been canny to resist showing off either cleavage or leg. She glided amongst them all with an aura of serenity and class. How ironic, thought Guy.

He wandered amongst the guests, realizing how few of these so-called celebrities he actually recognized, sickened at the thought that the nation was riveted week after week by their fictionalized antics or their ability to redecorate a house in twenty minutes. A few of them managed to do some good, no doubt, as their agents or managers would ensure they did a quick stint in some war-torn third-world country to plump up their image. But on the whole they were superficial and self-absorbed, unable to handle the attention or the money that went with meteoric rises that weren't underpinned by any particular talent. Guy felt a shudder of revulsion at the forced camaraderie, the shallow air-kissing, the false shrieks of greeting that ill-disguised the underlying rivalry. He wondered about moving through the glazed expressions and pinprick pupils to reach Richenda, but decided she would be able to work the room better without him standing like a lemon at her side. Not that he wasn't supportive, but no one was really interested in him. After all, *he* had no influence over the outcome of tonight's awards. Nor could he offer anyone a plum role in a forthcoming production, or write them a glowing review. He was just arm candy.

If he'd known it was going to be this ghastly, he'd have found an excuse not to come. There were a million and one things that needed doing at Eversleigh: they had a party of twelve coming this weekend, who'd emailed an endless list of dietary requests and peculiarities. He really could have done with going over it all with Honor – these were going to be difficult clients, and it was vital to get everything right at this early stage while they were establishing their reputation.

Slugging back his beer, he wondered if he was being sanctimonious and a bit of an old fogey. Who was he to look down on these people? What right had he to scoff at their success, just because it didn't fit in with his view of the world? After all, he came from a world of privilege and what had he actually achieved? Running a bed and breakfast wasn't something most people aspired to. He shouldn't be so smug and judgemental: if he wasn't careful, he could end up losing Eversleigh and it would more than likely end up in the hands of one of the people here tonight. As his mother had pointed out, they were the new aristocracy. They represented the nation's values.

And to be fair to Richenda, she handled her celebrity status with aplomb, or so it seemed to him so far. She didn't fall over herself to court publicity or exploit situations. She'd made as little fuss as possible over the engagement; the photo session hadn't been that much of an ordeal. And even though he'd been unsettled by her revelations earlier that day, Guy felt confident that Richenda would handle the knock-on discreetly. He resolved not to be petulant and self-righteous. He mustn't let this blip spoil their relationship. There were bound to be pressures all the way through their marriage. If he fell at the first fence, what hope did they have? She needed his support, not his judgement.

Resolved, he pushed his way through the jostling throngs until he reached her side. The way her face lit up when she saw him was reward in itself.

'Hello, darling,' he murmured.

After Ted had been tucked up safely in bed, Honor served supper. She realized it was years since she had done this: sat down at the table with another adult, enjoyed a simple meal and idly chatted about their respective days. Johnny was on top form, thoroughly appreciative of her cooking.

'This is way better than my curry would have been.'

'I still think it's a myth. I think you forgot accidentally on purpose. I don't think you've got a clue what's in it.'

'Ginger, coconut milk, lemongrass . . .' Johnny started reciting the ingredients indignantly, then ran out of steam.

'Chicken?' suggested Honor helpfully.

Johnny thumped her arm.

'I'll prove it to you Saturday. Definitely. Tell you what, why don't you ask some friends round? We could have a supper party.'

Honor didn't reply for a moment. She couldn't say that she hadn't actually mentioned Johnny to any of her friends yet. She'd been on the verge of telling Henty, but even then something was still holding her back. Like the fact that as soon as she publicly acknowledged his presence in her life she'd have to start making decisions.

'I don't think we'd better. They've got a big party at Eversleigh this weekend – they might need me till quite late. Why don't we wait till I've got a weekend free?'

Johnny looked a bit crestfallen. There was nothing he liked better than a party.

'I can hold the fort till you get back. Everyone will understand. And I can get to know your mates.'

She definitely wasn't letting Johnny loose without supervision. That was asking for trouble.

'No,' she said firmly. 'It's too early, Johnny. I think you should be spending the time with Ted, not showing off your culinary prowess.'

Johnny stuck out his bottom lip.

'I'd forgotten what a bloody school marm you can be,' he complained.

'I thought that's what you liked,' she flashed back with a mischievous grin, then stopped herself. Don't flirt, don't tease. That was dangerous ground.

Even though the hotel boasted four stars, dinner was far from impressive: chicken with a parmesan and polenta crust that tasted as if it had been picked up at the local KFC two hours before, then a raspberry mousse that resembled Instant Whip with a drop of crème de framboises mixed in. However, no one seemed bothered. Most of the guests didn't eat anyway as their outfits didn't allow it, and they were more intent on a liquid intake. When the time came for the awards to be presented the atmosphere was decidedly relaxed. Make-up was fading, guards were dropping, hairdos were drooping. Guy was relieved to see that Richenda was still as fresh as a daisy. Apart from a glass of champagne on arrival, she had wisely been sipping mineral water throughout the evening.

The ceremony began. It seemed tediously slow and repetitive to Guy, but everyone seemed to be on the edge of their seats as the Best Television Makeover Show or the Best Celebrity Chef was revealed. And the ritual really tested everyone's acting abilities: the agonizing expectation, the bitter disappointment, the delight, the fixed smiles, the false congratulations, the forced tears, the gushing. By the time the award for Best Actress arrived, Guy was thoroughly nauseated. Yet he still felt a flurry of nerves for Richenda. Of course it would be wonderful if she won. Not to mention awful if she lost. He squeezed her hand under the table and crossed his fingers secretly. She sat, straight backed and serene, the only sign of any tension the tightness of her fingers on the stem of her glass as the nominees were announced.

The award was to be presented by a young comedian whose filthy innuendo had made him a celebrity almost overnight. He bounced on to the stage in a dinner jacket, worn with leopardskin winkle-pickers and matching dickie bow. Which bit of black tie did these people not understand? wondered Guy.

'I have to admit, I was feeling a right tit earlier,' he said, then trailed off. 'Thirty-six double D,' he added helpfully, waiting for the audience to get the joke. Then he picked up the gold envelope.

'No point beating about the bush, is there? Anyway, I'm sure all the ladies here have had Brazilian waxes . . .'

The audience laughed again.

''Scuse me – I'm just fumbling with the flap . . . As usual . . .'

Another slightly nervous laugh. His jokes were getting a bit too close to the bone. Being a professional, he sensed this.

'And the winner of the Best Television Actress Award, as voted by the readers of the *Daily Post*, is . . .'

Everyone held their breath as he drew out a thick card.

'. . . the fox herself. Richenda. Richenda Fox, ladies and gentlemen. Congratulations, my darling . . .'

Richenda had a look of utter amazement on her face. She seemed slightly dazed. Guy leaned over and gave her a kiss on the cheek. She turned to him with a smile, shaking her head in bewilderment, then accepted a kiss from the delighted producer on her other side. Then she stood, gathered up her skirts and picked her way through the tables as daintily as a milkmaid picking her way through a field of buttercups. She ran lightly up the stairs on to the stage, accepted a congratulatory hug from the comedian, then took her place behind the microphone. She waited for a few moments before speaking, while she composed herself. Then she looked round the huge audience with a dazzling smile.

'Every little girl likes to dream. When we're dreaming those dreams, I don't think we expect them to come true. I invented many wonderful scenarios for myself as a child, but this is beyond my wildest imaginings. So thank you.'

She paused and a smattering of applause began, but

she put her hand up to show she hadn't finished. The clapping abated obediently.

'So . . . this is the fairy-tale ending. But what you don't know is that the beginning of the story is rather different from what you've been led to believe. The readers of the *Daily Post* gave me this award, so in return, I'm going to give them the truth. Tomorrow you can read all about my reunion with my estranged mother, and I hope you won't judge me too harshly for the past I invented for myself. I'm sure when you read what happened you'll understand why I felt the need to pretend for so long.'

She paused for a moment, the smile never leaving her face, while the audience digested this information, murmuring speculatively and exchanging surprised glances. Then she cleared her throat, to indicate that she wasn't finished. She carried smoothly on, before they'd really had time to digest the shock revelations, thanking the cast and production team of *Lady Jane*, name-checking the minions as well as the producer and directors.

'Finally, there's one person I'd like to thank in particular, without whose support I wouldn't be standing here, and that is my wonderful, big-hearted, generous-spirited fiancé, Guy Portias. Thank you a thousand times, my darling.'

A collective, heartfelt 'Aaah' swept the room at these words. Heads swivelled as she blew Guy a kiss, then rapturous applause broke out and hundreds of flashbulbs popped. She had the entire audience in the palm of her hand. She paused for a few more moments to ensure that every photographer had had their fill of her radiance, then she glided back down the steps and made her way back to the table, stopping en route to shake hands and receive kisses of congratulation with gracious modesty.

Guy felt slightly sick. How could he have misjudged Richenda like that? He had assumed that she would try and make as little as possible of the forthcoming revelations about her past. Instead, she had used her victory to blow it out of all proportion. Admittedly, it was a bloody masterstroke in how to manipulate the media. In one fell swoop she had ensured that the photographers would be falling over themselves to snap her: she wouldn't feature just in the *Daily Post*, but all the papers. The entire episode had been contrived and calculated – she had engineered the situation to bring her maximum publicity. Worse than that, she had used him; capitalized on their recent engagement with that nauseating name-check. He cringed as he remembered all those grinning heads swivelling round to look at him. Did she have any idea how that had made him feel? He thought not.

Guy topped up his glass, realizing that he was the only one left at the table. Everyone else was circulating. Richenda was surrounded by a huge crowd of sycophants. He watched as she embraced Cindy Marks from the *Daily Post*, and his stomach turned over. Was he imagining it, or did the two of them share a conspiratorial smile? Had the whole thing been conceived and engineered between the two of them from the very beginning? He remembered them directing him during the photoshoot a fortnight ago – at the time, he'd gone along with it with good-natured grumbling. Now he wondered if he'd been naive; if he was in fact part of a more sinister plan; an extra in a piece of theatre they had been rehearsing for weeks.

It suddenly occurred to him that perhaps the entire engagement had been a publicity stunt. But no – Richenda couldn't have engineered that. He'd proposed to her voluntarily, if a little rashly. Guy told himself now he was being paranoid.

Nevertheless, the entire incident was making him question everything that had happened between them. He urgently felt the need to escape. He couldn't go back to her apartment tonight. He didn't trust himself not to have a huge confrontation with her; a confrontation that would question her values and her motives. And in the mood he was in, he didn't think their relationship would survive. He needed to get away and think before he made his next move.

Resolved, he moved through the adoring throngs and reached her side.

'Listen, darling – I'm going to slip off and leave you to it.'

She looked startled.

'What? But we're going on somewhere to celebrate. You can't leave.'

'Honestly – I've got to be up early in the morning. We've got a huge party this weekend and I haven't done a thing yet. If I go out partying with you I'll be in deep trouble.'

'I want you with me.'

Her eyes were beseeching him. He had to be firm.

'I know it's a bore but it can't be helped.'

'But I wanted you to meet my mother. She's coming round in the morning.'

'I think it would be far better if I left you two alone. If it's all coming out in the paper tomorrow you won't want any distractions. Much better if we have a get-together when everything's calmed down. Maybe . . . bring her down for Sunday lunch or something?'

Richenda looked slightly mollified by this suggestion, though Guy could see she wasn't happy at being abandoned. But she couldn't protest, not in front of her adoring entourage. The press would pick up on any discord straight away. Well, she'd made her own bloody bed. She could lie in it.

Guy gave her a lingering kiss for the benefit of her onlookers.

'Well done, darling. I'm so proud of you. And we'll celebrate as soon as I've got this weekend out of the way. Have a lovely evening.'

He squeezed both of her hands in an affectionate gesture of farewell, and walked away swiftly. It was all he could do not to bolt for the exit as soon as her back was turned. He came out of the hotel, ran down the steps and breathed in the crispness of the cold night air, so refreshing after the smell of a hundred different perfumes, the lingering traces of cooking and the million cigarettes that were being smoked one after the other. A cab appeared around the corner with its orange light on. Guy stuck up his hand, leaped into the back and flopped on to the seat with a relieved sigh.

'Paddington Station, please. As quick as you can.'

*

When Johnny and Honor had finished supper, she plonked the dishes in the sink, then brought over the bottle of wine to top up Johnny's glass. To her surprise he put his hand over the top.

'I'd better get going. It's going to take me over an hour to get home.'

Honor knew that disappointment was spreading itself over her face.

'You could always stay,' she said softly. 'On the sofa,' she added hastily.

Johnny looked up and gave her his familiar lopsided smile.

'If I have another drink, I won't be responsible for my actions.'

'Oh dear. Well, we can't have that.'

She smiled down at him teasingly. He put a hand either side of her waist, his thumb massaging her hip bone. She could feel the warmth from his fingers diffuse right into her bones, melting her. All of a sudden she felt rather weak.

'What are we going to do, Honor?'

He was looking up at her, suddenly serious.

'I don't know,' she whispered, as he stood up and folded her in his arms. She leaned back slightly, panicking inwardly. 'I don't know . . .'

The evening had been perfect. Delightful. Easy. How fantastic if they could just repeat that formula day after day. Him getting in from work at about seven, getting quality time with Ted for half an hour. Then the two of them enjoying a relaxed meal. Honor sighed. If only she had a copper-bottomed guarantee that was how it would be, she'd suggest making a go of it again. But she was wary; very wary.

'I need time,' she told him.

'Of course you do. It's still early days.'

She looked at him, surprised. She was expecting pressure for a decision.

'It's totally up to you, you know that. And when you make up your mind what you want to do, I'll go with it. Because I know you'll make the right choice.'

She nodded her agreement, distracted by his hand massaging the small of her back, wanting him to explore further but knowing she should move away. Instead, to her horror, she found herself winding her arms around his neck and pulling him closer. She told herself it was because she wanted the comfort of human contact, the reassurance. But the tiny little tornado of white heat she felt deep inside made a mockery of this. It was all she could think of. She could hear Johnny talking to her, re-assuring her, in the special voice he used when he was comforting an animal in pain. She wasn't listening to him, though. All she could focus on was the incredible sensations, long forgotten, seeping through her.

She turned her face to kiss him. As long as she only kissed him, that was OK. A kiss didn't mean anything, especially to the likes of Johnny. She brushed her lips against his, once, then twice, then once more; random little pecks of affection. That was fine. Nothing too compromising. But the next kiss became lingering, sensual. She shivered as she felt his tongue against hers, told herself this was the moment she should pull back, then chastised herself as she responded and their tongues entwined slowly and languorously. She found herself coming to life inside as the flicker of warmth ignited into full flame and charged through her, as if her veins were filled with petrol and the fire was dancing along them, unstoppable. She felt his muscles through the soft cotton of his shirt and longed to feel his skin on hers. For a moment, she wondered if he'd slipped something into her wine. She'd heard about people using horse tranquilizers in nightclubs: maybe he'd got hold of something that turned women into sex fiends. Because she felt desperate. After years of celibacy, she craved abandonment.

Before she knew it, his hands were inside her jeans. She moaned as he made contact, then rubbed herself against his fingers as satisfaction became the only thing important to her. Nothing would make her turn back now. As she came, she hugged him to her, racked by the ferocity of the first orgasm to have been effected by another person for more than seven years. He brushed his fingers against her lips, then he kissed her again, and they shared the taste of her in a gesture that was incredibly intimate.

She laid her head on his shoulder for a moment, trying to recover her poise, then he disengaged her gently.

'I really had better go,' he whispered. 'I've got to be at work at half seven tomorrow morning.'

He drew away from her. She looked up. If he smirked, she'd slap him. But he didn't. He picked up their wineglasses and took them into the kitchen, washing them carefully under the tap and wiping them with a cloth and putting them on the draining board. Honor busied herself putting away the salt and pepper; pushing the cork back into the wine bottle. She could barely look him in the eye as he picked up his keys. He kissed her again, lightly, affectionately, just on the side of her mouth.

'I'll see you at the weekend.'

She nodded.

'Bye . . .'

As soon as he'd gone she sank down on to the sofa with her head in her hands. What on earth had she been thinking of? It was almost worse than sleeping with him, letting him get her off like that. It had been for her satisfaction alone. Her behaviour had been . . . well, wanton was the only word she could think of. And now he had the moral high ground, the smug satisfaction of knowing that she had been desperate while he'd exercised total self-control. Her cheeks rosy with shame, she reflected that she'd gone from cosy and contented to orgasmic to desolate in the space of one evening.

Then she remembered – that was life with Johnny. The bloody emotional rollercoaster, never knowing where you were. It hadn't been her at all – he'd engineered the whole thing. Ruthlessly exploited her weak spot. Literally.

Bastard. Bastard bastard bastard. He'd known exactly what he was doing, and she'd fallen into his trap. She could imagine him now, smirking at the wheel of his car, convinced he was well on his way to winning her round. Having given her all that blarney about the future being her choice. Well, bugger him. She wasn't going to be manipulated any more.

By the time she got to bed, she was freezing. She struggled to get to sleep, as guilt and self-reproach and indecision did nothing to warm her. Chilled to the bone, she searched in vain for a solution to this dilemma that wasn't going to cause one of them pain.

Rozzi Sharpe was incandescent with rage as she looked at the early edition of the *Daily Post*. A photograph of Richenda delivering her acceptance speech was emblazoned across the front, along with the headline 'Mother and child reunion: see full story inside'. Mick Spencer's story wasn't worth wiping her arse on now. Stupid, blithering drunken fool. It would have been a fantastic story – much better than the simpering, saccharine-sweet reunion plastered all over the *Daily Post*. People loved nasty stories much more than they liked happy endings – *schadenfreude* kept the British media afloat.

She wasn't even going to bother contacting Mick. His accusations were unfounded without the mother's backup; it would just look like petty sour grapes on the part of her paper. She'd find a better story. There was absolutely bound to be one. She wouldn't bother with Richenda: her guard would be up now. Rozzi knew exactly where she was going to concentrate her investigations – in deepest Gloucestershire, where the handsome prince was residing in his castle. She wasn't really bothered what came out of the woodwork: accusations of drug abuse, homosexuality or a family history of hideous war crimes. But she'd find something.

She phoned up her favourite reporter, a tenacious little terrier who she saved for the really juicy jobs. He always got results, but he made her pay.

'Guy Portias. Get me some shit. And make it stick.'

Bill Weeks's evil chuckle was all she needed to satisfy her that she'd have a big steaming mound of it before too many days had passed.

20

Guy woke on Thursday morning feeling guilty. Firstly because it was nearly eleven o'clock, and he had vowed to get up early and start work. But he hadn't got in until the early hours of the morning, and then he hadn't slept properly.

Secondly, he felt rather uncomfortable with his actions of the night before. Abandoning Richenda like that was hardly chivalrous. But he'd felt totally compromised. He wouldn't have trusted himself not to say something awful, especially if he'd had a few more drinks, which he no doubt would have if they'd gone on partying. It was best that he left when he did. Anyway, he consoled himself, she hadn't exactly been short of company.

Now he'd distanced himself from her, however, he realized he had to give her a chance. Both of them a chance. They had to get off the merry-go-round that was their life. He had to explain to her exactly how he felt about what had happened, and she in turn needed to defend her actions – he had no doubt that in her eyes it had been defensible. Then perhaps he would be able to understand her better. It was, after all, almost as if he'd fallen in love with someone from a different culture entirely. An alien.

What the two of them needed was time alone, away from both the pressures of Eversleigh and the public eye, to have a really serious heart to heart and lay down some ground rules. The events of the past couple of days were only the beginning; if Richenda continued on this upward path, life was going to become more and more tricky. He needed to book something romantic for the two of them. Paris was out: by the time they got there it would be time to come back. Lunch at the Honeycote Arms, by contrast, wasn't really special enough, and it was hardly private. He lay there for a few moments, musing on various possibilities, when inspiration hit him. He picked up the telephone by the bed and dialled a number.

'Eldenbury Wines.'

'Felix – it's Guy. Tell me, is your brother still running that crazy business of his from your parents' farm?'

'He certainly is. And don't mock – it's turning out to be very lucrative. More profitable than dairy cattle, at any rate.'

'Give me his number, will you?'

Ten minutes later, satisfied that what he had organized was the perfect antidote to their floundering relationship, he called Richenda. She answered on the first ring.

'Hey. How are you?'

'Guy! I was wondering when you'd call. I was getting worried.'

'Sorry. I'd have rung earlier, but I've been . . . seeing some suppliers.' He couldn't admit he'd been snoring his head off in bed. 'How's it going?'

'Great. Mum's here with me having a late breakfast. We've got the paper. Have you seen it?'

Shit. He should have had the foresight to get it from the shop before he phoned. He didn't want to look too uninterested.

'I've just sent Malachi down to the shop. I'm going to read it over a coffee.'

'Cindy's done a fantastic job. And the pictures are wonderful. I really think we've made the best out of a bad situation. In fact, Mick's almost done us a favour.'

Guy wasn't sure he liked the glee in her voice, but he murmured his approval nevertheless.

'We've had loads of calls from magazines wanting to do features,' she burbled on. 'But I've told them that's it for now.'

'Good.'

'I've told them they'll just have to wait for the wedding.'

She gave a merry little laugh and Guy felt his blood freeze. He tried to inject some warmth into his voice as he responded.

'By the way – I've booked us a surprise. For Monday morning. Just you and me.'

'Oooh – what?'

'I can't tell you, because then it won't be a surprise. Anyway, I've got to get on. Mum's tearing her hair out.'

'OK. Love you.'

She squeaked a kiss down the phone. Guy hung up, his heart feeling heavy. He'd persuaded himself to give Richenda the benefit of the doubt, but he hadn't liked her almost triumphant tone, as if she had milked the situation for all it was worth. And how many lies had he trotted out in just one phone call? At least three. This was not boding well. Never mind. They could iron things out, he was sure.

He slung on a faded grey sweatshirt and jeans and went down to the kitchen in pursuit of breakfast and his mother, who usually had her first pot of coffee at this time. But Madeleine was nowhere to be seen. Instead, he found Honor, carefully whisking up egg whites in a copper bowl.

'Morning!' he said cheerfully.

'Hi,' she greeted him back. 'How was last night?'

'Fine. Actually no, awful. The food was vile and the people were even worse. I felt a bit of a spare part.'

'Oh. But I bet Richenda looked lovely.'

'Yes. She won . . . Best Actress or something.'

He knew he was being deliberately dismissive, but that was the mood he was in.

'That's fantastic. You must be very proud.'

'Yes,' he replied, rather unconvincingly. 'You haven't seen the papers, then?'

'No.'

'There's a big piece in it about her reunion with her mother. They haven't seen each other for ten years, apparently.'

'I didn't know that.'

Guy didn't say that he hadn't known either. He'd already been disloyal enough. He told himself to bloody behave and not be so petulant. A slab of chocolate broken into rough pieces was nestling in golden foil rather temptingly next to a bowl, waiting to be melted. He pinched a square and put it in his mouth before she could stop him. Honor rapped him sharply over the knuckles with her wooden spoon.

'Ouch!' he yelped. 'That bloody hurt.'

'It was supposed to. There's not going to be enough now.'

'I'll go and get you a bar of Bournville from the village shop.'

'This is Green and Black's seventy per cent cocoa solids!'

'No one will know the difference.'

'I will.'

Guy shook his head in mock exasperation.

'What's it like to have such high standards?'

'Exhausting.'

He looked at her. She did look rather tired, he thought. Pale and drawn, with dark circles under her eyes.

'Actually, you do look shattered,' he said, immediately concerned. 'Are we working you too hard?'

'No,' she replied, and promptly burst into tears.

Guy was horrified.

'Hey! Don't cry, for heaven's sake. The recipe doesn't call for salt.'

Honor gave a helpless giggle through her tears, then dissolved again.

'I'm sorry. It's just . . . Shit. I don't know what the hell I'm doing. I'm making such a mess of everything.'

'No, you're not. You're doing a fabulous job.'

'Not this. I mean . . . my life.'

'Oh.'

She desperately tried to wipe her eyes with the corner of her apron.

'You don't want to hear about it. It's incredibly boring.'

'Try me.'

'It's . . . Ted's father.'

There was a pause while Guy considered this revelation. He realized he'd never given the idea of Ted having a father much thought. Ted and Honor belonged together and that was that. The idea of a third party wasn't one he warmed to much. Especially when whoever it was had clearly got Honor into a terrible state.

'Is he giving you trouble?'

'No. Not exactly. I just don't know what to do about him.'

Guy surveyed her gravely.

'I think we should go to the pub and talk about it.'

'No! I'm sorry. I shouldn't have said anything. You don't want to get involved in my problems.'

'Listen, it's in my interests to have happy staff. And if that means supplying them with half an hour's counselling in the local, that's fine by me. Anyway, I could do with a drink to get over last night.'

'Really?'

'Truly.'

Honor looked down at her egg whites.

'I can't go without finishing this. This is the crucial moment.'

'OK. Finish your whatever-it-is. Then we'll go. I prescribe double Bloody Marys and one of the Fleece's thoroughly inedible cheese and pickle sandwiches.'

'How can I say no?' said Honor.

'You can't. Simple as that.'

It was gone twelve by the time Honor put the finishing touches to her chocolate, prune and Armagnac parfait. She fled to the cloakroom at the end of the passage and dug around in her handbag to see if she could improve her appearance, but she hadn't brought her make-up bag with her. So she washed her face and ruffled up her hair, then went to find Guy.

He was in the small sitting room with Madeleine, going through the bookings diary. He jumped up as soon as he saw her.

'Honor. Good. I'm bloody starving.' He turned to his mother. 'Um – I'm taking Honor to lunch at the Fleece. I think she could do with a break.'

'Quite right,' said Madeleine. 'Though I don't know if I approve of the venue. Can't you go somewhere more salubrious?'

'It'll be fun,' said Honor. 'I haven't been out for so long that anywhere's a treat.'

Madeleine surveyed Honor discreetly. She might not have a huge clothing budget, but she knew how to put an outfit together. Today she had on linen drawstring trousers and a white shirt with the sleeves rolled up. A silk scarf tied round her neck and pale blue suede loafers finished off the outfit. Madeleine thoroughly approved: Honor knew instinctively what suited her, but didn't need to spend a fortune to look good. Which was a very good sign.

Madeleine knew it was a bad habit of hers, to judge people by what they were wearing, but actually you could gain a lot of insight into character by how people dressed. Richenda, for example, didn't fool her in the least with her understated perfection. It was all very calculated and preconceived: subtly done for effect, but at huge expense. Madeleine hadn't missed any of the labels so far; Richenda didn't go in for chain-store chic. She obviously needed the security of haute couture to maintain her image.

Madeleine hadn't said anything to Guy, but she'd already seen the papers that morning. And she'd found the revelations rather distasteful. There had been a certain gloss put on it all that made Madeleine feel there was more to the story than met the eye. Richenda might know how to dress and look the part, but that didn't guarantee propriety.

Madeleine was feeling increasingly uncomfortable about the whole relationship. And very protective, though she couldn't show that. Guy was old enough to make his own decisions, and his own mistakes. She wasn't going to interfere. She would just hover on the sidelines, watching and waiting . . .

'Please – do join us if you'd like to,' Honor was saying, obviously anxious that Madeleine shouldn't feel excluded. Thereby climbing up another notch in her estimation: the girl had lovely manners.

'That's sweet of you, but I've got a mountain of brochures to send off and some bookings to confirm. I promised myself I'd get them in the post this afternoon. You two go off and enjoy yourselves . . .'

The Fleece was a black and white thatched pub at the end of the village. It served dreadful food but delicious beer, which Guy considered to be every pub's duty. There were rumours that the brewery who owned it were lining it up for a revamp, mirroring the Honeycote Arms, their flagship gastropub. Guy hoped not. The whole point of the Fleece was its abundant shortcomings which kept out the Mercedes CLK brigade.

Guy ordered two Bloody Marys, two cheese and pickle

doorsteps and a bowl of chips to share, while Honor found them a place by the window.

'So,' he said, plonking a glass of thick tomato juice laced with a hefty kick of vodka and a shot of Worcester sauce on the sticky table in front of her. 'You can get it off your chest if you want. Or we can just get disgracefully plastered. It's up to you.'

'I could do with someone to talk to,' admitted Honor. 'It's been driving me mad, not knowing what to do. Basically, I bumped into Ted's dad at the ball the other night. I hadn't seen him for seven years.'

Guy raised his eyebrows.

'Do I gather from that you parted on bad terms?'

Honor gave a rueful nod.

'The day I found out I was pregnant with Ted, I found Johnny in bed with a nineteen-year-old girl.'

Guy winced.

'Shit.'

'I didn't give him a chance to defend himself. Because I couldn't think of any reason that would justify it. As far as I was concerned, it stripped him of any right to be Ted's father. I didn't want anything else to do with him. So I ran away. Here. To Eversleigh. And I hadn't seen him till the other night.' She sighed. 'Of course, he found out about Ted. And he was very angry with me . . .'

At that point in the story the sandwiches and chips arrived, allowing Guy to take in what he'd been told while they distributed the plates and administered salt and vinegar. He realized the object of Honor's angst must be the owner of the green scarf Ted had discovered the other afternoon.

'No wonder you've been looking pale,' he said, squirting a sachet of ketchup carefully on to the side of his plate. 'And there was me thinking it was the pressure of all those canapés.'

He hoped he didn't sound too flippant, but he wasn't sure yet what he was supposed to say.

Honor chewed thoughtfully on a chip.

'Yes, but do you think I was wrong? Was I too judgemental? Was what he did not actually that awful? I mean, we weren't married. But I did think we had some sort of commitment to each other . . .'

She looked at Guy.

'Would you do that? If you were in a long-term relationship? Would you sleep with someone else? Even if it was just a meaningless bonk?' Her questions were rapid fire. '*Have* you ever?'

Guy thought very carefully before he answered. He knew everyone's ideas of morality were different, but Honor was looking for guidance and he hoped he might give her some. He looked back on his past. He'd certainly been no angel. He'd had plenty of one-night stands and flings. But on close analysis he didn't think he'd ever cheated on anyone.

'I don't think I have, no.'

'Would you cheat on Richenda? If you were tempted and thought you could get away with it?'

Guy looked horrified.

'Certainly not!'

'So you think I had the right to cut him off?'

'I can't say that, Honor. I can't give you my approval. It's a pretty big deal, fathering a child. I can't help feeling that maybe he did have the right to at least know.' He paused. 'That wasn't what you wanted to hear, was it?'

'I don't know,' said Honor miserably. 'Johnny seems to think it was the crime of the century. And now he's putting me under pressure.'

'What sort?'

'I think he wants us to get back together. But he's too clever to actually say that's what he wants. He's trying to get me to think that's what I want.'

'And is it?'

Honor shrugged. 'I keep thinking how great it would be for Ted to have a mum and a dad. Not to be the odd one out all the time. For him to have a proper family.'

'But what about Johnny? How do you feel about him? There's no point in forcing yourself back together if you don't love him.'

'Johnny's a . . . loveable rogue with his own moral code. Though he seems to have grown up a bit. He certainly dotes on Ted: I think he'd make a good job of the parental thing. Up to a point. But he's tricky. He drinks for England. He flirts for Ireland. And he's totally irresistible when he wants to be.'

'You're not selling him to me,' said Guy bluntly.

'I'm just trying to put you in the picture.'

'What's he really got to offer you and Ted? That he can't give you if he does the part-time dad thing? He can see Ted at weekends and holidays, contribute to his upbringing.'

Honor was silent. Guy ploughed on.

'Don't be seduced into thinking that having him around is going to make life better for Ted. He doesn't know any different at the moment, remember. And you're a fantastic mum. If you ask me, the most important thing for Ted is that *you* are happy.'

'So you think I'm entitled to ask for more time?'

'Definitely. Whatever decision you make is going to shape the future for all three of you. It's not something you can decide overnight.'

Honor looked relieved.

'That's what I thought. But he makes me feel so guilty. The other day he said I'd deprived him of a third of Ted's childhood already, so I've got to make up for lost time.'

'Have you heard the term emotional blackmail?' asked Guy. 'Don't stand for any of it. You take your time.'

Honor looked miserably at her sandwich.

'I'm trying to keep my distance,' she said carefully, looking up at Guy, her huge brown eyes glassy with tears. 'But I think I made a monumental error last night.'

She bit hard on her lower lip, her face anguished. His heart sank.

'You didn't sleep with him?'

'No. Not quite. But I might as well have done.' She looked utterly shamefaced. 'That doesn't exactly leave me room for manoeuvre, does it? I mean, that's a pretty big signal. I can't behave like that and tell him he can't have anything to do with us.'

Guy decided it was time to speak plainly. It was the oldest trick in the book, getting into a girl's knickers in order to gain the upper hand.

'I'm quite sure, from what I've heard of him, that he put you under pressure. Or at least took advantage of your vulnerable position. He was trying to undermine you, Honor, and that's not fair. He's playing dirty.'

'So you don't think I'm a prick-tease?'

Guy winced. He couldn't think of anyone less of a prick-tease than Honor.

'No. But I can think of plenty of words for Johnny. I know he probably feels strongly about Ted, but he should have a bit more respect for you as his mother. He should stop toying with your emotions.'

He picked up Honor's glass to go and get her a refill. He didn't trust himself not to go and say too much. He was amazed at the strength of feeling that rushed through him, and how protective he felt. He hadn't met this Johnny yet, but he didn't like him already.

At three o'clock that afternoon, Bill Weeks slunk back behind the wheel of his Ford Focus, grinning gleefully to himself.

He'd come straight down to Eversleigh that morning after his conversation with Rozzi, to recce the manor house, get the lie of the land and perhaps do a little bit of digging in the village while he built up a profile of Guy Portias. What he hadn't imagined, in his wildest dreams, was Guy emerging from the manor with a tall, leggy brunette on his arm, entirely oblivious that Bill was in the bushes running off a few establishing shots of the old ancestral pile, including a close-up of the family crest and motto over the front door.

He'd disguised himself as a walker. You could get away with anything in sturdy socks and boots and an ordnance survey map round your neck. You just looked confused and said you'd got lost if you were caught somewhere you shouldn't be. He didn't even need to hide his equipment, for as well as a walker he was a keen birdwatcher and amateur photographer. Bill was a practised liar.

He'd strolled into the pub ten minutes after Guy and his companion. He loved that word: companion. It said so little and yet so much. He took up a vantage point on a stool at the bar, ordered a pint and a ploughman's, and spent the next hour pretending to read the local paper while watching the pair of them engrossed in deep soul-searching conversation.

She was a pretty girl. Bill ran through some adjectives in his head. Gamine, he decided upon. It had a Hepburn-esque ring to it, and it wasn't too hackneyed. Even if he did churn out scurrilous stories for the gutter press, Bill still had some pride in his work.

Now they were getting up to leave. Bill waited until the wooden door had shut behind them with the click of a latch.

'Blimey, isn't that a red kite?' he'd asked the startled barman, and bounded over to the window to run off half a roll of film of them leaving the car park. 'You wouldn't think you'd get them round here, would you?'

21

Honor went back to work that afternoon with a slightly heavy head from three Bloody Marys, but much lighter of heart. It had been wonderful to have an objective opinion about her situation. She'd nearly driven herself mad the night before, going round and round the alternatives in her head. Now she was happy she had the right to stand her ground, to insist that Johnny should stay at arm's length for a little while longer. She spent the rest of the afternoon showing Marilyn how to pipe choux pastry on to baking sheets for savoury éclairs, which she would then fill with a delicious creamy smoked haddock mixture. Marilyn was proving a quick learner.

'I quite like this cooking lark,' she admitted. 'All I ever do for Malachi is stodge – he needs it with all the physical work he does. But I could get into this.'

'Maybe I could train you up?' suggested Honor. 'There's going to be times when I won't be here. If I'm ill or something.'

'That's a very good idea,' said Madeleine, coming in on the end of the conversation. 'Marilyn could take the pressure off if you show her how to do the simpler stuff. I've got a feeling things are really going to take off here and you can't bear the whole burden. We are officially fully booked between now and New Year, and I can't expect you not to have some time off.'

Marilyn seemed thoroughly delighted with this new plan, and Honor was pleased. She and Malachi were a bit of an eccentric pair, but they were hardworking, and Marilyn was definitely wasted polishing the silver and changing bedlinen. Honor was also impressed with how eager Madeleine was to give them opportunities. They weren't, after all, to everyone's taste, but Madeleine seemed able to see beyond that. Honor knew for a fact that no one had wanted to employ Malachi when he'd come out of prison, because Marilyn had told her. But Madeleine had given him a chance. There was definitely more to her than met the eye, decided Honor. She might come across as the lady from the big house, but she had hidden depths.

At five, Guy and Malachi came in from building a huge bonfire of burnable rubbish they'd removed from the old garages: Madeleine was toying with the idea of converting them into further accommodation, but there were several generations of clutter to get rid of first. The six of them – including Ted, who'd been dropped off by one of the mothers from school – sat round the kitchen table devouring thickly buttered malt loaf and Jaffa Cakes.

'We better go in a minute, Maz,' said Malachi. 'Big night tonight.'

'It's fifties night at the Malmsley Working Men's Club,' explained Marilyn. 'There's a prize for the best-dressed couple. And the best dancers.'

'That sounds like fun.' Honor buttered more malt loaf for Ted, who was starving. Marilyn leaned forward and helped herself to a slice.

'Why don't you come?' suggested Marilyn. 'And you, Guy.'

She shot her boss a sly glance from under her long eyelashes. Guy looked at her askance.

'Fifties night? I haven't got anything to wear.'

'You don't have to be authentic; just look as if you've made a bit of an effort.' Marilyn waved her malt loaf excitedly. 'Go on, it would be a laugh. Anyway, we deserve an office outing. We've all worked hard this past couple of weeks.'

She sat back, satisfied that this last shot would provide the final turn of the screw. Honor and Guy were looking at each other, both obviously quite liking the idea.

'What about Ted?' Honor asked.

'I'll babysit,' offered Madeleine quickly. 'You wouldn't mind me coming to look after you, would you, Ted?'

'No – that would be cool.'

Honor hesitated.

'Honestly, I don't mind,' Madeleine assured her. 'You've worked your socks off for us. One night of fun is the least I can do to repay you.'

Ten minutes later, as Honor hurried Ted back up the street to get ready for her impromptu evening out, she reflected that there had been a definite sense of conspiracy in the kitchen.

At seven o'clock, there was a knock on the door. Honor answered it to Madeleine and, standing behind her, a self-conscious Guy in jeans and a tight white T-shirt, a packet of cigarettes rolled up in his sleeve. His hair was dishevelled, even more so than usual.

'I can't do the quiff thing like Malachi,' he complained. 'I've put half a ton of gel in it and it won't do a thing.'

'Just grease it back,' giggled Honor, pushing his hair back with her fingers. 'That looks great. James Dean, eat your heart out.'

'Hardly,' grinned Guy. 'But it's sweet of you to say so. You look fantastic, by the way. Like a fifties movie star about to jump on a Vespa.'

She was wearing three-quarter-length jeans, a red cardigan and matching sneakers, a red silk flower on a velvet ribbon tied at her throat. Swiftly, she showed Madeleine the kettle, the remote, the corkscrew, the telephone, the fridge –

'Just go and enjoy yourselves,' interrupted Madeleine, amused, as the bugling fanfare of Malachi's horn sounded outside.

'Eight o'clock bed for Ted, and don't let him tell you otherwise,' called Honor over her shoulder as Madeleine shooed them out of the door.

Pulled up at the kerb outside was a car as long as Honor's house was wide – an authentic Ford Zodiac, gleaming in the lamplight from its chrome grille to its fins at the back. The CD player – not original, but necessary, and cleverly disguised – was blaring out Eddie and the Hot Rods. The roof was down, as it was a mild evening, and in the front sat Marilyn in a vintage prom dress and Malachi in a Hawaiian shirt, their hair bouffant and quiffed respectively.

'This is like a movie set,' breathed Honor. 'How cool is this car?'

With a whoop of excitement, she jumped in the back behind Marilyn. Guy followed suit, springing lithely into the back seat without opening the door.

'Y'all ready?' drawled Malachi in his best Elvis, and the car accelerated away down the high street with a squeal of rubber.

Malmsley Working Men's Club was packed to the gunnels. Everyone from the village from eighteen to eighty was there. Quiffs, ponytails and sideburns abounded; there were drainpipes, brothel-creepers, winkle-pickers, drape coats, bootlace ties, bobby sox, saddle shoes, petticoats, baseball jackets, pedal-pushers – everyone had plundered their wardrobes, charity shops and jumble sales to make the effort. And the atmosphere was infectious: with a few well-chosen accessories, the room had been made to feel like a high school prom.

Halfway through the evening, Guy realized he hadn't called Richenda to see how her day had gone. He hadn't even read the revelations in the newspaper. He hadn't had the stomach for it. But he knew he should phone to see how she was, so he nipped outside and called her on his mobile.

'I've taken the staff out for the evening,' he said. 'Fifties night at the local working men's club. Mum wanted me to rally the troops. I think it's called incentivizing.'

He tried his best to sound like a patronizing, long-suffering boss who couldn't wait to dump his workforce and get back to his own bed. He certainly couldn't admit that he was having the best fun he'd had since a mojito-fuelled salsa session in downtown Havana. They'd eaten hot dogs and knickerbocker glories, and now Marilyn and Malachi, bless them, were doing their best to teach them the rudiments of rock and roll. Guy knew from the salsa experience that what he lacked in skill he could only make up for in enthusiasm, but Honor was very quick to pick up the steps. She and Malachi were twirling expertly on the dance floor; Guy had begged a moment's respite from Marilyn, who was quite happy to sit out and sip Coke through a straw in a glass bottle, her stiletto-clad feet jiggling in time with the slap of the double bass.

'Mum and I went out for a quiet dinner,' Richenda was saying. She sounded quite relaxed. 'There weren't any cameras, thank God.'

'Well, you've got nothing else to hide, have you?' answered Guy, hoping the remark didn't sound too loaded. 'I better go and buy another round of drinks for the workers,' he added quickly, seeing Marilyn come outside and look round for him. She waved enthusiastically as he hung up.

'There's a bloke from the local paper. He wants to take our photo.'

'Bloody paparazzi,' grinned Guy amiably as he wandered back in. Malachi, Honor and Marilyn were lined up in front of the stage, arm in arm, grinning. He slipped in between the two girls, curling an arm round each of their waists.

'That's perfect,' said the photographer, fiddling with his zoom. 'Perfect. Just hold it there while I do another, in case that one doesn't come out properly.'

Later, as they drove back home, the roof now up to protect against the drop in temperature, Honor fell asleep on Guy's shoulder holding the trophy she and Malachi had won for Best Dancers. Marilyn bore Guy no grudge for scuppering their chances, as she clutched to her ample bosom the much-coveted Best Dressed Couple trophy she and Malachi had retained for the third year running.

It was totally bizarre, Guy reflected, as Malachi drove the Zodiac smoothly through the country lanes that led from Malmsley back to Eversleigh. Last night he had gone to a glittering social gathering stuffed with famous names and faces that most people could only ever dream of attending. The evening had left him cold. Whereas tonight, in a dingy working men's club in a shabby village on the outskirts of Evesham, in the company of his cook, his cleaner and his gardener, he had had the time of his life. And he thought he knew the reason why. He looked down at Honor, her mascara slightly smudged, her lipstick worn away, and he felt his heart skip a momentary beat.

Honor had bared her soul to him in the pub earlier that day, and spared him little detail – though he'd been grateful that she hadn't elaborated on her skirmish with Johnny the night before. He could only imagine what had gone on, and every time he thought of her in the hands of the monster he had created in his head, he gritted his teeth. He told himself not to be so reactionary. Johnny was probably a perfectly reasonable bloke. Women always painted a black picture of people they didn't want you to like, especially when they were asking you for advice – to make sure you gave them the advice they wanted to hear. Besides, it was none of his business and he'd do best to keep out of it. It was a complicated enough situation and he was, he reminded himself, engaged to be married.

To Richenda. Richenda, who had kept her murky

secrets close to her until the very last – and who, he still felt strongly, would not have confided in him even now if her hand hadn't been forced. Richenda: calculated, rehearsed, word-perfect, in full costume and make-up for the performance that was her everyday life. Was that really how he saw her, he wondered? Had the scales fallen away from his eyes that quickly, because of one betrayal? What about the woman he'd fallen in love with? Had she gone for good?

To be replaced by another, perhaps?

Guy knew he was being ridiculous. Immature and over-emotional, losing his heart and his temper too quickly. Grow up, Portias, he told himself, then thought ruefully that perhaps there was something to be said for eternal bachelordom. At least that way you didn't get yourself into scrapes, even if people did talk and make ghastly suppositions about your sexuality.

As they pulled up outside Honor's house, Guy shook her gently awake. She looked at him, confused for a moment, then smiled with sheepish embarrassment.

'Oh God – I didn't fall asleep on you, did I? I hope I wasn't dribbling.'

'Of course not.'

Guy got out to escort Honor to the door. Inside the house, Madeleine was ready with her coat, alerted no doubt by the powerful roar of the Zodiac engine driving off at full throttle.

'He's fast asleep. I've just checked him,' she whispered at the bottom of the stairs, waving goodbye and slipping out of the house to spare Honor the awkwardness of offering to pay for her services.

Mother and son stepped along the street, breathing in the cold night air.

'How was your evening?'

'Great fun,' said Guy heartily, to avoid further questions and cover up the fact that, like Honor's organic chocolate earlier, his heart was slowly melting.

22

At three o'clock on Friday afternoon, Honor was fighting with a saucepan full of sugar syrup that didn't want
to caramelize. It had been a bad morning; everyone was
tired from the night before, and time was running out.
Gone was the soft and vulnerable creature of the day
before, Guy observed, as Honor whipped them all into
line. Marilyn had let a batch of shortbread stars burn to
a crisp in the Aga and found herself torn off a strip. That
prompted Madeleine to remember that one of the party
had a wheat intolerance – a vital piece of information
she'd forgotten to pass on to Honor. The resulting atmosphere was therefore a little tense as Honor re-jigged all
the menus.

'Shit!' she swore. 'I've got to go and pick up Ted. I'm
never going to get everything done in time.'

'I'll go and get him,' offered Guy. 'I've done my jobs.
The guests aren't arriving till seven. He can come and
help me in the garden for an hour while you finish off.'

'You're a star,' said Honor. 'Whose idea was it to do
spun sugar baskets?'

'Yours, I think,' grinned Guy cheerfully. 'See you later.'

As he left the house and made his way down the high
street, he realized he felt back on track today. His dis-
illusionment had abated somewhat, and anyway, with the
imminent arrival of another batch of guests, he didn't

have time to dwell on matters of the heart. He'd get the weekend out of the way, then he could focus on his private life. Richenda had phoned to confirm that she and her mother Sally were coming down for Sunday lunch. Guy had resisted the temptation to ask whether there was going to be a photocall capturing the happy moment for posterity. Sarcasm wasn't going to get them anywhere.

He took Ted back up to the garden, where they spent a good half hour scratting around for conkers until Ted's pockets were full to bursting. Guy smiled as he pictured himself doing the same thing nearly thirty years ago; the garden had barely changed. It was a paradise for children, with its secret paths and dens and hiding places. Then he remembered something.

'Hey,' he said to Ted. 'Follow me. I've got a surprise.'

Charles got his usual early train home on Friday afternoon. He leaned back in the comfort of his first-class seat, his eyes closed, not intending to sleep but just wanting to enjoy planning the weekend ahead in his mind. It seemed the perfect antidote to the utter hideousness of the past few days.

He couldn't even bring himself to think about Wednesday. He'd gone to bed that evening blind drunk, and all he could hear was the sound of Henty and Travis talking and laughing in the kitchen as he lay in his bed trying to stop it spinning. The day after had been horrendous. He'd had the most monumental hangover: champagne always gave him a blinder, and he hadn't been able to focus on anything. By the time he'd got home in the evening, children's activities took over and he hadn't actually clapped eyes on Henty until half nine, by which time he was ready for bed. The relief of waking up on Friday with a clear head had been marvellous. He'd spent a useful morning at the office, and now felt filled with resolve on the journey home.

They were going to have a good old-fashioned family weekend. Who needed thrills and excitement? The price was too high. He felt a desperate need for some stability after the recent turmoil. Perhaps they could make some plans for the house together. Henty was longing for a new kitchen, and the boys' bedrooms could do with revamping. He'd held off for a long time because of the expense, but a couple of his authors' royalty cheques had come in that week. Bugger it, he thought. He'd go off and get paint samples, pick up some kitchen brochures, get Robin and Walter the study bunks they'd been going on about . . .

As he idly ran through various possibilities he felt something brush itself against his leg. Without opening his eyes, he moved slightly, not wanting to embarrass whoever had inadvertently rubbed against him. Moments later, he felt it again, more insistent. Someone was running their foot up the inside of his trousers! This time he looked up with an indignant glare. Sitting on the other side of the table, fixing him with a sweet, innocent smile, was Fleur.

'Hello, Charles,' she said. 'Fancy us being on the same train. I've been up to town to do some shopping.' She indicated a clutch of carrier bags to prove her statement. 'I was just going to go and get a hot chocolate from the buffet car when I spotted you.'

Charles could only manage a strangled greeting from the back of his throat.

'Aren't you pleased to see me?' She leaned forward. 'We might as well take the opportunity to talk about our . . . project.'

Charles's eyes flicked wildly round the carriage. There could be any number of people on board that he knew. He didn't see anyone he recognized in the immediate vicinity, but he knew from experience that people listened in keenly to other people's conversations.

'Not here,' he muttered.

'What?'

'Not in here.'

With his eyes, he indicated behind him to the toilets. The sign luckily read vacant. Fleur nodded her understanding, got up and made her way down the aisle, then disappeared through the sliding door. Charles looked at his watch. They were at least half an hour from Eldenbury, or he might have done a runner. Instead, he gave it two minutes, then followed her, tapping on the door. She opened it up and let him inside, grinning mischievously. No sooner was the door closed than she pressed herself urgently up against him.

'Hold on, hold on!' he squawked in alarm, pushing her away. 'What's all this about?'

'We've got unfinished business.'

'I'm a happily married man.'

'And I'm a happily married woman. That doesn't stop us, does it? I don't want to marry you. I just want to fuck you.'

She leaned back against the sink matter-of-factly,

thrusting out her chest. Charles looked aghast.

'Not in here. I couldn't.'

'You don't want to join the 125 club?'

'No.'

Fleur surveyed him, a little smile playing on her lips, as if debating whether to pursue the issue, then relented.

'So – how's the pilot looking?'

The rushes were still sitting in Charles's study. He couldn't bear to look at them. In fact, he'd been meaning to erase them, destroy the evidence. He didn't want the tape getting into the wrong hands. There'd be a lot of explaining to do. He scolded himself. He really must learn to be more careful. What with the knickers, and the tape . . . he really was too careless for this infidelity lark. Not that he had any intention of taking it any further. Though he thought Fleur had other ideas.

He feigned a nod of enthusiasm, for the time being.

'It's looking good. There's still a lot of work to do, of course.'

'Can we have a private viewing? When it's ready?'

'Of course. Good idea.' Bad idea. Very bad idea. He looked at his watch. 'Hey look – we better get back to our seats. We're nearly at Eldenbury.'

Fleur went to unbolt the door.

'Oh dear,' she said after a moment. 'The lock seems to be stuck.'

Looking back on it afterwards, Guy was sure he had only been gone two minutes. But then, on reflection, you didn't leave six-year-old boys alone for even one minute. Especially not if there was an old tree house right in front of their eyes. Even if you had said don't go near it till we make sure it's safe. He'd gone to fetch a hammer and nails, and when he got back Ted was lying on the ground, perfectly still and as white as a sheet.

As he looked down at the little boy, Guy realized he had never felt fear before.

It had been quite possibly the most humiliating experience of Charles's life. He'd managed to stop Fleur pulling the communication cord. She'd insisted that otherwise they'd end up in Hereford, but Charles imagined everyone lining up on the platform to see what the emergency was, and the two of them filing out. Instead he had to stick his head out of the window at Eldenbury and call the guard's attention.

'It's a bit embarrassing,' he'd explained in a stage whisper. 'I'm locked in the lavatory.'

Behind him he could feel Fleur convulsed with giggles.

'*Oh dear, what can the matter be?*' she sang.

'Shut up,' he said. 'It's not funny!'

'Where's your sense of humour?'

The guard had done something magical with his penknife and the lock slid back. He looked a little taken aback when two people instead of one emerged from the cubicle, but by then it was too late to attract anyone else's attention to the situation and Charles barely thanked him before bolting off down the platform and mingling in with everyone else.

He hid in the waiting room until he saw Fleur climb into her Merc and drive off. Even now he wasn't convinced that her appearance on the train had been a coincidence. Charles remembered mentioning that he always got the three-eighteen on a Friday. His heart pounded. This was getting a bit spooky. He wasn't sure, but he thought he might have got himself his very own stalker.

Honor sat in the ambulance at Ted's side, utterly transfixed with terror. Her whole world was imploding; her mind whirling with random thoughts and images. Nothing was coherent because nothing was certain. The only thing that gave her any vague reassurance was the thought of Guy following behind the ambulance. Somehow that gave her a crumb of comfort, knowing he would be at her side throughout the ordeal. The ambulance men were kind, but refused to give any prognosis. She supposed they had to stay on the fence. They couldn't say Ted was going to be all right, because he might not be.

He was just so very still. She had never seen him so still. Even in his sleep he gave off a certain energy, his limbs occasionally twitching. He was a wriggler. There was no hint of wriggling now. Whatever state of consciousness he was in, there were no signals being transmitted. Her stomach churned. Her mouth was dry. And, strangely, her eyes. There were no tears yet. Presumably because she didn't know yet what to cry for. Without a diagnosis, you couldn't prescribe the amount or quality of tears needed.

She could feel the ambulance slow, feel it encounter the speed bumps on the hospital drive, and her heart began to pound. The agonizing limbo was at an end; the expertise and machines that would ascertain Ted's future were only minutes away now. The doors of the ambulance were opened and she climbed out to wait on the pavement, knowing that hanging over Ted would impede the work of the paramedics. She felt a strong arm round her shoulder. Without looking, she knew it was Guy, and she allowed herself to fall against his chest for a moment to draw some strength.

The stretcher went past. For a moment she had a flash forward to the future: a tiny coffin being held aloft by pallbearers. Then she told herself not to be stupid. He was still breathing. Where there was life there was hope. This was the twenty-first century. She grasped Guy's hand and hurried inside the hospital, trying to ignore the sympathetic glances of passers-by. Again she had the sense of mourners at a funeral, pouring sympathy on the grieving mother.

Once inside, protocol took over. The form-filling was interminable; the questions tedious and confusing – or was that just her state of mind? They mistook Guy for the father; she had to explain over and over again. At one point they asked her if she wanted to phone anyone and she said no, even though a small voice told her she should contact Johnny. Finally they were left to wait, on hard orange plastic chairs, in a small cubicle, listening to the mayhem of the accident and emergency unit: the barked orders, the complaints of the patients, the ringing phones, the two of them still and quiet amidst the chaos. Guy gripped her hand tightly but neither of them spoke. There was nothing to say.

At last, the curtain was drawn back by an authoritative hand. The swish was so certain, so definite, that Honor knew the perpetrator was the bearer of the verdict. She shut her eyes, not sure if she could bear it, and felt Guy's protective arm around her once more.

The consultant spoke, in the smooth modulated voice of one who couldn't be contradicted.

'I've got a little boy out here who wants his mummy.'

Honor slumped against Guy with a low moan. The joy that flooded through her made her feel sick. She could barely stand up. She took in several juddering breaths to steady herself.

'Is he going to be OK?'

The consultant nodded kindly.

'We're going to have to take him up to X-ray shortly – I think he may have cracked his collarbone. And we'll have to keep him in tonight for observation. But I think he's going to be fine.'

Henty stood in the queue at the post office in Eldenbury, clutching a large brown padded envelope to her chest. As she arrived at the window, she slid it carefully under the partition.

'Special delivery, please.'

She couldn't risk this getting lost. Ten thousand carefully chosen words. Words that had tumbled out of her mind in a glittering cascade, falling exactly where she had wanted them. She had reached a natural turning point in her story: before she poured her heart and soul into completing it, she needed to know if anyone would want to read on. Or was it meaningless, mindless drivel?

Harry Jenkins was her old editor, who'd steered her through the first two novels and had tried to coax a third out of her, who had been so patient and supportive and, in the end, when she had become thoroughly frustrated and miserable, had gently suggested she have a break. At the time she didn't think he'd meant fifteen years – he'd kept in touch every few months for the first two, but then his letters had trailed off. After ten years his Christmas cards stopped, though she suspected it was his assistant who had culled her from the list, not Harry himself. But she knew he'd be pleased to hear from her. He was an absolute sweetheart. Better still, he wouldn't be afraid to tell her it was absolute crap. He'd told her to throw her first attempts at a third novel straight in the bin. He didn't believe in writers torturing themselves to produce something they didn't believe in.

Henty had believed in what she was writing this time. It was why it had been so easy. The question was, would anyone else be interested? She didn't know the market any more. What she'd written wasn't exactly chick-lit – she was too old to be a chick. But it was fun. And there was a message underneath that she thought a lot of women would identify with. It was the tale of a Cotswold housewife who, devastated when her husband leaves her, embarks on a trail of sexual reawakening courtesy of a young garage mechanic. It was bitter-sweet, semi-pornographic but ultimately optimistic. Henty had a feeling in her gut that it would be a success: there must be hundreds of women out there who could relate to what her heroine was going through. She knew Harry would give her an honest appraisal. He'd always understood her work completely; the way she twinned naivety with naughtiness, then added an unexpected twist to the tale to show that what she'd been writing wasn't just superficial froth.

She'd printed out the opening chapters that morning, admiring the way the jet black letters covered the page so authoritatively, each word perfect in itself; so different from her earlier manuscripts, which had been covered in sticky blobs of Tippex. And although she knew she shouldn't, because it was unspeakably naff, she tied it up with a big pink ribbon, then added a label, writing on it with a thick fountain pen: 'To Harry – Part One. Only fifteen years overdue – love Henty.'

Resisting the urge to kiss the parcel for good luck – nearly as naff as the ribbon – she paid the cashier and left, retrieving Thea and Lily from the magazine rack, where they were drooling over photos of boy bands, and hoicking Walter and Robin away from the sweet counter.

When she got back, Charles was already home, sitting in the kitchen in his jeans. He looked very pleased with himself.

'What is it?' asked Henty, intrigued.

'I've decided you deserve a treat.'

'Oh.'

'I mean, bugger it, if you can't spoil your wife every now and again, then what's the point? And if you can't really afford it, so what? It's only money.'

'Goodness,' said Henty.

'We can go out and choose it tomorrow. Whatever colour you like, whatever extras – it's a big investment so I want you to have exactly what you want.'

Henty's eyes were shining with excitement. Charles felt hugely gratified.

'Is it what I think it is?' she asked.

Charles nodded.

'It's long overdue, but I think it's time. We'll go round the showrooms tomorrow.' He beamed. 'Like I said, whatever you want. It's your treat. A brand new, state-of-the-art kitchen.'

Henty's face fell.

'Kitchen?' she echoed. 'I thought you meant a sports car.'

Charles looked perplexed.

'Sports car? What on earth would be the point of that? It's totally impractical.'

'I kind of thought that *was* the point.'

'I thought you wanted a new kitchen?'

'Yes – but not for me. Not as a treat. Because we need it.'

Charles looked thoroughly crestfallen.

'I thought you'd be pleased.'

'Well, I suppose I am . . . pleased. But it's not something I can get excited about.'

'Forget it, then. I'm not forking out twenty grand if you're not interested.'

He pulled open a drawer sulkily to find the corkscrew. Henty sighed.

'Of course I'm interested. I'm sorry. I just got the wrong end of the stick, that's all.'

She didn't want Charles in a strop. Charles in a strop all weekend was hard work. Travis ambled in, and Henty tried to inject some enthusiasm into her voice.

'Hey, Travis. Guess what? Charles is going to buy me a new kitchen.'

The expression on Travis's face said it all.

*

Honor was going to spend the night at the hospital. Guy drove her back home to get her night things and the toy monkey that Ted couldn't sleep without. He felt rather subdued. The incident had shaken him. How could he ever have forgiven himself if Ted hadn't been all right?

He pulled up outside Honor's house. He had to speak.

'Honor – I'm just . . . so sorry. I don't know what to say.'

She smiled at him wearily.

'It was an accident.'

She spoke automatically. It was probably easy for her to say, now she knew Ted was all right. But what would she have said if he'd been killed? He could have been. Fifteen feet . . . Guy put his arms on the steering wheel and leaned his head on them for a moment, overwhelmed now it was all over.

'Hey . . .'

He felt her soft breath on his cheek, her arm slide round his shoulder. He felt something wet on his cheeks, and realized they were his tears. They were being brushed away gently.

'It's OK,' came the reassuring whisper, and as he turned his head and opened his eyes, their lips met. The kiss was intense, a moment of healing and forgiveness and relief that soothed both their hearts, wiping out the trauma. Shakily, they parted, and looked at each other.

'I shouldn't have done that,' said Guy. 'I'm sorry – it was just the relief . . .'

'I shouldn't either,' said Honor, flushed with embarrassment. 'I don't know what I was thinking of. It must have been the shock.' She opened the car door hastily.

'I'll go and get my stuff. Don't worry – I can drive myself back to the hospital.'

'No – you're in no fit state to drive.'

'I'll be fine. Honestly. You've got guests to see to. I can drive myself back in the morning.'

She insisted, and Guy had to accept that perhaps she didn't want him in the vicinity, not if he was going to pounce on her at every opportunity. Cursing his weakness, he drove off down the road, unable to believe what a complete and utter prat he'd made of himself. He should know better at his age.

Honor barely slept a wink that night at the hospital. She was on a deeply uncomfortable camp bed next to Ted's. Apart from feeling the need to check he was all right every fifteen minutes every time she shut her eyes she remembered kissing Guy, and cringed inwardly. He must think she was absolutely sex-starved, especially when she'd admitted getting embroiled with Johnny only the day before. Even now she didn't know what had got into her.

She fled the hospital as soon as she could on Saturday morning, once she was happy that Ted was a hundred per cent and had been discharged by the doctor. The atmosphere in there reminded her all too grimly of what might have been. She wanted to get the pair of them home, into a hot bath each, into their comfort clothes, in front of the telly.

At eleven o'clock the doorbell rang and she answered the door sheepishly, praying it wasn't Guy, even though she was fairly sure he would steer clear of her after her wanton behaviour. To her relief it was Marilyn, who'd come up to fetch a few things from her freezer.

'Madeleine says you're not to worry. She's cheated by buying a load of stuff in from the deli in Eldenbury, and Suzanna from the Honeycote Arms has sent over some puddings. She thinks we'll get away with it.'

'I'm so sorry to leave you in the lurch.'

'Don't be ridiculous. You can't leave Ted.'

'Actually, he's fine. He wants to go and play football with Walter. I'm the one that feels a bit shaky,' admitted Honor.

'You don't feel as bad as Guy, I can tell you,' said Marilyn knowingly.

'It wasn't his fault,' insisted Honor.

'I know, but you know what a lovely bloke he is. I can tell he's gutted.'

Honor didn't reply. She didn't want to talk about Guy. In fact, the sooner all the events of yesterday were eradicated from her memory bank, the better. She couldn't bear the thought of facing him again on Monday. Maybe she should resign? But perhaps that was making too much of it. No, she'd just keep her head down and keep out of his way. Keep things on a businesslike level.

'Honor?' Marilyn was looking at her, concerned. 'Are you OK?'

'Yes, I'm fine. Sorry. I didn't get much sleep in the hospital.'

'By the way, he sent these down for Ted. With lots of love.'

She held out a carrier bag. Honor peeped inside. *Beano*

annuals. His old *Beano* annuals. For some reason this made her want to cry.

'Say thank you to him, will you?' she asked rather shakily.

The two of them spent the rest of the morning devouring the annuals. After lunch Honor tucked Ted up in bed for a proper nap, then fell asleep herself on the sofa. She woke two hours later to find Johnny standing in front of her. She sat up, confused for a moment, then realized that of course he was there – they'd agreed he would come over again to look after Ted.

'Aren't you going to work?'

He looked her up and down, bemused. She was still in her tartan pyjamas and slipper socks.

'I haven't been at work. They've had to manage without me.' She sat up and stretched. 'Ted fell out of the tree house yesterday and broke his collarbone.'

'What?'

'He's fine. He's got his arm in a sling, that's all, and he's got to take it easy –'

'What do you mean, he fell out of a tree house? Where?'

'At Eversleigh.'

'Well, who the hell was watching him? You don't let six-year-old boys into tree houses unsupervised.'

'He wasn't unsupervised. Guy was watching.'

'What – watching him fall out?'

'It was an accident.'

'Why didn't you call me?'

'Because . . .' Honor stopped for a moment. She'd remembered thinking she should call Johnny, and realizing that he was the last person she wanted to see. And

406

now realized how selfish she had been. Of course she should have called him. 'It all happened so quickly. And once I knew he was all right – there didn't seem any point.'

'No point?' Johnny was shouting now, his eyes blazing with anger. 'Jaysus, Honor. What were you thinking of? I'm his bloody father!'

Honor flashed him a warning look, but it was too late. Ted was standing in the doorway, looking backward and forward between the two of them.

'Is it true?' he demanded. 'Are you really my dad?'

23

A deathly hush hung in the air for a moment. Honor looked at Johnny, aghast. He mouthed 'Sorry' to her, equally agonized, knowing that his outburst had brought the moment of reckoning. Honor gave a small, helpless shrug, mouthing back 'What do I do?' He gestured to indicate it was up to her. He wasn't avoiding responsibility, merely deferring to her. Meanwhile, Ted stood uncertainly in the doorway, clutching his monkey, hopping awkwardly from one foot to the other.

Honor made a split-second decision. She couldn't hide it from Ted any longer. To deny it would be to actively lie to him, and she'd never done that. She put out her arm; Ted scuttled over and tucked himself underneath it, instinctively knowing from the expressions on the grown-ups' faces that what was coming was important.

'Yes,' Honor said calmly. 'Johnny's your daddy. And very proud of you he is too. He's been wanting to tell you for a long time, but I asked him to wait. Because . . . I wanted you to get to know each other first.'

'So – does that mean I've got a proper mum and dad? Like everyone else?'

'Yes.'

'Is he going to live here with us? Are we going to be like a real family?'

There was such a look of hope and expectation in his

face, Honor felt a pang. Had he always felt as if he was missing out? How could she deny him what he obviously so badly wanted?

'We're . . . not sure yet. We've got a lot of important decisions to make. But the main thing is that Johnny will always be here for you from now on.'

Johnny was hovering awkwardly, wary of Ted's reaction. The little boy was surveying him, still a little unsure. He frowned.

'What do I call you?'

'You can call me what you like. Johnny. Or Dad. Personally, I like Mr Potato Head.'

Ted giggled. He took a step towards Johnny, the ice broken. Johnny knelt down and put out his arms.

'Come here, big boy. Come and give me a hug.'

Ted slipped obediently into his embrace. Johnny closed his eyes, overwhelmed by the emotion of at last being recognized. Ted seemed to sense how important this moment was, and snuggled into him. Honor turned away, choked. She knew in her heart of hearts that this was right, that Ted and Johnny should be united. But now she had to steel herself for the inevitable onslaught, the questions, the pressure. How on earth was she supposed to decide what was best for all of them? And did what was best for her come into it? She'd never resented making sacrifices for Ted before, but getting back together with Johnny might be going beyond the call of duty.

One thing was certain: life was never going to be the same.

*

Charles was feeling decidedly po-faced. After the damp squib of his offer to buy Henty a new kitchen the evening before, things had gone from bad to worse. Henty seemed rather excitable, like a skittish mare. He'd come down the stairs earlier and heard her giggling. The sound made him stop short, because he realized he hadn't heard it for a long, long time. It had been one of the things that had made him fall in love with her, her giggle. It wasn't silly or irritating, like it would be in some women. It was charming, infectious.

What the bloody hell was Travis doing to make her giggle like that?

Even more disconcerting, she stopped as soon as Charles came into the room. The two of them didn't look guilty, but he definitely got the feeling that he was an intruder. He bristled. This was his house. Henty was his wife. Why should he be left feeling like a gooseberry?

She was wearing a pink T-shirt he hadn't seen before, and a pair of black jeans that made her look . . . well, not thin, because Henty was curvaceous. But she'd definitely lost weight – or perhaps it was because she wasn't wearing one of her usual baggy sweaters. She'd tied her hair up in a butterfly clip, and a few tendrils hung down either side of her new fringe, giving her a glamorous, dishevelled look. And she was wearing lipstick. She didn't usually wear make-up unless they were going out. Charles felt a flicker of panic. Why the sudden interest in her appearance?

Travis slid off the kitchen table where he'd been perched.

'I'm off into Eldenbury for a few beers, if you guys don't need me tonight?'

Travis had already made himself a network of friends. He was one of those people that made new acquaintances easily: a couple of chats with the local farrier and he'd already been absorbed into his social circle. A gang of them met up every Saturday for a drinking session followed by an Indian – a high-spirited bunch, but good fun. Travis fitted in very well.

Charles didn't miss the look of disappointment on Henty's face.

'Shall I run you in?' she offered swiftly. 'You don't need to worry about driving then; you can get a cab back.'

'That would be great.'

Travis swung his battered leather jacket off the back of his chair and slipped it on, then ran his fingers through his hair nonchalantly. That was the extent of his grooming and he looked gorgeous. Charles gritted his teeth. If he hadn't lost his licence he could offer to drive Travis. Somehow he felt the less time Henty spent alone with him, the better.

'Aren't we going out?' he asked Henty.

'I hadn't organized anything. Unless you have?'

'No.'

'Shall I pick us up a video while I'm there?'

Yippee, thought Charles. Saturday night in with a video. Wasn't the whole point of having Travis to give them the chance of a social life, not give him the opportunity to go on the razz? But he didn't protest.

'If you like,' he replied.

Henty picked up the car keys.

'Can you give the kids a shout? There's a tuna bake in the oven – it should be ready in five minutes. I'll do us some pasta when I get back.'

A moment later she was gone. Charles didn't think he had ever felt the kitchen so empty.

At seven o'clock, Johnny and Ted went into Eldenbury for champagne and 7-Up.

'This is a Very Special Occasion. We need a toast,' Johnny had announced solemnly. 'Come on, big boy. We'll leave your mum to get the supper ready.'

Honor had opened her mouth indignantly, but Johnny gave her a wink.

'Only joking. We'll pick up a Chinese.'

'Chinese?' said Ted. 'I've never had a Chinese.'

'Well, this is where your education starts,' said Johnny. 'We need sesame prawn toasts and wonton and spring rolls and chow mein and prawn crackers . . .'

'Chicken and cashew nuts for me, please,' said Honor.

'I know,' said Johnny, holding her gaze. For some reason, she blushed. Of course he knew. How many take-aways had they had in the past?

As soon as they'd gone, Honor sat down at the kitchen table, chewing the side of her thumb. In some ways it was an enormous relief that the burden she'd been carrying round all of Ted's life was lifted. Oblivious to the fact that a can of worms had been opened, Ted had been thrilled, and now he wouldn't leave Johnny's side. There'd been a barrage of questions, some of which they'd been able to answer, some of which they hadn't. She had to admit that Johnny was brilliant at deflecting the trickier enquiries. He had a way of being able to explain things that satisfied Ted, for the time being at least. Probably because he behaved like a child himself much of the time, thought Honor ruefully.

'So, how are you my dad, exactly? I thought you had to be married to have a baby?' Ted had asked, his mind clearly working overtime.

'Sometimes God gets it a bit wrong,' explained Johnny. 'He's so busy, you see. He knew your mummy was the right mummy for you, but he forgot to check if she had a husband. By the time he realized, it was too late. You had arrived.'

Their eyes met over the top of his head, each of them aware that the questions could get more complicated and more biological the more Ted thought about the replies he was getting. Which was the point at which Johnny suggested a boys' trip into town, leaving Honor alone to take stock of the situation. She still couldn't believe it, even now. Ted was ecstatic; Johnny was equally enchanted. It was only Honor who was wary. Rushing off for champagne was fine, she thought, but this was only the beginning. It was all very well having a heart-warming, Disney-style reunion, but there were a lot of issues to address. Sighing, she got out some porcelain bowls and the collection of mismatched chopsticks she had accumulated over the years. No doubt the answers would come to her, she told herself sternly. In the meantime, she should just relax.

The Chinese was a huge hit. Ted was as high as a kite: the combined novelty of having a father, staying up late, being allowed 7-Up and getting to grips with chopsticks, all mixed up with lashings of monosodium glutamate, meant he was in seventh heaven. Johnny too seemed euphoric: he was making crazy plans with Ted. For some reason the warning 'It'll all end in tears', so beloved of parents with overexcited children, kept repeating itself in Honor's head as she ate her chicken and cashew nuts. But she didn't want to be a party pooper, so she kept quiet. Who was she to spoil their moment, a moment they would probably remember for the rest of their lives?

Henty was ages. Charles fed the children, then sat at the kitchen table getting angrier and angrier. He could hear Robin and Walter squabbling upstairs, and the thump of loud music from Lily and Thea's room, but couldn't be bothered to go and remonstrate. Getting the girls to wash up had been like getting blood out of a stone – they'd moaned and groaned and hadn't even touched the pasta-encrusted serving dish, leaving it on the side to soak. He couldn't bear the thought of going up to tell them to go to bed. He didn't need more abuse. He was starving, but it didn't occur to him to start getting the supper ready. Women, in his experience, hated it when you took the initiative in the kitchen. He always seemed to use some-thing that was being saved for a special occasion, or fail to use something that needed eating up that very day. So he opened a bottle of wine instead, and found some Carr's water biscuits to keep his hunger at bay.

An hour and a half later, Henty finally rushed in.

'Sorry. Travis made me come and have a drink with his friends. They wanted me to go into Evesham to a club. Can you imagine? Everyone would have thought I was his mother.'

She flopped into a chair. Her cheeks were slightly

flushed. Charles wondered just how much she had had to drink, then decided that she wasn't foolish enough to risk her licence when he'd already lost his. Her demeanour must be a result of the company she'd been keeping.

'The kids have had their supper. The washing-up's done.'

Henty looked at him.

'What's the matter? You look like thunder.'

'Nothing,' said Charles sulkily. 'Only it's gone nine o'clock. I just wondered when we were going to eat, that's all.'

Henty rolled her eyes and stood up.

'Nothing stopping you from cooking,' she retorted.

Charles only just managed to stop his jaw from dropping. She'd never spoken to him like that before. What on earth had got into her? He watched as she bent down and pulled a saucepan out of the cupboard. She was looking decidedly sexy. Charles felt a sudden urge for the comfort of her warm curves. He put his arms around her from behind and nuzzled her neck.

'Why don't we just have an early night?'

Henty turned her head and looked at him.

'I thought you were hungry,' she said coolly and, slipping out of his grasp, she walked over to the sink to fill the pan with water.

Charles felt as if she'd tipped an ice-cold bucket of water over him. That was an overt rejection of his amorous advances. He felt panic. He didn't know what was happening to his wife, but he didn't like it.

'I'd like to take Ted away for a couple of days.'

Honor and Johnny were still sitting at the table,

finishing the dregs of the champagne. Ted had been dispatched to put on his pyjamas and brush his teeth.

Honor looked at him, her glass halfway to her mouth. 'What?'

'I'd like to . . . you know, *bond* with him or whatever they call it. Have some guy time together. He could come and stay at my place – it's half-term this week, isn't it?'

'Yes, but –' Honor struggled to find a valid objection. Johnny gave her an easy smile.

'Don't panic. I'm really quite house-trained these days. My new flat is as clean as a new pin – I've a woman who comes in once a week to keep it spotless. He'd have his own bed. I can do sausages and fish fingers without burning the place down. And there's always McDonald's.'

'I don't know,' said Honor reluctantly. 'What about his collarbone?'

'I'm a vet, remember? I didn't do seven years of medicine for nothing. He'd be in good hands. Anyway, it doesn't seem to be bothering him all that much.'

'No,' Honor had to agree. Ted had been very brave and hadn't complained at all.

'I thought if we went away, even if it's just for one night, it would give you a chance to have some space and think things over. Without us breathing down your neck.'

He had a point. Honor was finding it difficult to be objective about her situation. Johnny made her nervous. Ted made her panic. Neither of them through anything they did, but because she knew their futures lay in her hands. Besides, she was tired. It had been a stressful week in many ways. Some time to herself would be very welcome.

'I think we should ask Ted,' she said. 'If he wants to go, then fine.'

Of course, Ted thought the idea of going to stay with Johnny was the most exciting thing to have ever happened. Honor wasn't sure if she was relieved or hurt by his enthusiasm. She wanted to cry, but told herself not to be so silly. Johnny worshipped Ted. There was no way he would let him come to any harm. And it would do Ted good to spend a bit of time away from her. She didn't want him to turn into a mummy's boy, after all.

Charles and Henty had a bowl of seafood pasta in front of the telly. At eleven, Henty announced she was exhausted and went to bed. There was no hint of invitation in her voice. Charles sat alone in the living room and ploughed his way through a second bottle of wine. What on earth had he done to deserve this treatment?

He thought back carefully. She'd changed ever since Travis had arrived. She'd gone from meek and biddable to . . . well, she seemed to have a sense of purpose. And drive. And she seemed to have blossomed. It wasn't just the haircut or the make-up she'd taken to wearing. She had an aura that didn't come out of a bottle. An aura that Charles was fairly convinced came from sex. Illicit and satisfying sex. Well, he wasn't having it. He wasn't having some Lady Chatterley scenario going on under his nose, especially when he was paying the wages.

At half past twelve he heard a taxi in the driveway. Travis was back. Charles shot out of the kitchen door, into the stable yard and blocked Travis's way into the flat.

'Hey, Mr Beresford. Everything OK?'

Charles took a step forward, realizing that the heavy Chilean Merlot had made him slightly unsteady on his feet.

'Are you fucking my wife?'

The question came out rather more belligerently than Charles had intended. He'd meant to sound casual with an underlying menace, not downright aggressive. But Travis didn't seem fazed. He looked at him levelly. Bloody cool customer for his age, thought Charles. He should be shitting himself.

'No,' said Travis. 'No, I'm not. But if I was I'd be a lucky bloke.'

Charles took another step forward, clenching his fists.

'Watch it. That's my wife you're talking about.'

'I know it is. And you should be careful.'

'What do you mean?'

'You treat her like shit.'

He spat out the last word in his guttural accent. Charles blinked in surprise.

'Shit?'

'You know what I'm talking about.'

'I most certainly do not.'

'Don't try and pretend. You treat her exactly the way my dad treats my mum. A new kitchen? That only means one thing. Guilt. My mum has a different rock for every one of my dad's affairs.'

Travis gave him such a look of distaste that Charles recoiled. How the hell could this kid have any inkling about what had gone on with Fleur? He laughed smoothly.

'I really don't have any idea what you're talking about,' he said.

'Oh, I think you do,' replied Travis. 'And I think you should watch out.'

Charles feigned puzzlement.

'Is that some sort of threat?'

'No. It's a warning. Henty isn't the walkover you think she is. You carry on treating her like this and you might just lose out.'

Charles strode over and jabbed him in the chest, angry now.

'I think you better mind your own business. I've a good mind to sack you. How dare you insult me in my own home?'

Travis put his hands up.

'Hey. Back off. I don't want to come to blows. I'm only telling you this because I care about Henty. And not in the way you think. She's a really great person. She deserves some respect. Not to be treated like a doormat.'

'I do not treat her like a doormat.'

'Yes, you do. She's only had a life since I arrived and took some of the pressure off.'

'Is that what she told you?'

'No. Of course not. She's far too loyal.'

Charles was struggling to make sense of what Travis was saying.

'There's *something* going on,' he persisted. 'I know there is. She's different. And I want to know why.'

The drink was making him insistent.

'Well, don't ask me,' said Travis. 'Ask Henty.'

He turned and put his hand on the latch of the door that led to his room.

'Try taking an interest in someone other than yourself

for a change,' he added over his shoulder, then pushed open the door and stepped inside, leaving Charles swaying gently in the pool of light from the security lamp.

Despite his initial instincts, he believed the boy's denial. Travis had stood his ground under questioning, and had even had the nerve to go on the attack. Charles felt slightly ill as he recalled his observations. Even more ill when he realized that the boy had spoken the truth. He was right. Charles was a miserable worm.

He'd ridden roughshod over Henty recently. He'd been an absolute arsehole, and all because of his own vanity and insecurity. It was an accumulation of things, he told himself. His lacklustre career – he wasn't a failure, but it had all become rather humdrum and there was no doubt he had lost pole position in the literary circles he moved in. His looks – he knew his middle was thickening and his hair thinning, not to mention becoming sprinkled with silver that Charles struggled to find remotely distinguished. His handsome features had always been a boon, and the prospect of losing them made him panic. To top it all, he even felt unsure about his position in the family. He had to admit that Thea and Lily, now they'd entered adolescence, rather terrified him. Thea was so confrontational and Lily so manipulative, both traits which he thought they'd inherited from him, which made it all the more frightening. He left Henty to deal with their incessant demands and threats, reasoning that a woman would understand their needs better. But even that argument didn't hold up. Walter and Robin still turned to Henty rather than Charles. They never came to him for man-to-man chats.

Charles put his hand over his eyes in despair. He was a useless husband and father. He was superfluous in his own family. They didn't need him. He'd felt more and more like an outsider recently. The atmosphere changed when he walked through the door; became heavier. Thea and Lily rolled their eyes; Robin and Walter became wary. And now even Henty, sweet-natured, long-suffering Henty, wasn't putting up with it any more. It was as if she'd finally realized what an utter knob she was married to, and had resolved to make the best of a bad job.

He stumbled back into the house, groaning. What an utter, utter mess. He'd behaved atrociously. Images of what he'd done with Fleur flashed through his mind and he batted them away with his hand, not wanting to be reminded. Panic and Merlot swirled together in his gut; he steadied himself against the wall, struggling not to be sick. He'd have to stop drinking. Alcohol was a fickle friend, enticing you into evil then laughing as you battled with the consequences; weakening your resolve and then amplifying your fears; promising reassurance but bringing you the demons of doubt instead.

He staggered up the stairs. Maybe it wasn't too late. If he confessed it all, then begged forgiveness, promised to start again, maybe it would be all right. They could be companions again. Laugh together, like they had in the old days. Share their dreams. They didn't seem to have any dreams any more. All his energies went into battling to survive; hers, he knew, went into looking after the family. They had no time to themselves.

He lurched in through the bedroom door, falling over his shoes where he'd left them earlier. It was pitch black in the bedroom, so he snapped on the bedside lamp, putting out a hand to steady himself.

'Henty!' he hissed urgently, in the loud whisper of the drunkard trying to be quiet. 'Henty – wake up!'

Henty sat up in alarm. She looked about twelve, with her tangled hair and her face free of make-up, wearing a long nightshirt with a picture of a snoozing teddy on the front. For a moment Charles imagined Fleur in bed, still perfectly made up and without a hair out of place, in a satin nightdress that would leave nothing to the imagination, and he shuddered.

'What's the matter?' she asked, alarmed. 'Is it one of the kids?'

'No. I need to talk to you. I've got something to tell you.'

Realizing it wasn't an emergency, and that Charles was roaring drunk, Henty flopped back on the pillow.

'For God's sake, not now,' she protested.

'No. It's important.'

'If it was that important, why didn't you mention it earlier?' Her voice was sharp. Charles winced. He flopped on to the bed and pawed at her arm pleadingly.

'You don't understand . . .'

'No, and I'm not likely to, with you in that state. Go to sleep, will you?'

'I've got a confession.' He stated it dramatically, then paused, waiting for a reaction. Henty just buried her head in the pillows. When she spoke, her voice was muffled.

'Tell me in the morning. When you're sober.'

After that, she absolutely refused to respond to any of his cajoling. He finally rolled on to his back, defeated, and stared dully at the ceiling. Henty was back in the land of nod within seconds. He lay there for what seemed like hours, battling with his demons, his conscience and the bilious Merlot. He remembered the early days, when they'd first moved into Fulford Farm. They'd had an ancient bed then, sagging in the middle. They would both lie in the dip, snuggled together, and she would tuck her hand into the waistband of his pyjama bottoms and hold him to her, as if she was afraid he would escape. She never did that these days. Their bed now was a kingsize, and she was as far over her side as she could possibly get without falling out.

24

Johnny arrived to collect Ted at eleven o'clock on Sunday morning, having gone home the night before to prepare for his son's visit. Honor tried hard to suppress her misgivings, telling herself she was over-possessive and clucky. It would do both of them good, she thought, as she packed an overnight bag with pyjamas and toothbrush and a spare change of clothes. Meanwhile, Ted had stuffed his backpack with all the essentials a little boy needed: half a ton of Lego, his cuddly monkey, his Action Man water bottle and several videos.

'You're only going for the night,' Honor smiled. 'You don't need half that stuff.'

'You never know,' said Johnny. 'Come on. The limo's waiting.'

Ted needed no second telling. He rushed outside and climbed into the front seat of the Audi. Honor leaned in and did up his seat belt, then turned to Johnny, who was waiting tactfully on the pavement for her to say goodbye.

'Don't forget to make sure his seat belt's done up properly. He can't do it himself.' She couldn't help feeling anxious. There were so many pitfalls and dangers that Johnny might not be aware of, practicalities and safety issues that just might not occur to him, just as they'd never occurred to her until she'd become a parent.

Johnny gave her a reassuring hug.

'Listen. I'm as concerned for his safety as you are. He's my son too, remember.'

'Of course. I'm sorry. It's just . . . it's the first time he's really been away.'

She was trying desperately hard not to cry.

'He'll be fine. I've promised him if he wants to come home he can ring you and I'll bring him back straight away. But that doesn't mean you have to wait by the phone. Go out and enjoy yourself. Have some me time, or whatever they call it.'

Honor just smiled. There was no way she was going to leave the house, but she wasn't going to tell Johnny that. It was going to take all her self-control not to follow the car back to his place and keep a pair of binoculars trained on the two of them for the next twenty-four hours.

The Audi drove away smoothly from the kerb. Honor waved madly, watched until it disappeared around the corner at the top of the village, then wondered what on earth she was going to do for the rest of the day. All the times she had longed for an afternoon to herself, and now she'd got one she had no idea what to do.

At Eversleigh, the house party departed at midday on Sunday. Compared to the inaugural visitors, they had been a dull bunch. Restrained, but picky nevertheless. Somehow the Black Country crowd had been less work: even though they had been noisy and boisterous they had been easy to please and relentlessly appreciative, which had been far more gratifying than mealy-mouthed nods of grudging approval.

'Goodbye. Lovely to see you. Fuck off and don't come back,' Guy muttered through his breath from the top of the steps, as their convoy of sensible saloons drove off through the gates. Marilyn giggled.

'You're wicked.'

'I'm not. I'm late. I'm supposed to pick up Richenda and her mum from the station in five minutes.' He looked at his watch. 'I promised them Sunday lunch and at this rate we won't get it.' He looked hopefully at Marilyn. 'I don't suppose you'd be an angel and peel some spuds for me, only Mum's still at church? I'll give you double time.'

'Sorry,' said Marilyn. 'I've got the beds to strip, then me and Malachi are going to a Zodiac owners' rally.'

'Oh,' said Guy, slightly affronted. Marilyn usually bent over backwards to help him out. He shrugged, and dug in his pocket for the car keys. It didn't matter if lunch was a bit late. There were loads of canapés left over from last night – they'd have to fill up on those while they were waiting.

As he swung the car out of the drive, he spotted a familiar figure making its way back up the high street. A familiar figure in a blue duffel coat, her long legs clad in multicoloured stripy tights and suede boots. He had only seconds to decide. He was already late. But to drive past would be rude and arrogant. Exactly the sort of behaviour one would expect from someone who jumped their own employee.

Honor was walking back home from the village shop with the Sunday papers in her arms when a car drew up beside her. Realizing it was Guy at the wheel, she felt pink and flustered as she remembered the last time she had seen him sitting in that very seat.

The car came to a halt and Guy wound down the driver's window.

'How's Ted?'

'He's absolutely fine. He's gone to stay the night with his dad.' She attempted a smile. 'Heaven only knows what the two of them will get up to. But at least it gives me an afternoon to myself.'

There was an uncomfortable pause.

'Thanks for the *Beano* annuals, by the way,' Honor added politely. 'Ted loved them.'

'That's OK. I'm glad they've gone to a good home.'

Guy slipped the car into first gear and raised his hand in a farewell gesture.

'I'd better go. I'm supposed to be picking up Richenda from the station.' He made a face. 'I'm meeting the future mother-in-law. Better not be late.'

'Have fun.'

'I doubt it. I've got to be on my best behaviour. I'll see you sometime next week?'

'Yes . . .'

The car drew away. Honor clutched the newspaper to her chest as she watched him go. He was such a gentleman. In one conversation, he had tactfully managed to remind her that he was still engaged to be married, that her behaviour had been forgotten and that her job was intact. She felt hugely relieved, yet as she started back towards home, she realized her heart was thumping. It was the stress of the humiliation, she supposed, taking several deep breaths to try and bring her pulse rate down.

She hoped she wasn't going to be overcome with confusion and embarrassment every time she saw him. It would be too exhausting for words.

Guy drove off with a heavy heart. For two pins he'd have told Honor to hop in, and driven her off somewhere for Sunday lunch. But she'd made it quite clear that she wanted to be on her own; that she was relishing the prospect of some solitude. And she was obviously going to pretend that Friday's disgraceful incident had never happened, for which Guy was very grateful. He didn't want to be reminded that he couldn't control his urges. She probably thought he did it all the time; that he was a randy old goat; that poor Marilyn had to fight off his lecherous advances as well.

Besides, he had to face up to his responsibilities. In ten minutes' time his fiancée was arriving with her mother in tow. Shit – what was her mother's name? Susan? Sarah? He was fairly certain it began with an S. He chided himself. Richenda deserved better than this from him. This was an important moment for her. And it was up to him to make sure everything went smoothly.

As the train slowed down and drew into the station at Eldenbury, Sally was tempted for a moment not to get off. She was more nervous than she liked to admit about meeting Guy and Madeleine. She and Richenda had spent a wonderful few days together. Over the past week they'd talked, shopped, talked, eaten, talked, drunk, talked, cried. They'd shared memories and confessions and home truths; hurled accusations at each other in their cups, then hugged each other fiercely. They'd realized they were very, very different, but in some ways the same – they both liked to keep their distance emotionally. Each day, Richenda had taken Sally on a spending spree. It was a useful way to give them something else to focus on, as sometimes the emotional turmoil became exhausting. Shopping was a suitably superficial distraction, and although Sally, very conscious that she might be perceived as a freeloader, protested that she hardly deserved spoiling, Richenda insisted.

'I've got nothing else to spend all this bloody money I'm earning on. Anyway, it's what celebrity mums and daughters do,' she added wryly.

At first when they went out, Sally had been a little freaked by the way people accosted Richenda to sign something or ask her a question or have their photo taken with her. But she loved the way they had the undivided attention of shopkeepers and waiters and doormen. 'I could get used to this,' she giggled, as they were ushered past a long queue of disgruntled diners into the inner sanctum of the latest restaurant, having deposited several expensive, rope-handled carrier bags in the cloakroom.

Thus the bond that had once been so strong between them was gradually re-soldered. Now, as they stood waiting by the doors for the train to finally stop, Sally was all too aware that she was going to have to share her daughter with someone else, someone who had a greater claim to her than she herself did. She looked out of the window and saw a tall, dark-haired figure waiting on the platform.

'There he is,' said Richenda excitedly, pushing open the window and reaching for the handle as the man went to open the door from the other side. Sally watched as her daughter was folded into the arms of her fiancé, and felt a momentary pang of jealousy that she didn't like herself for.

Quickly, the good-mannered Guy disengaged himself from Richenda and went to embrace Sally, who took a step back. She didn't kiss people she didn't know.

'Hi,' she said warily, crossing her arms in front of her to make sure he got the message. Guy seemed unfazed.

'In case you hadn't guessed, I'm Guy,' he grinned cheerily. 'Welcome to the Cotswolds.'

And with that he picked up each of their cases and led them to the car.

Back at home, Honor dumped the newspaper on the sofa and went into the kitchen to make a cup of tea. On the table, she saw a large white envelope, her name on the front in Johnny's inimitable scrawl. He must have put it there when she wasn't looking. Cautiously, she slid her finger under the flap and opened the envelope.

Inside were the details of a house, a pretty, square, Cotswold stone village house with a walled garden, and paper-clipped to them was a handwritten letter.

Dearest Honor

I want you to have a look at this and think about it ser-iously. It doesn't have to be this house, of course, but it's quite near Eversleigh and I didn't want to uproot you and Ted. The beauty of my job is I can work just about anywhere. There are plenty of practices I could join around here – I've already done my homework.

*I know we could make it work. We always had something
special, we had the spark, and if it went wrong it was entirely
my fault. I accept the blame, and all I can say is that I'm no
longer the selfish, self-centred, self-indulgent (what a lot of selfs!)
person I once was because I now realize what matters. In other
words, maybe I've grown up!*

*What is most important of all is Ted. He is ours, Honor.
Whatever happens I want to share him with you and be a part
of his life. And for what it's worth I think it would be in his
interests if we did that together.*

*I can put an offer in on this first thing in the morning. It's
up to you.*

Johnny x

Honor put the letter down with trembling hands. This
was serious. This was life-changing. This was commitment. And she still wasn't any clearer about what she
thought. She looked carefully through the details. The
house would be perfect. It had light and airy reception
rooms, a big kitchen with a conservatory off it, four
bedrooms, a study for Johnny, a pretty garden. A family
house . . .

She tried to imagine what their life would be like. The
whole atmosphere of the household would change with
a male presence. There would be rugby on Sky, the phone
ringing; lagers in the fridge, razors in the bathroom. The
girly haven that was her bedroom would be invaded: the
oyster-pink walls, the blue chintz curtains with the huge
cabbage roses, the piles of French embroidered pillows,
the scent bottles and silver-backed brush set would not
sit so easily with a man in her bed, and Honor resented

the idea that the place that was so resolutely hers would have to be shared.

Not just her bedroom, in fact, but her whole life. At the moment, she could please herself most of the time. She could make do with chicken nuggets for supper if she couldn't be bothered to cook once Ted had gone to bed. If Johnny moved in, meals would be dictated by when he got back from work, and she couldn't fob him off with nursery food. But on the plus side, it would be nice to have company. She'd enjoyed having supper with him recently – it made it worth the effort of cooking.

And there was no doubt that life would be easier in many ways. Financially, for a start. What a relief it would be not to have a slight sense of panic at the prospect of new school shoes *and* football boots in the same month. And it would be nice to have a proper social life again. Honor kept herself to herself, because she didn't always enjoy being the only single female. But with a partner things were different. Though Honor wasn't sure she wanted to be drawn into the social circles that Johnny had been mixing in. She'd seen him at the ball; the crowd he'd been with were notorious, people with pots of money who were determined to spend it as quickly as they made it, people who loved fast cars and fast horses . . . people who were as hard as nails, who would think nothing of bankrupting themselves if it was convenient, even if it meant bringing others down with them. Johnny couldn't keep up with them financially, but no doubt he was their darling, the one who looked after the tons of horse flesh that brought them more financial reward. Honor knew she would never feel comfortable with their dubious morals, and would always be wary that Johnny was being lured into nefarious practices. She wasn't sure what, exactly, but she'd read enough Dick Francis to know that some of the people mixed up in racing didn't always play by the rules. And Johnny was just the type to turn a blind eye for a substantial brown envelope.

Bloody hell, she thought. I really don't trust him. Not on any level. And it was totally unfounded. She had no proof whatsoever that Johnny was bent, but when she thought about it his Audi estate was top of the range, even if it was filthy, and his watch was expensive . . . She told herself not to be stupid. Johnny earned a good whack and he had no one else to spend money on and the car would be tax deductible. Of course he wasn't crooked. She was just looking for excuses . . . Her mind whirling, she flopped down on the sofa and closed her eyes, trying to make some sense of why she was so reluctant to give Johnny a chance.

In less than a minute, she had drifted off. It had been an exhausting and traumatic week, what with one thing and another. She had a lot of sleep to catch up on. But her mind didn't allow her any real respite: her dreams were a muddled re-run of the inaugural house party at Eversleigh, her skirmish with Johnny, the night out with Malachi and Marilyn, the night spent in hospital after Ted's accident. Like a video on fast forward, the images flashed through her mind until they eventually slowed down, and she dreamed of being fast asleep in a feather bed. Her bones melted into the downy mattress, and she snuggled into the warmth of a body lying next to hers. It was bliss; snug, contented bliss. She revelled in the luxury, until the body next to her rolled over to face her, and she found herself looking into a pair of eyes – not topaz as she might have expected, but sparkling navy blue.

It was Guy.

Honor sat bolt upright on the sofa, hot with embarrassment that she could have dreamed such a thing. Her heart was pounding, as if somehow her mind had been invaded and everybody knew its contents. She swung her legs off the sofa and walked to the kitchen, mulling over the subtext. Was this the reason for her wariness of Johnny? She couldn't deny the feeling she had in her dream was similar to the feeling she had when Guy had kissed her in the car: bliss, contentment, security, but with a frisson of excitement. She'd told herself at the time it was because he had been so masterfully in control in a time of crisis; that it was just a little crush because he was forbidden territory. After all, it was a ridiculous notion that he might be interested in her. He was practically the lord of the manor, he was engaged to a stunningly beautiful actress, and Honor was definitely below stairs. As he had subtly reminded her only that day. If she was clinging on to the hope of a relationship with Guy to avoid making a decision over Johnny then she was seriously deluded.

Gloomily she went into the kitchen and sawed at the remains of the baguette left over from breakfast. If only she hadn't gone to the ball, she thought. If she hadn't gone to the ball, then she wouldn't have bumped into Johnny. And Madeleine would never have asked her to work at the manor. She would be bumbling along quite happily just as she had for the past six years, with no dilemmas, no heartache, no crazy bloody Cinderella complex, and everything would be just fine.

At Eversleigh Manor, Madeleine immediately got up Sally's nose: the glacial smile that lacked warmth, the top-to-toe assessment of her outfit that took less than a second, the patronizing tone. She had absolutely none of Guy's warmth. He must have got that from his father, Sally decided. She followed Madeleine to the drawing room, wondering if she should have chosen something more conventional to wear than black leather trousers and a military jacket covered in zips, then scolded herself. She was forty-three years old; she could wear what she liked. She'd never pretended to be something she wasn't before, and she wasn't going to start now for Madeleine Portias, in her long camel skirt and silk blouse.

In no time at all, the two of them had perfected the art of winding each other up, much to Guy and Richenda's discomfort. Madeleine would kick off with a leading question and Sally would retaliate with an outrageous answer designed to shock. Over canapés, she boasted that she'd never paid rent or national insurance or taxes in her life.

'How very unpatriotic,' Madeleine responded icily. 'And short-sighted. I'm sure you'll expect a state pension when the time comes.'

'I bet you pay your cleaning lady cash,' Sally flashed back quickly. 'It amounts to the same thing. You're still cheating the state.'

By the time they'd finished their roast beef the two of them were embroiled in the great hunting debate. It promised to be bloodier than any fox being killed. Guy stood up to clear the plates away, hoping that lemon meringue pie left over from the night before would provide a distraction. But over pudding, Madeleine decided to go for the jugular.

'So, tell me.' Madeleine cocked her head to one side with an ingratiating smile. 'Who is Richenda's *actual* father?'

Guy cringed. His mother could be so insensitive at times. Richenda looked faintly startled, almost as if it was a question that had never occurred to *her*.

Sally prodded a potato with her fork, pretending it was Madeleine's hand.

'To be honest, I don't know,' she said airily. 'I was a bit of a wild child. Looking at her now, I think I've got a pretty good idea, but I couldn't prove it without a DNA test.'

Richenda dropped her spoon in horror. She now knew Sally was being deliberately provocative.

'Mum!' she protested.

'I wonder when he'll pop out of the woodwork, then?' persisted Madeleine, delighted she'd found a weak spot.

'Probably at the wedding,' said Sally cheerfully. 'That would be a laugh, wouldn't it?'

'For heaven's sake, you two,' said Richenda, unable to bear it any longer.

Sally pushed back her chair and stood up.

'Actually, I think it's time I went. I'm obviously not welcome here.'

'No. Please don't go.' Guy stood up as well, anxious to try and make peace. 'My mother doesn't mean to be rude.'

Madeleine sat at the head of the table, feigning bewilderment.

'I didn't think it was me that was being rude.'

'Rude? You're the rudest woman I've ever met.' Sally pointed a finger at Madeleine. 'You think I'm some promiscuous drop-out that's been walking the streets for the past twenty years.'

'I can only make assumptions on what you tell me,' said Madeleine icily.

'Well, at least I don't think I'm better than everybody else. And I'll tell you something else for nothing,' she added to Richenda. 'She doesn't think you're good enough for her son, either. She's only getting at me in order to get at you, because she knows Guy wouldn't stand for it.'

And with that she stomped out of the room.

'Gracious,' murmured Madeleine, pressing her napkin to her mouth.

Richenda and Guy exchanged agonized glances.

'I better go and see if she's all right,' said Richenda, and slipped out of the door. Guy glanced at his mother, who looked at him defiantly.

'All those questions needed to be asked,' she said stoutly.

'Yes, Mother, but it's the way you ask them,' he replied wearily.

'Well, I can't help that. It's just the way I am.'

Guy knew there was no point in arguing with Madeleine. There never had been.

Richenda found her mother rolling a cigarette on the front steps. Sally looked at her like a rebellious teenager expecting trouble, slightly defiant.

'I'm sorry. I didn't mean to spoil it for you. But I just couldn't sit there any longer listening to her patronizing us.'

'It's OK. I understand.' Richenda didn't admit that inwardly she had been cheering Sally's outburst. She'd wished on more than one occasion that she could stand up to Madeleine.

'She's a fucking cow.' Sally put out her tongue and carefully licked down the end of her Rizla.

'She's just protective of Guy, that's all.'

'Well, I'm protective of you. Ten years too late, maybe, but she didn't have to keep pointing it out.' She lit her roll-up and blew out a defiant stream of smoke. 'I'm going to go.'

'Where?'

'I'll get the train back to London. I'll go and stay with Ruth.'

'I thought she had no room?'

'She won't mind me kipping on the floor.'

'That's silly. Why don't you go and stay in my flat?'

Sally shook her head.

'I can't do that. It's taking advantage. And I'm sick of people implying that I'm taking you for a ride.'

'They aren't, are they?'

'They're all thinking it. I know they are.'

Richenda slid an arm round her bony shoulders.

'Listen – I know you're not and that's all that matters. I've told you, if I want to spend money on you, it's up to me. And what's the point of you sleeping on Ruth's floor when there's a spare bed in my flat?'

Sally looked doubtful.

'If you're sure . . . ?'

'Of course I am. Do you want me to come back with you?'

'No. I'll be fine. Anyway, you need to spend some time with Guy. I think he's lovely, by the way. Nothing like his cow of a mother.'

'I know he is.' Richenda sighed. 'But we've got a few things to sort out. It's been a stressful couple of weeks.'

Sally stubbed her roll-up out on the bottom of one of her new Hobbs boots, then stuck the nub end back in a Golden Virginia tin, which she slid back into her matching handbag. She suddenly felt the need for the security of her old jeans and leather jacket. She'd felt as if she'd been parading round in a costume for the past few days. It had been exciting initially, but she didn't feel like herself any more.

'I'm really proud of you, you know that?' she said to Richenda. 'Not because of your acting and stuff, though that's fantastic. But because you've been able to forgive me.'

'You're my mum,' said Richenda simply.

'Yeah, but I haven't been a very good one.'

'Life wasn't easy for you, though, was it?'

'Only because I chose not to make it easy. At least that's how it seems looking back on it. I made some really crap decisions. Especially where men are concerned. And it was you who paid the price.'

'No, it wasn't. Look at me now. I'd never be here if it hadn't all gone wrong.'

'There's not many people who would look at it that way.'

Richenda shrugged.

'I don't really see the point in getting bitter and twisted.'

At that point a battered taxi pulled in through the gates. Sally picked up her bag.

'This is my cab. I'll see you in a couple of days, OK?'

Mother and daughter embraced on the step tightly, then Sally disengaged herself quickly and scrambled into the front seat of the taxi before the tears that were threatening to escape made her lose her cool. She didn't want Madeleine looking out the window and thinking she'd got to her.

'To the station, is it?' asked the driver.

Sally just nodded, not trusting herself to speak, then watched in the wing mirror as Richenda waved frantically from the steps until she disappeared from view altogether.

To Honor's relief, Johnny finally phoned early that evening. She'd resisted calling to see if they'd arrived safely, and instead sat there in agony waiting for the phone to ring.

'He's absolutely fine,' Johnny assured her. 'We've been playing football in the garden all afternoon, he had sausage sandwiches for tea, and he's going to have his bath in a minute.'

'Great.'

'Have you had a good day?'

'I haven't done much. But then it's nice to do nothing.'

There was a small pause.

'Did you read my letter?' Johnny asked lightly.

'Yes.'

'And?'

'I don't know . . .'

'You must have had some time to think about it.'

'Yes, but I'm just not sure whether we could make it work. It would be awful for Ted if we got together and it all went wrong.'

'Why would it?'

Honor felt irritated. Johnny was so unrealistic. When he made a plan, he refused to see any possible snags.

'It did before, didn't it?'

Johnny sighed.

'Not that again. Can't we wipe the slate clean?'

'Up to a point. But we can't pretend it didn't happen.'

'You have to keep going on about it. Can't you be more positive?'

'You can't expect me to go into this without any thought.'

'No. But do you have to harp on?'

'Sorry.' Honor didn't think she was harping, but Johnny was obviously sensitive. 'Look, let's have a chat tomorrow night when you bring Ted back. I'll have had more time to think it all through then.'

'Grand. And don't worry about the little fella. He's as happy as Larry. Whoever Larry is.'

Honor laughed.

'Give him a big kiss from me.'

'I will. And remember, Honor. You won't know unless you try.'

Honor put the phone down. Johnny always wanted things to happen now. He had no patience. In his head they could settle down and start playing happy families straight away. He had no streak of caution. But perhaps she should take a leaf out of his book. Maybe he was right: they wouldn't know until they tried.

She looked at her watch. It was only just gone six. The evening stretched ahead of her, lonely and empty. She couldn't bear the thought of sitting down to watch *Heartbeat*. It wouldn't provide nearly enough of a distraction. What she needed, she decided, was a girls' night out. Female company and a few drinks. If she sat in alone all night she'd mope about Ted and mither over Johnny's letter. She needed to talk it all over with someone who could give her an objective viewpoint; someone who would sympathize and wouldn't judge.

She phoned Henty.

'I know it's short notice. And Charles will probably be furious with me. But do you fancy going out for a drink?'

'I'm sorry about my mother.'

'I'm sorry about mine.'

Guy and Richenda had finally made it to the privacy of their bedroom, having spent the afternoon clearing the manor house of the debris from that weekend's guests. Mindless graft had seemed the best recourse after the dramas over lunch. Now they had flopped, exhausted, on to the bed. Richenda rolled over on to her side, putting her head in one hand.

'You can see why people sneak off and get married in the Caribbean, can't you?'

Guy just nodded without saying anything. He didn't really want to talk about weddings, not at the moment. He slid his hands round Richenda's waist.

'Let's not talk about it now. We'll leave it till tomorrow.

You haven't forgotten about the surprise I've booked for the morning?'

'What is it?'

'It won't be a surprise if I tell you, will it? But it'll just be you and me with no interruptions and we can talk and make plans, and we don't have to worry about paying guests or intrusive photographers or interfering mothers . . .'

'It sounds heaven.'

'You'll need to wrap up warm.'

Richenda frowned, trying to puzzle out what he'd got planned.

'A day trip to Lapland?' she asked.

Guy shook his head, grinning.

'There's no point in guessing. I'm not telling you what it is. You'll just have to wait.'

Richenda reached out and started tickling him.

'Please. I'm dying to know.'

'No way.'

'You've got to!'

She bore down on him, pulling up his shirt so she could get at the bare skin underneath. He rolled on to his back, laughing, trying to wriggle away from her. In two moments she was on top of him, sitting astride his stomach. Her hair had come loose from its chignon, her eyes were shining with laughter. He could feel the warmth of her against his flesh. Guy found his heart was beating faster than was healthy as she bent over him and spoke in a low, suggestive voice.

'Well, if I can't tickle it out of you, maybe I can bribe you . . .'

Like most men, Guy could resist anything except the promise of sex.

Charles sat in the kitchen staring at the handset, willing himself to have the nerve to dial the number.

Thankfully, Henty hadn't remembered his drunken attempt at a confession the night before. When she announced she was going out for a drink with Honor, Charles had surprised himself by suggesting she take along Travis. Henty's eyes had sparkled at the suggestion.

'What a great idea. You'll love Honor. She's gorgeous. And she's totally single.'

She turned to Charles.

'What do you think, Charles? Honor and Travis?'

Charles couldn't resist a dig.

'She's far too old for him.'

'There's no such thing as too old,' Travis assured him.

The two of them had driven off in the Land Rover, leaving him with absolutely no excuse.

If he was going to save his marriage, he needed closure with Fleur. He couldn't risk leaving her ricocheting about the county, thinking she had some sort of hold over him because of their business together. It had been a mistake right from the start. But he was fairly sure he had the means to knock it on the head. And he was pretty confident that once he'd put Fleur in the picture, she'd lose interest. Charles had just enough humility to realize that she was dazzled by the prospect of fame, not him. He took a swig of red wine, then prodded out the six numbers that would determine his future.

Thank goodness Fleur answered the phone. His nerve might have failed him if Robert had answered.

'Fleur. Charles Beresford here.' He sounded as businesslike as possible.

'Charles.'

Her voice dripped honey and innuendo. He plunged straight in before he could fall under her spell.

'Bad news, I'm afraid. I talked to my contact, gave him a brief appraisal of our project. But someone's beaten us to it, sadly. They've already shot a pilot. Called *Petal Power*. We're too late.'

'But surely there's room for two? I mean, there's room for Delia and Nigella.'

'Not at the moment, I'm afraid. I don't think they feel that floristry has quite got the *legs* that cookery has.'

'Oh.'

'I'm terribly sorry. Perhaps I should have had the chat with him before getting your hopes up. But then you always run the risk of someone pinching your idea.'

'Oh well. C'est la vie.' Fleur sounded matter of fact rather than totally crushed. 'Never mind. Nothing ventured, as they say. See you around sometime.'

'Yeah. Maybe. Um . . . cheers.'

Charles put the phone down with a trembling hand. Hopefully, that would be it, and there wouldn't be any hideous repercussions. He could work on his marriage with a clear conscience, with no need for a messy confession. He shuddered when he thought how close he had come to spilling the beans the night before.

'Dad?'

Charles looked up to see Thea standing in front of him

with the expression of total outrage that only a teenage girl can perfect.

'I've just been into the ironing room to get my denim skirt. You've got to come and see. It's really weird.'

'If it's a spider, just pick it up in a duster.'

'It's not a spider.'

'What could there possibly be in the ironing room that's of interest to me?'

Charles could be as difficult as his daughter when he liked. What he'd forgotten was she didn't take no for an answer.

'Do you want another pink drink?'

Honor knew she shouldn't. The concoction that Travis had introduced her to – some sickly raspberry alcopop – was slipping down too easily and she was already slurring her words slightly. But what the hell? It stopped her thinking about things, which was ideal.

'Why not?'

Travis went off to the bar. Henty and Honor watched his perfect bum beadily, then looked at each other and burst out laughing.

'Isn't he just edible?' asked Henty.

'You haven't!' said Honor, shocked.

'No way. I don't need any complications in my life. But you're a free agent.'

Honor wondered if now was the time to come clean about Johnny. But somehow, now she was out, she didn't feel like it. She was having too much fun. Bringing it all out into the open now would alter the frivolous atmosphere. And the whole point of going out tonight was to forget.

'How's the book?' she asked.

Henty winced.

'I've sent the first few chapters off to my old publisher,' she admitted. 'He'll get it on Monday morning. I'll soon know if I've been wasting my time.'

'I'm sure you haven't,' said Honor. 'I'm sure it's brilliant.'

Travis reappeared with the drinks, and distributed them round the table. Honor found herself admiring his brown wrist, the bracelet made from blue and pink silk thread that had no doubt been a love token from some previous conquest. She looked up and Travis raised his bottle in a toast to her with a wink that was cheeky rather than lascivious, but still brought a blush to her cheeks.

For a moment she was sorely tempted. That would definitely take her mind off things. He'd be the perfect antidote to Johnny. He was young and uncomplicated. He'd want no-strings sex. She felt her mouth watering as she watched him put his bottle to his mouth, imagining those lips on hers. What would it take? She felt sure Henty would turn a blind eye; would drop Travis off at her house without being judgemental. She had practically told her to help herself, after all.

Then Honor came to her senses. She'd already made a fool of herself twice this week, and she needed her life to be less complicated, not throw a randy twenty-one-year-old South African into the equation. Dragging her eyes away from his sculpted jawline, with the dusting of golden stubble, she decided perhaps after all these years she should invest in something discreet and battery-operated if she was going to keep herself out of trouble.

*

Charles stood open-mouthed in the middle of the erstwhile ironing room. So this was her secret. His darling, clever Henty had done all this behind their backs. Correction – she'd done it under their very noses, and the fact that none of them had noticed the ironing room had undergone a transformation said it all. He ran his hands over the lid of the silver laptop on the desk under the window. He had no idea that she knew how to use one – she'd obviously sorted it out somehow.

On the desk next to the laptop was a folder. Tentatively he lifted the flap, and saw inside a printed manuscript. He drew out the title sheet. *Diary of a Cotswold Housewife* by Henty Beresford. He felt the thickness of the manuscript – about sixty pages, he reckoned with a literary agent's precision.

He knew he shouldn't. For ten long seconds he battled with his conscience. But how could he resist? How could he walk away without getting some idea of what she had been doing in here? After all, if she really didn't want anyone to see it she should have kept it under lock and key. Perhaps it was sitting so temptingly on the desk precisely because she did want him to read it.

He told himself he would just skim the front page. After all, he was skilled at judging most manuscripts on the first few hundred words. Hungrily, he began to read.

Some time later – it felt like no time at all, which in itself was a good sign – he put down the last page reverently. The hairs on the back of his neck were still tingling. He could barely contain his excitement. She'd done it again. He might be biased, but the fact that he was absolutely desperate to know what happened next meant there was no doubt she had hit the jackpot. Better than that, it was totally original: nobody could dismiss this as a pale imitation of any other writer on the shelf today. She had her own voice, and it was loud and clear.

He felt pride. And shame. And relief. Relief that somehow this explained her behaviour of the past couple of weeks. He recognized the signs now: this was how she always used to be when she was in full creative flow, when she was writing something really good. Her eyes sparkled, she was ebullient, mischievous, crackling with a mysterious energy. It was only when she'd struggled to write her third book that her aura had dimmed, and Charles realized that over all the ensuing years it had never been relit.

He felt a surge of fury and self-loathing. As her husband, her agent, her fucking Svengali, for God's sake, he should have done everything in his power to help her. But he never had, because he had been too self-absorbed, and perhaps it had suited him to have her at home looking after the children. Perhaps he'd been afraid of being in *her* shadow, for her career had had stellar promise in the early days. Promise that he had failed to nurture.

Yet all these years later, she'd had the courage to do it for herself. Shamefaced, and in total awe, Charles crept from the room. He shuddered when he thought how close he had come to spoiling it all for them with his sulky, self-centred behaviour, his shameless flirtation, his lack of responsibility. His petulance when he thought she was paying too much attention to Travis. Now he realized what it was the boy had been driving at last night: Charles cringed when he remembered how he'd accosted him in the stable yard. Travis had dropped pretty heavy hints to him, and it had gone right over Charles's head. Take an interest in someone other than yourself, he'd said. And all the time Henty had been pouring her heart and soul into a work of what Charles fondly considered to be pure genius.

Respect. It was about time he treated her with a little respect. Even if he didn't deserve any in return.

25

On Monday morning, Richenda hurried down to the kitchen to make tea. She smiled as she pulled her dressing gown tightly round herself and ran down the stairs. Everything was going to be all right. You didn't have sex like that if it wasn't: her insides were still fizzing, her knees were weak. She had shagged senseless written all over her, but she didn't care, not even if Madeleine fixed her with one of her disapproving looks.

She pushed open the kitchen door. Marilyn was sitting at the table reading the paper, with Malachi reading over her shoulder. They looked up as she bounded in, smiling brightly.

'Tea, anyone?'

Malachi leaned over Marilyn and snapped the paper shut. Marilyn looked horribly guilty, as if she'd been caught with her fingers in the till. Richenda looked from one to the other, puzzled.

'Is something the matter?'

The two of them exchanged glances. Malachi gave a small shrug followed by a nod, and Marilyn held out the paper as if it had been used to line a cat-litter tray.

'We might as well show it to you,' she said in her soft burr. 'Because if we don't, someone else will.'

Richenda took the paper gingerly, pulled out a chair

and sat down at the table, smoothing it carefully out in front of her.

UPSTAIRS, DOWNSTAIRS AND IN MY LADY'S CHAMBER! blazed the *Voice*'s headline.

Darling of the small screen Richenda Fox has been busy over the past week, collecting awards and reuniting herself with her estranged mother Sally Collins. But has she been neglecting her fiancé in the process? Guy Portias, owner of the impressive Cotswold pile Eversleigh Manor, seems to have been spending rather a lot of time with his housekeeper, single mother Honor McLean. The gamine brunette has been cooking up a storm in his kitchen lately. The question is, has she been busy in the bedroom as well?

Time for Lady Jane to investigate, we say . . . !

Accompanying the article were three photographs. One of Honor and Guy emerging from the Fleece. One of Guy with his arm around Honor at the fifties night, both of them smiling widely. And the last, and most incriminating, was the pair of them sharing a kiss in Guy's car.

'I'm really sorry,' said Marilyn.

'It's OK,' said Richenda calmly. 'You didn't have anything to do with it, did you?'

'Of course not!' said Marilyn indignantly. 'It's rubbish, anyway.'

'Is it?' Richenda met Marilyn's gaze coolly with her green eyes.

Marilyn looked away for a moment, flustered.

'Honor just works here. They have to spend a lot of time together. But there's nothing going on.'

Richenda smiled her thanks.

'You're very loyal,' she said gently. 'I wouldn't expect you to tell me if there was.'

Marilyn opened her mouth to protest further, then shut it as the door swung open again and Guy came in, his hair damp from the shower.

'Come on. We need to get going. No time for breakfast – I've got that sorted out. Just a quick cup of tea –'

He realized that there was an icy atmosphere in the kitchen, and that Marilyn, Malachi and Richenda were all looking at him with equally doom-laden expressions.

'What?'

Malachi and Marilyn decided simultaneously that it was time to make a hasty exit.

'I'll go and sweep up the leaves,' said Malachi.

'I'll start on the vacuuming,' said Marilyn.

A moment later they were gone, and Richenda held out the *Voice* with a resigned sigh. Guy took it wordlessly, somehow knowing instinctively that he was in hot water.

How hot he couldn't have imagined. Bile rose in his throat as he examined the article. Combined panic and outrage paralysed him momentarily. The three photos together looked more than incriminating.

'I can explain all of these,' he croaked.

'Then please do,' replied Richenda coolly.

He cleared his throat, desperately wanting to sound unperturbed.

'That's just us leaving the Fleece. I took her there for lunch, because she was upset about something and wanted to talk . . .'

'Uh huh,' Richenda nodded.

'That was taken at the fifties night thing I told you about. The photo's been taken totally out of context. I had my other arm around Marilyn – it was a picture of all of us. Just having a bit of a laugh.'

'Right.' Richenda nodded again. 'And that one?'

She pointed at the picture of them kissing.

'That's . . . not really what it looks like. We'd just got back from the hospital. We'd heard Ted was going to be all right. It was just the sort of kiss that friends give each other when . . . well, you know . . .' He trailed off, knowing he sounded thoroughly unconvincing. He picked up Richenda's hands. 'Richenda, you know what the press are like. They can twist any situation when they put their mind to it. This . . . bastard obviously came down to Eversleigh looking for a story.'

'Looks like he found one.'

'No. There's nothing going on between me and Honor. We spent a lot of time together this week because of work and then Ted fell out of the tree . . .'

Guy suddenly felt annoyed.

'I don't see why I should have to stand here and defend myself for something I haven't done. If you choose not to believe me then there's nothing I can do, is there?'

'Guy – look at these pictures. I'd be a fool if I didn't think something was going on.'

Guy picked up the paper in a rage.

'Who is this Bill Weeks? I'll bloody sue him for invasion of privacy. I'll sue him first and then I'll kill him. Fucking bastard – anything for a headline in his scummy paper. Who reads this shit anyway?'

'Millions of people,' said Richenda calmly. 'Which is why you should really have been more careful.'

Guy stared at her.

'You believe this?'

'I don't know what to think. But I do know things aren't right between us.'

Her chin trembled. Her icy demeanour was dissolving. Guy suddenly felt very sorry for her. Didn't she realize this was setting the pace for the rest of her life? If she remained a success then her private life was going to be picked over constantly; allegations and implications would be made.

'Come on,' he said gently. 'We mustn't let them win. We've got a day out planned, remember? Go and wrap up warm. I'm not going to let this spoil our day, and neither should you. We're going to sort it all out, I promise.'

Honor was in a deep alcohol-induced coma when she heard the phone ringing. She looked at the clock, which promptly moved before she could discern the time. She groaned. Raspberry Reefs had seemed such a splendid idea at the time, but she was unused to spirits and they had slipped down all too easily. Before she knew it she had drunk far too many, and now she could hardly lift her head off the pillow. She reached out an arm to answer the phone. She couldn't ignore it; it was probably Johnny calling to make arrangements to drop Ted back later.

'Hello?'

'Well, good morning to you, Miss McLean.'

It was Johnny. Honor ran her tongue over her teeth. They felt sticky and furry.

'Hi,' she managed.

'Did you have a good night?'

'Fine.'

'You managed to get some sleep, then?'

Honor was puzzled. Johnny's voice sounded a bit edgy.

'Well, yes. I knew Ted was in safe hands.'

'And whose hands were you in?'

'What?'

'While the cat's away, eh?'

Honor was immediately on her guard. She recognized the silky aggression in his tone, and her stomach contracted with fear. Did he have his spies out? Did he know she'd gone out? That wasn't a crime, was it? He was the one who'd told her to enjoy herself.

'What do you mean?'

His voice oozed vitriol.

'You're a hypocrite. You've hung me ten times over for my mistake. Made me feel like a worthless worm. Not good enough for you. And all the time you've been screwing the lord of the manor –'

This really was too confusing for Honor's addled brain.

'What?'

'Does he know I had my hand in your knickers only last week? You're nothing but a little slut, really. A slut and a cock-tease. But I'm not surprised you're holding out for him. I'm sure you fancy yourself as Lady Muck.'

'Johnny, what are you talking about?'

'You haven't seen the papers yet, then?'

'No.'

'Well, it makes very interesting reading, I can tell you. And the pictures are even better.'

456

'What pictures?'

'You'd better get down to the shop and see for your-self.'

'I don't understand. How can there be pictures? I haven't done anything.'

'Well, it must be your identical twin sister with her tongue down Mr Portias's throat, in that case.'

Honor gripped the phone tightly, desperately trying to make sense of what Johnny was saying. She tried to keep her voice calm and no-nonsense.

'Look, this is silly. Why don't you bring Ted home and we can talk about this sensibly.'

'Bring Ted home?' There was a bitter edge to his laugh. 'Do you know, I don't think I will.'

Honor felt as if she was falling through the air. Icy panic flooded her insides.

'What?'

'For six years I had to live without Ted because of one small mistake. I don't think the punishment really fitted the crime. But you considered that to be justice, so I might as well judge you on the same basis. I was condemned as an unfit father. Well, now you're an unfit mother.'

'Johnny, what do you mean? Don't be ridiculous –'

'Let's see how you like it. Being deprived of your own flesh and blood.'

'You can't do this to Ted!'

'Ted's quite happy. He's having the time of his life. He hasn't asked for you once.'

Honor struggled to sit up. Her head started spinning. She closed her eyes to try and make it stop, but that was worse.

'Johnny, please. Let's talk –'

'Did I get the opportunity to talk? I don't think so. You judged me, Honor. And sentenced me. Remember? Well, now the boot's on the other foot.'

The line went dead. Frantically, Honor redialled Johnny's number.

'Sorry, but the number you are calling is unavailable . . .'

Honor gave a sob of terror.

The balloon stood in the field, patiently awaiting the arrival of its passengers, its magnificent red and yellow stripes bold against the bright blue autumn sky. The air was crisp and still; the only sound was birdsong and the occasional whoosh from the gas canisters that kept the canvas aloft.

'It's absolutely beautiful,' whispered Richenda in awe.

Next to her Guy smiled, gratified that his surprise had had the desired effect, as the balloon's pilot hurried forward to greet them. Matt was twenty-nine, but didn't look a day over sixteen, with his pageboy haircut and baggy hand-knitted jumpers.

'You're very lucky,' said Matt. 'It's always touch and go whether you can fly at this time of year, but today's conditions are perfect. Come on!'

It was obvious that he hadn't seen that morning's paper. Or perhaps he had, but didn't see it as being of any consequence when there was a balloon ride in the offing. He ushered them excitedly towards the basket, eager for them to start their journey. Matt was evangelical about ballooning; he'd started up the business two years before, when his parents' farm had been on its knees, and it was now more than buoyant. He'd been fully booked all summer with weddings, family outings, corporate days out, and had only managed to fit Guy in because he didn't normally fly on a Monday. They were old mates: Matt and his older brother Felix had grown up with Guy, the three of them terrorizing the local pubs together in their teenage years. Matt noted wryly as he helped Richenda into the basket that Guy had done it again. She was just as stunning in real life as she was on the telly. Guy was a jammy bastard. But then, he remembered from their teenage escapades, he'd always nabbed the good-looking birds.

Half an hour later, the balloon was gliding regally over the fields, above the treetops, the landscape below a glorious tapestry of greens and golds. Richenda and Guy stood side by side, looking down at the scenery: the sparkling silver thread that was the river, the cattle like lead animals in a toy farm. Eventually Eversleigh hove into view, and the manor appeared below them, perfectly symmetrical, surrounded by the sprinkling of houses that made up the village. It occurred to Guy that if it hadn't been for the hideous cost of upkeeping the manor, if he hadn't had to hire it out, this mess might never have happened. But it was no use blaming an inanimate object. In fact, if it was anyone's fault it was his – if he'd gone and got a proper job . . .

He gave a heavy sigh. Richenda turned to look at him. 'Are you in love with her?' she asked softly.

'No, of course not,' said Guy, not giving himself even a moment to consider his reply. He was shocked that

Richenda could think such a thing. 'I thought I explained – those pictures were a total set-up.'

'Let's put it another way,' said Richenda, her green eyes surveying him gravely. 'Are you in love with me?'

The question almost took his breath away. He should have been able to reassure her at once. But he couldn't. His response stuck in his throat. The words he wanted to utter wouldn't come out.

Because he didn't love her. Not properly. He'd thought he had. He'd truly thought she was the one. But now he realized that he hadn't understood the meaning of true love. He wouldn't lie down and die for her, move mountains for her. How the hell was he going to tell her that? He certainly loved her enough not to want to hurt her.

She was looking at him, waiting for an answer. There was pain in her eyes, but understanding as well. Which made it all the more difficult. Guy tried to come to his senses, telling himself he was being illogical. He couldn't throw everything back in Richenda's face because of a fleeting kiss.

For try as he might, he couldn't get the moment he'd kissed Honor out of his head. In those brief few seconds, he'd felt everything he knew he should be feeling for Richenda. A burning desire to protect Honor for all of her life. To scoop her up and treasure her. To kiss away all her fears and worries. It had made him feel giddy; had quite literally taken his breath away. Seeing the pictures of the two of them together had brought it all back to him. He might be vehemently denying it to the rest of the nation, but it was proof, in black and white, of what he felt. Even though, for all he knew, Honor hadn't given him a second thought since that moment.

How could he commit to Richenda while he nursed those feelings? It would be cruel, to exchange vows with someone when your heart belonged elsewhere. He couldn't make her a hollow promise; lure her into a marriage that was a sham. But could he bring himself to break off their engagement because he was being fanciful? Perhaps it had been the drama of the situation that had made him read so much into it; the relief that Ted had been all right. Emotions had run high that afternoon. Maybe the brief encounter in the car had been the remnants of the adrenalin they'd both had charging through their veins – it had needed somewhere to go, and the resulting endorphin rush had given him a false impression. It was just a crush, he told himself firmly. A silly little schoolboy daydream.

But if it was all a fantasy, why did he keep thinking about her? Why had he continually wished that she'd been in the kitchen on Saturday night? Because she kept her cool while everyone else panicked, and brought an air of calm to the chaos? Or so he could watch her as she carefully dressed each plate, admiring the curve of her neck as she bent her head over her handiwork. And hadn't there been a moment in bed with Richenda last night, when he'd imagined dark eyes fringed with spidery lashes gazing into his?

Seconds ticked by as they drifted through the sky. He had to decide what to say. If he ignored his doubts, and assured Richenda he loved her, that would seal their fate. There would be no going back. And he would never know . . .

Somewhere in his consciousness, Guy heard a phone ringing. It was so out of context that he looked around, confused, then realized it was his mobile. He rummaged in the pocket of his coat and pulled it out. He didn't recognize the number.

'Hello?'

'Guy?' The voice on the other end was small. 'Guy – it's me. Johnny's seen the paper. He's seen the paper and he's got Ted. He says he won't bring him back.'

Guy didn't hesitate for a moment.

'I'll be with you as soon as I can.'

He hung up the phone and looked at Richenda.

'I'm sorry,' he said simply. 'That was Honor. She needs me.'

Richenda just nodded. She didn't look surprised or angry. She put her hands in her pockets and turned away, looking out over the countryside.

Guy turned to Matt.

'Is there any way we can land this thing quickly?'

26

Honor answered the door to Guy, as pale as a ghost, her eyes huge in her face. He put one arm around her and gave her a comforting squeeze; for a moment she rested her head despondently on his shoulder, then looked up.

'I'm sorry to drag you into this,' she half whispered. 'But I didn't know who else to call.'

'That's OK. It's all my fault anyway. You're the one who's been dragged into this appalling mess.' He saw the paper on the sofa in the living room. 'You've seen it, then?'

Honor nodded.

'Yeah.'

'I don't know what the hell these people think gives them the right. It just goes to show you, doesn't it? You can't believe what you read.'

'I know. The only problem is, Johnny does . . . Believe it, I mean.'

'I'm so sorry, Honor.'

'And I can't blame him for being angry. He's so desperate for us to get back together . . .' Honor swallowed hard. She could feel a lump of tears the size of a peach stone sticking in her throat. 'He says I'm an unfit mother. He says he's not bringing Ted back. He can't mean that, can he?'

'I don't know. You know him better than I do.'

'He's very volatile. He's got a bit of a wild streak. But I don't think he'd do anything to hurt Ted. Even if he'd quite like to kill me.' Honor twisted her hands nervously. 'Do you think I should go to his house? Try and talk to him?'

'You might pass him on the way. Then if you weren't here . . .'

'Then maybe I should call the police?'

Guy realized she was starting to get distraught.

'Calm down a moment. Let's think about this logically. What time was he supposed to bring him back?'

'After lunch. We didn't say an actual time.'

Guy looked at his watch.

'So he's not technically missing yet. The police won't be interested.'

'But what happens in the meantime? What if he takes him out of the country? What if he takes him to Ireland?'

'Has Ted got a passport?'

'No . . .'

'Well, he won't be going anywhere. You can't fly anywhere without paperwork these days.' Guy tried to think rationally. 'Why don't we give him another couple of hours; see if he does bring him back? If he doesn't, then we can make a plan. Until then, there's nothing we can do.'

He put his arms round her and gave her a reassuring hug.

'I'm sorry I can't be more help.'

'It's OK. It's nice that you're here. I'd go mad if I had to wait on my own.' She smiled at him bravely. 'I haven't interrupted anything important, have I?'

'No, no,' lied Guy. 'Nothing at all.'

Honor bit her lip anxiously.

'Has Richenda seen it?'

'Yes, but she knows it's all nonsense,' Guy assured her. 'She's used to this sort of thing.'

'That's OK,' said Honor, relieved. 'It would have been awful if she'd thought there was something going on between us.'

'Quite,' said Guy. 'But you don't need to worry.'

Richenda had to smile at the irony. Most people came back from being whisked off in a hot-air balloon betrothed, not dumped. As a dramatic end to a relationship, it took some beating. For she knew that it was all over. And she wasn't going to demean herself by protesting or fighting or throwing a tantrum. She was going to make a tactical and gracious withdrawal, and be grateful that this had happened early on in their engagement, before the stakes had got too high. She'd be able to turn it to her advantage somehow, she felt confident of that. Not by exploiting Guy, of course. Or by bleating about the pressures of the media; she despised people who courted publicity then complained when the press turned on them. She thought it would be fair to explain their split as a temporary respite while she explored her past and rebuilt bridges with her family. That should satisfy the nation's curiosity, and eventually they would lose interest, until the day she found love elsewhere.

Richenda stood in the master bedroom at Eversleigh, looking round for the last time. She'd gone into the small sitting room, taken a sheet of notepaper out of the bureau and spent half an hour agonizing over what to put in her letter, painstakingly choosing every word until she'd got it just right. Now she placed the letter on the dressing table, next to the little leather box that held Guy's cufflinks and his loose change. She slid the ruby ring off her finger and placed it carefully on top of the letter, feeling a sudden calm as she did so.

She'd always felt out of place at Eversleigh. She neither belonged there as part of the family or a member of staff or a guest. The only time she'd felt comfortable was as Lady Jane, when the cameras were rolling and the lights were burning and she was moving round the room in character. Even Malachi and Marilyn had been wary of her; she'd been aware of their complicit glances, their tacit disapproval. And she certainly knew that Madeleine had never considered her good enough for Guy, for she'd never gone to any great lengths to hide it. Richenda knew she would never have broken down those barriers. She would never have felt mistress of Eversleigh. As she picked up her bag, she felt a huge relief that she didn't have to struggle to fit in for a moment longer.

Honor didn't think that the hands on the clock in the kitchen had ever dragged themselves round so slowly. Each minute felt like an hour. And there was nothing either of them could do to kill the time. Conversation was pointless; reading was futile. She spent the first half an hour tidying up the kitchen, then sat on the sofa chewing her nails, jumping up every time a car went past, willing the phone to ring. Five times she tried Johnny's mobile but was met with the same polite voice telling her he was unavailable. Guy did his best to calm her, but there was nothing he could say to reassure her. Every trashy made-for-TV movie she had ever seen flashed through her mind. She had visions of Johnny helping Ted into a helicopter, loaned to him by one of his flash clients, and flying him over to Ireland. At one point she even imagined Chloe escorting them, she and Johnny exchanging affectionate smiles over the top of Ted's head. Then she saw herself in court engaged in a long drawn-out custody battle, with Johnny's brief producing evidence of her wanton behaviour.

'Hey,' said Guy, and she realized she had dug her nails so hard into her hands that they were practically drawing blood. 'Don't torture yourself.'

At twenty past three, there was the rumble of a diesel engine outside the front door. Honor looked at Guy and flew over to the window. She saw Johnny getting out of the car. And Ted in the front seat.

'He's brought him back.' A sweet relief flooded through her, but she resisted the urge to go rushing out. She wasn't going to give Johnny the benefit of knowing how much agony he'd put her through. Instead, she composed herself and opened the front door, pale but cool, acknowledging him with a tight smile that didn't quite reach her eyes. He responded with a twitch of his mouth that was more of a grimace than a smile; they both had to pretend to be civil in front of Ted, who shot straight into her arms without noticing any atmosphere. She bent down and hugged him to her.

'Mum – we had such a cool time. We went to see some Labrador puppies and I slept on a . . . what was it called?'

He looked unsurely at Johnny.

'A futon.'

'Goodness,' Honor laughed. 'Now listen – go upstairs and unpack your things. Put your dirty clothes in the laundry basket and put everything else back in the right drawer. I just want to talk to Johnny for five minutes, then you can come down and give me all the gory details.'

As Ted pounded up the stairs she stood up and looked Johnny in the eye coldly.

'I suppose your conscience got the better of you.'

The look she gave him was so withering that even Johnny had the grace to look a little shamefaced.

'I was always going to bring him back. You know that.'

'How do I know that?'

'You know I'm impulsive, Honor. You know I've got a temper.'

His freckles stood out in stark relief against his skin, which was white with tension.

'So that makes it all right, does it? Do you know what I've been through today?' She couldn't help blurting it out, even though she'd sworn to herself not to let him see she'd been out of her mind with worry. But Johnny was impassive to her plight.

'What about what I went through?' he demanded. 'I got a bit of a shock over my morning coffee, I can tell you.'

'The difference being I didn't go out to make you suffer.'

'Oh yes. Honor McLean. The professional victim. Always wronged, but never in the wrong.'

Her distaste was palpable as she pushed past him into

the living room. Johnny followed, and stopped short when he saw a figure standing rather awkwardly by the fire-place. It was Guy, half wishing he'd slipped out the back door to leave them to settle their differences, but know-ing that Honor deserved his support.

'Surprise, surprise,' said Johnny, raising a sardonic eyebrow.

'Actually,' said Guy, 'I'm just here to explain.'

'Nothing needs explaining. It was all there in black and white and words of one syllable.'

Guy tried to hide his exasperation. He was hoping to get through this encounter without losing his temper, but he was already prejudiced. He'd hated seeing Honor suffer over the past couple of hours, trying to remain brave while inside she was obviously in turmoil, her little face set in a mask of distress. And he didn't think you could sink any lower than to use a child as a weapon; it was despicable. But if he was going to convince Johnny, he had to remain cool.

'You know, that's why papers like the *Voice* survive,' he said calmly. 'Because the people that read them choose to believe the rubbish they read, instead of chucking it in the bin where it belongs.'

Johnny looked at him sharply. Was he being patronized?

'There's no smoke without fire, surely?' he retaliated, a trifle smugly.

'I can assure you – there's absolutely nothing going on between me and Honor. She's my employee and that's the extent of the relationship. The whole story's been cooked up by the paper and I just want to apologize for any distress it's caused you.'

'*I'm* not distressed. Though how Ted will feel in the playground next week I can't say. I'm sure word will have got round.'

Honor stepped forward, her fists clenched. It was typical of Johnny to be able to go straight for the Achilles heel. But Guy shot her a warning glance. He'd got her into this and he was going to get her out.

'If anybody's spiteful or unkind enough to say anything, I'm sure Honor will do a great job of explaining how the truth's been twisted. The paper lost out on a scoop on Richenda last week and this was their retaliation. Unfortunately they specialize in insinuation that isn't underpinned by anything remotely resembling the truth. They present it as fact, and unless you've got the time and patience to read between the lines you can come away with the wrong impression. Which is understandable: they do a very good job.'

Despite himself, Guy managed a self-deprecating grin; a blokey attempt to get Johnny on his side.

'I can tell you, I had quite a bit of explaining to do myself. Richenda wasn't remotely impressed. But I'm afraid it goes with being engaged to a celebrity. I don't suppose I'll ever be able to look at another woman without it being all over the front pages.'

Johnny nodded his acceptance of Guy's explanation.

'Yeah, well, life's a bitch, eh? I suppose you weighed it all up before you asked her to marry you. I'm sure she's got a lot of other attributes that more than make up for the inconvenience.'

Guy's face remained remarkably impassive.

'I just want to be sure that you're quite happy Honor

is the innocent party in all of this? It's my fault – I should have realized they'd be looking for an angle. I should have done more to protect her.'

'I'm sure it happens all the time,' said Johnny. 'Occupational hazard.'

'Quite,' said Guy, relieved that Johnny seemed mollified. He raised a hand in farewell. 'Right, well, see you. Take care. I'll see myself out.'

A moment later the front door clicked shut.

'Wanker,' Johnny muttered under his breath.

'What do you mean?' demanded Honor indignantly.

'All that bloody pseudo-apologetic Hugh Grant frightfully-sorry waffle. You watch, I bet in six months' time he'll be caught in a brothel wearing ladies' knickers.'

'Johnny!'

'He's the pervy public-school type. You can see it a mile off.'

Honor suddenly found she'd run out of patience with Johnny and his conspiracy theories. She rolled her eyes and stood up.

'Whatever you want to think. I'll go and get Ted so he can say thank you. Then I think you better go.'

'Hang on – we've still got some talking to do.'

'Have we?'

He dropped his voice, so it was low and persuasive.

'Honor. You read my letter.'

She stared at him in disbelief.

'You honestly don't think that after today we can make it work?'

Johnny sighed, and took her hands. Honor tried not to snatch them away.

471

'Listen, I misunderstood. You can't blame me for misunderstanding. I've forgiven you.'

Honor looked at him incredulously. That wasn't what she'd meant at all. She hadn't committed any crime, yet here was Johnny still implying she was the guilty party. While all along he had done something so hideous that it made her feel sick even now to think of it. She had been terrified when he threatened not to bring Ted back. Even though it had been a hollow threat. And what it made her realize was that Johnny was capable of incredible cruelty while remaining oblivious to the distress he caused. That was no basis for a relationship.

Nevertheless, she needed to be cautious. He was still prickly and defensive, on his back foot. She had to couch her rejection in general terms, not point the finger of blame at him. She didn't want to make an enemy of him. There was Ted to consider, after all. So she had to tread a careful path through this minefield.

'Johnny – I've given it some really serious thought. I don't want to share my life with anybody at the moment. What Ted and I have got is perfect. I don't want to risk spoiling it just so I can have the benefit of a relationship. You can see him as often as you like – I don't have a problem with that. We can even go on holiday together if you want. But I think we'd be better keeping things as they are, rather than putting ourselves under pressure. Do you understand?'

Johnny's face was bleak. He didn't respond. Honor ploughed on, desperate for him to see her side of the story.

'We've barely managed to get through one week

without ending up hurting each other. We can't put Ted through that again and again. Or ourselves.'

Johnny finally spoke.

'Is there nothing I can say to make you change your mind?'

'No. I think I'm a good mother to Ted, and you'll be a great father. But I don't think we'd work as a team. We're both too set in our own ways – I know I am. I'd find it incredibly difficult to fit someone else into my life after all these years. I'd be impossible. We'd squabble and fight. And sulk. But if we do it my way . . .'

'OK,' said Johnny, pulling away from her sharply. 'Let's do it your way. That seems fair.'

He turned to walk towards the door, but not before Honor had seen a tear glistening in the corner of his eye.

'Don't you want to say goodbye to Ted?'

Johnny shook his head, his voice choked as he reached for the door handle.

'Tell him I had to go. I'll call him later.'

Honor waited until she heard the door close, then blew out her cheeks in a puff of relief and flopped down on the sofa. She wasn't too taken in by the dramatic exit. Johnny was very good at milking situations.

She heard Ted pounding down the stairs and burst in through the door.

'He hasn't gone, has he?'

'He had to, darling. He'll phone you tonight.'

'Was Guy here?'

'Yes, but he had to go too.'

Ted looked away, frowning. Honor could see there was something going on in his little head, and wondered if

Johnny had said anything to him. Worse, if he'd actually seen the paper. She wouldn't put it past him to embroil Ted in his games.

'Is there something the matter?' she asked, sick with anxiety. The poor kid could be imagining all manner of things.

Ted nodded.

'Tell me.'

Ted slid on to her lap.

'Monkey's got a hole in him. Right near his tail. Johnny said he couldn't fix it, but I thought he was a vet. And there's all stuff coming out.'

Honor hugged her son to her, trying not to laugh with relief. The entire episode had passed him by. If only Ted's life could stay that simple for ever. Well, as long as it was just the two of them, maybe it could . . .

Guy walked back down to Eversleigh Manor with a heavy heart. The urge to punch Johnny right in the nose had been hard to suppress. He'd hated trying to placate him; the words had stuck in his craw, but he thought he'd managed to convince him of Honor's innocence. Hopefully, they could now iron things out between them, if only for Ted's sake. Guy sighed: he'd got some ironing of his own to do now.

The house was eerily quiet. He wondered where Richenda might be. There was no trace of her in the kitchen or the small sitting room – nor of anyone else. He ran lightly up the stairs to the bedroom and pushed open the door.

He knew immediately that she was gone. All traces of

her had been eradicated: her silk dressing gown, her shoes, the cosmetics that were usually scattered on the bedside table. There was no evidence at all that she had ever been there – except for a piece of cream notepaper on his dressing table, pinned down by the small leather box he had opened so proudly when he'd asked her to marry him.

He flipped it open, turning the ring over and over, admiring the deep redcurrant glow of the ruby, rubbing the cool gold against his fingers as he read the blue ink spread across the letter underneath.

Darling Guy

Everything that has happened recently has forced me to make a choice. I don't think I'm the right person for you, or for Eversleigh. I simply don't belong in your world. My career, my schedule, the publicity – the whole circus! – don't allow me to compromise, and I can't give it all up – not yet. It is the only thing I have ever had that is my own. It's my security, my identity – it is me. I hope you understand.

We had a wonderful time and I will never forget you. I know you will find the right person to look after Eversleigh for you.

Love,

Richenda

There was no hint of reproach in the letter. No malice or resentment. It was typical Richenda: calm and gracious. Guy sat down on the bed. Half of him thought that he should go after her, insist they could work it out, but he knew his heart wouldn't be in it. Their engagement would lurch on, only to come to a more unpleasant end sometime in the future. Richenda didn't deserve that.

She'd had the sense to realize they weren't compatible. She'd put her finger on it. She didn't belong in his world, any more than he belonged in hers. He wasn't turned on by auditions and film schedules and premières, any more than she was interested in the politics of the village fête or how high the hedges should be cut. They had high maintenance lifestyles that couldn't run in tandem, and neither of them could be expected to sacrifice their existence for the sake of the other.

Guy felt a sudden surge of gratitude to Richenda for having the balls to call it off. He wanted to ring her, to make sure there were no hard feelings, but it might be best to give her some time to lick her wounds. He felt sure she'd be in touch when she felt up to it. She was, after all, no coward. What she'd done had been incredibly brave.

He put the letter back on the dressing table, then picked up the little leather box and slipped the ring gently back inside. As the lid snapped down, he gave a wry smile.

He was a bona fide eligible bachelor once again.

Richenda arrived back at her flat exhausted. All she could think about was opening a bottle of cold white wine and having a good weep on her mother's shoulder. Thank God Sally was going to be there, she thought. For the first time in her adult life she felt as if she needed her mum. She needed a shoulder to cry on belonging to someone that wouldn't judge her. She knew she'd handled the day's events with a cool dignity, but she didn't think she had the strength to carry on pretending. It was so exhausting, being Richenda Fox. For just one night she wanted to be Rowan Collins again, take off the mask, drop the facade. And there was only one person she could do that with.

She stuck the key in the lock and pushed the door open.

'Hello!' she called, dragging her case in after her and dumping it in the hall.

The flat was decidedly empty. Checking her watch, she saw it was only just after five and Sally could be out somewhere. She'd go and have a shower, get changed and nip down to the deli to get some bits and pieces for supper. She realized she hadn't actually eaten anything all day.

She dragged her case into her bedroom. There was a note on the bed.

Dear Richenda

I'm going off for a few weeks to get my head together. I'm really grateful for everything you've done but it would be too easy for me to hitch myself to your wagon, and I don't want to do that. I need to prove that I can stand on my own two feet and do something for myself. It's the only way I'm going to get back my self-respect. When I come to your wedding I want to be ME, not just your mother. Though I'm very proud to be that, of course! I hope you understand . . .

I'll get back in touch when I've sorted myself out. In the meantime, you've got my number, but you're only to use it in an EMERGENCY. Please respect me for this.

Lots and lots of love

Mum xxxx

Richenda put the note back on the bed. With shaking hands she took her mobile out of her handbag, scrolled through until she found the number she wanted, and pressed the call button.

'Mum?' she said plaintively when Sally answered. 'This is an emergency . . .'

27

On Tuesday morning, Honor woke up and groaned. Absolutely the only thing she could think of to be grateful for was that there was no school. She didn't have to go and face curious stares at the gates. She did need to go and get milk and bread, though, and she didn't think she could brave the village shop. She'd have to get in the car and drive to Eldenbury. Even then she risked being spotted by someone she knew.

The full import of what had happened yesterday had taken until now to hit her. The paper's revelations had been rather overshadowed by Johnny's reaction – or rather, his over-reaction. But now she had to accept that the whole village – the whole county, the whole country! – thought she had been at it with Guy. Who had made it abundantly clear that he was, quite literally, otherwise engaged. It was a bit like walking round with your skirt tucked into your knickers. Honor felt humiliated, exposed. She never wanted to show her face in public again.

Worse than that, she was supposed to go and work at Eversleigh Manor this morning. But wild horses wouldn't drag her there. What if she bumped into Richenda? Not what if – she was bound to! What the hell could she say? She wouldn't be able to look her in the eye. Even though she was technically innocent of what the papers had insinuated, Honor knew the sort of thoughts she'd been

479

having about Guy over the past few days. Completely preposterous fairy-tale daydreams worthy of a teenage magazine.

She looked at her clock. It was five past nine. At half past nine every Tuesday the Eversleigh team were supposed to meet to discuss the weekend ahead, after which Honor would spend the rest of the day planning menus. She pulled the duvet back over her head. She was going to go back to sleep. She could hear Ted downstairs watching telly – he'd be quite happy there for another hour.

At nine thirty-five, the telephone rang.

'Hello?' said Honor warily.

'I hope you haven't had any ridiculous ideas about not turning up for work.' It was Madeleine, who never felt the need to announce who she was on the telephone.

'Um . . . well, I didn't really think it was . . . appropriate.'

'It's quite simple,' said Madeleine crisply. 'We can't do without you. The whole place will fall apart. Apart from anything, you haven't done a thing wrong. You're the innocent party in all of this.'

Obviously they all considered it quite unthinkable that Guy would be involved with her.

'I want you here for a meeting at ten o'clock. We've got another big weekend ahead of us. And I know it's half term, so bring Ted along. Malachi needs a hand draining the fishpond.'

'It doesn't sound as if I've got much choice.'

'None whatsoever. And please don't worry – nobody blames you for anything. We all know the bloody papers will cook up anything for a headline.'

Honor put the phone down, slightly mollified. It was a relief to know that she hadn't been made quite such a fool of as she thought, although there would be those who would be more than happy to believe what they read. But following Madeleine's vote of support, she thought she could face them. And she was secretly relieved that her job was intact. She'd already got used to the idea of the money coming in on a regular basis, and now she didn't have her contract with the craft centre she would have been really stuck without it.

She leaped out of bed and into the shower, calling down to Ted to get himself dressed. As she pulled on her jeans, the phone rang again.

'Honor?'

It was Henty. Shit – of course she should have called Henty. What kind of friend would she think she was? She would have seen the papers yesterday.

'Henty – I meant to call you.'

'No mention! No mention whatsoever! We spent all night getting plastered and you didn't squeak a word!' Henty sounded mildly indignant rather than downright furious.

'What was I supposed to say? Anyway, none of it's true.'

'None of it?'

'Absolutely none. And I was going to tell you . . . about loads of other stuff. But I couldn't in front of Travis.'

'You're a dark horse,' said Henty.

Honor looked at her watch. It was quarter to ten. No time to go into detail now.

'Listen, I've got to go to a meeting. But why don't we meet up later? Bring Walter round for lunch.'

'Actually, I was going to ask *you* for lunch.' Henty sounded rather smug. 'Guess what?'

'What?'

Henty couldn't keep the excitement out of her voice any longer. 'Harry – that's my editor – just phoned Charles. He wants to buy my book. He actually wants to buy it!'

'That's completely amazing.'

'I know. But I can't bang on about it now – the kids all need taxi-ing here, there and everywhere. This would bloody happen at half term. I just wanted to ask you over for a celebration.'

'Of course! Try and stop me!' Honor was thrilled for her friend. 'Look, I've got to go or I'm going to be late. I'll see you later . . .'

Honor arrived at Eversleigh Manor at ten past ten, hot and bothered, with Ted in tow. Malachi appeared from nowhere with a fishing net.

'Ted. Just the man. I need someone to scoop the fish out. They're too fast for me.'

She burst into the kitchen, apologies on her lips. There was only one person at the table.

It was Guy.

He looked at her, frowning.

'Hello.'

Honor felt her cheeks flaming red as she ventured into the room. He didn't look very pleased to see her.

'I'm really sorry about this. I don't want to cause any trouble. Between you and Richenda, I mean. And I totally understand if you want me to hand in my notice.

It was Madeleine who insisted I came into work –'

Guy was looking at her evenly. She took a step back again.

'But it was a really silly idea. I should have just been more firm. I don't think your mother really understands quite how embarrassing this all is.'

Her hand was on the doorknob, ready to make her escape.

'Honor.'

'What?'

'Richenda and I . . . it's all over.'

'Oh God.' Honor put her hand to her mouth, horrified. How could she have thought that awful article had done no damage? Now she was going to be branded a marriage wrecker, or worse. 'Guy, I'm so sorry. Is there anything I can say, or do, to convince her?'

'Richenda doesn't need convincing. The article had nothing to do with it, really. It just brought the day of reckoning forward a bit. Things . . . weren't working out between us.'

'Oh.' Honor struggled to take in everything he was saying. 'So . . . it wasn't my fault?'

'No,' said Guy. 'Sit down. I'll make some coffee while we wait for the others.'

Honor sat down obediently while Guy went to put the kettle on. Then he sat down again. There was a long silence. Honor tapped her pencil against her notebook.

'I wonder where everyone is?'

They both looked at the clock.

'Madeleine said to be here at ten or else.'

'She said the same to me,' said Guy.

Honor snapped her notebook shut and stood up.

'Well, if there isn't going to be a meeting, I've got to get on. I'm going out to lunch. I need to go and make myself presentable.'

Guy looked at her. To him she looked perfect.

'Special occasion?'

'Yes.' Her eyes sparkled.

Guy's heart sank. She and Johnny had obviously patched up their differences.

'My friend Henty. She's just sold her book. She's asked me over to celebrate.'

'Oh.' Guy managed a smile. 'I thought you might be having lunch with Johnny.'

'You're joking.' Honor looked suitably unimpressed. 'It's going to be a while before Johnny and I are on proper speaking terms. Obviously we've got to pretend to be civil, for Ted.'

'But you're not . . . ?'

'Not what?'

'I don't know. Whatever you call it. An item.'

Honor shook her head.

'The only thing Johnny and I are is history. For good, this time. I'm not going to get in the way of him and Ted, but I'm keeping him at arm's length, I can tell you –'

Honor stopped, aware that Guy was staring at her.

'What?'

He gave a funny little twisted smile.

'I've just realized when it was.'

'When what was?'

'It was when you hit me over the back of the hand with your spoon.'

484

'Sorry?'

Guy pushed back his chair and walked over to her. She looked up at him, but she didn't flinch. Didn't step away. He put up a hand and brushed her fringe out of her eyes. She blinked once or twice in surprise and smiled, a little unsure. He bent his head and kissed her, just once, on the lips.

'That was when I fell in love with you,' he explained. 'When you whacked me for pinching your chocolate.'

She breathed in, shakily, and Guy steeled himself. He was ready. He could take the rejection. But he had to take the risk. It would be crazy not to, after everything that had happened. And Richenda had known how he felt all along. He couldn't let her sacrifice their engagement for nothing. She'd done the noble thing. It was up to him now.

Honor was looking up at him, obviously trying to figure out the best way to let him down gently.

'You can pinch my chocolate any time,' she smiled.

Guy swallowed. His throat was dry. He wasn't sure what she meant. But as she curled her arm around the back of his neck, and pulled his head towards her until their lips met again, he finally got the drift . . .

Moments later, Madeleine swept in through the swing door of the kitchen, then promptly turned on her heel and walked out again.

She met Marilyn in the corridor, bearing the candelabra from the dining room table.

'I was just going to give this a polish.'

'I wouldn't go in the kitchen,' said Madeleine. 'Not just yet.'

Marilyn looked at her quizzically, and Madeleine gave an imperceptible nod, accompanied by a smile.

'About bloody time,' pronounced Marilyn.

Two hours later, wrapped in Guy's arms, Honor called Henty.

'Henty – don't kill me, but I can't do lunch. I'm really, really sorry. I'll explain everything later . . .'

Henty just giggled. She sounded rather drunk.

'That's OK. I'm actually doing a bit of research anyway.'

Honor was scandalized.

'Not with Travis?'

'God no, darling. How deadly dull and predictable. With my husband, actually . . .'

Epilogue

Charles looked out of the kitchen window. Henty was climbing into the driving seat of her Alfa Romeo Spyder. She pressed the button that rolled back the roof, revealing Travis in the passenger seat. She was driving him to Heathrow; he was off to university in September, and was going to travel for the next three months, so his stint at Fulford Farm was over. The agency was sending them a Swedish girl as his replacement. Charles hoped she was capable rather than comely: they needed the extra pair of hands more than ever.

Henty was flying high. He'd brokered the most fantastic three-book deal for her with *Cotswold Housewife*. She had a column in a newspaper; she was an agony aunt for a magazine. And things had snowballed for Charles off the back of it. Whether because it had given him confidence, or because success breeds success, he couldn't be sure. But already he'd picked up three fantastic new clients and done deals for them too; business was looking up. He was back on the circuit and he felt on top of the world.

Not least because he and Henty had rekindled their marriage. Things were now on a more equal footing, and both of them felt comfortable with their status and therefore each other. They were each enjoying their own renaissance, and now the children were growing up it was possible to make the most of the lifestyle that went with it: launches and lunches. They were enjoying family life as well. Only last week they had gone to Sports Day. Charles decided that Henty was the most glamorous mother there, curvaceous in her red silk halter-neck with the white polka dots. Fleur, by contrast, had looked decidedly ropey, obviously a few weeks behind with her Botox. She'd hovered next to them with her picnic basket, angling for an invitation to join them on their rug now Henty was the closest the school had to a celebrity, and Henty, warm-hearted and generous to the end, had made room for her.

The postman arrived, with a hefty parcel. Charles ripped it open eagerly; it was the cover proof for *Cotswold Housewife*, and he couldn't wait to see what the publishers had done. Henty had hinted that he would be very surprised.

Charles picked up the proof. It was satisfyingly glossy. On the front was an illustration of a harassed-looking housewife pushing a Hoover, her hair in a headscarf, and tiny little motifs of her life were scattered around – scrubbing brushes, can-openers, shopping lists, car keys.

On the back was the rear view of a shapely woman, dressed only in –

For a moment, Charles thought he was going to faint. It must be a coincidence, surely. For the woman was wearing a pair of knickers exactly like the pair Fleur had abandoned that night in the Honeycote Arms. Black satin, with ribbon bows tied at each side. Then he read the tag line at the top: 'For abandoned housewives everywhere.' And he knew. This was a message. Henty had known all along about Fleur, and this was her revenge.

Despite himself, he grinned. It was a tiny little dig at him that she hadn't been able to resist, but he admired her for it. And their marriage was strong enough now for him to be able to take the joke.

In the departure lounge, Henty waited by Travis's luggage while he bought chocolate and a new CD for the journey. She hoped she wasn't going to cry when he left. She was hopeless at airports. There always seemed something so final about someone getting on a plane. The best thing to do, she decided, was to leave before his flight was called, so she didn't make an idiot of herself.

'I'm going to get off,' she said briskly as he reappeared with his booty. 'You'll be OK, won't you?'

'I don't know,' he replied. Henty felt unsettled. He was looking right into her eyes, and he suddenly seemed very serious.

'Of course you will,' she laughed nervously.

He didn't answer, just slipped his arms round her waist and drew her to him. She giggled, and went to give him a peck on the cheek. Suddenly, she found his warm lips on hers. For a full ten seconds they kissed. She drew away, breathless, unsure what to say.

Travis was staring at her.

'I've been wanting to do that for months,' he said. 'You don't know how much self-control it took to keep my hands off you.'

He turned sharply, picked up his rucksack and strode off towards the departure gate without a backward glance. Henty watched him go, her heart still pitter-pattering, her tummy jumbled upside down.

She didn't know what to think, but she could definitely feel a sequel coming on.

Sally looked ten years younger. She'd lost her bedsit pallor, her skin was starting to tone up from all the swimming and the massages, her hair was glossy and her eyes bright from the healthy food they'd been eating: steamed fish and vegetables and rice and fruit so fresh it had barely left the tree. She hadn't had a cigarette for days, or even a drink apart from the occasional glass of wine. Her mind was clearer than it had been for years. The future seemed bright, not blurry. The past was behind her; issues dealt with or buried.

She was sitting on the sand next to Richenda's sunlounger, sketching ideas. She was going to open a boutique. It was going to be called Ravers, and stock sexy, well-cut clothes for middle-aged women who didn't want to look middle-aged. Even though Richenda was bank-rolling it, Sally had done all the hard work: the market research, the sourcing, the deals, the décor. It had already created a lot of interest and it wasn't due to open for another four weeks. Which was why they'd escaped for a week on holiday to Thailand: once it was open there would be no respite.

Next to her, Richenda put down the script she was reading with a sigh of satisfaction. It was perfect. Absolutely perfect. Swashbuckling and bodice-ripping, of course. But witty and stylish too. Deeply romantic. With a tear-jerking ending that would have the entire nation sobbing into their handkerchiefs. Correction, the entire world. For this script was a blockbuster. A lavish, big-budget production with American money and a huge distributor behind it. Richenda knew in her gut that this was the platform she had been waiting for, the one that would launch her as an international superstar. The project was a remake of the black and white classic, *The Wicked Lady*, with Richenda in the title role. The leading man hadn't been pinned down yet, but some heavyweight names were being bandied around. Richenda had a sneaking hope for Russell Crowe – there was something about him that reminded her of Guy, with his dishevelled devil-may-careness.

She picked up the phone that was lying on the arm of the sunbed next to her and pressed the number that would put her through to her agent.

'I love it,' she gushed. 'I love it and I want to do it. Fax me the contract now.'

Guy carefully turned the dial, opened the safe and drew out the little leather box.

He had long been in a dilemma. Was it bad luck to use a ring again, when it had already been returned to you once? What exactly was the etiquette? He took it out of its velvet bed and turned it over and over in his fingers. It was stunning; far more beautiful than anything he'd seen in the shops. And if he didn't use it, then it would stay in its box for ever. Jewellery like this was made to be worn.

He put it back carefully and snapped the lid shut. He'd go and ask his mother. Madeleine always knew the right thing to do.

Veronica Henry

about Veronica Henry

diary of a cotswold housewife

the books

read more

When did you first start writing?

My first job after university and secretarial college was as a Production Secretary for *The Archers*. The producer at the time, William Smethurst, came from a writing background, and was very keen to nurture any of his employees who showed promise. He encouraged me to start by throwing me in at the deep end, writing scenes for *The Archers Roadshow*, where members of the public could record scenes with their favourite character. When William was subsequently made producer of *Crossroads*, he offered me the job of script editor – a sure-fire way to learn hands-on about writing! Several years later, when I was expecting my first child, I left script editing to become a script writer.

He encouraged me to start by throwing me in at the deep end, writing scenes for *The Archers Roadshow*

What sparked the idea for *An Eligible Bachelor*?

My husband and I went to view a manor house that was for sale deep in the Cotswolds – it was far out of our reach financially but we had a sneaking fantasy to run an upmarket B&B. The house was absolutely divine – perfect, in fact – but no matter how we did the maths it was out of the question. I kept the particulars for years, and the house became the setting for Eversleigh Manor, the seat of eligible bachelor Guy Portias!

Your characters are always so vivid and real. Where do you draw your inspiration from?

I consider myself to be working all the time. Whoever I meet, wherever I go, whatever I read all goes into my mental database, and, luckily for me, I have a good memory for detail. But I never carbon copy a person I have met or what they have told me into my work – all my characters and their situations are fictional, patch-worked together from experiences I have had, whether first or second hand. I also do a fair amount of background research – the brewery run by the Liddiards in *Honeycote*, or the Bugattis raced in *Wild Oats* – and these worlds often open up new possibilities for stories and characters.

> Whoever I meet, wherever I go, whatever I read all goes into my mental database

Out of all of your novels, do you have a favourite character?

I do adore Patrick Liddiard: so arrogant yet so vulnerable; so desperate to do the right thing but unable to resist temptation. Sadly I think I am getting too old for him now. Though he does have a history with older women!

If you had to choose, which character would you secretly like to be?

Lucy Liddiard, with her rambling, chaotic house, constant flow of family and friends, her gorgeous clothes and her ability to produce a feast at short notice without turning a hair. But I could do without her unfaithful husband . . .

What is your perfect writing environment?

I need absolute silence and no distractions, a tidy table, plenty of coffee, a fresh note pad and pen for scribbling, and my laptop, which must not be connected to the internet! Every now and then I escape from my family for two or three days, which means I can devote myself entirely to writing as soon as I wake up – I am definitely a morning person – rather than running around buttering toast and doing the school run!

What is the best thing about being a writer and the worst?

The best thing about being a writer is earning your living by writing out your fantasies – creating wonderful worlds and then causing chaos by turning your characters' lives upside down. What could be more fun? The downside is that you can't delegate any of it – from start to finish, the book has to come from you, and that can be very daunting.

I do adore Patrick Liddiard: so arrogant yet so vulnerable; so desperate to do the right thing but unable to resist temptation.

Do you ever get writer's block? And, if so, how do you deal with it?

Absolutely! I get varying degrees of writer's block. Sometimes it can be dealt with by moving to another point in the story, then going back to the sticky bit later on. At other times, I just have to walk away and come back with a fresh eye. If it is a truly dreadful block, it often means there is something wrong with the story or a character isn't working – if this is the case, then sadly they have to be killed off. I have learnt that being a good writer means not being afraid to chuck out what you have done. In other words, there is no point in flogging a dead horse.

Diary of a
Cotswold Housewife

Henty Beresford wrote the bestselling *Diary of a Chelsea Virgin* in the 1980s. The story is now continued in *Diary of a Cotswold Housewife*. Henty lives in organized chaos with her husband and four children in, coincidentally, the Cotswolds.

ACKNOWLEDGEMENTS

I don't know what the record for writer's block is, but the last time I put pen to paper, or should I say finger to keyboard, the word processor had only just started easing its way into public consciousness. Having spent the past fifteen years or so pretending that *Chelsea Virgin* was a fluke, I finally found the courage to write again. There are several people I want to thank for giving me the courage to do this:

My husband Charles, who despite his vested interest never put me under any pressure.

My best friend Honor, for not laughing when I told her what I was doing.

My children, for not disturbing me while I locked myself away.

My editor, Harry Jenkins, for being so patient.

Gary, of Eldenbury Computer services, for technical support.

And finally Travis, cook, bottle-washer, babysitter, groom and all-round uncomplaining dogsbody – every home should have one.

Finally, I would like to stress that this is entirely a work of fiction, and any resemblance to any persons living or dead is the most extraordinary coincidence.

DIARY OF A COTSWOLD HOUSEWIFE

It is hard being married to a god.

It is even harder, as I may well find out, not being married to one.

For Tom is a god. It is official. He has, after all, brought people back from the dead. He has given them the gift of life when their every last hope had long been extinguished. I can see it must be hard to feel like a mere mortal when all around you people are prostrating themselves in awe and gratitude. But does it really absolve you from the washing up for the rest of your life?

Apparently, yes.

Tom is a heart surgeon, you see. He has taken the pulsating, still warm life-force from a recent corpse and placed it gently in the gaping cavity at the centre of his patient, then meticulously stitched the veins and arteries into place. But has he ever sewn a nametape into one of his children's Aertex shirts? I think you know the answer.

You'd like Tom. Everybody does. He is charm personified. He has twinkly blue eyes and soft brown hair that sticks up and a dimple in his left cheek and he looks about twelve. Well, maybe fifteen. And he doesn't talk like a heart surgeon. He talks about football and the new White Stripes album and who should win *Big Brother*. He never mentions aortas or ventricles in public – unless somebody asks him first. But he'll soon change the subject, turn it back round to the other person, quiz them gently about what it is they do. Being such a modest man. And when his bleeper goes at a dinner party, he makes as discreet an exit as possible: no fuss, no drama, no hint that he is off to play god yet again. Which of course leaves all the women misty eyed and sighing. And me having to cadge a lift home.

People often don't believe me when I tell them what he does. One woman was convinced he was a personal trainer at our local gym. That would be because he spends so much time there, honing his own heart muscle into perfection when he's not saving other people's. And he's often giving the ladies there tips on their technique, spurring them on to go the extra mile. At the last count he had seven gym buddies.

I don't go to the gym. I don't have time. I've got four children.

What else to tell you about him? Oh yes. He is having an affair with Alicia Birtwhistle and he thinks I don't know. Alicia Birtwhistle is a lawyer. She specializes in alimony. Which when you think about it is ironic. Not to mention massively irritating, as she is shit hot. There was a rumour she was headhunted by Mischon de Reya. You know, the people who looked after Princess Di's divorce. Apparently she said no, because she didn't want to work in London. She only works part-time and she still earns six figures. And she is always at the school gate to pick up her children. I know, because I have to pretend to be nice to her. Even though in her spare time [!] she is screwing my husband.

So apparently it is possible. To have a career and children and go to the gym and have an affair. But I don't know how. I can only manage one of the above. Clearly I am incompetent. Or lazy. Or just plain thick.

Tom obviously thinks I'm thick. Because the other day when he said he was going to the gym, I took his shorts out of his sports bag and replaced them with a pair of my eldest daughter's hockey knickers. He didn't say a word. The next time, I replaced his Nike t-shirt with a Funky Monkey crop top. Still no reaction. Finally, I put bright pink laces in his trainers. So unless he is jumping on the treadmill dressed like Britney Spears, he is definitely up to no good.

Clearly, shagging Alicia is the only form of exercise he needs at the moment. But then he has always claimed that plenty of sex is the best way to keep fit. Which would explain why I am two stone overweight while he is as sleek and as streamlined as an otter. And why Alicia can get away with having her belly-button pierced for her fortieth birthday. I keep telling myself that is massively tacky and common, but deep down I know that if I could get away with it, I would. However, the thought of anyone even trying to find my belly button makes me shudder. It would be like ploughing through several pounds of pizza dough. And when it was finally unearthed, I'm not sure it would be physically possible to pierce it. The sides have totally caved in.

Oh God, here I go. Tom is always telling me to stop moaning about my appearance and do something about it. Is that before I get up, make your breakfast, lay out your clothes, get your children up, get them breakfast, wash up, take them to school, come back, clean the house, go to the supermarket, come home, do the laundry, collect the children, cook their tea, wash up their tea, take them to their after-school activities, come back, supervise their homework, prepare our supper, supervise bath-time, read bedtime stories, put them all to bed, and have a glass of chilled sauvignon blanc ready for when you walk in the door? I want to ask him. Or after?

We had a cleaner once. Five years ago, before I had Clemmy, when I had a silly idea about going back to college to learn sports massage. Overnight, my life changed. In fact, I actually had one. But after the cleaner had been with us about three weeks, I found Tom in the bathroom holding up a bottle of Domestos.

'That's it. You can phone her up and tell her not to bother coming back.'

'What?' I wailed in protest.

'I'm not paying her six quid an hour not to bleach the bog!'

He brandished the Domestos at me in evidence. He'd marked where the bleach was. Like you would a gin bottle if you thought someone was an alcoholic. So you see, everyone else sees a twinkly-eyed, dimpled god. Whereas I know the truth – that he is a marker of bleach bottles. The sort of man who sets a trap for a cleaner who definitely needs the six quid an hour he was paying her more than he does.

To me this proves two things. That he doesn't want me to have a life [I had to sack the cleaner and give up college]. And that me replacing his gym kit was learned behaviour. Entrapment, I think they call it.

Ok. I need to stop here. All this is making Tom sound like a self-centred, controlling bully. He didn't actually make me sack the cleaner. I did anyway, because she smelt of stale smoke, and, even though I have been known to have the odd sneaky Silk Cut after two bottles of Blossom Hill on a girls' night out, I don't think someone who cleans your house should reek of fags. And I didn't have to give up college because of it. I gave up because I was pregnant with Clemmy and couldn't step out of the house without throwing up. Not ideal when you're practising sports massage on someone.

Which reminds me, I haven't actually introduced myself properly. My name is Amelia, but everyone calls me Millie. Or Mills, depending on how well they know me. I'm thirty nine, which is a coincidence, because that happens to be my chest, waist and hip measurement and my shoe size. In other words, I am shaped like a cork. My hair is brown and shoulder-length and I am proud to say that I no longer hold it back in a velvet Alice band. But only because the dog chewed up my last one and they don't seem to sell them any more – believe me, I've looked everywhere. Not even in Claire's Accessories. It's very annoying. As a last resort, I have been known to tie a pair of tights around my head to keep my hair out of my eyes. It's not a good look. It might also explain why Tom has decided to look elsewhere.

Alicia has sleek, golden hair – a subtle, natural sun-kissed shade of blonde that falls just below her jaw-line and is chipped into by the Man With the Golden Scissors, Alberto. He's got an incredibly trendy salon in Cheltenham, all rubber floors and see-through sinks and music that makes your ears bleed. I daren't go in there. I'd have to have my hair done somewhere else first. A bit like cleaning your house before the cleaner comes [if you have one, that is!]. I couldn't bear the humiliation otherwise: him running his fingers through my hair in distaste, clocking the threads of silver [I try and pull them out but it's getting painful], tutting over the split ends, discovering the bald spots where it all fell out after Clemmy and hasn't grown back yet …

Maybe you've guessed by now that my self-esteem, on a scale of one to ten, is about zero. Sometimes it overwhelms me and I go upstairs and lie on the bed while this big black cloud rolls over me. No matter how hard I try, I can't push it away. No matter how much I try and count my blessings, tell myself to pull myself together, be positive, blah blah blah, I feel completely overwhelmed. Sometimes, the thought of being smothered for ever by the big black cloud is the only comfort I can find, and frankly if it wasn't for the fact that I'd have to go and get the children from school …

The bottom line is I've decided to write this diary, because sometimes I think I am going mad. Sometimes I think I'm imagining things. Tom often tells me I'm over-reacting. I'm haunted by this sense of paranoia, which makes my heart pound and my palms go sweaty. I think this might be the start of a panic attack, but am I panicking because of something real? Or is it all in my head? Everything whirls round and round and gets out of proportion, and that's when I start reading into things and go off at the deep end and Tom looks at me as if I am completely losing the plot. So I thought if I started writing the plot down, I couldn't lose it.

But hey-ho. Not too much time to wallow in self-pity. Off to Tesco for me, because we've got eight for dinner tomorrow night. And no prizes for guessing who is on the guest list. And as Tom left this morning, he asked me not to make lamb tagine again.

Lamb tagine is my signature dish. It's about the only thing in the world I can do better than Tom. It's also incredibly easy and everyone likes it. Except, I happen to know, Alicia, who is not over keen on apricots. Not actually life-threateningly allergic to them or anything. Just not over keen. So basically he has asked me to rethink my entire menu, because his mistress –

Hang on. The phone's ringing. I'd better go and answer it because it might be the Aga man about a service and if you miss him he puts you back to the bottom of the list …

Bloody hell. Talk of the she-devil. That was Her. She was phoning to offer to bring a pudding on Saturday. Why?

There you are, you see? Paranoid. No-one else would see anything suspicious in the offer of a tarte au citron. But I can't help wondering if it means Tom has been bleating to her about my complete inability to function. [Though she probably doesn't need to be told. She just needs to look at me.] Did he ask her to offer to bring a pudding? To take the pressure off me? Which in turn will take the pressure off him. I always get panicky before a dinner party. But doesn't everyone?

Bugger. Thinking about it, I should have said yes. Why didn't I? I hate doing puddings, and round here you can't get away with buying from M & S and trying to disguise it. I should have gracefully, gratefully, said 'That would be lovely. Thank you.' Then Alicia would have had to spend Saturday morning making pastry and squeezing lemons and wouldn't be able to meet Tom. Though thinking about it, she's not that dumb. She wouldn't actually do it herself, would she? She's bound to have a little woman somewhere who churns out home-made puddings for her, that she can then pretend to have made.

Anyway, I've said no, because I just couldn't bear it. I couldn't bear the tiny complicit glance between Tom and Alicia as she handed me the tart. The triumph in her eyes, the gratefulness in his. No – I've decided on Nigella's orange and almond cake with clementines drenched in a boozy syrup. It looks easy, and

I've already got the ingredients. So I'm not going to give her the opportunity to gloat.

Right. Before I brave the supermarket, I'm just going to re-read everything I've written so far and see if it makes things any clearer. Seeing it in black and white might help me focus. Otherwise everything just whirls …

Ok. The way I look at it, I have two choices.

Or as Tom the pedant would point out, I have one choice.

Two options.

And the options are:

1. Do nothing, shut up and get on with it.
2. Snap out of it and win him back.

You might ask, after everything I've told you, why I'd want to bother with the second option. But I'm only bitching about Tom because I want sympathy. Telling you the bad bits so you will gasp in horror and wonder how on earth I cope. It's the oldest trick in the book, and I hate myself for it because I've always loathed women who moan about their husbands. But reading back, everything I've said makes me sound as if I don't love him. And I do. I absolutely do, deep down. After all, nobody's perfect and there are things to dislike about everyone on the planet. But sadly the things I dislike about Tom are stacking up at the moment, and the more you start noticing …

The only thing I *really* don't like about him is the fact he is screwing Alicia Birtwhistle.

So. Here we go. Decision time.

Option 1 sounds like misery and torture. I'm sure eventually they'll get bored, but in the meantime I will have driven myself mad imagining him with her legs around his neck or whatever so in the end he will want a divorce anyway because I will be a basket case, unable to get out of bed.

Option 2, on the other hand, is even more terrifying. I've got a pretty fierce opponent, after all. Though I have got one advantage over Mrs Alicia Birtwhistle and that is the fact that I'm actually married to Tom and I have four of his children.

But I don't know if I've got the courage or the energy to fight. I can't even bring myself to go over to the mirror and assess the situation. It will just be too depressing for words. Oh God. I hate making decisions. I've got enough to make as it is. What to make instead of lamb tagine. What to wear tomorrow night … groan.

What do you think? What would you do?

HONEYCOTE

The Liddiards have lived at Honeycote House for generations.
But all that might be about to change …

Mickey Liddiard adores his wife, Lucy. So why is he cheating on her with Kay? He knows
it's wrong, but he can't help himself.

James, Mickey's brother, has been in love with Lucy since the day he met her. He can't
betray his brother – but he's not going to stop the truth coming out.

Kay only married Lawrence Oakley for his money, and he knows it. But is it Mickey who
holds the key to her happiness?

For each of Mickey's misdemeanours, somewhere in the seemingly peaceful village of
Honeycote there is a knife being sharpened. Ambition, greed and good old-fashioned
revenge all conspire to bring about his downfall – but will true love save the day?

MAKING HAY

Suzanna and Barney Blake are swapping city life for the countryside – determined to
breathe new life into the Honeycote Arms and a marriage touched by tragedy.

Newly separated Ginny Tait arrives in Honeycote at around the same time – with very
nubile twin daughters and an awful lot of baggage.

If the newcomers expected to find a sleepy English village, they quickly discover that a
whole host of colourful characters have long woken up to more interesting ways of using
the bedroom. Throw in a dodgy businessman with a secret past, and Honeycote is soon a
veritable hotbed of passion and intrigue.

Will Ginny be blinded by choice and go for Mr Wrong again? Will Suzanna and Barney
find happiness in Honeycote? And if they do, will it be with each other?

An intoxicating blend of true love and hidden agendas, *Making Hay* proves once and for
all that village life doesn't necessarily mean the quiet life …

read more

WILD OATS

Life in the bosom of the Wilding family has its ups and downs ...

From the moment she arrives back to find a half-naked man in the kitchen, nothing about returning to the Shropshire village of Upper Faviell is quite what Jamie Wilding expected. For much has changed at Bucklebury Farm in the months she's been travelling the world since the death of her mother ...

Her best friend's wife has gone completely off the rails, her father is behaving like a love-sick teenager – and he's about to sell off the farm. What's worse, the shark threatening to take away Jamie's family home is the man who made off with her heart twelve years ago.

To defend her legacy and have a chance to discover the true love she craves, Jamie will have to confront a long-running family feud, her father, and her own past.

And she'll have to answer the question: is home always where the heart is?